AND THERE HE KEPT HER

JOSHUA MOEHLING

Poisoned Pen
PRESS

Published by Poisoned Pen Press, an imprint of Sourcebooks
P.O. Box 4410, Naperville, Illinois 60567-4410
(630) 961-3900
sourcebooks.com

Library of Congress Cataloging-in-Publication Data

Names: Moehling, Joshua, author.
Title: And there he kept her / Joshua Moehling.
Description: Naperville, Illinois : Poisoned Pen Press, 2022.
Identifiers: LCCN 2021023658 (print) | LCCN 2021023659 (ebook) | (hardcover) | (epub)
Subjects: GSAFD: Mystery fiction. | LCGFT: Detective and mystery fiction. |
    Novels.
Classification: LCC PS3613.O3344 A85 2022 (print) | LCC PS3613.O3344
    (ebook) | DDC 813/.6--dc23
LC record available at https://lccn.loc.gov/2021023658
LC ebook record available at https://lccn.loc.gov/2021023659

Manufactured in the UK by Clays and distributed by Dorling Kindersley Limited, London
10 9 8 7 6 5 4 3 2 1
001-329482-June/22

For Chris

CHAPTER ONE

4:30 A.M.

RAIN LASHED THE BOY as he ran from his car back to the old man's house. It was cold enough that he could see his breath. Water dripped from the ends of his shaggy hair, ran down his scalp and under his shirt. At least the clouds had hidden the moon. The news had called it a *supermoon*. All night it had followed everywhere he went, an ivory face watching him, reading his mind.

The road was gravel and getting muddier by the minute. Jesse tried running along the edge, but the ground was soft and soon his feet were as wet as his hooded sweatshirt.

On his left, houses faced the lake. He ran by a mailbox that said MILLER in faded letters and then by another mailbox that said MADIS N, this one pitched forward with its door hanging open like it was about to be sick. He stopped in front of the small gray house set back from the road and realized he was looking right through a hole where the door should have been and out the other side at the water beyond. He looked back at the MILLER house and noticed it was missing most of its roof and all of its windows.

Jesse ran on, already wet to the skin. He turned off the road and followed two muddy ruts past a stand-alone garage. The house ahead of him was a dark-brown rectangle without a straight line or a sharp corner. A wooden staircase went up the front to a sliding glass door and small windows with the blinds drawn.

Jesse stopped to catch his breath. In the dark, the house looked like it had climbed out of the mud or was sinking back into it. No part of him wanted to be here, to have to pay back his debt like this.

"In and out. Get it over with," he muttered.

He bypassed the staircase, pulling up his hood as he skidded down a muddy set of uneven steps alongside the house.

The lower level of the house was cement block. A narrow yard widened in the direction of rusty metal chairs overturned around a fire pit before gradually descending to the lake. The house had another deck on the back. Underneath were the remnants of a depleted woodpile and a battered storm door with access to the basement.

Jesse pulled open the storm door and set the clip that propped it open. The back door had individual glass panes set in a crosshatch pattern. Jesse hit the window closest to the dead bolt with his elbow. The sound of breaking glass made his breath catch in his throat. He counted to ten, waiting for lights to come on. Nothing happened. He reached inside, undid the bolt and the twist lock on the doorknob. Thunder rolled overhead as he pushed the door open and stepped over the broken glass.

It was pitch-dark inside. A clock radio on a shelf flashed red numbers 12:00...12:00...12:00. It smelled like cigarettes and garbage and wet, rotten things. Jesse took a penlight from his back pocket and used it to sweep over a workbench on his left littered with scattered tools and boxes of nails and spools of wire and plastic grocery bags. A telephone with a tortured, twisted cord hung on the wall. On his right an old refrigerator droned. He pulled open the door hard enough to make the beer cans inside dance on their wire racks. The light reached all but the basement's darkest corners. He left the door open.

Shelves made from concrete blocks and long sagging planks split the room in half lengthwise. In front of the shelves he saw a rocking chair with cracked leather on the seat and on the back. A sawed-off section of tree trunk was being used as a side table. He saw an enormous ceramic ashtray filled with cigarette butts and a garbage can overflowing with beer cans and crushed cigarette packs and boxes from microwave meals. On the floor behind the chair, a damp cardboard box had split its seams and let slide an avalanche of magazines. Nearly nude women stared up from the covers. Jesse picked up one closest to his foot—a moldy *Penthouse* from August 1981. More than twenty years before he was born.

He circled behind the shelves, past a wall-mounted sink and an open toilet in one corner. The other corner of the basement was built out into a small room with a metal door. It could have been for storage, but his gut told him it was something else. Jesse shivered at the threshold, his skin clammy and prickling with a million hairs. He made a sideways fist around the door's sliding bolt and pulled it backward, stepping out of the way as the heavy door swung open on silent hinges.

He thumbed the penlight again. He wasn't sure but he thought the walls were painted...pink. The color had peeled away in places, leaving discolored spots that looked like scabs. He saw a thin mattress covered in dark stains on a metal frame. A heavy chain hung limply through a steel ring bolted on the wall at the head of the bed.

Nothing about the scene in front of him made sense. He wasn't sure what he was looking at, but he knew the last thing he'd ever want was to be left alone in this room, in the dark, with the door shut. He blindly reached for the inside door handle to pull it shut again and found there wasn't one. He shined the penlight on it just to make sure.

This was a prison cell of some kind. A cage. How else to explain a door with no handle, no way to get out from the inside?

He shined the weak penlight across the blistered pink walls again. He felt like he was staring into the mouth of something that wanted to swallow him. When he killed the light, the darkness inside seemed to go down and down to a place that had never known the sun.

Behind him, the furnace made a loud ticking sound, then *whoomp*ed to life. Jesse turned away and shook off the bad thoughts. He stuck the light in his pocket and headed for the stairs that went up to the main floor. At the bottom, he stared at the closed door above him. He'd been told the old man would be drunk, at least. Passed out, if Jesse was lucky.

He labored up the first three steps, pausing on each one to talk himself out of turning around and making a run for it.

He turned one last time toward the dark room in the corner and thought about the stained mattress and the door with no handle.

Someone stepped on the broken glass by the basement door.

Jesse crouched and froze like a rabbit with no cover. The refrigerator door was still open, spilling light into the room. Behind it he saw a dark silhouette through the window in the basement door. The shape paused with one foot on the broken glass, then took another step into the room.

Jenny.

"What the fuck are you doing here?" Jesse hissed. He took out the penlight and flashed it at her so she could see where he was standing against the wall on the stairs.

"I got worried," she whispered.

Jenny was much less wet than Jesse was, thanks to the oversize letter jacket with sleeves that went down past her fingertips and made her look like she had no shoulders. In the dark he couldn't see her freckles, or her green eyes, or the eye tooth with the twist to it, the imperfection that made every one of her smiles perfect.

"Where's the car?"

"I moved it a little closer. I have the keys."

She came over and stood by his side at the bottom of the stairs. They both looked up at the door overhead. "We shouldn't be here," she said.

"I don't have any choice. He's threatening my family."

"We can figure out something else."

"No, we can't. He doesn't want money. It's this or something bad happens to my sister."

"Jesse, come on. He's messing with you. If you go back and say—"

The floor creaked over their heads.

They stared at each other, wide-eyed, frozen. One second passed. Another. There was only the sound of the furnace blower and the drum of the rain, coming down hard again at the open basement door.

Jenny put a hand on Jesse's arm and eased him a step backward.

The door at the top of the stairs crashed inward with enough force that it hit the wall and tried to bang shut again. The double-barreled shotgun leveled down at them kept it from closing all the way.

Jenny screamed and ducked behind Jesse. Jesse raised his hands in a pleading gesture. He waved the penlight at the fat, naked man standing above them with the shotgun and an oxygen mask over his mouth.

"Hold on, hold on! We made a mistake. We were just leaving," Jesse pleaded. He felt Jenny's body small and hard against his back, her hand tight around his arm.

The shotgun boomed like the end of the world. The light went out and fell from Jesse's hand. Jenny screamed again when Jesse crumpled without a sound, all his weight falling back against her. They went backward down the steps, Jesse on top of her. Jenny hit her head on the concrete with the bright crack of a glass jar breaking.

The fat, naked man stepped down through the cloud of burning gunpowder and fired the second barrel.

CHAPTER TWO

7:00 A.M.

THE CALL ABOUT THE bear came over the radio as Ben Packard was on his way to see the sheriff. He listened as dispatch directed it to another deputy on duty. "Caller says she and her husband were walking their dog when a large black bear came out of the trees and charged their animal. Her husband grabbed the bear around the neck to make it let go of the dog. The husband has a bite or a scratch on his belly. He's bleeding but not seriously wounded."

Packard picked up the mic. "This is 217."

Dispatch came back. "Go ahead, 217."

"I'm 10–8. I can take the bear."

"You're not on the schedule, 217."

"Yeah, yeah. I'm suited up and nearby. Let me take it."

"Copy, 217."

The bear was gone by the time Packard arrived at the address. The house was a boxy, manufactured home on a grassy lot with a ring of ornamental grass surrounding a flagpole. Packard stood with an elderly man and his wife in a kitchen that smelled like lemon dish soap and coffee, waiting for the ambulance to arrive. The old man had taken his shirt off and was holding a wet paper towel to his wound.

The wife looked in the fridge and asked Packard, "Can I make you a breakfast sandwich? Eggs and bacon on a biscuit. I could wrap it up and you could take it with."

Packard said, "No thank you. That's very kind of you to offer."

"You can make me a breakfast sandwich," the old man said.

"Hush. You'll get your sandwich after the ambulance looks at you."

"They better not think they're taking me to the hospital." The old man pulled the pink paper towel away from his sunken chest to look, then put it back. "There's nothing wrong with me. They'll do a bunch of tests and send in three doctors to ask me questions so each one can bill me. That's how they fund Obamacare. Charging guys like me three times."

Packard *hmm*ed, trying to sound sympathetic. "How's your dog?"

The wife turned from the fridge, put the tips of her fingers over her mouth, and shook her head. The old man stared out the window over the sink and kept blinking.

"I'm sorry," Packard said. "I know how hard it is to lose your dog."

After that, the wife continued her verbal inventory of the fridge. He politely declined a slice of pie, a piece of fruit, and a cup of coffee to go—she had real cream if that's how he took it.

When the EMTs arrived, Packard excused himself and left to find the bear. He drove slowly with the window down, watching the trees and the ditches for the animal. There had been a full moon the night before, followed by a fair amount of rain. The bear's tracks were easy to follow in the soft ground on either side of the road.

A half mile later—thin, shrubby trees on one side, small homes spread far apart on the other—he came upon two men standing at the end of a driveway. One had a bloody rag wrapped around a hand he was holding against his chest. A blue pickup was backed into the driveway next to a chop saw and a pair of sawhorses set up outside a partially sided garage.

"Is that from the bear or the saw?" Packard asked as he rolled to a stop.

"Bear," the bleeding guy said. "We were just getting started. I was up on the ladder when the bear come across the road. I yelled but Jim was running the saw and had his ear protection on. I came down and tried to chase the bear away. Got too close and got raked across the back of my hand."

"Where did the bear go?"

"It's in the garage," said Jim.

Packard could see a boat on a trailer, a four-wheeler, and a riding mower packed into the two-car garage. "What's in there that a bear would want?"

"Fifty-pound bags of dog food and birdseed."

Packard parked the county SUV. There was no chance of making it to the sheriff's house by 7:00 a.m. He texted the sheriff's wife to let her know he was running late, then asked dispatch to have the ambulance at the old man's house sent to his current location when they were done. He had the number for the county conservation officer in his phone. He called her to confirm what he should do about the bear.

"Any idea if it's a male or female?" Theresa Whitaker asked.

"Haven't got that close yet," Packard said, keeping an eye on the garage, watching for any sign of movement.

"Cubs?"

"Not that I've seen."

"You have to put it down," Theresa told him. "It's attacked two people. I'll call the university and have someone come pick up the carcass. They'll test it and see if they can find a reason for the aggressiveness."

Packard gave her the address and then got out of the vehicle, taking the twelve-gauge shotgun from the rack behind his seat. He asked the men if there was anyone else on the property. Both shook their heads. Packard told them to stay where they were. "Where's the dog food?"

"Back right, behind the boat," Jim said.

"Is there a garage door opener in that truck?"

"Yeah."

"Let's get it."

The guy with the bloody hand followed Packard to the truck in the driveway and unclipped the opener from the visor. Packard asked him to shut the garage door once he was inside.

"Try not to shoot my boat," the guy said.

Packard approached the open garage with the shotgun raised. He stepped inside, nodded back at the man behind him, and waited as the door lowered. In twelve years as a police officer in Minneapolis, he'd fired his service weapon once. In the last eighteen months with the sheriff's department in Sandy Lake, he'd already shot two deer and a moose, all mortally wounded after being struck by cars. A bear was another first.

The weak light on the overhead garage door unit stayed lit. Packard hugged the wall to his left, skirting the four-wheeler and the riding mower, since he didn't know exactly where the bear was. The trailered fishing boat was a red Lund with a 60-horse Johnson tilted over the stern.

He could hear the sounds of plastic being dragged and the crunch of dry dog food. Near the back wall, he got his first glimpse of the bear—its snout buried in a torn bag—pinned in the far corner by the boat's motor. Packard pegged its weight somewhere north of three hundred pounds. Its fur was deeply black and glossy. It smelled musky.

As soon as the bear realized he was there, it rose up on its hind legs, taller than Packard, who was six four. Packard kept the gun up but paused to marvel at the size of the animal. It moved its pale snout this way and that, sniffing the air. Nothing in its shiny black eyes gave any hint of what it was thinking. In such an enclosed space, they could have been in an interrogation room back at the station. Packard had a ridiculous urge to try to negotiate a deal with the bear. Let it off with a warning if it promised not to attack little dogs or cranky old men again.

The bear dropped its front paws on the motor's lower unit, hard enough to bounce the front end of the trailer, then rose up tall again.

Packard took two quick steps forward and pulled the trigger.

The twelve gauge thundered. The bear curled like a question mark, then collapsed, boneless, to the floor. Packard waited for a few seconds, then hit a button on the back wall to raise the garage door. Daylight raced across the floor like a sunrise at high speed. He squatted next to the dead bear, his ears ringing. The animal already looked diminished in death. Packard put his hand on top of its head. "I'm sorry," he said.

Packard was hours late by the time he turned into the sheriff's driveway. A decorative split-rail fence ran a short way on either side, then ended abruptly, keeping nothing in or out. The house was a brick rambler with green shutters that backed up against acres of thick woods five miles outside of town.

Marilyn Shaw answered the door. Early sixties. Hair dyed red with gray roots. Wearing blue slacks and a cardigan sweater over a green shirt. She had a dish towel over one shoulder that she used to finish drying her hands before she took Packard's between hers and stood on her toes to kiss his cheek. "You get taller and more handsome every time I see you."

Packard towered over her. He had dark hair that had started to recede at the temples in his twenties, then decided to hold its ground, leaving him with a slightly irregular hairline in the front. He kept it short, just this side of a military cut. He wore a trimmed beard almost year-round now that beards on men were the style again. Eyes blue or gray, depending on the light. Women were drawn to the size and shape of him. Men were intimidated by it. He was an imposing figure in uniform, even the brown one worn by the sheriff's department.

Packard followed Marilyn inside. "How's he feeling?" he asked, keeping his voice low.

Marilyn shrugged a bit and waved her flat hand side to side. Packard nodded and followed her to the kitchen.

"Can I get you a cup of coffee?"

"If it's not any trouble," Packard said. Waiting with the old man and his wife at the scene of the bear attack had taught him it was easier to accept the first offer than decline ten more.

"No trouble at all. Go on in. He's watching TV."

The family room was on the back of the house. The Shaws' decor was classic country. Varnished beadboard. A wallpaper border of chickens and checkerboard hearts that circled the ceiling. The family room was heavily carpeted, with bookshelves and an overstuffed sectional and framed wildlife prints. Scented candles in glass jars perfumed the air. Packard had to duck to avoid hitting a low bulkhead. Stan was lying back in a recliner, television remote on his belly, looking drowsy. He slowly turned his head. When he saw Packard, his face lit up. He struggled for a moment to right himself in the recliner. "Hey, you giant sonofabitch."

"Hey, yourself."

The sheriff had been a walking bull of a man. Only five foot nine but broad shouldered and wide through the chest, shaped like a potato on toothpick legs. Before the chemo, he had thick dark hair, gray just over the ears, that he kept swept back with pomade in a tamed pompadour. He was a foul-mouthed bullshit artist with men, a gentleman to the ladies, and a hard-ass on criminals. He and Marilyn taught Sunday school and marriage preparation classes at the Catholic church. The people of Sandy Lake loved him. He could have run for sheriff and won, uncontested or not, until the sun burned out.

Stan sat up in the recliner, a blanket over his legs. He looked more diminished every time Packard came by. A February snowman in March. His hair had come back thin and white. His scalp had spots and odd scaly patches crusted with blood.

Packard took a seat on the end of the sectional. A bass fishing show was on the flat-screen TV in front of them.

"You just missed that guy in the orange hat pull up a seven-pounder," Stan said.

"Where they at?"

"Uh… Hell, I don't know. I thought it was Minnesota. Could be anywhere."

They watched TV for a couple of minutes; then Stan pointed the remote at the TV, turned down the volume, and asked what was new.

Packard told him about the budget review with the city council. They were underspent in overtime and fuel costs. "Warmer temps forced the ice fishing festival to be canceled, which helped keep overtime down. We've been so fiscally responsible I thought it was a good time to pitch the idea of hiring two new deputies. I assume they'll approve only one. You all right with that?"

Stan shrugged. "You're the one who has to be all right with it," he said.

Packard had been hired by Stan Shaw eighteen months earlier as an investigator for the Sandy Lake County Sheriff's Department, but for the last four months he'd been serving as acting sheriff, covering as many of Stan's duties as possible while the sheriff went through a second round of treatment for colon cancer.

Shaw's decision to appoint Packard came as a surprise to the county board of directors. Off the record, Shaw had told them his deputy with the most seniority was six months from retirement and didn't want the job. The one with the second most seniority wasn't fit to plan the holiday party let alone run the whole department. Shaw liked Packard for the job because he worked hard and came with no baggage. The sheriff, or the acting sheriff, had to be unpopular at times. Packard had no alliances, no grudges, no debts. He hardly knew anyone. Shaw told the board its options were Packard or no acting sheriff at all.

The other investigator in the department, and Packard's closest ally at work, was Detective Jill Thielen. She was one who told Packard about the other deputies, all of them male, claiming it wasn't fair the single guy who worked all the time got the acting sheriff job. They couldn't be expected to put in the same hours he did.

"Congratulations," Thielen told them. "Now you know how every working mother feels."

That shut 'em up.

Marilyn came in with his coffee. Stan said, "Sweetheart, I just thought of another positive thing about colon cancer. This guy has to review the budget with the board. Not me."

Packard smiled, then tried to swallow it when Marilyn tsked and shook her head. "We heard you respond to the bear call this morning on the scanner," she said, changing the subject.

"Yeah, damn. I forgot to ask about the bear," Stan said.

Packard told them about the old man with the dog and the other guy with the bloody hand. "I cornered the bear in the guy's garage and shot it," he said, sipping his coffee.

"What did you use?" Stan asked.

"Twelve gauge."

Stan nodded his approval.

"What I want to know is why you're in uniform and responding to calls on your day off. I heard that on the radio, too," Marilyn said.

"I was coming here so I thought I'd be ready just in case."

"Benjamin, someone else could have responded to the bear. You need to take time off. You can't work seven days a week."

Oh, but he could. Not all of the work was as exciting as coming face-to-face with a seven-foot black bear, but it was still work. It gave him a sense of purpose. The things he did in his time off—working out and remodeling the house he'd bought—were solitary activities. Too much time alone gave him too much time to ponder whether moving to Sandy Lake after Marcus was killed had been the right decision or not.

"You'll never meet someone if you don't take off the uniform and get to know people socially," Marilyn said.

By *meet someone* she didn't mean friends—not that he had a lot of those either. She meant romantically. Packard shifted nervously in his seat. Stan did the same, but probably because of the cancer.

"Marilyn, don't pester the man. He's doing his job and my job. That's a lot of responsibility."

"All I'm saying—"

"I hear you, Marilyn," Packard interrupted, smiling. "I'll work on it."

He changed the subject by asking how her seedlings were doing. Marilyn was a master gardener who could put dirt in a shoe and grow a foot. She asked him if he'd started swimming yet.

"A week ago," he said.

"What's the water temperature?" Stan asked.

"Above forty-five degrees. That's the magic number."

Marilyn crossed her arms, grabbed her elbows, and shivered. "Mother Mary and Joseph. I can't even imagine. You must be blue as a berry coming out of that water."

"I wear a wet suit. It keeps a layer of body-temperature water next to your skin. Once you get going, you can stay warm for twenty minutes or so."

"Benjamin, that sounds perfectly dreadful to me."

Packard smiled and shrugged and visited with the Shaws for a while longer. The purpose of these visits had started out as a way to keep his boss informed about what was going on at work. Lately, he could sense Stan was less interested in work, and so the conversation wandered from town gossip to the weather to stories they'd heard from deer hunters or people ice fishing. Stan had another treatment scheduled for the next day. Packard didn't ask how the chemo was going. He could see how hard it was on Stan. If they were still treating him, it meant they hadn't given up. That's all he needed to know.

When it was time to go, Packard handed Marilyn the empty coffee cup and shook the sheriff's hand. "I'll see you again soon. Let me know if you guys need anything."

Back in the truck, Packard listened to the radio chatter as he tried to decide whether to go home or to the station. No one was expecting him to come in, and they wouldn't be particularly thrilled to see him if he did. A day off for the boss was a day off from the boss. He could give them that at least.

His personal cell phone rang just as he was putting the truck into reverse.

"Ben, this is Susan Wheeler."

The few times Susan had a reason to call him, she always introduced herself by her first and last name, like it was their first meeting. She could come off as humorless if you didn't know her. Also, if you did. She and Packard were cousins.

"Hello, Susan Wheeler. What's up?"

"Jenny is missing."

"What do you mean, 'missing'?"

"I mean she wasn't in her bed this morning, and she didn't go to school. No one has seen or heard from her since last night."

The clock on the dashboard said it was just after 11:30 a.m. Packard already had questions but decided to hold them until he could meet Susan face-to-face.

"Do you want me to come to your house, or do you want to meet me at the station?"

"I'll meet you."

"I'll be there in twenty minutes."

CHAPTER THREE

THE SANDY LAKE COUNTY Sheriff's Department was part of a larger complex that included City Hall, the license bureau, and the county public works department. The two-story blond-brick building sat a block north of the highway, surrounded by a large parking lot.

Packard walked a white-tiled hallway past glass doors and a community bulletin board that flapped with flyers for fundraisers, lost pets, and an upcoming sheriff's sale. In the department's reception area, Kelly Phelps was sitting at the front desk. She didn't look happy to see him.

"I heard you were on the prowl. You're supposed to be off today." Kelly had been with the department for thirty years and had as much authority as the sheriff, if not more. Get on the wrong side of Kelly, and you'd ask to be locked in a jail cell for your own protection.

Packard held up two fingers and tried the sheriff's line on her. "I'm doing two jobs."

Kelly shook her head, not buying it. She waved a hand at Packard, pushed a button on her phone, and said, "Sandy Lake Sheriff's Department."

Susan was sitting in one of the waiting-area chairs. A petite woman with straight brown hair parted on one side and tucked behind her ears. She was dressed in jeans and a green T-shirt with a bike on it. She held a red zippered case in her lap.

Packard knew his cousin didn't like being touched so he didn't try to hug her or shake her hand. She didn't like small talk either. "Let's go back to my office," he said.

Packard waved a security badge in front of a card reader and led Susan through the door and down a hallway past a large open room with desks arranged in rows, past a conference room and a break room, finally coming to the sheriff's office in the back. The framed photos and articles on the walls were about Stan Shaw. Packard wanted everyone to know he considered his use of the sheriff's office to be temporary. He hadn't even wanted to clear Stan's papers off his desk. Kelly had done it for him.

Packard sat and flipped his yellow pad to a clean piece of paper. "You said Jenny's missing. Tell me the details."

"I got up at six thirty this morning to go for a bike ride. At six forty-five I knocked on Jenny's bedroom door to get her up for school. When I opened the door, she wasn't there."

"What time did you last see her?"

"It was around eleven thirty last night, just before I went to bed. She was still doing homework."

Packard wrote the time on his notepad. "Did you hear or see her get up in the night at all?"

"No."

"Has she done this before?"

Susan blinked and nodded slowly. "I've caught her sneaking out at night, yes. She ignores her curfew whenever she feels like it. Since Tom died."

Susan and her husband, Tom, had moved to Sandy Lake more than a decade ago. Susan was familiar with the area from summers at the family cabin, same as Packard. His mom and her dad were sister and brother. Their father—Packard and Susan's grandfather—had built a house on Lake Redwing back when you didn't have to be a millionaire to do so.

Susan and Tom owned a restaurant, the Sweet Pea, that served elevated comfort food. A bit fancy for Sandy Lake but the summer tourists loved the place. Susan developed recipes and cooked. Tom was front of house.

Before moving to Sandy Lake himself, Packard had last seen Susan at her wedding. She and Tom, both avid cyclists, had biked from the hotel where the wedding party was staying to the park where the ceremony was held, then stood before an officiating friend in cycling kits—all black for the groom, all white for the bride—proving Susan had a sense of humor after all; you just had to be patient to get a glimpse of it.

He'd only had one social visit with his cousin and her family since arriving in town. Last summer he'd gone to the Sweet Pea and sat at the bar with Tom, who had recently been diagnosed with an aggressive brain tumor. Tom wore a baseball cap to hide where they'd shaved the top of his head and implanted a reservoir under his scalp that would deliver drugs right to his cerebrospinal fluid. He talked like a man with miles of road ahead of him, offering to help Packard remodel his house and to take him ice fishing in January. His daughter, Jenny, was waitressing that night—a pretty girl with short brown hair and a spray of freckles who took her phone out and looked at it every time she stopped at the end of the bar to pick up an order.

Susan was cooking the whole time and only stopped by long enough to bring Packard his food and ask Tom if he was feeling okay. When he said he'd had enough, Packard drove him home.

The next time he saw Susan and Jenny was at Tom's funeral.

Packard made some notes on his pad. "What did you do when you saw she wasn't in her bed at six forty-five?"

"I called her. No answer. I texted her and asked where she was and told her she better not miss school."

"No response?"

Susan shook her head.

"Then what did you do?" Packard asked.

"I went on my bike ride."

"Did you stop anywhere?"

"Not really."

Not really was not really an answer. That and the sudden slump in her shoulders told Packard she was lying. He pushed back. "You know as well as I do that when kids go missing, the first people scrutinized are the parents. If you were with someone this morning who can corroborate any part of your story, you might want to tell me."

Susan sat up straighter. "I rode about forty miles and then I stopped to see Sean White Cloud in St. Albans. I was at his house for an hour or so before I rode home."

Packard knew Sean White Cloud. He was an EMT. Young American Indian guy with a chest like a whiskey barrel and a big smile. They'd worked a number of emergency calls together.

Sean was also on the sex offender registry.

"How do you know Sean White Cloud?"

"He was our in-home nurse while Tom was in hospice. When it was all over, I told him to come to the restaurant so I could cook for him. He came by a couple of times."

"And then what?"

"What do you mean, 'And then what'?" Susan asked.

"I mean what's your relationship now?"

Susan was getting visibly frustrated with his questions. "What does this have to do with Jenny?"

"It establishes your whereabouts at a critical time. It gives me another potential source of information from someone who knows you."

She gave him a hard look and very purposefully said, "The second or third time Sean came to the restaurant, he sat at the bar and we talked after the rush ended. We had a couple of drinks, and I asked him to take me back to his house and fuck me to a fare-thee-well. He has continued to do so, upon my request, for the last couple of months."

Packard resisted the urge to gape. He still thought of his cousin as the introverted, bookish girl shivering and scowling in a blue swimsuit at the cabin. Their shared childhood meant little after so many years apart. They had a blood connection, but they didn't know each other at all.

"Does Sean have any kind of relationship with Jenny? Are they friendly?"

"No."

"Did they spend time together while he was taking care of Tom?"

Packard could see Susan visibly start to shut down, either from exhaustion or frustration. "Jenny was gone from home as much as possible while Tom was going through the worst of it. Her interactions with Sean were limited."

"Does she know about your relationship?"

"It's not a relationship. But yes."

"You told her."

"No. She found out a few weeks ago from a text she saw on my phone. Nothing obscene. Just…confirmation that we were seeing each other in a capacity that had nothing to do with taking care of her dad."

Packard made some more notes. "How do you know she didn't show up at school today?"

"I got a text while I was at Sean's from the school that she had an unexcused absence. I sent her more texts after that. I texted her boyfriend. No response from either one."

"Who's her boyfriend?"

"Jesse Crawford."

"How long has she been going with Jesse?"

"Less than a year. Eight, nine months," Susan said.

"What are your thoughts on that relationship?"

"They make each other happy. Do they smoke pot? Yes. Are they having sex? Yes." Susan stared at him defiantly, like she was daring him to criticize her parenting.

"Any signs of physicality between them? Fights? Bruises? Yelling?"

"No. They think they're in love."

She gave him Jesse's cell phone number and the numbers of Jenny's two closest girlfriends who had already confirmed for Susan that they hadn't seen Jenny or Jesse at school. Packard said he'd try contacting all of them again later in the day if Jenny didn't show up. He asked Susan if she knew what car Jenny and Jesse were in.

"They're not in Jenny's," she said. "Her car is in the garage. I don't know what he drives. It's red or maroon. Sedan of some kind."

"Know anything about Jesse's family?"

"Almost nothing. He lives with his mother. There might be a sister or a brother."

Packard thought for a minute, circled the last name Crawford. "I only know a few Crawfords in town. I wonder if his mom is Ann Crawford."

Susan said she didn't know.

"Ann used to raise a lot of hell. She's been banned from every bar in Sandy Lake. Does her drinking at home now. She had an old man who was trouble, too. He took off before my time."

The more they talked, the more Packard had a feeling these were two kids tired of everyone's bullshit who wanted to be alone together. He boiled it down for Susan. "You don't need me to tell you Jenny's been through a rough patch. Jesse... I don't know. If his mother is Ann Crawford, his whole life has probably been a rough patch. Maybe they just want some time on their own and never mind where they're supposed to be or who's worried about where they are. I doubt they've gone far. They might be holed up in a cabin around—"

Susan angrily unzipped the padded case she was holding and laid it flat on the desk between them. "What about this? She needs this stuff to stay alive."

Packard studied the case's contents held in place under elastic bands: a blood glucose meter, syringes, glucose tabs. There were loose alcohol swabs and Band-Aids and test strips.

"She's a type 1 diabetic?"

"Yes!" Susan said, like Packard was supposed to know this already.

"How long?"

"She was ten when she was diagnosed. We got her on a pump a year ago while we still had Tom's insurance and were maxing out the deductible with his care."

"The pump carries a supply of insulin, right?"

"About three days' worth depending on her activity level and how well she eats. But she still needs to check her blood twice a day to make sure the sensor is calibrated."

"Is there anything here she couldn't buy in a drugstore if she needed to?"

"She could buy everything but the insulin. You need a prescription for insulin. There's some older formulations that you can buy over the counter, but she's never used them."

"Do you know how much insulin was in the house before today? Do you know for sure she didn't take some with her? Besides what was in her pump?"

"No."

"Okay. Here's what we know. Jenny's snuck out before. She snuck out again last night at some point. We assume she's with her boyfriend because neither of them is answering their phone. She didn't go to school this morning and still isn't there for all we know. She didn't take her diabetes supplies with her. Given all that, you give me a number of how concerned you are from one to ten."

"Seven."

"Okay. I'm a seven, too." He looked away quickly and wrote on his pad so she wouldn't see in his eyes that he wasn't a seven. He was a four. Susan's first reaction after finding her daughter had snuck out in the night and still wasn't home was to go for a bike ride and get laid. That didn't sound like a seven to Packard. The situation might not warrant the full attention of the Sandy Lake Sheriff's Department, but he was going to look into things because Susan was family. And because—as a family—they'd been through something like this before.

Packard stood up and walked Susan back to the reception area. "I'll make some phone calls and check back in with you later this evening," he said. "Call me if she shows up. If she doesn't, I'll want to come by the house and go through her room."

Susan walked out without a goodbye. Packard watched her go, hand half-raised, thinking about what else had gone unsaid between them during their meeting. Neither one of them had mentioned Nick.

Behind him, Kelly said, "She's an odd one. What did she want?"

"Her daughter snuck out last night and didn't come home."

"Oh god," Kelly said, crossing herself and looking up at the ceiling. "I hope we don't have another one."

"Another what?"

"Another missing woman. Like the others."

Kelly was remembering two local women who had vanished without a trace a couple of years apart, the first one almost two decades ago. "Those gals were way before my time," Packard said. "They hadn't even crossed my mind."

Kelly grunted. "Let me tell you, as a woman who was here then, it crosses your mind every time someone is five minutes late getting home. Or doesn't call when she says she's going to. Even all these years later. You don't forget a time like that."

"Susan's daughter is with her boyfriend. They'll turn up," Packard said.

Kelly seemed doubtful but she changed the subject anyway. "Here's your reward for coming in today, Big Shot. You get to put your coat back on and go see Gary Bushwright."

"Now what?"

Kelly picked up her pad and read from it. "Cora shot his garage with a crossbow. This is a quote: 'Honey, you better tell Packard to get out here and talk to this crazy woman. I'm about to take my earrings out and fight a bitch.'"

"What does he mean, 'take my earrings out'?"

"It's what women do before they fight. If they're wearing hoops or dangling earrings, they take them out before fighting so they don't get snagged and their earlobe torn."

Packard grimaced at the image. "For chrissake. What's Stuart doing? Send him."

Kelly shook her head. "Stuart's in court this afternoon. And Roger called in sick this morning."

Early on, Packard thought being the acting sheriff meant he'd be able to delegate stuff like this. The reality was, in a department this small, there were few people to delegate to and even fewer that he trusted to do the job the way he'd do it.

"All right, I'm going. One more thing. Do you know Ann Crawford?"

Kelly went *pffff*. "If you've set foot in a bar in this town, you know Ann Crawford. She's either tried to get you to buy her a drink, fought you, or thrown up on your shoes."

"Does she have kids?"

"Yeah, high schoolers I think."

"Text me a number for her. I want to find out if her son is Jesse Crawford. He's the boyfriend in question."

Kelly shook her head while she made a note. "Gary Bushwright and Ann Crawford on the same day? You really should have stayed home."

CHAPTER FOUR

THE CABIN PACKARD'S GRANDFATHER had built on Lake Redwing was once the center of all their family activity. The house hummed like a hive May through August, swarmed by friends and relatives, turning over almost daily as people landed or took off. They pitched tents in the yard when the house was too full or too hot. Someone was always going to town for ice or beer or Popsicles.

In the winter, just the immediate family gathered for Christmas and New Year's. They spent the short, cold days snowshoeing or cross-country skiing. The woodstove gave off a crackling dry heat while they played games or watched movies late into the night.

It was Packard's favorite place until the year his oldest brother, Nick, snuck out of the house two nights after Christmas and never came home.

Packard was twelve at the time and the last family member to see Nick alive. He'd begged Nick to take him with him. Nick had refused, admitting only that he was meeting a friend and they didn't want him hanging around. They'd fought at the back door, Nick finally yanking Packard outside and shoving him in the snow in his pajamas so he'd be too cold and too wet to do anything but go inside and change. Nick took off on a snowmobile that divers found three days later in open water after a searcher spotted one of Nick's gloves frozen at the edge of the ice. It looked like someone had struggled to climb out.

Divers searched underwater for days, and again in the spring, patrolling the shoreline in boats labeled SHERIFF. The lake was over ten thousand acres and more than one hundred feet deep in spots. Nick's body was never found.

After three years of no answers and a law-enforcement budget that couldn't afford to spend any more money on the search, Nick's case was closed. Packard's family—once racked as tight as billiard balls—spun off in fifteen different directions after that. Grandma and Grandpa did their best to keep up the family tradition of summers at the cabin, but each year it got harder, not easier. People felt the strain and stopped coming. The thought of getting in the same lake that refused to give up his brother's body had terrified Packard as a kid. He had nightmares about a white, gloveless hand grabbing his ankle while he tried to swim for the shore.

He was a senior in high school when his grandparents finally decided to sell the cabin. Packard's parents divorced a year later. They kept in touch with police until they got tired of hearing there was still nothing new to report. Sandy Lake became a time and a place in family history that no one talked about. Nick was still out there, forever seventeen, even as life moved on for the rest of them.

Packard had put Sandy Lake out of his mind for almost two decades. It wasn't until Marcus was killed that he thought of it again.

Back in Minneapolis, most people Packard mentioned Sandy Lake to had never heard of the town. *Is it up north?* they'd ask. Everything this far from the cities was "up north." Duluth was up north. Grand Marais was up north. Brainerd, Hibbing, Thief River Falls. Hell, if you were from Rochester, St. Cloud was up north. Only politicians and reporters bothered to think of any place farther than commuting distance from the Twin Cities as anything but a homogenous north.

There used to be agriculture, mining, and logging jobs in this part of the state. People could live comfortably with a certain degree of economic security and raise children who wouldn't immediately flee the area. Now what could be sold had been sold, consolidated into fewer hands, and what remained supported a dwindling number of jobs. There was a poultry processing plant twenty miles to the south, and an outdoor Sportcraft manufacturer forty miles north. Most other employment around Sandy Lake was in the service industry, tourism, and retail, none of which paid for shit.

From Packard's limited perspective, the economy was the kindling that fueled almost all the crime in the area. Chronic unemployment and under-employment made it difficult to raise a family. Financial uncertainty made people do crazy things. Hopelessness made them indifferent to the consequences.

Then there was random nonsense like the ongoing feud between Gary and Cora, two people who just plain-old-fashioned hated each other.

————————

Fifteen miles out of town, off a two-lane highway that ran east–west, he came to Gary Bushwright's house. It was set back from the road at an angle, a single-story rectangle painted yellow with green trim. A wheelchair ramp ran up to the front door, with mulched flower beds on either side. The wide, unfenced yard was mowed prairie grass and weeds.

Packard pulled up behind a Peterbilt cab and chassis parked beside the house. Gary was sitting on one of the chassis's eight rear tires, smoking a ciga-rette. He was bald with a reddish-brown beard that blanketed the top half of his chest, and dressed in a quilted jacket and denim overalls. He had a birthmark on one cheek the size and shape of a chocolate thumbprint. A white pit bull was stretched out on the gravel at his feet.

Packard checked his phone as he got out of the sheriff's SUV. He had a text from Kelly with Ann Crawford's home number.

"What's going on now, Gary?"

Gary ground his cigarette out on the bottom of his boot and stuck the butt in his pocket. He was indistinguishable from any other overweight, bald, bearded trucker in his sixties until he opened his mouth. "Honey, let me tell you something. I have had it with that bitch next door." He gave a dismissive point in the direction of Cora's house and turned on his heel. "Follow me. Let me show you something. You, too, Baxter. Come on."

The pit bull got up and followed even more reluctantly than Packard. The three of them went around the semi cab to the back of the house.

"Feast your pretty blue eyes on that," Gary said.

He pointed at the orange shaft of an arrow with green fletching sticking into the back wall of his garage. "This is a whole new level of nonsense. She could've put that arrow right through me."

Gary Bushwright and Cora Shaker had been neighbors for more than two decades, ever since Gary had come back to Sandy Lake in the early 1990s to help his mother after she had a stroke. He used to be a commercial truck driver, on the road for three or four days a week, then home with his mother the rest of the time. He took care of her for twelve years until a heart attack punched her clock for good. After she died, everyone expected Gary to tear up the road in his hurry to get out of Sandy Lake. They assumed he'd move to a big city, or at least Minneapolis, where there were more of his kind. Instead, he did the unthinkable. He kept driving his truck and he kept coming home to Sandy Lake.

"And don't you dare tell me I'm overreacting," Gary said.

"I'm counting on you not to respond in kind," Packard said.

"I'd have to go out and buy a crossbow in order to respond in kind!"

"I meant stand down. I need you not to retaliate."

Gary stood with his hands on his hips. "I am doing my best to take the high road, but she has pushed me. To. The. Limit!"

On the acreage behind his house, Gary had built a white aluminum building, out of which he ran a dog rescue. The building was the size of a small barn with a row of windows around the middle and a fenced dog run off the back. Packard could hear dogs barking inside.

He turned from the kennel building and looked down the dip in the land to Cora's blue, two-story house with its three-car garage and concrete driveway. The two lots sat on acres and acres of land, but only a few hundred feet separated the houses.

Cora must have been watching them the whole time. She came out of her house just then with the crossbow by her side. "I didn't do nothing wrong," she yelled across the way. "It was an accident. I got my rights. Second Amendment."

"Good god. 'Second Amendment,'" Gary said. He touched the side of his face and rolled his eyes.

"If you want to press charges, I'll take her in for reckless discharge of a dangerous weapon."

Gary hooked his thumbs inside the front of his overalls and stared up at the sky. His beard lifted off his chest. "I don't know. I don't want that woman to go to jail on my account. I just want her to leave me alone."

"It's up to you."

Gary kicked at the gravel with his boot and shook his head. "No, I don't want to press charges."

"You sure?"

"I'm sure."

"Stay here. I'll go down and talk to her."

Packard grabbed the arrow by the fletching and pulled it out of the wall, then went down the hill toward Cora's. He'd been mediating things between these two since arriving in town, with no end in sight. His last visit was to negotiate a mutual de-escalation involving warring yard signs. Cora's went up after Thanksgiving—a large hand-painted message on canvas strung between two trees in her yard with a Bible verse about the sexually immoral and idolaters and men who have sex with men not inheriting the kingdom of God. Gary retaliated by making his own giant sign on canvas that said HONK IF YOU'RE HORNY! He wrapped his in blinking lights and put an eight-foot-tall inflatable Santa next to it. The sheriff's department would have stayed out of it had Cora not kept calling and complaining about the honking keeping her up all night.

Cora was barely five feet tall, with short red hair curled tight. On a previous visit she'd come to the door with little green rollers pinned in rows all around her head and a clear plastic shower cap over it. She shouted her defense as Packard closed the distance between them. "It was an accident! I didn't mean it! Greta is my witness."

"Cut the crap, Cora. Put down the crossbow and step away from it."

She did as she was told, then stood there with her jaw set.

Packard pushed up his sunglasses and pointed the arrow at her. "I should be arresting you right now for violating Minnesota Statute 609.66, which calls for a $1,000 fine and/or ninety days in jail for handling a dangerous weapon in a manner that endangers the safety of another."

"It was an accident. Me and Greta was gonna go out and shoot at the hay bales. I was carrying the bow over my shoulder and it went off."

"Why did you have a loaded crossbow over your shoulder, Cora? What sense does that make?" He took a step closer so there was almost no space between them at all.

She had no response. Packard looked past her at the picture window in her living room. He saw Greta standing a few feet back. She was a giant woman, over six feet tall, built like a lumberjack with long brown hair she kept pulled tight in a thin braid long enough to sit on. There was a hulkiness to her that spoke to some kind of thyroid or pituitary condition. She stepped back and disappeared in the shadows when she saw him looking.

"Cora, I'm telling you this for the last time. I'm tired of this nonsense."

"I'm tired of living in the shadow of sin. There's improper traffic in and out of that house at night. Other sodomites. The Bible says in Ephesians chapter five, verse eleven, 'Have nothing to do with the fruitless deeds of darkness, but rather expose them.'"

"The Bible also says, 'You shall love your neighbor as yourself. There is no other commandment greater than this.'"

Cora gave him the stink eye while she struggled to find a retort. He cut her off. His own quiver of Bible quotes didn't hold many arrows. "It's only Gary's kindness that's keeping you out of jail right now, Cora. He doesn't want to press charges. Now listen to me. If I get called out here again—for any reason—I'll arrest both of you for wasting police resources. You think being his neighbor is bad? Wait 'til I put you both in the same jail cell."

"You can't do that."

"I'm the acting sheriff for this whole county. I can do whatever I want."

He put the arrow under his heel and bent the shaft ninety degrees, then gave it back to her. "I'm not kidding, Cora. If you or your family or any of your possessions end up on Gary's property, you're going to jail. Count on it."

Cora snatched the bent arrow. He saw her eyes shift from him to something behind him, probably Gary. "Of course you take his side. You're just like him," she spat out.

Packard pulled himself up taller. Speculation about his life out of uniform had started almost as soon as he arrived in town. *What brings you to Sandy Lake? Where you from? No wife? No kids?* Packard had answered some of their questions and ignored others. Silence, he thought, would stonewall them. A long enough silence would bore them.

He unsnapped the cuffs on his belt and pulled them out. "Say one more word to me, Cora. I dare you."

She turned and hurried toward the house, shaking the bent arrow over her head. "'Vengeance is mine. I will repay, says the LORD!'"

Packard went back up the hill to find Gary standing outside the dog kennel. "I was hoping you'd put her over your knee and whip her ass with that arrow."

"Mr. Bushwright, I'm gonna tell you the same thing I told Cora—"

"'Mr. Bushwright'?" Gary looked taken aback. He put a hand on his chest. "How very formal of you. Sorry, please continue, Mr. Deputy Packard, Acting Sheriff, sir."

"Knock it off, Gary. You need to know I'm not on your side. I'm not on her side. I'm out here to represent the law. I'm tired of babysitting you two."

"Honey, I know you're tired. I'm tired, too. But am I supposed to just let her get away with this shit? Do you know what I've put up with over the years?"

"I do know. You've told me."

Gary kept going without taking a breath. "I've been called names. I've been told I'm going to hell. I have had flaming bags of feces left on my doorstep. I had F-A-G-I-T spray-painted on my garage. Things have gotten better since I put in the security cameras and sent them a nice stack of photos showing them all the land covered by the system. But it feels like she and that Sasquatch daughter of hers are always testing my defenses."

"I think she'll behave. I threatened to arrest both of you and put you in a cell together."

Gary tried to hide his smile behind his bushy beard, but it got away from him. He howled and slapped his leg. "I would love to share a cell with Cora. I could teach her how to knit." He put his hands out, palms facing each other eighteen inches apart. "She could hold my yarn while I scandalized her with stories from my wild youth when I worked in the skin trade."

Skin trade? Packard opened his mouth, closed it, deciding not to take the bait. "I gotta go," he said. Gary and Cora could turn into a full-time job if he let them.

"Wait, you gotta see the dogs before you leave."

"Gary, I don't have time."

"Honey, you have two minutes. Two. Minutes."

"All right. I'll look. But you gotta stop calling me honey. Seriously. You can call me Ben or Packard, you can call me Deputy—"

Gary gave him a dismissive wave. "Honey, I call everybody honey. You aren't special."

———

Packard followed Gary inside the kennel. The steel door made a sweeping sound as Gary pushed it open and closed it behind them. It smelled like dogs and dog food and laundry soap inside. Twelve fenced kennels filled half of the building. The rest of the building contained a business office, a table where dogs could be treated or examined, a supply room, a bathing station, and a washing machine and a dryer. A door at the far end led to the outdoor dog run.

"I got a black lab in number four, pretty old, arthritic, and the worst god-damn breath you ever smelled in your life. Lord have mercy," Gary said.

Packard walked up the aisle between the kennels. Marcus had had a golden retriever named Jarrett—after Keith Jarrett, the jazz musician—that became Packard's dog after Marcus was killed. Packard had brought the dog with him when he made the move to Sandy Lake. Jarrett used to sniff along the shoreline and wait at the end of the dock while Packard swam laps.

He stopped in front of the kennel holding Jack, a husky-poodle mix that looked all husky but was poodle-sized. He put the back of his hand out and let Jack lick it. In the next cage, a black Rottweiler-Lab mix named Captain came over to get his share of the attention.

Jarrett had developed a cancerous obstruction in his bowel and stopped eating last fall. He was twelve years old. Dr. Weiss, the vet in Sandy Lake, told Packard this was a common occurrence in the breed. When there was nothing else to be done, Packard sat with Jarrett on a blue blanket while Weiss gave him two injections. It took everything Packard had to keep it together long enough for Weiss to confirm Jarrett had no pulse, then leave him alone with his dog. Packard moved to Sandy Lake to get away from everyone and everything he knew. He'd wanted to be alone. But not this alone.

In the last cage on the right was a white-and-brown Welsh corgi gnawing on a pig's ear pinched between his front legs. One of his legs was wrapped in a bandage and significantly shorter than the other. The whiteboard was blank.

"What happened to that dog?"

"Just came in yesterday from a puppy mill in Missouri. He was in a too-small cage and got his paw stuck between the bars. A dog in the next cage started eating it."

The corgi's other legs had white feet that looked like socks. His fur was brown and black across his back and white on the belly. "He looks like a cartoon. I've never seen a dog so…" He struggled to find the right word.

"He needs a forever home. And you need someone to keep you warm at night, Deputy." Gary elbowed him.

Packard shook his head. "I just put in a sauna at my place. I'm good."

"Oh Lord. Spare me the sauna talk, okay? You're talking to a man who saw the inside of every bathhouse from LA to New York back in the day. I know from saunas."

"That's not what I was talking about."

"What I'm saying is there's no sauna that can keep you as warm as the love of a good dog. You had Jarrett so you already know that."

The corgi hobbled to the cage door. Packard squatted and scratched the top of the dog's head with his finger. He suddenly had a vision of their whole life together—walks through sun and leaves and snow. Dog bowls and leashes. Napping on the couch. He saw a table set for two with half-empty beer glasses and the corgi begging for table scraps.

Gary said, "You think you're hiding behind those sunglasses, Deputy, but I see you. I think you just fell in love."

Packard stood up. Yes, he was hiding. From his life and his past. Hiding who he was since moving to Sandy Lake. Police departments and small towns were notoriously conservative places. A certain amount of camouflage was always required. Even in Minneapolis, his relationship with Marcus had been very much on the down low in the interest of their careers. When he interviewed for the job in Sandy Lake, he'd kept his family's connection to the area to himself. Most people still didn't know he and Susan were related. His plan was to come in as an outsider, be the best deputy possible and nothing else. The solution for the pain and confusion caused by Marcus's death was not to get involved like that again. In Sandy Lake, he wouldn't have a choice.

"I gotta go, Gary. I've got work to do."

Packard led the way out. Gary took the half-smoked cigarette butt out of his pocket and relit it as they stepped into the sunshine. "So if someone comes by to adopt the corgi, should I let him go?"

Packard turned but kept walking backward. "Not yet. I might need to question him if this business with Cora and the crossbow escalates. Understand?"

Gary folded an arm across his belly and propped the elbow of his cigarette hand on top. He thumbed the butt and knocked the ashes loose. "Honey, I understand plenty."

CHAPTER FIVE

PACKARD DROVE HOME, PONDERING the idea of getting a dog again. Not having to scoop Jarrett's winter poop this spring had been nice, but he missed their walks. He missed the sound of another living being in the house.

To describe where Packard lived as "under construction" would imply that any part of it was fully constructed. It was not. He'd bought the house at a bank auction knowing full well what he was getting into. The house needed a roof, windows, flooring, mechanicals, and siding. He'd started by renting the largest dumpster available and gutting the place from top to bottom. He was slowly finishing it one room at a time. Throughout the house, furniture sat on plywood subflooring, and plastic sheeting hung in doorways. He was nearly finished turning one of the bedrooms into the master bath. It had a two-person shower, a cedar sauna, two sinks, and a hammered copper soaking tub sitting on a bed of smooth river rocks. He'd built a bathroom for two just for himself. Marcus would have loved it.

Packard parked in the garage and brought in the twelve gauge for cleaning. Shooting the bear already felt like another day. It was only 3:00 p.m.

There was no word from Susan by the time he'd changed clothes and cleaned the gun. He made a list of Jenny's girlfriends, Jesse's mom, and their phone numbers. He added Sean White Cloud's name to the list, then texted Kelly to ask for his number.

He waited until the end of the school day before calling Jenny's girlfriends. Neither one answered her phone, but the first one called him back as he was still leaving a message for the second.

Her name was Taylor. The last she'd heard from Jenny was via text the night before. Packard asked her to read their exchange, which Taylor did reluctantly. She had to spell out all the abbreviations and describe the emojis used. It was a lot of nonsense about another girl and the homework that was due the next day. Taylor's parents had a rule about no phones after 10:00 p.m., so the messages stopped then. Jenny made no mention of Jesse or of sneaking out to meet him.

"Were you surprised she wasn't in school today?"

"Kind of. She doesn't miss very often. She has diabetes, you know, so she can get sick suddenly. I've seen her when her blood sugar is really low, and she's disoriented. I texted her today to make sure she was okay, but she never responded. I know Carrie hasn't heard from her either."

"Where would Jenny and Jesse go if they wanted to be…together?"

Taylor seemed embarrassed by the question. "I don't… She wouldn't. I don't know."

"Come on, Taylor. Now's not the time to play dumb."

"I mean…there used to be a cabin that kids would go to. It's kind of remote, owners were never around, and there was a hidden key. Everyone called it the Love Shack. After that old song, you know."

"I know the song. It's very old."

"Too many people found out about it. Some kids ended up having a party there. The owners put in cameras and changed the locks. That was, like, six months ago. I don't know where they would go now."

"Tell me about Jesse," Packard said.

"I don't know him other than through Jenny. We don't all hang out together. They do their own thing."

"What kind of kid is he? Jock, nerd, pothead?"

"None of those really. He's just a guy. Kind of cute. Smokes weed, I guess. Who doesn't? My dad vapes it out in the garage every night. Like we don't know what he's doing."

Packard asked a few more questions, but Taylor didn't give him much else to go on. Carrie, by the time he got hold of her an hour later, was even less helpful. She confirmed the Love Shack story but didn't know of a new place. She couldn't identify any of Jesse's friends, wasn't even sure he had any. She called Jenny and Jesse's relationship intense and weird.

"Weird how?" Packard asked.

"Just how into each other they are."

"In a good way or a bad way?"

"A good way, I guess, unless you're the one who's left out because Jenny doesn't have as much time for you."

After talking to Taylor and Carrie, Packard found tasks to keep himself busy, realizing the whole time that he was waiting to hear from Susan, and that every hour that went by made his shoulders feel tighter, like he was bracing himself for something to come at him but he didn't know what or from what direction. He was still convinced Jenny and Jesse had taken off somewhere to be alone, but he also thought someone would have heard from them by now.

He made himself dinner in a kitchen where all the upper cabinets and drawers and lower door fronts had long ago been hauled to the dump. His meager collection of dishes was piled on green linoleum countertops begging to be put out of their misery.

He texted Susan, knowing she'd be cooking at the restaurant. He heard back half an hour later that she still hadn't heard from Jenny. She said she could meet him at her house at 9:00 p.m., after the rush had ended. He said he'd see her there.

His next call was to Ann Crawford, Jesse's mom. "Ann. It's Ben Packard with the sheriff's department."

There was a pause. Packard knew she was trying to place a face with the name. She should know who he was. They'd had a memorable encounter. How long it took her to remember would depend on how much she'd had to drink. "Whadda you want?"

"Ann, is Jesse Crawford your son?"

"Depends on what he's done."

"He hasn't done anything. I'm just wondering if you've seen him today."

"No."

"Any idea where he might be?"

Ann scoffed. "Boy treats this place like a flophouse. Comes and goes as he pleases 'cause he thinks he's a man now. Takes my car without asking. Don't clean up, don't do nothin'. I usedta could whoop his ass, but he's too big for that now." Her accent had a lingering flavor of the South. He had a vision of someone driving Ann Crawford all the way to the north woods of Minnesota and leaving her on the side of the road, far enough away to make sure she'd never find her way back.

"One more month 'til graduation and then I'ma start charging him rent to put up with his shit."

"When did you see Jesse last?"

He heard the scratch of a cigarette lighter and a weary exhale. "Yesterday, I guess. Why? Wait, have you found my car?"

"What kind of car?"

"'95 Grand Am. Maroon. Rhymes with *varoom*." She laughed at her own joke, then stopped to take a drink of something.

"I haven't seen your car, Ann."

"So why are you calling me?"

"Jenny Wheeler's mom is looking for her daughter," Packard said. "We think Jenny and Jesse went out sometime last night. No one has seen or heard from either of them today. They both skipped school. They're not answering their phones."

"Skipped school? That's your big worry?" She made a laugh that sounded like a bark. "You have no idea what that boy gets up to. He's got weed. He's got pills."

Packard wrote *weed* and *pills* in his notebook. Susan and Taylor had both mentioned smoking weed in relation to Jesse. This was the first he'd heard of pills. "What kind of pills does he have?"

Ann wasn't listening. She was on a rant now, a well-worn one by the sound of it. "He thinks I'm stupid. That I don't know what's going on. I know things. Trust me. And when I ask if he's got something for his old mom, something for my back, you know what he says? 'Pay me.'"

"Where does he get the pills?"

"'Pay me.' Like I'm some junkie off the street. 'I'm your mother,' I said."

She paused to catch her breath and take a drink.

"What else can you tell me about the pills, Ann?"

"I'm not telling you anything. I know you. You threw me on the ground." She was remembering when he tried to break up a fight between her and another woman at Bob's Bar. He was doing a patrol rotation back then, still getting to know Sandy Lake's roads and rhythms. During the incident, just when he thought he'd had her calmed down, Ann had literally climbed the front of him to get at the other woman, ending up folded over his shoulder. He started to carry her out of the bar like that when she bit him on the ass, right below his vest. He'd dropped her onto the floor, then roughly cuffed her before putting her in his car. It was his own fault for carrying her like that. He should have known better.

"I was just doing my job, Ann."

"Do your job and find my car, how about? That boy stole it. Find it and drive it over here, okay? So I can get to work."

Packard paused, then thumbed the phone off. Ann wasn't much use to him in her current state. He'd get more out of her if he could catch her tomorrow before she got too many under her belt. At least he'd been able to confirm no one had heard from Jesse today, either, and now he knew what car they were driving. The pills were an interesting lead, too.

He called dispatch and asked them to pull the registration information for Ann Crawford's vehicle, then requested a BOLO go out for the car and the two teens. He gave the description of Jenny and Jesse that he'd gotten from Susan. A BOLO meant everyone on duty would be on the lookout.

After that, he made the twenty-minute drive back to town to meet Susan at home. He parked in the driveway. The garage door was open with a Jeep Grand Cherokee and a gray Camry parked inside. He imagined a bear crouched in the back corner, waiting to stand up and fall on top of anyone who came through the door from the house.

Susan answered the door wearing the same green bike T-shirt she'd had on earlier. She smelled like roasted meat and pasta steam. Her face was red, like she'd been warmed under a heat lamp.

It was his first time in his cousin's house. It was neat and orderly, as he knew it would be. She had low furniture against the walls, a modern couch, and midcentury tables.

"Still no word?" he asked.

Susan shook her head and walked away from him, heading for the kitchen. "Do you want something to drink?"

"No, thanks. I'd like to look through Jenny's room."

Susan got herself a glass of water from the tap, then led him to a bedroom just down the hall from the garage. She flipped on the light, revealing a room painted light blue. The queen-size bed was neatly made with a yellow bedspread. A desk next to the door had a MacBook Air and a lamp and books stacked on it.

Susan turned on the desk lamp and walked around the bed to turn on the lamp on the far side.

"What do you notice is missing?" Packard asked her.

Susan looked around. "Her letter jacket. Her purse." She noticed a blue container on the bedside table and opened it. "Her retainer."

Packard pulled out the three desk drawers as far as they would go. Mostly pens and pencils, old school notebooks, batteries, hand lotion, lip balm, a box of thank-you cards, outdated electronics, and charging cords.

Her backpack was on the floor beside the desk, split open like it had been gutted, its contents a notebook and an AP English textbook and a paperback copy of *David Copperfield* by Charles Dickens.

On top of the dresser was a sharps container filled with needles, discarded infusion sets, and used reservoirs from her insulin pump. There was also an old square TV and an even older VCR. "This is ancient technology," Packard said.

"She's got Star Wars VHS tapes that Tom bought long before she was born. We watched them a million times when she was little. She still likes to put on *The Empire Strikes Back* when she can't sleep. She doesn't want new DVDs. I asked."

Packard pulled out the dresser drawers, went through them methodically, but found only clothes. He stopped for a minute to look out the bedroom window. If it were January, he would have been looking at a neighborhood buried waist-deep in snow and imagining winter's worst reasons why these kids didn't make it home. A car sliding sideways into a deep ditch. An icehouse with a leaky propane heater.

A snowmobile dropping into open water.

It was almost May 1. The snow and the ice were gone. It was dark out, but he could see tulips in the neighbor's yard across the street.

Packard lifted the mattress on one side, walked around the bed, and lifted the other side. Nothing. Susan was sitting at the desk, looking at Jenny's computer. Packard pulled away the pillows at the top of the bed and froze.

"Susan."

She turned in the chair, got up without a word. She put her knee on the edge of the mattress as she reached for what Packard had uncovered.

Jenny's phone.

———————

Packard and Susan sat at her dining room table, Jenny's phone in front of them, shiny and black and inscrutable on its surface. Susan had poured herself a glass of red wine. She hadn't offered Packard any.

Susan had the password to Jenny's phone, so they were able to unlock it. Jenny had nine missed calls and twenty-three unread text messages, mostly from friends wondering where she was and why she wasn't replying. No calls or texts from Jesse.

Under her recent calls, Packard could see Jenny and Jesse had talked for forty minutes around midnight. The last text Jenny received between when Susan saw her before bed and when she noticed Jenny wasn't home at 6:45 a.m. came from Jesse at 1:38 a.m. It said, **On my way.** Jenny had responded with **Meet u @ the corner.** Nothing in their previous messages gave any hint about where they were going or what they were doing.

Packard and Susan went through Jenny's photos and emails. They checked her social media accounts. There had been no recent activity on any of them.

There was an app that gave them access to Jenny's bank account and credit card. "She took out $100 in cash a week ago. She used her credit card three days ago to buy gas for her car and pay for food at Hardee's. Two days ago she got charged the monthly fee for her Apple Music. Nothing since. Nothing today."

After they went through the phone, he'd told Susan about his phone call with Ann Crawford and the BOLO he'd put out on her car. He sent himself several photos from Jenny's phone of her and Jesse that he then emailed to dispatch to update their files. He called to see if there had been any sightings in the last couple of hours, shaking his head for Susan when he was told that, so far, no one had seen anything.

It was nearly 10:00 p.m. Packard got lost in thought for a minute about how the size and shape of the object in front of them now represented the idea of a phone—it had become a symbol of itself—and how odd it was that we still called them phones even though that was probably their least used feature.

Susan said, "This changes everything." She nodded at the phone as she set down her wineglass. "I assume I don't need to explain to you about sixteen-year-old girls and their phones."

Packard shook his head. What he knew about the internal lives of modern teenage girls would fit in a single tweet with characters left over, but he knew everyone these days—himself included—was glued to their phones. Even his memory of first meeting Jenny was of her working at the restaurant and looking at her phone every chance she got.

"Let's think about why she might leave it behind," Packard suggested.

"She wouldn't. That's the problem."

"But she did. So…it's almost two o'clock in the morning. She's meeting her boyfriend. Maybe she decides she doesn't need it. Who's she going to call or text at 2:00 a.m.?"

"But it's not just about calling or texting. She and her friends don't go anywhere without their phones. They're constantly taking selfies, recording, snapping, posting, chatting. Any chance she gets, she's scrolling and scrolling."

"The phone still has a charge, so she didn't leave it behind because the battery was dead."

"She could have charged it in the car if she needed to. If she walked to the corner to meet him, she would have been looking at her phone the whole way there. Or at least while standing there and waiting for him."

"Maybe she forgot it and didn't want to risk getting caught going in and out of the house again."

Susan shrugged.

"Another thing…a phone can store a history of where you've been if the GPS is recording. You can leave a trail of cell-tower pings even if you're not actively using the phone. Maybe they were going somewhere and didn't want to leave a record. Or be tracked."

Susan drank her wine. "You're not going to convince me she ran away from home and left her phone behind. Her diabetes kit? Maybe, but I find that almost as implausible. Whatever they were doing, they were supposed to be gone for an hour or two max. She could live without her phone that long if she had to. Something happened to them."

Packard sat and stared at the phone. Being in Susan's house was reminding him of all the ways he hadn't been there for her after Tom died. He'd called a couple of times after the funeral and left messages that Susan never returned.

Was offering help when it wasn't wanted its own kind of burden? He didn't know. It was different when Marcus died. Their relationship had been a secret. He'd been alone in his grief by default. Susan seemed to have chosen the isolation. After a certain amount of time went by, Packard had felt awkward reaching out to her again, so he didn't.

Jenny's phone suddenly buzzed with a text message, causing both of them to jump. Susan picked up the phone and read the message. "It was Carrie. She saw Jenny was on Snapchat twenty minutes ago. That was us looking at her account."

Packard got up to leave. "I'll call you first thing in the morning, news or no news. Call me anytime tonight if you hear anything."

Susan sat there and said nothing. Packard waited for a moment, then assumed he was getting another one of Susan's goodbye-less goodbyes. She spoke just as he got to the door. "You asked me this morning how concerned I was on a scale from one to ten. I'm at an eleven now," she said.

"I am too," Packard said.

This time he wasn't lying.

CHAPTER SIX

SOMETIMES EMMETT BURR HAD pain the pills couldn't touch. Usually, when he was fully loaded, they dropped a shroud between him and the things hurting him, so that he felt like a boat lost in fog, and the pain was a ringing bell that he could hear but couldn't locate the source of.

It was nearly 11:00 p.m., and the pills he'd been taking all day hadn't done anything for his back. Something had gone *fwaaapp* when he'd tried to help move the boy's body earlier that morning. Now he was barefoot and shirtless, leaning on the deck railing. It hurt to sit, and standing always hurt because of his enormous weight. Leaning on his forearms allowed his pendulous belly to hang like a swollen udder, which helped relieve the pressure in his back. It was the best he'd felt since blasting those kids with the shotgun.

The night air chilled his bare skin as he smoked. He heard a cough and turned to look through the leafless trees that separated his property from his neighbor's. The red eye of a cigarette burned on Ruth Adams's front porch. Ruth had been the town librarian for the last hundred and forty years. The two of them shared this shallow, muddy part of the lake. He could have called out and said hello, but Ruth had been Myra's friend, and Emmett hadn't spoken a word to Ruth since Myra left him almost twenty years ago.

Emmett blamed Myra for the mess he was in, just like he blamed her for all the ones before. He wouldn't have a dead body in the garage and a girl in the pink room again if Myra had stuck around. Yeah, they'd made each other miserable, but goddamn…wasn't that what a marriage was?

Their union had been the product of overbearing mothers who knew each other from bridge club and who saw no hope for their awkward, misshapen spawn—Emmett with hips and breasts and the pink complexion of a woman; Myra flat as a new road with a man's height and jaw and hands. They conspired to push Emmett and Myra together, one Sunday supper at a time. Ernestine did her best to convince her son that Myra was his best and only option. *I don't exactly see the ladies ah…lining up for a date, Son. You're doughy and shifty and the only thing you can do for yourself involves your hand in your pants. You could do a lot worse than Myra, Emmie. You get a job after your apprenticeship, and she'll keep you a good home. You could be happy together.*

When the time was right, Ernestine had all but proposed on his behalf. "Listen, Myra. Emmett has something to ask you. Go ahead, Son. Say it like we practiced."

Once married, he found that the sex with a real live woman he'd dreamed of having all his life couldn't have been more disappointing. Even while horizontal, it was no easy feat climbing Mount Myra. The physical act left him stunned at the end, more like a sudden collision than the warm pistoning he'd always imagined. Who knew what Myra had imagined? The way she squeezed her eyes shut and turned her head away while he was on top of her, like she was trying not to smell something bad, said plenty. They quickly set aside the sex that neither one of them enjoyed and focused on their roles inside their Jack Sprat marriage. Myra's interests were gardening, canning, and tuneless humming. Emmett's welding business paid the bills with enough leftover that he could submerge himself to the eyeballs at the end of the day in alcohol and mail-order pornography.

The day Myra finally decided she'd had enough, Emmett had passed out in his rocker, wearing stained boxers and nothing else, while a dirty movie played on the basement television. He came awake to the squeal of aluminum and the smell of cheap beer as sharp as the stink from a urinal. Struggling up from his chair, he found Myra in the backyard, red-faced and gasping, a pitchfork in her hands. The beer from the basement fridge was scattered on the lawn. Cans geysered white foam from where they'd been stabbed. The shiny entrails of a shattered VHS tape moved like hair in the breeze.

"The hell has gotten into you?" Emmett asked. "That's my goddamn basement beer." He glanced back at his television and knew where the videotape had come from. "Christ. Wha'd I do?"

Myra was dressed in a plaid western shirt buttoned to the throat, a frill of lace at the collar and the cuffs her one nod to the idea that she had a feminine bone in her body. She held the pitchfork up and glared at him through her splattered glasses. A can caught in the tines poured beer down her sleeve. "You've done nothing, Emmett. For decades, nothing. That's the problem." Myra pushed up her enormous glasses with a knuckle. "Why do I continue to live like this? Why do I work so you can spend all your time watching filth and getting drunk in your underpants?"

"'Work,'" he scoffed. "And I do nothing? Who do you think pays for this house?"

"Don't kid yourself. You do the bare minimum to keep us out of poverty. You might make the money, but I put it to work. We're not starving or sleeping in a ditch because of me."

"Baaaah," he said, turning away from her and pulling at the back of his underwear.

"*Baaaaah*," Myra aped as she pushed by him. "You sound like an old goat. That's the sound you'll make the first night I'm gone when you realize there's nothing to eat." She stomped up the basement stairs to the kitchen, rolling up her wet sleeve like she had work to do.

Two weeks later, her sister and brother-in-law came from Iowa with a moving truck. Emmett stayed in the basement while they loaded Myra's things. The next time he went up the stairs, she was gone.

He never saw her again.

It took him a month to get used to feeding himself and doing his own wash. The dusty rectangles on the floor where Myra's furniture once stood made it easy to remember things the way they used to be. He walked around the missing love seat and sometimes reached up to turn on the lamp by his chair only to find empty air where the knob used to be.

A year after she'd gone—when clutter and a creeping filth had wiped out all traces of Myra—he started construction in the basement. Sandy Lake Building and Supply delivered the load of concrete blocks and bags of cement. He used his own skid loader to bring the pallets around to the back side of the house. It took six months for him to wall off the corner into its own room. Many nights, he'd collapse in his rocking chair with a beer and a cigarette, while a bright work light illuminated the staggered blocks climbing as high as the floor joists. He felt like a pharaoh watching his pyramid go up. He felt like he'd been waiting all his life to do this for himself.

When construction was done, he rested for two months while he planned his next step.

Then he kidnapped Wanda from the gas station.

———————

Emmett flicked his cigarette butt into the yard.

How long ago now since Wanda? he wondered. *Fifteen years? Twenty?*

He went to his bedroom, dropped his pants, and lay down on a sagging mattress. The girl had been locked up for almost eighteen hours now. What happened in that room was supposed to be long behind him. He was an old man now. If it had come down years ago like it should have, he wouldn't be in this mess.

He'd been lying in this same spot when he was wakened by the storm last night. His chest hurt and his breathing felt labored, so he'd gone to the living room and was sitting in the dark with his oxygen on when he saw a car with just its running lights go back and forth in front of his house. A few minutes later he saw someone dressed in black come down the driveway.

"Sonofabitch," he said as he struggled up from the chair. He forgot the oxygen mask on his face and had to yank the hose from the machine before he could get the shotgun from where he kept it in the kitchen cabinet with the broom.

A chance to finally catch the cocksucker who'd been breaking into his house had felt like a stroke of luck at the time.

He hadn't stopped to consider what would come next.

Just putting on pants and going down the basement stairs left Emmett exhausted and breathless. Looking at the dead boy and the unconscious girl, he knew immediately he was in trouble. Calling the police wasn't an option. He'd managed to stay off their radar all these years. He wasn't about to invite them into the basement where he'd kept Wanda and the others. One look into the pink room and he'd be done.

He needed help.

An hour later, a '70s-era Ford long-bed truck rolled into Emmett's yard. It had a yellow body, a gray hood, and a red driver's side door, all scavenged from other wrecks. Its owner called the truck Frankenstein.

Everything about the man who ducked through Emmett's basement door was just as monstrous—his height, his hands, the crowded teeth in his mouth. A dark beard tried to obscure a face that had been ravaged by acne. He was wearing a hunting coat spotted with old blood, a gray T-shirt, and dirty jeans. A camo cap topped a sloped-back forehead and a prominent brow ridge. Over one shoulder he carried a blue backpack heavy with something inside.

Carl took cigarettes from his shirt pocket and lit one as he surveyed the scene in front of him. Emmett had taped the girl's mouth and cuffed her hands behind her back while she was still unconscious. She had a lump on the back of her head as soft as old fruit. Since coming to, she hadn't moved much beyond rolling on to her side. One of her ankles was chained to a steel pole holding up the floor above them.

"You got a red Pontiac sitting up the road just past your place," Carl said. "I grabbed this out of the front seat." He unshouldered the backpack and left it on the workbench.

"Find the car keys," Emmett said. "They gotta be on one of them."

The boy's very dead body was awkwardly crumpled on the landing at the bottom of the stairs. Carl pinched the pants pockets and felt inside the front of the boy's sweatshirt. He turned to the girl, his rubbery clown face and the dangling cigarette as close to the side of her face as he could get without burning her. She closed her eyes and tried to curl up tighter. "You sure this one ain't a boy, too? Gots awful short hair. Tiny titties."

Carl stuck two thick fingers in the front pocket of her jeans, pulled the keys out, and jangled them in the air. "What's the plan?"

"What makes you think there's a goddamn plan?" Emmett asked. "You think I was expecting something like this?"

Carl smoked and towered over the girl, chin pinned to his chest. She rolled to one side to look up at him. "This one's your problem," he said. "It would have been better if you killed 'em both."

"I didn't know there were two of them until after."

"It's not too late. You could just…" Carl made a trigger-pulling motion with his finger.

Emmett imagined putting the shotgun to the girl's head. She turned to him, pleading with her eyes. He looked away and rocked. "I can't kill a girl cuffed to a pole."

"You sure as shit killed that one over there," Carl said, pointing with his cigarette.

"That was an intruder. I was protecting myself."

"What about that one gal way back? Shot her point-blank while she was chained in that room."

Emmett stared at Carl like he had no idea what he was talking about. The girl was sobbing now, louder and louder behind the tape over her mouth. *Wanda cried like that, too, but I never shot Wanda. The hell is he talking about?*

His memories from the time before he started taking so many pain pills were slow to come back. Sometimes it felt like the last six, seven years of his life—trapped in this house, in this body with every kind of pain imaginable—was the only life he'd ever lived. Sixty years of this, not six.

Then he remembered the jogger.

"That was different. I was cleaning up your mess. You wrecked that woman, coming back here day after day."

Carl shook his head and hitched up his pants. "So what are you gonna do? You can't call the cops. You get one of those K9s snooping around, it'll find them three you got buried out there."

"One of 'em belongs to you," Emmett said. "I had nothing to do with that third one." He squirmed in his rocker, trying to get his hand down in the pocket of his pants for the handcuff key. He tossed it to Carl. "I'm not calling anybody else." He regretted calling Carl, the sonofabitch. "Lock her in the room until I can think of something."

At the mention of the room, the girl started thrashing. The handcuffs around her ankle rang against the steel pole. Carl put a big boot on her shoulder and pressed it to the ground so she was flat on her belly. The boot was almost the same length as her back. "Now you got her going," he said. He stepped on his cigarette, then got down with his knees in the girl's back, almost all his weight on her as he uncuffed her from the pole.

She was breathless, sobbing soundlessly when he got up, flung an arm around her neck, and dragged her backward. Emmett turned in his chair as far as he could to watch them go. One of the girl's shoes peeled off and lay sideways as she was carried away.

Carl came out a minute later, asked Emmett for a rag or a towel of some kind. Emmett pointed him to a box above the washing machine. Another minute and then Carl shut the door on the room and ran the bolt. The volume of the girl's cries went down by more than half. Emmett took a deep breath and slowed his rocking.

"You winged her on the right side. She's bleeding some from her hip and thigh. Her hand is pretty tore up," Carl said. He took off his hat, wiped his forehead.

"Get me a beer outta the fridge. Get yourself one if you want," Emmett said.

They drank and filled the basement with cigarette smoke. The sun had come up, turning the sky gray-blue. Emmett was thinking about the view his neighbor Ruth would have of his place if she happened to look this way. Plenty of trees between them but no leaves out yet. They should have moved the car and the body while it was still dark.

Carl started laughing to himself as he tipped the last of his beer back.

"What's so goddamn funny?" Emmett asked.

"Just thinking about how you got a new bird in your cage. She just flew through the window. Not like them other two. It's like my wife tells our daughter— you don't find love, love finds you. You lucky bastard."

Emmett rocked in his chair and seethed. He'd never been lucky a day in his life. He didn't feel lucky now.

"Shut up, Carl."

CHAPTER SEVEN

PACKARD GOT UP EARLY, put on his clammy wet suit, and walked down to the lake. He did a shallow dive from the end of the dock, surfaced, then moved through the water with the grace of a kayak. His arms arced and plunged in a steady rhythm, pulling him through the forty-seven-degree water to the center of the lake and back.

Since buying the house, he'd already developed a reputation as being the crazy guy who swam from April to November. He'd swum in high school and college, well enough for a scholarship but not fast enough to break any records or be much more than a reliable leg in the relay.

When he was done with his laps, Packard put his hands on the end of the dock and lifted himself out of the water and into a sitting position. He peeled off his goggles and wiped his face.

A great gray owl roosting in the open, not far from her nest at the top of a dead tree, watched him as he toweled his hair. He'd first noticed her there a week earlier, a sign that her clutch had hatched. A fish flopping on the surface of the lake caught her attention, but then she turned her large facial disk back in his direction, rings of black and white feathers receding toward two yellow eyes.

Packard gave her a nod, like a neighbor.

Susan hadn't called or texted during the night so Packard knew Jenny still wasn't home. When he got to the station, he checked on his BOLO and found out there'd been no sightings of the car or the two teens. No reports from any of the local hospitals either.

He reviewed the other news from the overnight shift, then made a list of what he wanted to do next. He wanted to talk to Ann Crawford, Jesse's mom, when she wasn't drunk. He wanted to talk to Sean White Cloud to see what he knew about Jenny from the time he was in their house regularly, taking care of her dad. Sleeping with Susan might also have given him some insight into her and Jenny's relationship.

The address on record for Ann Crawford led him to a place five blocks off Main Street. The house was a tan box in need of paint and a new roof. The yard was more dirt than grass. He climbed two steps and banged on an aluminum storm door. A mountain bike lay on its side next to the steps. He looked back across the street and saw an old woman watching from her front window.

The front door pulled open with a *hoosh*ing sound. A teenage girl with long, straight hair stood in the doorway. She had eye makeup on only one eye.

"I'm Deputy Packard with the sheriff's department. What's your name?"

"Alissa."

"Alissa, is your mom home?"

The girl shook her head. She had thick lips covered in pink gloss, and a look on her face like she didn't appreciate the interruption. "She's at work."

"Your brother home?"

"Nope."

"You seen him at all today? Heard from him?"

"Nope."

Packard pulled open the storm door and climbed the top step. Behind the girl, he caught a glimpse of a shirtless teenage boy with buzzed hair and lots of red acne duck away from an arched doorway into the kitchen. On the coffee table, two cigarettes smoldered in an ashtray next to a game controller and a scattered collection of makeup products. The girl took a step back, unsure whether she should try to stop him from coming in or not. He stayed just outside the door. "No text messages, nothing from your brother?"

"No."

"Who's that in the kitchen?"

Alissa looked over her shoulder like she had to be sure who he was asking about. She shrugged and gave him a weary look. "No one. A friend."

Packard nodded. "Shouldn't you and your friend be in school?"

Alissa shrugged again. It seemed to be the primary form of communication for her species. "We're sick," she said.

"I see. Remind me where your mom works."

"At the lumberyard."

"Wellards?"

"That's what I said."

Packard nodded as if the mistake had been his. "I appreciate your help, Alissa. I hope you and your friend feel better. Giving up the cigarettes might help."

He let the storm door close behind him as he went down the steps. The old woman in the window across the street was still watching, shaking her head.

Wellards was a big-box hardware retailer with a new store half a mile east of town on Highway 18. Packard parked close to the main entrance. The car and the uniform caused people to tap their brakes and slow their pace as they watched where he went. He stopped at the service counter and asked a middle-aged woman with blond hair and a green apron where he could find Ann Crawford. She asked him to wait while she picked up a white phone hanging on the wall. "She's out in the lumberyard in the inventory control booth," she said, hanging up the phone and smoothing her apron. "I can have someone take you back there if you want."

"I know where it is."

The blond woman leaned across the counter. "Is she in trouble? Did she do something?"

"No, ma'am. She is not in trouble," Packard said.

The blond looked disappointed by the news. Or by being called *ma'am*.

Packard walked up the main aisle, past pallets of blue wiper fluid, aerosol cans of flat-tire fixer, and fifty-pound bags of lawn starter. A recorded ad on the overhead speakers encouraged shoppers to apply for a Wellards credit card and receive 2 percent cash back on all their purchases.

At the rear of the store, he passed through a towering glass door that slid open to a lumberyard surrounded by a twelve-foot wooden fence, the planks set edge to edge like the wall around a frontier fort. Lumber was slotted into wood racks along the perimeter, protected from the elements by an overhang. A small guard shack with a bright-orange traffic arm controlled the vehicles leaving the yard.

It was warm in the sun, but the creeping shade within the tall walls chilled the damp air. Ann Crawford was wearing a black coat with a hood. When she saw him coming, she stamped her foot and threw her head back, a you-gotta-be-kidding-me gesture. He could tell she wasn't entirely surprised to see him. Alissa might have warned her he was on his way. The nosy blond at the service counter didn't strike him as the type who would do Ann Crawford any favors.

Ann handed her bar-code scanner to a skinny bald guy breathing through his mouth. "I'm going on break," she said. She grabbed her purse from the guard shack and walked away from Packard. He followed her off the property. "Can't smoke in there by the wood," she said over her shoulder.

They went around the traffic control arm and crossed the street. They stood by the curb on the other side as she lit a cigarette.

Hard living had aged Ann's thin face with lines and wrinkles and dark rings around her eyes. Her hair was shot through with streaks of gray, and she wore it pulled back, with long straight bangs that covered her eyebrows. She was only a year or two older than Packard, but she looked old enough to be his mother.

"How long you been working at Wellards?"

"Since the beginning. Put in my application when they were hiring for the grand opening. I like working the yard. You get more smoke breaks if it's not busy."

Packard nodded his understanding. "I wanted to talk to you about Jesse."

"Figured as much. He turned up yet?"

"No. I assume you haven't seen or heard from him either?"

Ann shrugged. Now he knew where Alissa got it from. "Alls I know is I woke up yesterday and my car was gone and so was he."

"How'd you get to work yesterday and today?"

"Yesterday I got a ride from a girlfriend. Today she had to take her kid to the doctor so I walked. It's only a mile and some."

"Why didn't you report your car or your son missing to the police?"

Ann took a long drag on her cigarette. She had a wide upper lip, deeply crimped from years of sucking air through a tiny filter. Smoke came out of her in sputtering clouds as she talked. "You think this is what I needed today? A cop showing up at work to question me about where is my lazy pothead son? You think my boss is going to be happy about this?"

Packard couldn't argue with that. He asked her to check her phone for the last time she'd had a call or a text from Jesse. She started to look it up on her phone, then stopped. "He can't call or text me because his phone is in my purse. I found it in his room and kept it."

Both Jesse and Jenny were without their phones. Intentionally.

"Can I have it? I'll make sure he gets it back."

Ann rooted in her purse and handed him a Samsung phone with a cracked screen. She didn't know the password. "You can keep it far as I'm concerned. He don't own nothing until I get my car."

"Where's Jesse get the pot?"

Ann shrugged again. "I don't know no names."

"Is he dealing or just smoking?"

"When you find him, you can ask him."

"You mentioned pills last night. Where does he get those?"

Ann looked away and smoked the last bit of her cigarette. She dropped the butt and stared at the ground while she stepped on it. "Like I said, you gotta ask him. I don't know and I don't want to know."

Packard believed her. Ann Crawford would rather maintain her ignorance than take responsibility for the actions of her almost grown son. He was going to do what he wanted, and the less she knew about it, the better. She had her own problems.

Packard pocketed his notebook and pen and followed Ann back inside the lumberyard. She went up to the skinny, bald guy covering for her. "Give me my scanner," she said. He handed it over and slouched away.

"I'd like to go with you back to your house and go through Jesse's room. I can get a warrant if I have to, but it'd be a lot easier if I can just get your permission. Can we do that?"

"Damn it, Packard. You're gonna get me fired if you haul me out of here right now when it's not my break."

"When is your break?"

Ann pulled the flip phone from her pocket and looked at the time on the front. "I get lunch an hour from now."

"I'll come pick you up in an hour. I'll bring you a burger or a sandwich, whatever you want. We'll go back to your house, have a look at Jesse's things, and then I'll drive you back. How's that?"

A navy-blue pickup pulled up to the gate with a load of drywall in the back. Ann took the printed receipt from the driver, scanned the bar code printed at the bottom, and looked over the load in the back before she pressed a button in her booth that raised the traffic arm. They both watched the pickup drive away.

"I want Arby's roast beef. Large curly fries. Diet Sprite," she said.

"Deal."

Ann scratched at her bangs and shook her head. "Pick me up in back by the goddamn loading dock. The last sonofabitchin' thing I need is everybody seeing me get in a police car."

Packard walked back through the store and called Sean White Cloud once he got in his vehicle.

"I need to ask you about something. Where you at right now?"

"Chillin' at the station. Quiet so far today."

"I'll be there in ten minutes. Meet me out front."

"What's it about?"

"I'll tell you when I get there."

It only took him five minutes to cross town and arrive at the Sandy Lake Fire Department. The station was built in the late nineties with three large bays for fire trucks, two smaller stalls for ambulances. All the doors were open and the ladder truck was in front, being scrubbed down by two firefighters in blue T-shirts. Packard parked and kept an eye on the station in his rearview mirror until he saw Sean step out of one of the bays into the bright sunlight. A blond woman in jeans and a sleeveless blouse, accompanied by two miniature versions of herself, approached him, carrying three pizza boxes. Sean smiled at her, got down and talked to her kids for a minute, then pointed the way to go inside the bay. Locals loved first responders in Sandy Lake. A steady stream of takeout and home-baked goods made their way to the fire station and the cop shop. Nobody with a badge was in danger of going hungry while on duty.

Packard waited until the pizza lady was gone before he got out of the SUV and waved Sean over. He came striding across the lot, all smiles, dressed in black pants and a white short-sleeved button-down with EMS patches on the shoulders. He had perfectly black hair swept back effortlessly from his face.

Sean said, "Haven't seen you in a while, Chief. Not since you moved up in the world."

They shook and bumped shoulders. "I could say the same. I heard you're a shift captain now," Packard said.

Sean shrugged. "I do my best," he said. "So what's up?"

Packard paused, looking for any sign Sean was anticipating what was coming next. He just kept smiling, squinting in the afternoon sun. "Susan Wheeler came in yesterday morning and reported her daughter missing."

Sean's smile faltered, then vanished. A storm of emotions raced across his face like clouds on a weather map.

"You asking me 'cause I'm on the list?" Sean hissed. His accent was suddenly full-on rez.

"Get in for a minute. We'll talk."

Sean brushed by him and went around the hood. "The front or the baaack?" he asked.

"The front, Sean."

They both got in and Packard started the engine to run the air conditioner. Sean said, "You didn't answer my question. You coming at me 'cause I'm on the list?"

"I'm coming to you because of your connection to the family. Not because of the list. I know you were Tom's hospice nurse. I also know you're sticking it to the widow upon request," he said. "That's why I'm here."

It was true and not true. If those kids didn't show up in the next day or so, Sean would be a prime suspect because of his connection to the family and because he was in the sex-offender registry. Sean's offense happened when he was eighteen and living in South Dakota. He'd texted nude selfies from his sixteen-year-old girlfriend to her friends in retaliation for her cheating on him. Her parents had him prosecuted for distribution of child pornography.

"Where were you Tuesday night and early Wednesday?"

"Working hospice. Edna Mallory passed at two thirty in the morning. Her son-in-law called me at midnight and I went over. After she passed, the family sat with her for a while; then we cleaned her body and dressed her and called the mortuary. I stayed with the family until they picked up the body around 4:00 a.m., then went home. I still hadn't been to sleep when Susan showed up at my place. I was there when she got a text that Jenny had an unexcused absence."

"What do you know about Jenny from your time with the family?"

"Not a lot. She wasn't around much. She did everything for her dad I asked her to. Tom was on lots of meds. In and out of it."

"What kind of drugs was he on? Anything go missing or come up short while you were there?"

"Absolutely not. Trust me. I've been to some shit shows where more of the pills went into the family members than the person dying. I know what that looks like. Tom was mostly on morphine toward the end. Knowing Jenny had no fear of needles because of her diabetes made me extra careful. There was a lockbox for all the medication. Only Susan and I had keys to it. I came back and grabbed everything after Tom died."

"Have you had any interaction with Jenny since she found out about you and her mom?"

"None. I haven't seen her in person since I quit working there. I've seen Susan at the restaurant and at my place. Never at her place."

Packard had hoped Jenny would have told Sean something that she would have kept from her parents. He was good looking, not that much older than Jenny, and had that aura that medical professionals have that either intimidates people or makes them open up.

Sean said, "You didn't tell Susan about me, did you?"

Packard shook his head.

"You don't think you should warn her about sexting me?"

"Does she sext you?"

"No."

"I didn't think so."

Sean reached forward to adjust the dashboard vent away from him. "She's an interesting person. I'm not sure she has much use for people outside the purpose she assigns them. My purpose is to make her eyes roll back in her head every couple of weeks."

Packard drummed his fingers on the steering wheel, thinking. "Jenny left without any of her diabetes supplies. She and her boyfriend both left their phones behind. It doesn't make sense."

Sean said, "We should all run off and leave our phones behind. The Lakota didn't even have a Native word for 'smartphone' until recently. *Omás'apȟela*."

"Why'd it take so long?"

Sean gave him a raised eyebrow. "Near the start of the twentieth century, the U.S. government actively suppressed Native customs and language while it continued to disregard treaties and push the tribes off their land. Indian kids were sent to boarding schools where they were forced to speak English and beaten when they didn't. A hundred years later, the number of motherfuckers sitting around, thinking up new words for shit is pretty small. They only meet once a year. They're a little behind."

Packard was embarrassed by his thoughtlessness. "That was a good answer to a dumb question. Sorry."

Sean had his hand on the door handle, ready to go. "That's all the Indian wisdom I got for you, Chief. You need anything else from me? Are we good?"

"We're good."

"Do me a favor and keep me out of this if you can. I care about Susan and I hope nothing bad has happened to Jenny, but I don't need the words 'Sean White Cloud' and 'sex offender' on the lips of everyone in town. I'm two years from the end of my registration period. After that I should be free and clear. I don't need this hanging over my head for the rest of my life."

"I'll do what I can."

Sean paused before he slid out. "Is it irony when you're on the sex-offender list for child pornography but in real life you're banging a middle-aged white woman old enough to be your mother?"

"Sounds like irony to me," Packard said. "The Lakota have a word for that?"

Sean White Cloud shook his head.

Packard put on his sunglasses. "Maybe next year," he suggested.

Packard went through the Arby's drive-through before heading back to Wellards to pick up Ann by the loading dock. She climbed in the passenger seat and took the white bag he handed her. Two of her coworkers smoking by the dumpster watched them drive away.

Ann ate the fries and peeked at her sandwich on the way back to the house. "You didn't get me cheddar cheese?"

"You didn't say beef and cheddar. You said roast beef."

"It's just plain meat."

"That's how they make 'em. There's Arby's sauce in there."

"Arby's sauce," she said, disgusted.

It took only minutes to get back to her house. Packard pulled up to the curb in front. The mountain bike was still on its side by the front door.

"There was a boy in there when I stopped earlier," Packard said. "Short hair, lots of zits. No shirt."

"That peckerwood," Ann said. She grabbed her soda from the holder between them and pushed open her door. "Come on. I'ma kill his ass unless you stop me."

Packard followed her up the front sidewalk. Ann walked, shoulders hunched like it was raining hard. He pictured her walking that way her whole life, from a little girl in a dress to the woman he saw now, like she was marching into the wind, into battle.

Alissa met them at the front door. She'd put makeup on the rest of her face. A lot of it.

"What are you doing home?" She sounded like she was confronting an inconsiderate roommate. "Why are you here again?" she asked Packard.

"Get out of my way," Ann said and pushed past her.

Packard kept his mouth shut and came in behind her. Over the top of Ann's head, he saw the boy slumped at the end of the couch, his head in one hand. He'd put on an orange T-shirt. He looked pissed but there was no fight in him.

Ann stared at him and her daughter. Her nostrils flared. She took a drink of her soda through the straw. "Smells like cigarettes and fucking in here," she said.

"Mom!"

"You," Ann said to the boy, "do not have permission to be in my house when I'm not here. Ever. If you're not out of my sight in ten seconds, you will leave here without your dick." She turned sideways and showed him the box knife in its canvas holster on her belt. "I'll nail it through the head to the wall. See how much fucking you do then."

The boy wrenched himself up from the couch and went out the front door without a word. Packard watched him pedal away, sitting low in the bike's dropped seat.

"You're supposed to be sick," Ann said to her daughter.

"I am sick."

"You ain't sick if you can spread your legs for that boy."

"Stop saying that."

"Why? Is this how you want to live for the rest of your life, Alissa? In a house like this? Having nothing? Keep it up. Have a baby when you're fifteen. You'll never get out of this prison."

Ann went through the arched doorway to the dining room table and pushed back a pile of clutter far enough to unpack her food.

Alissa flopped down in the spot on the couch vacated by her boyfriend. "Did you bring me any Arby's?"

"Nope."

"What am I supposed to eat?"

"They serve lunch at school. Second lunch ends at one. You better hurry if you're going to make it."

Alissa twisted over the arm of the couch. "Mom, the day's half over."

"There's still half to go then."

"How am I supposed to get there? Jesse has the car."

"Walk."

Packard wasn't as interested in the family drama as he was in getting a look at Jesse's room. Down the hallway on his left he saw two doors opposite each other and a bathroom at the end. "Which room is Jesse's?"

"On the right," Ann said.

Alissa pushed past him down the hall to her room and slammed the door. Packard followed her and turned on the light in Jesse's room. He saw a twin bed, a short table next to it, and a four-drawer dresser. The bedsheets were pulled off the corners and bunched in the center of the bed like they'd been stirred together. The floors were painted wood. A blackout shade covered the single window.

He opened the closet door and saw more empty hangers than clothes. He looked for an opening in the back or loose floorboards. Nothing. The top two dresser drawers had socks and underwear and T-shirts. The bottom two were empty. He felt underneath each drawer and pulled out the one on the bottom. Nothing between the mattresses or under the bed. It looked like the room of a transient. Packard looked at the closed bedroom door across the hall and wondered where Ann slept if the kids had the two bedrooms.

He was about to leave when he noticed two phone chargers pinned down by a lamp on the nightstand. The two cords had different ends.

Two charging cords. Two cell phones.

He went back to the dining room. Ann had finished her food and had a beer open in front of her. She gave him a look like he was another man in her house who didn't belong there.

"His room is pretty empty," Packard said.

"He must be keeping the rest of his things at our lake home," Ann cracked.

"I found two phone chargers by the bed. Does he have two cell phones?"

Ann lit a cigarette and shook her hair out of her eyes. "He's got one number I call him at. That's all I know about."

"What about things he usually carries with him? Schoolbag or something like that?"

"There's a blue backpack that goes everywhere he does," Ann said.

"Seen it since he's been gone?"

"No."

Packard nodded, looked around. The house was small, full of clutter, unhappiness, and cigarette smoke. "You ready to go back?"

Ann drank her beer and washed it down with the soda from Arby's. "I'm gonna walk so I can smoke on the way. You can take Alissa to school if you're looking to do a good deed."

"Will she come?"

Ann got up from the table and went down the hall to the bedroom. "The cop is leaving in two minutes. You need a ride if you're going to make it for lunch."

He could hear Ann's side of the conversation but only the muffled sound of Alissa's replies. "I don't care… Too bad… Alissa, keep talking, keep it up and I'll throw everything you own in the garbage. You know I'll do it again."

Ann came back and sat at the table again and drank her beer. She smoked her cigarette and let out a long, weary exhale. "I would appreciate it if you would find my fucking car. I can't keep on like this forever. People need transportation, even in a town this small."

"If we can find Jesse and Jenny, I'm sure we'll find your car."

Ann scoffed like she wasn't so sure. Packard heard banging from the back bedroom. He shifted on his feet. "I'll be in the truck. Tell her to hurry up."

"How's that bite mark I put on your ass? Did it leave a scar?"

Packard shook his head. "It scabbed up but didn't leave a mark. Not that I can see anyway."

"I'll bite you harder next time."

"Stay out of trouble, Ann. Let me know if you hear from Jesse."

———————

He was just getting in on his side when Alissa barreled out of the house, head down like she didn't want to be recognized. The old woman in the window across the street was still at her post. Packard saw her turn her head to say something to someone behind her. Packard wasn't the biggest fan of Ann Crawford, but he figured she had enough problems without the constant surveillance and judgment from the neighbors.

When Alissa was in her seat, reaching for her seat belt, he backed up far enough to be directly across from the neighbor's perch. He lowered his window, took off his sunglasses, and locked eyes with the woman. Alissa suddenly reached across him and shoved her middle finger out his window.

"That nosy cunt needs her goddamn face smacked," she said, settling back into her seat.

Packard put the truck in drive and they pulled away. Alissa had a big, red zippered bag between her feet. She smelled strongly of perfume and cigarettes. He rolled his window back up but left it cracked an inch.

"Tell me about your brother's drug dealing," he said.

Alissa turned away. "I don't know what you're talking about," she said.

"Come on, Alissa. There are only a few reasons to have two cell phones. One is you have a separate phone for work. I fall into that category. Then you have guys who are cheating on their wives. Your brother's not old enough for that. That leaves drug dealers."

"It must be nice having such a simple view of the world," Alissa shot back.

Packard laughed. "It's called experience. It comes with getting old."

"Whatever."

"Your mom said he carries a blue backpack everywhere. Seen it anywhere?"

"No."

"Where do you think he is?"

"I wish I knew." She sounded like she meant it.

They rode in silence for a minute. Packard said, "Your brother's a senior this year. What's his plan?"

"He's saving all his money to move to Minneapolis this summer."

"How does he make money?"

Alissa gave him a look like *Nice try*.

"You think you'd know if he was into harder drugs? If he and Jenny were using?"

"Jenny doesn't use shit. She's been getting my brother to clean up his act. He's not dragging her down. She's lifting him up. He has a plan to get away from this town and it's because of her."

Alissa sounded both bitter and sad. When her brother was gone, it was just going to be her and her mother. Who would look out for her? Who would try to lift her up? Probably not the boy with the zits and the dirt bike.

They were getting closer to the school. Packard purposefully slowed down to give them more time. "Look, I'm not here because your brother sells drugs. I could give a damn about that right now. I'm trying to find him and Jenny. Neither one of them has their cell phone on them. Jenny doesn't have her diabetes supplies. Right now that other phone is the only way to get hold of them. That's all I'm interested in."

"I've been calling it. He doesn't answer."

"Give me the number. I have other ways to track it besides just calling."

The school was three blocks ahead on the left. "Stop here and let me out," Alissa said.

"Give me the number and I'll stop."

"I'm not a narc."

"The whole school's going to think otherwise when I pull up front and we get out together. I'll walk you to the cafeteria to make sure you get your lunch."

"You're an asshole."

"Don't make me be an asshole. Give me the phone number."

Alissa sighed and reached into the bag between her legs. She took out a cheap smartphone and scrolled through the contacts. She shoved it at him in her left hand and stared out the window on her right side.

Packard turned right at the next corner and pulled over. Alissa had the number saved on her phone as Jesse2. He dialed the number on his own phone and let it ring. It went to voice mail after four rings. He ended the call, then dialed his own number from Alissa's phone so her number showed up on his when the call connected. He hung up again and handed the phone back to Alissa. "Thank you," he said.

She shoved the phone in her bag, gathered up the straps, and pushed her door open.

"Your mom's right about getting pregnant. You'll be trapped here forever if—"

Alissa slammed her door. She showed him the same finger she'd shown the nosy neighbor.

Packard pulled away from the curb, laughing. This was why the sheriff hadn't assigned him to cover the high school. He didn't know how to relate to kids at all. They were all criminals or morons in his mind.

CHAPTER EIGHT

THE FIRST WOMAN EMMETT kidnapped worked at the gas station where he bought beer once a week. Wanda. Late twenties. Blond hair, wide hips. She had giant breasts, just like he liked. Not very bright—she had a hell of a time counting change.

He'd never been good at talking to women. The last decade of his marriage had passed more or less in total silence. Between visits to the gas station, he practiced things he would say to Wanda, imagined whole conversations they might have, but when the time came, standing there with his wallet out, he could only manage a few croaked words. *Busy today? Snow's coming.* Wanda wasn't particularly chatty. She had a pretty smile but not the kind that invited you to linger.

The run-down gas station where she worked was on a rural road between towns, backed into a clearing and surrounded by trees. A yellowing sign on a pole advertised CANOOS 4 RENT and CHAINSAW SH RPNING. The two red pumps out front had mechanical dials that spun the gallons and the price. Most of the customers were out-of-towners who stopped to buy alcohol, or gas for the boat, or something from the dusty shelves they needed for a weekend at the cabin.

The day he came in with his arm in a sling, Wanda said, "Oh...hi..." Her voice trailed off as she blanked on his name. Did she know his name? He didn't think so. He didn't remember ever telling her.

"What happened?" she asked.

He went to the beer cooler against the wall to her left, using the tail of his long shirt to grab the handle and open the door. "I hurt my arm," he said as he dropped the first case on the counter.

"But how?" she said.

"Missed the last step," he said. His flat feet scuffed across the floor as he made the round trip for a second case. He handed her his wallet and asked her to take out enough money to cover the cost. She whispered his name to herself after seeing it on the driver's license in his wallet. She took out a twenty and made change.

"Can you carry one of these for me?" he asked.

"I can carry both," she said, coming around the wooden counter. "When I worked at the sawmill, I had to grab sheets of plywood off the conveyor belt and stack them on pallets. Grab, turn, stack, turn, grab. That's how fast they came off the line. Two cases of beer is nothing."

He led the way, pushing open the door with his hip, careful not to touch anything.

"Did you break it?" she asked.

"Break what?"

"Your arm?"

It's in a sling, not a cast, he thought, but he kept quiet as they walked to his car. He opened the back door and stood behind her, looking up and down the road as she bent over to put the beer in the back seat.

When she stood up again, he was holding a gun.

"Get behind the wheel. You're going to drive," he said.

He sat in the back seat, and they drove in silence except for when he told her to turn. He kept the gun pressed to the back of her neck. She didn't fight and she didn't ask any questions, as if lacking the ability to imagine what was coming next. She wasn't the only one.

He led her back to his house. Inside the room he'd built in the basement, now in the presence of an actual woman, he realized for the first time how bad the pink paint he'd chosen was. It wasn't the pink of a woman's bedroom, like he'd intended. It was hot pink. Vulgar. No woman was going to like that color.

There was a cot pushed into one corner with new sheets that still had fold lines from the packaging. On the floor next to it were some magazines he thought she might like to read. The restraints—bolted to a boat chain that went through an iron ring on the wall—were heavy manacles he'd rolled and welded himself at his shop because he couldn't buy the things he'd imagined.

"Put those on," he said. "I'll kill you if you don't."

Once she was secure, he left her in the room and locked the door. He tried to keep his hands from shaking as he lit a cigarette. He'd done it. He had a woman in his room. She was perfect. He liked everything about her. Her face, her body, her name.

Wanda.

Invisible fingers played piano keys in his belly. His thudding heart pushed heat to his face. Was this what it felt like to fall in love?

He had none of the same excitement when it came to the new girl. He felt dread, and it felt like cold skin touching his skin.

He sat in his rocker and smoked a cigarette. He could hear the girl moaning through the door. It was midday and still he hadn't gone in to look at her. She'd been alone in the dark since Carl locked her up yesterday morning.

Emmett hadn't slept most of the night. After lying in bed for a while, he'd gone back to his recliner and watched the channel that showed reruns of shows he remembered as a kid—*Gunsmoke, The Rifleman,* and *McHale's Navy.* Flickering light from the television had animated the gauzy cigarette smoke that swirled in the darkness around him. He watched *I Dream of Jeannie* through heavy-lidded eyes and remembered when he saw the show in color for the first time. He was thirteen. He'd seen Barbara Eden plenty in black and white, but his first time seeing her pink bra and red panties broke something loose inside him. It changed him, kept him up at night, breathless and sweaty, rubbing a stuffed teddy bear against his erection.

A genie in a pink bottle who called him master and made all his wishes come true.

A woman who would do whatever he wanted.

It was the fantasy that gave root to the hundreds that followed and led him to build the pink room.

He felt no sympathy for the moaning girl, only a growing unease that climbed his insides. Finally, he got up and found a large, square flashlight on the shelves behind his chair. The batteries were weak but good enough. He slid back the bolt and let the steel door swing on its hinges. The room was pitch-dark. Light from the basement stretched across the floor in a golden rectangle with his shadow a dark silhouette at the center.

He found the girl with the flashlight. She was flat on her back with her hands shackled over her head. A gag made from one of Emmett's old T-shirts ran across her mouth.

She turned toward him, and light shone back from a pair of animal eyes in a face shiny with sweat. She growled through the gag. Emmett smelled piss.

This was no genie's bottle. It was an animal cage at the zoo.

He suddenly remembered the last time he'd been in this room. A decade ago, with a power washer to clean the blood and shit off the walls from the jogger. The room had filled with steam that dripped down on him from above. The pink paint came off the wall like strips of torn skin. That was supposed to be the end of things.

Emmett left and came back a minute later carrying a white five-gallon bucket. The flashlight was pinned under his arm. In his other hand was the jackknife he always carried, its four-inch blade locked into place.

He saw the girl imagine the worst possibilities. She bucked her hips and dug her heels into the mattress.

Emmett dropped the bucket and held the flashlight close to her face. "You want to keep wearing those bloody, pissed clothes?"

The girl froze.

"Do you?"

She didn't respond.

Emmett set the flashlight on the overturned bucket, then reached for the collar of her sweatshirt. He brought the knife to her throat. "Don't move. Don't even breathe," he said.

The girl shook uncontrollably. When she closed her eyes and turned away from him, he felt the urge to pause, to study her face, but didn't.

The knife was sharp as could be. He slit the girl's top from the neck to the hem at the bottom, then laid it open. He felt something heavy in the front pocket but was distracted by the sight of her body and the things attached to it. Her abdomen was covered in bruises in different shades of purple and yellow. To the right of her navel was a gray disk the size of a silver dollar held in place under clear adhesive tape. On her left side was a similar-sized button, but this one had a thin tube coming out of it that disappeared into the folds of her sweatshirt.

"The hell is all this?"

He followed the tube through an opening inside her sweatshirt to a blue device smaller than a pack of cigarettes. Shining the flashlight on it, he squinted through one eye to read the buttons and the small screen. "Insulin," he read aloud.

He dropped the device and got a finger between her cheek and the gag and pulled it below her chin.

"You got diabetes," he said.

She nodded.

"This thing gives you insulin through this tube?"

Nod.

She was wearing some kind of athletic bra underneath the sweatshirt. He cut the straps and the sides and pulled it away. She bucked and said "No, don't!"

as he yanked at the buttons on her jeans. He knocked her on the side of the head with the back of his hand.

"Don't fight me."

She stilled and he sawed through the thick fabric near the fly, then all the way down her damaged leg. Dried blood had glued the fabric to her skin. She screamed when he peeled it away and revealed a constellation of red welts in her thigh from the birdshot. Fresh blood rose from her wounds.

He cut away her jeans on the other side. She was wearing blue panties, stained with blood and urine. He took a long look between her legs at the mound of flesh and the crinkle of hair under the fabric before he cut the panties on both sides.

The dying flashlight gave off only the faintest orange glow as Emmett stepped back and looked at what he'd uncovered. The girl was naked, stretched long and taut like a pig carcass. She was sobbing and shaking, but Emmett could only hear the sound of his own breathing and the roar of blood in his ears. She looked alien in this room, in this light, with her buttons and tubes, like something that should have been under glass or preserved in fluids.

The room felt smaller than usual with the two of them together in the near dark. He ran his fingers across her bruised belly and watched her skin break out in gooseflesh.

He put away the knife. Her clothes were in a pile on the floor. He pushed them through the doorway with his feet and came back with a brown wool blanket that he dropped on top of her before unlocking the padlock keeping her hands pulled behind her head. Now she had enough slack in the chain to sit up with her hands in her lap or stand next to the bed.

"I need...water," the girl whispered.

"What?"

"Water...please," she said.

He left her, taking the flashlight, and found an empty beer can in the garbage and filled it with tap water from the basement sink. When he came back, the girl was sitting with the blanket pulled up to hide her nakedness. She shivered and winced in pain as she took the can of water and drank it quickly. "Please take me to a doctor. It hurts so bad." She cringed as her raw nerves lit up again.

"I'm the doctor around here."

"*Please.*" Her voice was barely more than a whisper. "I'm sorry… I just want to go home. We didn't mean any harm."

Emmett grabbed her by the ear and twisted it. "It harms me when my pills get stolen!" he thundered. The girl shrank from his touch, small enough he thought he could swallow her whole and suck the meat off her bones.

He yelled into her face. "Why couldn't you leave me alone? I'm an old man. I wasn't hurting anybody."

Three times before now they'd broken into his house and stolen his pills and anything else of value they could get their hands on. He couldn't figure out why him or what he'd done to draw their attention.

"Do you know what it's like to come home and see your door standing open? Your windows broken? I've been afraid to leave my house. Now you come in the night while I'm sleeping because I never leave my pills behind when I'm gone. I need those pills for my pain," he said. "I need to live in peace."

The girl sobbed. "I'm sorry," she cried.

Emmett leaned against the wall next to the door. Wanda had cried like that, begged him to let her go. Nothing he did to make this room less sad or scary for her had worked. It was never supposed to be a dungeon. He'd built it and painted it and put nice things in it for her. The chains were supposed to be temporary. Until there was trust.

He turned the knife in his pocket a few times, then took it out and scratched under his belly with the hilt. "What's your name?"

The girl's breath hitched in the middle of the word that came out. Emmett grunted in surprise, pushing himself away from the wall. "Did you say Jeannie?"

"Jenny," she said louder.

"Mmm," he said. He left her and locked the door. She cried out for him to come back, to please leave a light. He ignored her.

Jenny, he thought as he slowly climbed the stairs back to the kitchen. The first time she said it, it sounded like she'd said Jeannie.

Wouldn't that have been the goddamndest thing?

———————

He came back hours later, after he took more pills and nodded off in front of the TV. When he woke, he made himself a lunch of frozen garlic cheese bread that he ate with six hot dogs cut up into jarred spaghetti sauce and microwaved.

The girl needed to eat. They always needed to eat. The reality of meals and trips to the bathroom hadn't figured into his plans when he built the room. A genie in a bottle was supposed to take care of her own needs. Even Myra had gone to the trouble of hiding her bathroom habits from him through their whole marriage.

He microwaved a breakfast sandwich in a plastic wrapper and took it downstairs with the last of the hot dogs and spaghetti sauce scraped into a coffee mug. He waited while she struggled to sit up and keep herself covered with the blanket, then handed her the food. While she ate, he found a lamp and an extension cord to bring more light into the room. He watched her use her good hand to take apart the sandwich in her lap and pick at the egg and sausage.

"You flipped over the mattress."

She nodded and set aside the plastic wrapper and biscuit halves. "What's this?" she asked about the coffee mug.

"Hot dogs in spaghetti sauce."

She looked at him in disbelief, then flinched as the pain hit her again.

"I forgot a fork. Use your fingers."

She smelled it, picked out a piece of hot dog with her good hand, then set the mug aside. "How long are you going to keep me here?"

"As long as I want."

"I'm going to need insulin."

"How much is in your thing?"

The girl pinned the blanket under her chin while she rooted under it for her device. "It's almost half gone."

"When will it run out?"

"Maybe two more days."

"Then what?"

"If I don't have insulin, I'll go into a coma and die," she said.

"You sound like a problem that's going to take care of itself," he said.

She stared at him in horror as he took away the remains of her meal. He avoided her eyes. *She broke into your house*, he reminded himself. *Not just the boy. Both of them.*

He filled her beer can again with water from the bathroom sink. When he came back, she was crying. "Please don't let me die in here," she pleaded. "I'm sorry we broke into your house. It was wrong. Jesse already paid with his life," she sobbed. "This shouldn't be a death sentence for both of us."

"Drink this."

He watched her coldly as she drank the water. She was a thief. Here in this room because of her own actions. Why would he do anything for her? Just keeping her fed and watered was work.

"Use the bucket next time you have to go. That's what it's for. I'll be back tomorrow."

She looked stunned by his indifference. "Can't you leave the lamp?" she asked as he carried it out.

"No."

Emmett bolted the door, leaving the girl in darkness. He grabbed a beer and fell heavily into the rocking chair across from the basement door. There were still shards of glass in the window and on the floor from the break-in. The lake was smooth as a mirror, reflecting the dark trees against a pink and gray sky. Emmett lit a cigarette and watched the sun set.

You really going to let that girl die, old man?

Why not? He had no use for a genie—or a Jenny, for that matter—at this point in his life. So far all she'd done was cry, piss the bed, and pick at her food. It was like taking care of a goddamn baby.

Out on the water, a loon made its two-tone wail, asking its mate *Where are you?* A second later, she responded with her own haunting call. *Here I am.*

Behind him came the sounds of the chain sliding through the ring and the scrape of the bucket against the floor.

CHAPTER NINE

THE MONTH OF MAY started with snow. Not unusual for Minnesota, not even unexpected, but still an unwelcome reminder of how short the time was from the last snow of spring to the first flakes of fall. Packard stood at the patio door and watched the cotton-ball clumps come down and decided to pass on the swim.

In the basement, he did his winter workout. Burpees, squats, lunges. Hanging from the pull-up bar, he closed his eyes and tried to imagine Jenny and Jesse's actions the night they snuck out.

Jenny's standing on the corner in her letter jacket at 1:30 a.m., waiting for Jesse to pull up in his mom's car. She's got no phone. The fact they both left their phones behind meant it was intentional. They didn't want to be tracked or leave a cellular record of where they were going. It was planned and Jenny had agreed to it.

They'd talked on the phone for a long time before this. That could mean the plans weren't solid. Things were being discussed and debated. Whose idea was this? Jesse's—because he was driving? Jenny's—because, whatever it was, she needed or wanted to be there?

It was the night of the supermoon. It started raining hard around 3:30 a.m.

*They went out of town and stopped somewhere secluded or private. Not in town
or a public place, otherwise the car would have been spotted by now. Someone's
house. Someone not expecting them because no one expects visitors at 3:00 a.m.
They get out of the car together. Or one of them gets out, followed later by the
other one. If one had stayed behind and something happened, he or she could
have driven away.*

They're both out of the car. It's dark. It's pouring rain.

Something happens.

Another option was there was some kind of accident that hadn't been
found yet. If it was raining hard and they were speeding, there were plenty of
places where they could miss a curve in the road or a narrow bridge and wind
up in the trees or a stormwater pond.

He kept coming back to the phones and how many times drugs came up
in connection with Jesse's name. They still could have been in an accident, but
this felt like something else.

After dropping Jesse's sister off at school yesterday, Packard had gone
back to the station. He and Kelly had spent the afternoon pulling together the
paperwork for a court order for the records from both of Jesse's cell phones. His
second phone—the one Alissa gave him the number of—intrigued Packard
the most. Finding out who called or texted him on that phone might be the
break they needed.

At the end of the day, he'd caught up with Ron Callahan, the sheriff department's school liaison, as the shifts were changing. Callahan was the best deputy
in the department. He had the most seniority after the sheriff. Packard knew
the only reason Stan Shaw had made him acting sheriff was that Callahan had
turned it down first. Before joining the department, he'd spent twenty years in
the army as a drill sergeant, turning teenagers into soldiers. He had a gray, bris-
tled flattop and ruddy jowls. He carried seventy-five pounds more on his frame
than the army would have allowed. Packard had liked him from the minute
they first met.

Callahan told Packard that Jesse had only recently shown up on his radar.

"A few weeks ago someone left an anonymous tip that Jesse was dealing. I decided to have a talk with the boy, so I went to the school and asked Principal Overby and the counselor to pull him from class. The point was to give him a shot across the bow. Let him know that I'd heard about him and that this was to be the one and only warning.

"The two of them went to get the boy. A few minutes later, they all three came around the corner, and Jesse got his first look at me standing outside the administration office. I felt like we almost had a moment of telepathy when our eyes met, like we both knew he was going to make a dash for it almost a second before he did it. That's probably all hindsight, but I swear I saw it coming.

"Anyway, he suddenly paused, hopped back two steps, and slammed through the door of the girls' restroom. By the time I ran down there and got my hands on him, he was standing in one of the stalls and both pockets were hanging inside out. He'd kicked the flush lever two or three times. Whatever he had on him was gone."

"So we know he was carrying at a minimum, probably dealing."

"He didn't run into the girls' bathroom to fix his hair."

Packard picked up a jump rope from the workout equipment in his basement—spread his arms wide enough to keep it from hitting the low ceiling—and added what he'd learned from Callahan into his vision for what happened that night.

Jesse had had to flush his stash days earlier. Pills or heroin—he's not walking around school with a bag of smelly weed in his pockets. Might have flushed his money, too, if he'd been carrying enough to be incriminating.

What they're doing has something to do with the drugs. If there's a supplier he's working for, why wait until the middle of the night to meet? And why bring Jenny? He wouldn't want her there if it's dangerous. Maybe she insists. Maybe she's hoping to talk him out of whatever he has planned. Maybe he wants to be talked out of it.

It's not his supplier they're meeting. A supplier knows you're coming.

*He's identified a source of something he needs. Something he can take if he
shows up unexpected at three in the morning.*

They're both out of the car. It's dark. It's pouring rain.

Something happens.

Packard finished his workout with push-ups and crunches, then called
Kelly on his way up the stairs from the basement. "Those phone records for
Jesse's phones come in yet?"

"They're here. I didn't know if you were coming in or if you wanted me to
email them."

"Email 'em to me. I'm heading up to the school to talk with the principal. Do
me a favor and make sure she knows I'm coming. I'd like to see her at eight thirty."

"Done."

By the time he'd shaved and dressed in his uniform, there were two emails
on his computer from Kelly. The first one said *Principal Overby is expecting you
at 830A* in the subject line. He went to the kitchen, made toast and scrambled
eggs, then came back to read the other email.

Packard printed the phone records on his home printer. The data was
separated by phone and by calls and text messages. Jesse's second phone had
received only one text message. People who had the number were probably
given explicit instructions not to send texts asking for drugs. Two nights before
he and Jenny disappeared, Jesse had gotten a message from someone that said
Whatup? When you going? Jesse's response was **Tomorrow night.**

Someone else knew the plan. The message said **When you going?** Not
Where you going? Not **When you coming?**

No more texts after that. The phone was still active. It had received eight
more calls since that night, including two from the *Whatup?* number, three from
Alissa's phone, and one from Packard's. None were returned. All were coming
in on CT233A, a tower almost ten miles north of Sandy Lake that picked up a
lot of the Lake Redwing traffic and points north of there. Packard knew a lot
of factors could influence which tower picked up which calls. It wasn't an exact
science. If nothing else, it told him they had stayed nearby.

He cross-referenced the call logs from all three phones. The *Whatup?* number didn't appear in Jenny's contacts or call history. It showed up once in Jesse's records as a missed call on Thursday night, the night after they didn't come home. Someone was careful about what they used that phone for and who they contacted with it. Someone who had both of Jesse's numbers.

Packard called Kelly at the office. "Do me a favor and open the file for the phone that ends in 9329."

Kelly clicked her mouse. "Okay, I got it."

"Pretty obvious pattern here. There's an incoming call; they wait for voice mail and hang up. See how they all have a call length of 0?"

"I do."

"Then this number—Jesse Crawford, we're assuming—calls back. Sometimes within a minute or two, sometimes longer. They talk for a couple of minutes, long enough for someone to say I need a hookup and Jesse to ask what they need. They settle on a price and make a plan to meet."

"I follow you."

"What I need you to do is run all those incoming phone numbers through the databases and get me as many names as you can. Call the high school and cross-reference the list with them. I'm sure they maintain contact numbers for parents and students. Hundred bucks says more than half of those numbers belong to high school kids. I want to meet with the kids on that list at the school today. Not Monday. Not over the weekend when they can hide behind their parents. Get me as many names as you can by one o'clock."

"I better get busy."

"One more thing. Jesse got a text message from someone on Monday night. Make sure that number is on the list. Make sure that one's at the top."

———————

Besides the court order for Jesse's phone records, Packard had also gotten warrants to search both Jenny's and Jesse's physical phones. The department's digital forensics tech had downloaded and scrutinized all the data from Jenny's phone but hadn't come up with any new leads. Jesse's phone needed a fingerprint or a password, which kept them from getting any of its data. Packard had the tech transfer the SIM card into another phone that he could take with him so he could monitor any new calls or messages that came into Jesse's number.

Packard took out the clone of Jesse's phone and checked the time. Just before 8:00 a.m. If the *Whatup?* number was owned by a student, he had minutes to catch them before the first bell.

Packard entered the number and put the phone on speaker.

Ring.

Whoever owned the *Whatup?* phone had been trying to find Jesse, too, based on the missed calls to both of his phones.

Ring.

Whoever owned the *Whatup?* phone would recognize Jesse's main number or have it in their phone as a contact.

Ring.

Someone answered.

Silence.

Packard waited. The person on the other end was waiting, too. No *Hello.* No *Where you been, motherfucker?* Just silence.

"Who is this?" Packard asked.

Silence.

"I'm looking for Jesse Crawford. I have his phone. Do you know where I can find him?"

Nothing.

"This is Ben Packard with the sheriff's department. I just want to know where Jesse went. I saw your text message. You don't have to tell me your name. Just tell me where Jesse was going."

The line went dead.

CHAPTER TEN

SANDY LAKE HIGH SCHOOL was a mile north of town, a T-shaped brick and glass building dating back to the 1980s when taxpayers had approved a plan to build a new school and consolidate the students from several neighboring towns into one district. Where the building made a turn to the right, a short glass breezeway went the opposite direction and connected to a gymnasium with an indoor pool, track, and hockey arena. Behind the school were playing fields and bleachers.

Packard parked the sheriff's SUV in a spot marked ADMINISTRATION ONLY. He went up a few concrete steps and through a double set of doors. A short distance down the hall, he came to the administrative office behind a wall of windows. There were three open desks and then private offices beyond that. He saw Principal Overby talking to one of the admins, her back to the door. She turned and greeted him with a bulletproof smile as he came through the door.

"Detective Packard. Nice to see you."

They shook hands. Principal Overby was in her midfifties, with short gray hair blow-dried into a poof and a receding chin that made her look like a peacock. She was wearing a pink sweater and a skirt with a large floral print that would have looked better on a bedspread.

"Is it still snowing out?"

"Nope. Done and melted," he said.

They went back to her office. The overhead lights were off, and the room was as gray as the overcast sky visible through the windows. When they were both seated and the door closed, her smile disappeared. "Tell me you know where those children are. Tell me something good," she said.

Packard shook his head. "Between you and me, we've got nothing right now. Neither one has been in contact with any friends or family that we've been able to verify. That's why I'm here. I think it's fairly obvious that Jesse Crawford is the rhyme and reason at the center of this. What can you tell me about him?"

"He's a smart boy. He could do anything if he would only apply himself, and that's not a line of nonsense that I say about all the children. I mean it."

"I heard the girls' bathroom story from Ron Callahan yesterday. Was he in any trouble before that?"

"Not at all," Overby said.

"Who else in this school is dealing?"

Overby sat up taller. She buried her chin in her throat, and her head twitched like a pigeon's. "I beg your pardon. You make it sound like the school is just a front for the Chinese opium den I'm running in the basement."

Packard held up his hands. "I didn't mean to imply that at all. It sounds to me like Jesse made a rookie mistake—he sold on school grounds, someone narked on him, and he almost got caught. I'm just wondering… If he's the new guy, who's training him? Who did he take over for?"

"I'm not naive. I know there are drugs in this town, and I know students are using them. We *both* know about the Wilson girl who overdosed at the start of the school year. But where the drugs are coming from? And who? I honestly don't know."

"No suspicions? No rumors?"

Overby looked like she was thinking, like she was about to speak, but then she shook her head. "No. Nothing."

"You sure?"

"I don't have a name to give you. I'm sorry."

Packard told her about the phone records and the pattern of calls to and from Jesse's burner. "I'm going to come back after lunch with a list of names who've called him most recently. I want you to tell me which ones are students, and which ones you're most surprised to see on the list. Then we'll call them to the office and have a chat, one-on-one."

"What about notifying their parents first? What if they want a lawyer present?"

"Nobody's being charged with anything. Nobody's going to need a lawyer. Whether they've bought or used drugs is the least of what I'm interested in."

Overby looked dubious. "You already have a pretty good suspicion that Jesse sells drugs. So what are you hoping to find out by questioning the other students?"

"Anything. Anything at all."

———————————

A green minivan with *Sandy Lake Gazette* printed on the side pulled into the parking lot as Packard was backing away from the school. Ray Hanson leaned out of the minivan's window and waved at Packard to get his attention. Packard stopped reluctantly.

"Detective," Ray said. "What's going on?"

"I don't know. What's going on with you?"

Ray was wearing a thin blue windbreaker with a white VFW logo on the front. He had a graying beard, thick lenses in oversized wire frames, and a bald spot on the back of his head. Ray was owner, publisher, and editor of the *Sandy Lake Gazette*. If you called it a newspaper you'd be half-right. It was little more than an ad rag filled with syndicated content, a community calendar, and high-school sports scores. Ray Hanson was no journalist.

"One of my delivery girls says two of her classmates are missing. One of 'em is Tom and Susan Wheeler's daughter. Is that why you're here?"

Packard stared straight ahead. "Nope."

"Who's the other kid? My girl didn't know his name for sure. Are they together?"

"I don't know what you're talking about, Ray."

Ray scoffed. "So what are you doing here then?"

"Playing Officer Friendly. Stay in school, kids. Don't do drugs."

"Bullshit. That's Ron Callahan's job. You know, all I have to do is call my source in the department to find out what's really going on."

Packard's dislike for Ray Hanson was warranted. Ray used his paper as a lever for or against you, depending on what you would or wouldn't do for him. After Packard was appointed acting sheriff, Ray had approached him about writing a monthly crime column for the *Gazette*. ("I can't pay you, of course, but think of it as a public service to the community.") When Packard passed, the next issue of the *Gazette* contained an unsigned editorial accusing the county board of making a mistake by allowing the newest member of the sheriff's department to be appointed acting sheriff while Stan Shaw sought treatment for his cancer.

"Let me tell you something, Ray. Your source in the department is Kelly, and she doesn't tell you anything I haven't told her to tell you."

"You're wrong. It's not just Kelly. Besides, the community deserves to know—"

"Ray, when I have something to tell the community, I'm going to reach out to a real newspaper, not one whose front page is entirely covered by an ad for used cars."

Packard took his foot off the brake and put up his window. In his side mirror, he saw Ray leaning out of his car, his mouth still moving as the SUV left him behind. Packard smiled. Pissing off Ray Hanson was one of the perks of the job he enjoyed the most.

———

As much as he wanted to, Packard couldn't ignore the rest of his responsibilities and just focus on the whereabouts of Jesse Crawford and Jenny Wheeler. He drove out to Lake Redwing and posted a foreclosure notice on a luxury cabin whose out-of-town owners had stopped making mortgage payments. He peered through a narrow window alongside the door into a large room with cathedral ceilings built from yellow knotty-pine logs. All the furniture was gone. A vacuum cleaner with its cord unspooled looked like a lonely robot that had had an accident.

Back in town, he delivered divorce papers to Kay Wells at her home. She and her soon-to-be ex-husband, Mike, owned a bait and tackle shop. The rumor in town was that Kay had been having an affair with the guy who drove the Coca-Cola truck that stocked the bait shop's coolers. Packard knocked hard, and Kay came to the door with dark circles around her eyes, her mouth thin and drawn down. She looked disoriented. She took the manila envelope he offered and quietly closed the door in his face before he finished his speech about acting as law enforcement on behalf of Mr. Wells and his attorney.

Lunch was a turkey sandwich at Subway that tasted like food science. Packard ate mindlessly, staring out the window and thinking of Marcus. The look on Kay's face when she opened the door reminded him of the haze he had moved through after Marcus was killed. Time had stopped making sense. There were times when he was in the car, wearing his uniform, when he couldn't remember if he was on his way to work or heading home.

He and Marcus had met at the Minneapolis police academy and connected over the fact that they'd both been premed at one point in college, before switching majors and moving into criminal justice. The other recruits in their class called them the Twins, even though Marcus was as black as Packard was white. They were the same height and build, same buzzed haircuts, same intense personalities.

Marcus had grown up poor in Mississippi. He told Packard everyone in his immediate family—including his mother, father, a brother, and a sister—had all passed away from old age or violence. He never talked about the specifics. Packard took the hint that the subject was off-limits.

Besides the story about his brother Nick's disappearance, he didn't have much to say about his own family—parents alive, divorced, retired far from Minnesota. He had a younger sister in Wisconsin and an older brother who was a cop in the Saint Paul suburbs. Everyone had their own lives, and little effort was put into making them intersect.

After the academy, he and Marcus were assigned to precincts on the opposite ends of Minneapolis. They'd run into each other at a gym downtown and sometimes got together with the other recruits from their class. Packard sensed the connection between him and Marcus from the day they met—that knowing sense of what else they had in common that neither one was going to be the first to admit. Nothing happened for years. It was after a bachelor party for one of their mutual friends that Marcus invited Packard to crash at his place at the end of the night, and, finally, loosened by alcohol, they stood too close together just inside the door, toe-to-toe, hesitant until the last second, until something invisible slapped them together like strong magnets. They grabbed for each other and staggered toward the bedroom, fighting to get out of their clothes.

They kept their relationship hidden from everyone they knew. Lived separately. Met when they had time. They went on one vacation during the thirteen months they were together, lying to others about where they'd gone and who they'd been with. They never talked about what it was they were doing, or tried to put a name on it. It was what it was. Fun. Casual.

Or so Packard thought.

Four months before he was killed, Marcus took a job with the Saint Paul police. A domestic disturbance brought him to a run-down two-story house in the West Seventh neighborhood. As Marcus approached the house, he was shot with an automatic weapon from an upper window. Another officer who had responded separately was wounded just as he was getting out of his squad.

The man inside had already shot his pregnant girlfriend. He shot himself last. Marcus died at the scene.

Once news spread of officers down and who they were, Packard went to the scene, but his Minneapolis badge barely got him past the yellow perimeter tape. They wanted him to stay back. After they loaded Marcus in an ambulance, he followed it to the hospital, hoping to get one last look at him. He was turned away there, too. The price of their secrecy was that Packard had no connection to the fallen officer. Not knowing what else to do, he went to Marcus's house and got his dog and brought him home.

Things went completely upside down a few days later when he was called by the City of Saint Paul's HR department and told that Marcus had listed him as his emergency contact, beneficiary, and legal representative in all matters, including power of attorney and health directives. Packard was stunned into silence. Marcus had never mentioned any of this. Had their relationship meant more to Marcus than he'd let on? Did it not mean enough to Packard? He consulted on the funeral arrangements but stayed in the background during all the media coverage of the fallen hero. Hundreds of officers lined the roads and followed the casket on its way to the cemetery.

In the weeks and months that followed, all the things said and unsaid, the things they did and didn't do came flooding back to Packard. He was angry at Marcus for putting him in this position. For making him question what he should have been feeling when they were together and how he should feel now.

He sold Marcus's house and possessions, donating the proceeds to the Fraternal Order of Police. He kept Marcus's badge, his dog, Jarrett, and an album of family photos. Everyone in the pictures was dead now, including Marcus.

Packard got to where he couldn't stand the job anymore. It wasn't the fear of being ambushed like Marcus. It was an absence of any feeling at all. For his partner at work, his CO, the people of Minneapolis he was sworn to serve and protect. There were whispers and rumors about him and Marcus that probably had existed before Marcus was killed but seemed louder now. He overheard two cops refer to him as the widow Packard in the locker room when they didn't know he was in the next row.

He imagined himself walking Jarrett on a dirt road surrounded by fall trees, coming home to an empty house, and having no commitments because he knew no one. Whatever it was he'd had with Marcus had cost too much—now he wanted the opposite of that.

Six months later, he saw the job posting for a deputy in Sandy Lake, the same town where he'd spent his summers as a child. The same town where his brother had disappeared.

He jumped at it.

It all felt like a lifetime ago. Marcus was gone. Jarrett was gone. Packard had been living like a monk for two and a half years. It was only a few months ago that he'd gone online and met Michael, a nurse in Minneapolis. Six years younger than him, stocky and hairy as a werewolf. He'd indulged Packard's unwillingness to send either a photo of his face or his dick, and still didn't disappear when he found out how far apart they lived. They chatted online, then via text. Packard finally sent a photo of himself. The last time he'd been down to Minneapolis, a month ago for the birthday of one of his brother's kids, he and Michael met for coffee.

Finally we meet.

Yeah, it's been a long time coming.

Neither one of them could quit smiling. One cup and they were out of there, back to Michael's house, naked in no time. Michael was aggressive and submissive simultaneously, and Packard felt the urge to use him up. When they were done, he was reluctant to leave. He felt like he'd walked into a clearing and was feeling the sun on his skin for the first time in years. He spent the night at his brother's house but met up with Michael again the next day before driving back to Sandy Lake.

It was fun, but Packard didn't expect to see Michael again. They'd kept in touch via text, mostly in the form of explicit selfies that Michael liked to send without provocation. *Bait*, he called them, to lure Packard back to Minneapolis again. Packard stayed noncommittal. There was something he was avoiding. Something tangled up in his unresolved feelings for Marcus and what had happened last time he got too close to someone.

On an impulse, Packard put down his sandwich, took out his phone, and texted Michael that he wanted to see him again.

That wasn't so hard. Why default to going without rather than take the steps to figure out what he wanted? He saw three dots indicating Michael was reading his message. A few seconds later his response arrived.

Funny, I was thinking the same last night.

It was followed immediately by a photo of Michael naked in the bathroom mirror, his dick in the sink like it was looking for water.

Packard heard steps over his shoulder and laid the phone facedown just as a voice behind him said, "A cop should do a better job of watching his back."

Susan slid into the booth across from him. He still had half a sandwich in front of him. He felt the heat rise in his face at the thought of her seeing the photo Michael had just sent. "That...wasn't me," he said.

"Too hairy to be you," his cousin said, matter-of-factly, looking inside the messenger bag she had flipped open in her lap. "I saw the SUV parked out front. Sorry to interrupt your lunch."

Was she? Her frankness sometimes made it difficult to parse her intentions. She'd been brutally honest like this since they were kids, doing or saying what she wanted with little regard for how others might take it. Packard had been the opposite. By the time he was a teenager, every word, every action and reaction was carefully considered before being revealed, lest anything give away his big gay secret.

Susan took a stack of bright-yellow paper out of her bag. "I made these on the computer last night and ran off copies this morning. I'm stuffing them in mailboxes and asking businesses to put them up."

On the front was the word MISSING and two photos of Jenny and Jesse together. Underneath that was a description of both kids and their car, and two phone numbers, one for the nonemergency number at the station and one for Susan's cell phone.

Her face was blank. He could tell she was tired and doing whatever she could to make something happen. Packard couldn't help but feel like the stack of yellow paper between them was an accusation. This was what she was doing while he was sitting at Subway looking at dick pics.

"These are great, Susan. Doesn't hurt to get more people keeping their eyes open."

Packard told her the story he'd heard from Deputy Callahan about Jesse flushing his stash in the girls' restroom. He told her about Jesse leaving his phone at home, same as Jenny, and about the second phone Jesse's sister had given him the number for. "We got his phone records this morning. We also know the second phone pinged a tower north of town in the last two days."

Susan brightened. "Can't you get a location from that? Don't all cell phones have GPS now?" she asked, nodding at his.

"Jesse's other phone is a burner. It's likely a cheap prepaid thing not registered in anyone's name. It's got no GPS. It's meant to be disposable."

Susan stared at the photos on her flyers. "The signal suggests they're nearby. I was right about that."

"It tells us the burner is nearby. They could have left it somewhere, or someone else could be carrying it now."

Packard told Susan about his meeting with Principal Overby and that he was on his way back to the school to meet with the owners of the phones that had been in contact with the burner. He held back the part about the *Whatup?* text message and his call to that number.

"I'm coming with you," she said.

"You are absolutely not coming with me."

"Jenny's been gone two whole days. We're entering the red zone as far as her diabetes goes if she doesn't have access to her supplies."

"You told me two days ago you weren't certain that she didn't take extra insulin with her."

Susan let out a frustrated sigh. "Don't repeat things back to me that I said. I know what I said. This isn't about how much insulin she has in her pump." Susan reached into her bag and started pulling out boxes of medical supplies as she talked, banging them on the table. "This is an infusion set. It needs to be replaced every two or three days to avoid infection. This is the insertion device for the infusion set. She needs reservoirs. She needs medical tape. She needs to replace her CGM sensor. This is the inserter for the sensor. She needs to charge her transmitter." She pulled out the padded portfolio he'd last seen in his office and unzipped it again to show him everything inside. "Needles, swabs, glucose monitor, test strips. Listen to me when I tell you this is not just about the god-damn insulin!"

Those were more words that he'd heard Susan say at once since he'd moved back to town. Packard leaned back, surveying the pile of boxes and strange plastic between them. "Why are you carrying all of this?"

She looked at him like he was an idiot. "In case I find her."

———

Packard finished his sandwich while Susan repacked everything she'd taken out of her messenger bag.

"Tell me more about Jenny," he said between bites.

"What do you want to know?"

"Tell me about her personality. Her interests. We're family, but I don't know a thing about her."

He thought he saw Susan flinch at the word *family*. It hadn't occurred to him that it might have a different connotation for her. "She's got my analytical mind and her father's extroverted personality. She's smart and she knows it. She can easily back you into a decision without you knowing you're being led."

"She does that to you?"

"No. I'm still much smarter than her. I can see her coming."

"If she's so smart, what does she see in Jesse? He's probably an average student at best. Part-time drug dealer, it appears."

"What does anyone see in anybody? What does she see in him?" She pointed at an elderly couple in a booth across from theirs. He was staring out the window. She was eating potato chips at the speed of a tree sloth. "What do you see in the hairy guy on your phone?" Susan asked.

Packard put his hand over his phone. "I don't… Forget about that."

"I'm the wrong person to ask about why people get together," Susan said. "Tom was attracted to me when we met. I went out with him because I was interested in his usefulness. Yes, I grew to love him. Having feelings of love and affection for someone has its own uses."

"Sean White Cloud used almost those exact words when he described your relationship. He said you had a use for him."

Susan was unapologetic. "It's easier for me if people know what I expect from them."

Packard wondered how much like her mother Jenny was. What use did she have for Jesse? Did he get her out of the house, out of her head, when everything was going south with her dad? It wouldn't matter what kind of student he was if that was the case. If he had access to drugs—another kind of escape—even better.

Packard said, "Jenny's not home. She's not in touch with her friends. What is she missing the most?"

"Her phone. It's practically her whole world. Texting. Social media. The camera. Music. She was in the chorus until it wasn't cool anymore. Music, audiobooks, and podcasts are her favorite things. There are audiobook readers whose books she listens to regardless of what the book is about. She's got an interest in using her voice in some way. Drama, singing, voice work."

"Any interests you two share or do together?"

"Almost nothing. I can get her to play tennis every once in a while. She works at the restaurant when she needs money, but she's definitely not into cooking. Or cycling. She wants nothing to do with my interests."

"Are you sure she isn't furious at you over Sean White Cloud? Mad enough to run away?"

Susan thought for a second. "I don't know that for sure. No."

———————

Susan handed Packard a flyer before putting the rest in her bag. He gathered up his trash and followed her outside. It wasn't until she grabbed the helmet hanging from the handlebars of a bike leaned against the building that he realized she was going around town with her flyers on her bike.

"I've been wanting to ask why you and Tom decided to move to Sandy Lake. You could have opened a restaurant anywhere. Even before what happened with my brother, I never really could tell whether you enjoyed coming here as a kid or not."

Before Nick disappeared, Packard had loved every day at the lake, reading Hardy Boys books on the screened porch and riding bikes on gravel roads to the bar by the railroad tracks that let them buy sodas and play Ms. Pac-Man. When he was older, his activities were more clandestine—stealing beer and trying pot. He spent long, humid nights thinking about the older boys on the lake going in and out of the water like otters in wet swimsuits that kept no secrets.

Susan never seemed to be having a good time. She always wanted to be alone. She went on long walks and was often seen talking to herself. She might sit down for a board game, but then played with an overbearing intensity, as if real money stood to be won or lost.

"Coming here as a kid was a break from the intensity of home," Susan said. "Dad could pretend his drinking was social, and Mom put on a happy face lest anyone see how miserable she was. You guys were the closest things I had to siblings. Or friends."

She clicked the helmet strap under her chin. "Moving here with Tom didn't have anything to do with the years spent at Grandpa's cabin. I knew the area;

we researched the economy, analyzed the cost of living. It was a very practical decision."

Packard said *hmmm*. "I did the opposite. Someone I was close to was killed. He was a cop, too. I was flailing back in the Cities, and when I saw the job posting with the sheriff's department, I jumped at it like it was a life preserver."

"So moving here to be a cop didn't have anything to do with finding Nick?"

Packard shrugged. "It's been over twenty years since Nick disappeared. I don't know what can be found out at this point. I came here because it was a familiar place. And because there was a job. I'm not sure those were the best reasons."

"You're regretting it."

"I don't know if 'regret' is the right word. I've been wondering if I can be happy here."

Susan put on her sunglasses and spun her bike away from the wall. "Don't expect Sandy Lake to wrap its arms around you and make it easy. It's not summer vacation. It takes hard work to make a life in a small town. You'll figure it out." She threw her leg over the bar, mounted the pedals in one smooth move, and rode away without another word.

Packard smiled and shook his head. If he was looking for comfort or a warm hug, he'd gone to the wrong person.

She was right, though. He'd figure it out. One way or another.

CHAPTER ELEVEN

BACK AT THE STATION, Packard pinned Susan's flyer to the hallway bulletin board. In reception, Kelly was talking into a Bluetooth headset screwed into her ear. She held up a piece of paper and flapped it at him. "All right, I gotta go, Mom. Packard is here... I said I would... Mom, he's giving me a look like he's going to make me answer this phone from inside a jail cell if you don't stop talking right now... Okay, goodbye."

"Maybe I should lock your mom up so you can get some work done."

"You know what? You could do that and she'd still think we should get married. She's crazy about you. She thinks it would be good for me to have an authoritative man in my life."

"You're old enough to be my mother, and you push me around like a schoolboy. I don't think it would work out between us." He took the piece of paper she was holding.

"Those are the names and numbers that called Jesse's phone. Principal Overby was a big help in cross-referencing the numbers with the school's database. Unfortunately, none of us could find anything for the number that sent the text message. It's probably another burner."

"I knew it wasn't going to be that easy."

"I recognize some of the last names on this list," Kelly said. "I keep thinking these are going to be my friends' kids, but these are probably their grandkids for god's sake."

"Kelly, you have grandkids about to start high school. Of course these aren't the kids of your peers," Packard said.

"I know. I forget how old I am sometimes," Kelly said. She pushed back the feathered wings of her hair and stuck out her chin to tighten the loose skin around her neck. "When the mirror says late thirties, it's easy to get confused."

Packard folded the list of names and headed for the door. "You're telling me you have a mirror that can see forty years into the past?"

"FORTY?"

The students were between classes by the time Packard got back to the school. He sat in the SUV and watched them move in clumps through the glass breezeway toward the gymnasium. He listened to dispatch on the radio request someone to check on a stalled vehicle on Highway 18. A minute later, dispatch sent another car to an address west of town. "Occupant is Mrs. Alice Enderall. She's eighty-four, lives alone. Her daughter says she hasn't been able to reach her on the phone for the last couple of days."

Packard waited until the breezeway emptied before making his way back to the administration office. He had a seat again in Principal Overby's office. It smelled like microwaved tomato sauce and hot plastic. He pulled out the list of names Kelly had pulled together. "I have fifteen names here. I know some of the last names but I don't know who these people are for sure. Except one. I see Darrel Johnson."

Principal Overby rolled her eyes. "Big surprise," she said.

"I'm pretty sure he's on probation. I want to lean on him first and see where that gets us."

He read through the rest of the list, and Principal Overby wrote a couple of names on the pad in front of her, saying nothing until he finished. "I hate to assume the worst, but if we are, then I'll say I'm most surprised to hear Virginia Stevens is on that list. She's a very good student."

"Have someone pull Mr. Johnson from class. While we're talking to him, I want Virginia waiting outside. Is there a conference room we can set up in?"

"Yes. Next door. I have to say I don't have a good feeling about this, Detective."

"Yeah, well, every hour that goes by I have an even worse feeling about Jesse and Jenny."

———————

The Johnson boys were the product of crazy, doomsday-prepping parents obsessed with surviving some imminent calamity that was going to bring about the downfall of society. Their dad rambled on about conspiracies involving Chinese hackers, a nuclear Iran, and a super stock-market crash, his understanding of the issues barely extending beyond the two or three words it took to name them.

Darrel Johnson was the older of the two Johnson brothers. He came into the conference room in a black T-shirt with a worn Chevy logo on the chest, smelling like cigarettes and unwashed clothes. He had a goatee and a buzzed haircut that couldn't hide the fact that he was already balding.

Darrel collapsed into a chair across the table from Packard. Overby sat at the head with a legal pad and a pen in front of her. Packard had tried to convince her to let him talk to Darrel alone but she'd refused. "Parents will have my head if they find out I let their kids be questioned by the police without a school official present."

Packard and Darrel regarded each other with mutual disdain. The silence stretched out long enough that Principal Overby pushed up her sleeve to check her watch twice. Finally, Packard said, "Any plans to graduate this year?"

Darrel shrugged. "If I feel like it. Not like it matters. This place is bullshit." He cast an accusatory glance in Overby's direction.

"Yeah, it's terrible how the taxpayers of this county want to give you a free education to keep you from being so goddamn stupid."

Now it was Packard's turn to look at Overby. He'd tried to warn her.

"Nothing this school teaches prepares you for the real world. When the end comes, nobody's gonna care if you have a high school diploma."

Packard nodded. "You're right. When the end comes, why would you want to know anything about basic chemistry or biology or math?"

Darrel didn't say anything. He slowly blinked his eyes and sank deeper into himself.

"Listen," Packard said. "I'm not here to express my concern about your grade point average. I could give a shit. I know Jesse Crawford has been dealing, and I've got your name and number coming up in the log of calls made to his cell phone. So why don't you tell me about that?"

"What do you want me to tell you?"

"What did you buy from him?"

Darrel scoffed. "I didn't buy shit from him."

"Why'd you call him?"

"To talk about homework."

"Was he tutoring you? It couldn't be the other way around. There can't be someone dumber than you."

"Deputy," Principal Overby warned.

Darrel moved his mouth like he wanted to say something but couldn't find the words.

Packard pushed on. "You're still on probation for drag racing and marijuana possession, if I remember correctly. So why don't you tell me what I want to know, or we can go find out what Judge Parker thinks about you fraternizing with a known drug dealer."

"Man, it ain't against the law or the terms of my probation to call somebody on the phone."

"That's true. Maybe it's time for a random drug test. That is a term of your probation, and I know most people don't think twice about it because they know the county doesn't have the resources to run around collecting piss in a cup from a bunch of dick drips like you. But I think we'll make an exception in your case. I'm going to find the money in the budget to have you tested weekly from now until I say so."

Darrel shifted in his seat and sulked.

Packard leaned forward in his chair. "What did you buy from Jesse?"

"Nothing. I already told you."

"Who else is dealing to high school kids?"

Silence.

"Where do you think Jesse and Jenny Wheeler have been for the last few days?"

"I think he took her to a hotel and he's nailin' the hell out of her." Darrel pounded his fist into the open palm of his other hand and grunted.

Principal Overby put a hand over her eyes and exhaled. Darrel smirked.

Packard said, "You don't want to help me, that's fine. What about your buddy Jesse? He could be in trouble."

"Man, he ain't my buddy. I don't hardly know him or the chick. They ain't got nothin' to do with me so fuck 'em."

Packard leaned back. He tapped his finger on the table and stared at Darrel. He looked at the clock over Darrel's head and watched the red second hand swing around. The silence stretched out.

"Can I go?" Darrel asked.

Packard took out his cell phone and started typing a message. "Just making myself a reminder to have the lab contact you for a sample. Should be any day now. Expect their call."

Packard stood up, walked around the table, and opened the conference room door. "Go," he said.

Darrel stood up, tried to stand tall and straight, but only came up high enough to make eye contact with Packard's chin. Outside the door, Virginia Stevens was sitting in a chair with a textbook and an iPad in her lap. Darrel laughed when he saw her.

"Vagina Stevens is on that list, too? That's fucking hilarious," he said. "Don't tell them nothing, Vagina. Keep cool."

"Keep walking, Mr. Johnson."

Darrel strutted across the administrative office with a bouncing gait. The secretaries at the front desks stopped their work and watched him go. At the glass door, he turned around again and yelled, "Know your rights, Vagina! You don't have to tell them nothing." He flipped Packard two fingers as he crossed in front of the office's glass windows and disappeared down the hall.

Packard, stone-faced, turned his attention to Virginia. "Ms. Stevens. We'll be right with you."

He closed the door as the color drained from her face.

———————

Packard sat at the table again. Principal Overby didn't look much better than the girl waiting outside.

"I work with these kids every day. You hear things in the halls that would singe your eyebrows off," she said. "But that was beyond the pale. To be trapped inside this room with such an absence of intelligence and compassion. It's frightening."

"It wasn't for nothing."

"What do you mean? He didn't tell you anything."

"Listen, I knew Darrel Johnson wasn't going to spook. He's got no respect for authority. Virginia, on the other hand, is sitting out there right now trying not to wet her pants."

Overby put her head in her hands. "That poor girl. She's a straight-A student. How did she get mixed up in this?"

"I don't know, but spare me the 'poor girl' business while she's in here. I'm going to come down on her just as hard as Darrel, and I don't want her looking to you for sympathy. Now that she's seen the company she's being lumped in with, she's going to break like cheap pottery. That was my intention the whole time."

"I don't want any of my students *broken*, Deputy."

"Figure of speech. Let's bring her in."

———————

Virginia already had tears in her eyes as she sat down at the conference table. She had long dark hair, parted on one side and tucked behind her ears. She was wearing a light-blue silk blouse and black pants, and looked like she was already dressing for the role of corporate attorney. A tiny gold cross on a thin chain sat right below the hollow of her throat. She set her books and iPad in front of her, aligned them with the edge of the table, then pushed them slightly away. Principal Overby watched her out of one eye while she wrote something on the yellow legal pad in front of her.

Packard finally broke the silence. "Why are you crying, Virginia?"

"I'm scared?" she said, a statement that sounded like a question.

"What are you scared of?"

"I'm scared of why you want to see me?" Again with the raised inflection at the end. It was like a round of *Jeopardy!* She was going to phrase all her answers in the form of a question.

"Why do you think we wanted to see you?"

She was too scared or too smart to venture a guess. She hadn't made eye contact with anyone since she sat down. She stared at her hands in her lap. Her hair fell from behind one of her ears.

Packard leaned across the table. "I'm sure you've heard Jesse Crawford and Jenny Wheeler are missing."

At the mention of Jesse's name, Virginia let loose a sob and the tears raced down her cheeks. Her shoulders jumped up and down. Overby turned to a row of cabinets behind her, opened one, and took out a box of tissues. She slid it toward Virginia and sat down again without a word.

Packard said, "Virginia, I need you to pull it together."

She grabbed a bunch of tissues and pressed the wad against her eyes.

Packard waited while she fought to get her breath back and stop shaking. After a minute, she sat up taller and tucked her hair behind her ears again. Her face was bright red.

"We've got Jesse's cell phone records. We know he was dealing. Your phone number came up on his call log. Tell me what you bought from him."

Virginia looked like she was going to crumple again. She squeezed her eyes together and bit her bottom lip hard enough to leave tooth marks once she released it. She smashed the wad of tissues against her eyes again. "Is this going to be part of my record, what happens here today?" she asked.

"I'm not here to charge you with a crime. Right now I don't care if you did drugs, bought drugs—"

"No, I meant part of my school record?" she said and cast a terrified glance at the yellow legal pad in front of Principal Overby.

"Virginia, I'm here because you're my responsibility while you're at school. Whatever you can tell Deputy Packard that might help find Jesse and Jenny—"

"Would it be possible for me to talk to the deputy alone?"

Packard leaned back, glanced at Overby, and gave her a small nod. Despite his big, mean cop routine, it wasn't him Virginia was afraid of; it was the principal. If he could get Overby out of the room, he might have a chance at getting some honest answers from Virginia.

Overby pressed her lips together, obviously displeased. She took a deep breath and gathered her legal pad. "If that's what you prefer. I'll be right outside if you need me."

Virginia just nodded. She touched the corner of her books and sat mutely until Overby closed the door on her way out.

Packard said, "What was it? What did you get from Jesse?"

"Nothing bad. Just, like, study drugs?"

"Adderall?"

She nodded. "Sometimes I have so much homework to do, you know?" She sighed and rolled her eyes up. "The pills help me focus."

"When did you start buying from Jesse?"

She shrugged. "Beginning of the school year, I guess?"

"Who did you buy from before that?"

"I don't know. It was totally different before Jesse came along. I think he started out doing it the same way as the other guy, but he wasn't as discreet. It didn't take long to figure out Jesse was answering the phone number, mainly because he told everyone. He kinda started doing things his own way after a while."

"What was the old way?"

"The old way was you had to get the phone number from someone? You'd call and hang up, and someone using some kind of app to disguise his voice would call you back to find out what you wanted. If he had it, the price was nonnegotiable. If you agreed, he'd text you a random address out of town where you would drive by and leave the money in a mailbox by the road and keep going. It was always a different address—some lake house with no one home, some lot for sale. A few minutes later, after he drove by and grabbed the money, he'd text you again and tell you to turn around and get the drugs either from the same mailbox or another one close by."

"How'd you get the number?"

She thought for a minute. "I don't remember," she said. "People just knew it. It changed every once in a while and people still managed to find out."

"Any guesses who the old guy might have been? Any rumors?"

Virginia shook her head. She reached up and twirled the gold cross at her throat. It winked from the overhead lights.

"You're shaking your head no, but you look like you're remembering something."

"It's just… I don't know. I saw something once that stuck with me, especially once I realized Jesse had taken over for whoever was the old dealer."

"Tell me about it."

The tears long over, Virginia was unrepentant, matter-of-fact. "Okay, so, like, my sister is a nosy little bitch, right? She's a sophomore this year. Last year she was snooping through my stuff and found my pills. She said she was going to tell our parents unless I told her what they were for and let her try them. It turned into this big deal between the two of us, her taking my pills, her trying to blackmail me all the time. She wanted some for herself and made me take her with me next time I was scoring. So we ran through the whole deal—drove out of town, put the money in an envelope and left it in a mailbox, and then went to the new location to pick up the stuff.

"The mailbox was on my sister's side. She grabbed the bag and stuck it in her pocket. I started driving away but I wanted her to give me the pills. They were mine—she'd only come up with enough money for three, and there was no way I was about to let her hold the whole bag, not even just for the drive home."

Virginia kept fiddling with her necklace. She flipped open the cover of her iPad to check the time. "I really don't want to miss the start of my next class?"

"Finish the story; then you can go."

She sighed. "At the next stop sign, I turned right, drove a little ways, then turned off the ignition and killed the lights. I said, 'We're not going any farther until you give me my dru—my pills.' She said, 'Fine, we'll sit here all night.' We sat there for five minutes in the dark, completely quiet; then I got mad and grabbed her by the hair. I got a finger through one of her earrings and threatened to rip it right out if she didn't give me the pills."

Packard had to keep from smiling as he remembered Gary's comment from the other day about taking his earrings out before going over to fight Cora. Funny how you could go your whole life without hearing about women fighting and their earrings, and now he'd heard about it twice in two days.

"So she turned over the pills and her earlobe stayed intact?"

"Yes. We were still sitting there, trying to fix the tangles in our hair when a car came up to the stop sign behind us. It continued in the same direction we had been going before I turned. It was a bright-red Mustang. The classic kind."

Something about the red Mustang was setting off alarm bells for Packard. He knew a classic red Mustang. Driven by someone not far from Jesse's age. If he could close his eyes and think for a minute, he could come up with the name himself.

"I didn't think much about it right then, but when we got back to town, we saw the same red Mustang at a light. I saw them clear as day under the street-light. Jesse Crawford was in the passenger seat."

"Who was driving, Virginia?"

Now she seemed like she didn't want to say. "I'm not saying they sold us the drugs, right? I'm just saying a red Mustang came down the road we had been on where we made the buy. Could have been a coincidence."

"Who was driving?" The name came to him at almost the exact moment she said it.

"Sam Gherlick."

Of course.

The sheriff's grandson.

Packard let Virginia go to her next class after a few more questions about Jesse and Jenny and where they hung out and who they hung out with. She didn't know anything. The only time her world intersected with Jesse's was when she needed more Adderall. Outside of that, she made a conscious effort to avoid him. She had a reputation to maintain.

He let her go with a warning. "Let's get one thing clear. You don't ever want to get caught in this town with prescription drugs on your person or in your car that you don't have a script for. I will make things extra hard on you because you've had this warning. Do you understand me?"

For a second, Virginia sat petrified, looking like she might start crying again. "Get out of here," he said before she broke down again. She grabbed her books and practically ran out of the room.

After Virginia left, Principal Overby came back to the conference room and made a show of adjusting the scarf draped around her shoulders and straightening the bracelets bangled up her wrist. She was unhappy, but Packard didn't care. He had what he'd come for. Chances were very good that the unidentified cell number that texted Jesse the night before he disappeared belonged to Sam Gherlick.

"I'm going to throw a first name out to you that belongs to a known associate of Jesse, probably taught him everything he knows about selling drugs, might even be supplying him. Your job is to throw out the last name. First thing that comes to mind. Ready?"

Overby nodded and twiddled the pen in her hand.

"Sam," Packard said.

"Gherlick?" Overby asked, then immediately put a hand over her mouth, trying too late to stop what had already been said.

"That's it."

"My God." Overby craned her neck so she was staring at the ceiling. "I know it came right out, but I don't want to believe it."

"Why not? You said it. You must have had some suspicion."

"He graduated last year near the top of his class. He was such a good student, but there was something about his smile and his earnestness that always made me think of a politician or an insurance salesman. Sincere but phony at the same time, you know?"

"I don't know him that well," Packard admitted. "I've been to a couple of family functions with the sheriff where his kids and grandkids have been present. Fourth of July picnic, his birthday, stuff like that. I talked to Sam about his car once. He's got a '65 Mustang that he's restoring himself. I remember him saying that's what he wanted to do—fix up and restore old cars."

Overby nodded knowingly. "He graduated last year. He had acceptances from several schools, a few scholarships, too, if I remember correctly. I seem to recall there being some drama over his desire to take a year off. His parents were up here to talk to Mr. Wilson, our guidance counselor. I think they calmed down after he helped Sam get things deferred for a year."

"So he was dealing to the high school kids for two, three years, and put Jesse in his place after he graduated."

"I'm so disappointed," Overby said. "Even the good ones are up to something. You can't turn your back on these kids for a minute."

Packard stood and pushed in his chair. "You're a high school principal. I imagine you figured that out years ago."

––––––––––

Back in the parking lot he called the sheriff's wife. "Marilyn, it's Ben. I'm wondering if I can come by and talk to the old man."

"Oh, Ben. I know he'd love to see you again, but he's wiped out from the chemo. He's been nauseous and asleep all day. He usually rebounds on the third day. Call again tomorrow and make sure."

Packard thanked her and hung up. If drugs connected Sam to Jesse, then Packard had to follow the lead, but he wanted the sheriff to hear about it from him first. It wasn't true that Packard was without loyalties or debts, as Stan Shaw had told the county board when nominating Packard for the job of acting sheriff. Packard was indebted to Stan for hiring him when he needed a job and for trusting him with the responsibility of the county's top law-enforcement job. The least he could do was give Stan a warning about where things were heading. How he would react was the question. All bets were off when family was involved. The worst thing that could happen was he and Stan ending up on opposite sides of the investigation, both dug in on behalf of family.

He got a call from Kelly before he could decide what to do next.

"We've got an all-hands situation," she said. "There's an overturned logging truck on the ramp from Highway 8 onto Highway 2 westbound. It tipped over onto a car. There's at least one person inside the car who isn't responding. The truck driver is injured and can't be moved. It sounds really bad."

"Who's on the scene?"

"No one yet. Everyone's in route. All the info so far is what came from a motorist who called 911."

Packard rubbed a hand across his face. This was the last thing he needed right now. Sam Gherlick was the priority, but a priority was only a priority until something bigger came along to knock it down.

"I'm on my way. Get the emergency management team on standby. Sounds like we might have a major mess on our hands."

CHAPTER TWELVE

THE GIRL WAS SINGING.

Emmett sat in his rocker and tried to remember the last time there was music in his house that wasn't the theme song to a television show or the background to a dirty movie. The closest thing was probably Myra humming like a belt sander.

The door to the pink room was open and so was the basement door. Fresh air warmed by the afternoon sun lingered at the threshold. Emmett lit a cigarette and cracked a beer and listened to the girl sing. She had a nice voice. She'd been singing since earlier that morning when he brought her breakfast. Thinking of songs and trying to remember the words helped distract her from the pain, she'd said.

He'd spent most of the morning in the basement, too nervous to let her out of his sight for too long. Breakfast was another egg-and-sausage sandwich and a can of peaches in syrup that had probably been in the cupboard since before Myra left him.

His own pain, in his back and down his leg, was a dull buzz thanks to the pills. He'd topped four hundred pounds the last time he went to the doctor to have his ailments cataloged as part of getting his prescriptions renewed:

emphysema, type 2 diabetes, an enlarged heart, arthritis, and psoriasis. His knees and hips were all bone on bone, his fingers knobby claws that could still hold a beer or a pinch a cigarette but not much else.

Pull a trigger. They could still do that.

The girl suddenly moaned loudly, causing Emmett to twitch in his chair. He reached for the cigarette in the ashtray and found it had burned down to the filter and gone out. He was on pill time again. Cigarettes burned down, TV shows ended, rooms got dark without him noticing. Keeping track of time on oxycodone was like trying to carry water in his hands.

Emmett crushed the empty beer can, tossed it on the overflowing garbage pile, then rocked a couple of times to get the momentum he needed to propel himself from the chair. His breath came in quick, shallow gasps as he shuffled back to the room.

The girl was on her side under the blanket, her back to the door. The fresh air hadn't done much for the smell inside.

"You should get clean," he said. "There's a place to shower out here. We should look at that hand, too."

The girl sat up and unwound the bandage on her hand, revealing something that looked like it had been chewed by a dog.

"It hurts so much," she said.

"It's supposed to hurt. You were shot. Not supposed to feel like getting licked by kittens."

Emmett put her in leg irons and handcuffs before unlocking her from the chain on the wall. He pulled the blanket away and helped her rise up and steady herself. Her naked body made both of them uncomfortable. She hunched forward while he tried not to stare. She twisted the plastic port on her belly and detached her insulin pump, leaving it on the cot.

They made their way to the sink where a length of green garden hose went from the faucet up and over a hook in the floor joists. Emmett turned on the tap and adjusted the temperature.

The water made the girl jump and yelp like a rake was being drawn across her wounds. Emmett stood close by, prodding her with a finger to stay under the downpour. He grabbed her by the wrist and shoved her hand directly under the water when he saw she was trying to keep it from getting wet.

Suddenly she stopped fighting and went completely limp. Emmett let go and let her crumple to the floor.

"Sonofabitch," he said.

He turned off the water. She was clean enough. He found a first aid kit on the shelves behind his rocker, took out a brown bottle of hydrogen peroxide, and poured its contents over her hand and her leg. If she wasn't already passed out, she would have been after that.

In another part of the basement he rummaged through a bag filled with old T-shirts Myra had set aside to be used as rags. He grabbed one the girl could dry off with and one to wear. He left them on the bed in the cage, along with the gauze and the tape and the bandages from the first aid kit.

He went back to the girl. She was on her back, twisted to one side on the wet floor. Her short hair was wet and flat against her head. Pink streams of blood thinned by water and peroxide ran in rivulets from the wounds on her leg. The flesh around the pellets under her skin was bruised and red.

Emmett staggered to his feet and eased down low enough to where he could reach her. He smacked her cheek a couple of times. "Come on. Wake up. Get up, girl."

She stirred. Her eyelids fluttered, then filled with hopelessness as she came to and moved her shackled hands and feet.

Emmett helped her up and led her back to the cage. She sat on the edge of the bed, shivering and silent. She reached up with her handcuffed hands and brushed the hair out her eyes. She did as he told her, using one of the T-shirts to dry off. Every few seconds she cringed in pain.

"What is all that?" he asked as she reconnected her pump and checked the tape around the button on the other side of her navel.

"This is a continuous glucose monitor," she said, pointing to the button. "It tells me if I need more or less insulin. This tube delivers insulin from the pump as I need it."

"I'll be damned," he said. "No needles?"

"Both of these have needles embedded in me," she said. "It's fewer needles overall. Fewer injections."

"I'm supposed to test my blood and use needles but I don't."

"You have type 2. It's still bad if you don't control it."

"Costs too much. Can't afford to treat the diabetes and the pain."

"My insulin pump is down to thirty percent," she told him. "I'm turning the power off and only giving myself minimal boluses to make it last. I get tired and weak when I don't get enough insulin."

Emmett didn't have any response to that so he ignored it. He undid the handcuffs so she could put the other shirt on. It came down to her knees and elbows, fitting her like a nightgown. It was yellow with a Ferris wheel on the front and the words *Sandy Lake Labor Day Festival 1986*. This girl wasn't even born when he got that T-shirt.

He lit a cigarette and leaned against the far wall while he watched her dress her wounded hand. He could feel the need for another pill coming on. His back was tight from all the walking and bending. Pain traced a red-hot wire through his right buttock and all the way down his leg.

"How come you two focused on me?" he asked her. "You broke into my house at least three times—"

"Not us," she insisted. She closed her eyes and hung her head while she waited for a wave of pain to roll over her. "We were never here before."

Emmett stared at her in disbelief. The first break-in had happened a year and a half ago while he was out shopping for groceries. He'd come home to find the sliding door wide open, the yellowed curtain billowing halfway across the deck like a ghost caught in the act. Inside, the house was a bigger mess than usual. Drawers were pulled out, all the cabinet and closet doors open. The contents of the medicine cabinet had been dumped in the sink and scattered over the bathroom floor. The pills by his bed and by the kitchen sink were gone.

OxyContins and Percocets and Valium, even his blood pressure and arthritis medication. Also a 1.75-liter Jim Beam bottle full of change and a handgun from his nightstand.

A few months later, someone forced open the garage door and made off with welding equipment, a bunch of old copper pipe, tools, and a rolling creeper for sliding underneath a vehicle.

Then they broke into the house again, took his pills again. He'd started locking the sliding door when he left and ended up with a broken window in his bedroom for his trouble. He had Carl help him screw a piece of plywood over the window and tape a black garbage bag around the frame to keep the cold air out.

It got to where Emmett didn't dare leave home. Meals on Wheels brought him lunch three days a week, but it wasn't enough to live on. When he had no choice but to leave the house, he tried to make it as early or as late as possible, and he took all his pills with him.

If the girl was telling the truth, she and the dead boy weren't behind the other break-ins. Someone else was. The thought turned him cold to the core.

"How did you know I had the pills you were looking for?"

The girl had her bandaged hand in her lap and was struggling to tear off a piece of tape to secure the wrapping. Emmett stepped forward with his knife and sliced it. He helped pin one end to her wrist with his thumb while she wrapped it around.

"Who told you to come here?"

"No one." She stared at her bandaged hand. She was lying.

Emmett reached into his pocket and showed her the pills he was carrying for himself. "This is what you came here for. This could take your pain down to nothing. You want me to help you, tell me who told you to take my pills."

The girl hung her head. When she looked at him again, he could see her doing desperate math in her head. Balancing the cost of telling him what he wanted to know versus not. Estimating how bad her pain was now and how much worse it could get.

"Jesse never told me—"

Emmett pocketed the pills and reached for the light. "You're lying. I'll let you sit in the dark for a couple of days and think about it."

"No! Please don't," she begged. "I'll tell you. I'll tell you what I know."

CHAPTER THIRTEEN

PACKARD WOKE SATURDAY MORNING feeling like he'd stood out in the rain all night, which he had.

The overturned semi ended up being a bigger mess than anyone could have imagined. The truck driver broke his leg and his pelvis in the rollover. In the ambulance he told them the white Chevy Cobalt had tried to pass him on the single-lane ramp coming down to the highway. He was taking the curve wide and jerked the wheel in surprise when he saw he was about to crowd them off the road. He was hauling a load of thirty-foot lodgepole pines, some as big as twenty-four inches in diameter. When the wheels on the inside of the curve lost contact with the road, the whole load landed on top of the car. It was clear that both people in the car were dead.

The scene already smelled like marijuana when the first deputies arrived. A peek with a flashlight into the car's crushed trunk showed it was full of green bricks wrapped in black garbage bags.

At the hottest part of the afternoon, the air was ripe with the skunky smell of weed and pine sap and sawn wood. It got late and started raining while they waited for another logging truck and a forestry crane to arrive on scene. Traffic on the highway and the overpass backed up in all directions for miles. The truck came but they were still waiting for the crane when the water-slicked logs, some weighing more than a ton, suddenly shifted. Everyone shouted, "Whoa! Look out!" and jumped back as more logs rolled on top of the Cobalt.

It was dark by the time the fire department guys were able to get to the car and cut the roof off. Sean White Cloud was standing next to Packard as they watched the jaws of life in action. The sound of the rain pelting their waterproof gear sounded like static from a radio.

"Has Susan heard from Jenny yet?" Sean asked.

Packard shook his head. "Not a word."

"Damn."

The roof of the car came off like the lid of a box, giving them their first look at the pulped bodies inside.

"I need a bucket for these two, not a stretcher," Sean said.

It was 1:00 a.m. before Packard got home and into bed. His alarm went off at seven. He made breakfast, dressed in jeans and a black T-shirt, and called Marilyn to make sure it was okay to stop.

At ten he found himself back at the Shaws' for the second time that week. Stan didn't bother trying to sit up in his recliner this time. He looked grayer than just a few days earlier.

"Who was in the crushed car? Locals?" Stan asked.

"Not that we can tell so far. The car's plates were registered in Duluth, but the vehicle information doesn't match the car involved in the accident. Both were probably stolen. The driver had an ID with a Fargo address. The female passenger had no ID at all."

"What about those missing kids? Wasn't them, was it?"

The thought hadn't occurred to Packard. He hadn't had more than a quick look at the smashed and bloody bodies, but he was sure they weren't teenagers. "Good question, but it's not them. I'm still looking for those two."

Packard filled Stan in on the time line so far. He was telling him about interviewing Darrel Johnson and Virginia Stevens at the high school when Marilyn came in with coffee in a white porcelain mug the size of a soup bowl.

"I just got these new mugs on Amazon," she said. "You can use them for so many things."

Packard took the mug with both hands and thanked her. He sipped his coffee. Marilyn stood there, waiting for the conversation to start up again.

Stan made a slight motion with his head. "Give us a couple minutes, honey. Would ya, please?"

"Oh sure. I understand. You let me know if you need a refill," she said.

"It'll be Wednesday before he needs a refill," Stan said.

Packard set the mug down on the end table between them. Stan said, "Coffee gets cold too fast in a cup that big. Might as well serve it in a five-gallon bucket."

"It's fine. I appreciate it."

Stan turned on his side, trying to get comfortable. His face and the loose skin on his neck seemed to hang free from the musculature underneath. Before he got sick, Stan weighed two bills. Now he looked like a buck and a quarter, if that. Bit by bit he was leaving them, picked up and carried away a little at a time.

Packard remembered the day he bumped into Stan hitching up his pants as he came out of the men's room. "Packard, tell Kelly I'm heading over to see the doc," he'd said. "I just took a mighty shit full of blood. That can't be good."

Packard had offered to drive him but Stan waved him off. "Nah. I'm fine. Just bleeding out of my bunghole. We'll see what the doc says."

The doc said it was colon cancer. They took out twenty-three inches of Stan's intestines and sent him home with a colostomy bag as a parting gift.

"So the boyfriend is dealing. That puts an interesting twist on things."

Packard nodded. He said, "Listen, Stan. I gotta ask you a sensitive question."

"We still talking about them two kids or not?"

"We are. The story I got at the school is that Jesse was the new guy inside this year. Took over for the guy who graduated last year."

"And who was that?"

Packard clasped his hands together, looking like he was about to arm wrestle himself. "One of the kids at the school seemed to think it was Sam Gherlick."

Stan didn't say anything at first. His eyes got flinty. He pressed his lips together and stuck them out like he was trying to form the words in his mouth before letting them out. "Let me tell you something about my grandson. About both of Patty's kids. I wouldn't give you five dollars for either one of 'em. She's ruined those kids."

Packard didn't know what to say, so he drank his coffee and waited for Stan to continue.

"I was strict with my kids. Curfews, bedtimes, church every Sunday. You bet I whipped their asses when they had it coming. I pushed those kids to be the best they could be. The boys went to college, got good jobs, married nice gals, and have smart, respectful kids of their own. But my daughter. Goddamn." He shook his head then coughed into his hand. He found a handkerchief somewhere under his blanket, wiped his hand, wiped his mouth, tucked it away again.

Stan said, "Ever since Patty turned eighteen and left home her every action and thought has been with the intention to rebuke me. She thinks she got a raw deal having to grow up in a small town the daughter of a cop. She holds me personally responsible for everything she felt left out of. She didn't get invited to parties because her dad was a cop. She didn't have more friends because her dad was a cop. She's done the opposite of everything I wanted her to do. She knew I wanted her to go to college so she decided not to. I said, 'Fine, take some time to figure out what you want to do. Just don't get married and have kids right away.' What does she do? She gets her claws into Danny Gherlick and she's married and pregnant at twenty years old."

Packard knew the Gherlick family had money dating back a generation or two from timber and mining rights on land the family owned further north. Danny and his brother had taken over the Sandy Lake Building and Supply business from their old man in the midnineties. They also owned a contracting business that had won the bid on just about every major construction project within one hundred miles. The family had wealth above and beyond almost every other family in Sandy Lake.

"So now she's got a family and they got all the money in the world. Those kids were dolls growing up, but Patty went out of her way to parent them opposite of the way I would have. No rules. No confirmation in the Church. Never heard the word 'no.'"

Packard had had a hard time imagining how the sheriff's grandson ended up dealing drugs. The picture was getting clearer by the minute. A sense of entitlement. The idea that rules didn't apply to him. Enough smarts to be discreet about it.

"Now she and those kids are reaping what they've sowed. My granddaughter is twenty-one and working as a part-time cashier because she never learned a thing in school and has absolutely zero skills. Were you here when she got the DWI?"

Packard shook his head. "Doesn't ring a bell."

"Pulled over with four other girls in the car. Blew .19. I think she was expecting to get off with a warning because her grandpa was the sheriff. She got the opposite. She got the full treatment. Still doesn't have her license back because she violated the terms of her parole. I personally called the judge and told her to suspend it for six more months."

Now he knew where Stan stood when it came to his grandkids breaking the law. "What about Sam? He been in any trouble?"

"Not that I've ever heard about. That boy is slick, like a politician. He'll grab your hand and ask you how you're doing but you can see in his eyes he doesn't give a shit about the answer. He's not even listening because he's trying to figure out what you can do for him."

"So it's not out of the realm of possibility that he's been dealing."

Stan looked incredibly tired all of a sudden. He shifted in his recliner. Something was giving him pain.

"Hell, I don't know. Anything is possible with that boy. His mother, too. If he came home and confessed he'd murdered a nun, his mom would ask him what the nun had done to provoke him. Then she'd try to sue the Catholic Church. That's the mentality you're dealing with in that bunch."

"Is he still living at home?"

"No. He's at the blue house that Dan's folks owned. It's out on County Road D and 105th. You can't miss it."

"I'm gonna drop in on him unannounced. I didn't want you to be surprised if word about this gets out or his folks try to get in my way. If nothing else, he's a known associate of Jesse Crawford. I've got one witness who's seen them together in Sam's car. It's thin but it's all I got."

"Do whatever it takes. Get in his face. You're the sheriff now," Stan said.

"Acting sheriff," Packard reminded him. He wanted to say *Until you get back* but he knew better. And he knew Stan knew better.

"Just do your job, Acting Sheriff. No preferential treatment because he's my grandson."

"Understood."

Stan rolled on his back again, his face scrunched in pain. Packard stood up. "I'm gonna say bye to Marilyn. Let me know if there's anything me or the gang can do for ya."

"Just keep the peace," Stan said. His voice was weaker, as if he was already almost asleep.

"Copy that," Packard said.

Packard dumped a half gallon of cold coffee in the kitchen sink and found Marilyn clearing the flower beds in front of the house.

"The sheriff's fading," he said. He meant getting tired. Marilyn took it the other way.

"He's giving up," she whispered. "He's only doing the chemo this time because I want him to. It's just a few spots on his liver. I think there's still a chance, but he's losing hope. That can be more fatal than the cancer itself."

"I'm sorry, Marilyn. I wish there was something more I could do. We're all here for whatever you need. Whatever Stan needs. Let me know and I'll make it happen."

She put a garden-gloved hand on his arm and stood on her tiptoes to kiss his cheek. "Thank you, Ben. Thank you for coming to see him. It means the world to him. And to me. It really does."

"I'll be back soon," he promised.

He gave Marilyn a wave and walked back to his truck. He'd left both his phones in the center console. He had three missed calls and a text from Kelly:
CALL ME BACK!!

"I'm supposed to be off today," she said when he got her on the phone. "I'm getting tons of voice mails on my work cell from the press looking for a statement about those missing kids."

"Shit. Why now?"

"Our own Ray Hanson was the first to call this morning. He said he interviewed Susan Wheeler and wanted to confirm some of the facts with someone from the department. I guess he shook the tree and was able to rouse enough interest with the real media. I've had phone calls from the St. Cloud station and the paper in Fergus Falls and a few others. They're all looking for a statement from us."

Packard watched Marilyn kneeling on a foam pad, digging in the dirt with a small shovel. Holding a press conference was the last thing he'd intended to do today. He said, "I know it's your day off. Can you come in and get the community room set up?"

"Yeah, that's no problem. What time?"

"Tell everyone to be at the station at four. I'll make a statement then. They'll have to rush to make the five o'clock news, but that's not my problem."

———

Packard went home and changed into his uniform for the press conference, then headed back out to drop in on Sam. He called Susan on the way and caught her at the restaurant prepping for the evening rush.

"Just wondering what you told Ray Hanson."

She said Ray had called her that morning after seeing her flyers around town. Her first inclination had been to tell him to go to hell. "Ray and I have a history. He called after we first opened the restaurant and pressed me hard about advertising in the *Gazette*. When I told Ray advertising wasn't in our business plan right now, he asked if he could talk to my husband instead. I suggested he go fuck himself."

Packard was glad to know he wasn't the only one who had it in for Ray Hanson.

"I told him the kids have been missing since Wednesday and that you're looking for them. He said he was going to write a story for the *Gazette* website and reach out to his contacts at the regional newspapers to see if he could get them interested in the story. He said to me the Twin Cities papers won't take an interest in missing teens until there's a pedophile or a dead body involved."

"Ray's an asshole even when he thinks he's helping," Packard said.

He told Susan about the press conference and that she didn't need to be there and hung up just as he pulled in front of the baby-blue house on County Road D. Four narrow arborvitae towered behind the house like the fingers on a hand raised in oath.

The garage door was open at the top of the sloped driveway. The red Mustang was backed into the stall with its hood open. Packard took off his sunglasses and started up the steep grade. "Hey, Sam, you around?"

Movement on the ground caught his eye. A trail of liquid came running down the driveway just to the left of his shoe. He followed it up and spotted the feet under the car, realizing at the same moment that the car was too low to the ground to have someone underneath.

"Goddamn it!" Packard clicked the two-way on his shoulder and requested an ambulance, Detective Thielen, and any available unit. He backed up from the garage a few steps until he could see the house numbers. "One sixty-five County Road D. Light-blue house near the intersection with 105th." The trail of piss running down the driveway told him there was no hurry. It would take a time machine to save whoever was under the car.

Packard went around to the driver's side of the car and got down on one knee. He put both hands down and leaned forward until he could see under the car. He recognized Sam even with the blue color to his face and blood running from his smashed nose. The wheels on this side of the creeper had pushed out from the weight of the car but hadn't dropped low enough to keep the heat shield from smashing Sam's face. Packard touched his wrist. The body was cooling but not cold. Packard noted two car jacks tipped backward and a wood block that might have been a chock for the back wheel slid out to the side.

He didn't need a warrant to search the house for other victims or a suspect so he let himself in the back door of Sam's house. He had his gun unstrapped, hand on the grip. "Anybody home?" he called from the landing just inside the door. A set of raw wood stairs went down to an unfinished basement. To his right two steps went up to the kitchen. The walls were the same baby blue as the house with white painted cabinets that were dirty around all the handles. Linoleum floor, unwashed dishes, old mail. A lot of empty beer cans for a guy only one year out of high school.

Through an arched doorway he went into the living room. It smelled like marijuana and microwaved burritos. A 50-inch flat-screen TV had a video game paused with armored soldiers wandering back and forth in the background. On the coffee table were a vaporizer and a baggie of weed. Packard used a pen to flip the lid of a cigar box sitting next to the vaporizer. Inside were a wooden dugout, a lighter, a marble-sized amount of white powder twisted into a plastic knot, and a tiny, clear zip bag with three green pills in it that he recognized as 80-milligram oxys.

He called out again and got no response. Sam's bedroom door was open. It had plastic blinds, clothes all over the floor. In the closet he spotted a hotel safe on the floor. Locked. At the other end of a short hall was a bathroom, a bedroom full of old furniture and packed boxes, and finally a third bedroom with a sleeping woman twisted into the sheets of a twin bed.

Packard said, "Hey, miss. Wake up."

She didn't move. She was wearing boxer shorts and a white tank top. Her face was buried in a pillow and covered by greasy blond hair. He knew the slack stiffness of a corpse when he saw one. This woman wasn't dead. Just completely passed out. He grabbed her exposed foot and shook it. She didn't move. He put two fingers on her throat just above a green *Princess* tattoo. She had a faint pulse. She wasn't cold.

He went back out the back door and saw an ambulance idling. Detective Jill Thielen arrived next in an unmarked Dodge Charger, lights flashing. Deputy Howard Shepard was right behind her in a sheriff's car.

Packard was surprised to see Shepard, who was usually the last person to show up when there was actual work to be done. Responding to calls took him away from his primary duties of smoking cigarettes and spreading gossip from inside the sheriff's department around town.

Packard motioned them over to the garage and filled them in on why he was there and what he'd found. Thielen was blond, five feet tall in shoes, and all business. To her he said, "There's a nonresponsive female in the back bedroom. See if you can rouse her and find out who she is. She obviously doesn't know what's happened out here so…use your judgment on how much to tell her."

Thielen nodded and headed for the house.

"Shepard, get your camera out. I want photos of everything before we raise the car. I want the hood and grille dusted for prints. Look for tracks before you go any further around the car. It's pretty dusty and dirty in there. There might be something we can photo if not lift."

Shepard was shaped like a snowman, circles stacked on circles, dressed in a deputy's uniform. Bald. Goatee. He hitched up his pants and scratched the side of his face. "Why do you want prints? It's pretty obvious that the car fell off the jacks on the poor bastard."

"That piece of wood is a chock. It was moved out of the way before the car fell. Even if the car managed to tip and roll with the chock in place, it would be under the car, not to the side like that."

"Who would want to kill Sam Gherlick?" Shepard asked.

"I don't know. That's why I'm asking you to collect evidence so we can figure it out."

Packard took out his cell phone and found the email from Kelly with the phone records. He repeated the *Whatup?* phone number in his head until he could remember it long enough to dial it. He told Shepard about the *Whatup?* message someone had texted Jesse the night before he and Jenny disappeared.

"Besides Jenny, this was the last number to be in contact with Jesse before they disappeared," Packard said. He put his phone on speaker so Shepard could hear it ringing. A second later a muffled ringtone sounded beneath the Mustang. Packard let it ring three times.

"That's the phone," he said, pocketing his. "Sam Gherlick knew where Jenny and Jesse were going the night they disappeared. Now he's not around to tell us."

"You're suggesting that someone who knew what Sam knew did this," Shepard said.

"I don't believe in coincidences. Seems as likely as the idea that a kid who's probably been under this car a hundred times would accidentally pull it down on himself just now."

Shepard fished a pack of cigarettes from his uniform shirt pocket and shook one out. "Sounds like you're inventing boogeymen, if you ask me. I know he's the sheriff's grandson and all, but he was probably high or thinking about pussy, and forgot to chock his tires before crawling underneath. Now he's got a Mustang parked on his face. I'll get the fingerprint kit if that's what you want, but if you ask me—"

"I didn't ask you anything, Shepard. Put the cigarette away and get the camera and the crime scene kit. We're not taking a smoke break. We're working."

Shepard shrugged and headed down the driveway, tucking the cigarette back in the same shirt pocket.

"Watch where you're walking, Deputy. You just stepped in piss," Packard said. Shepard looked down at the wet streak striping the driveway, shook his foot, and sidestepped the rest.

When Thielen came back from the house, she handed Packard a driver's license. "I can't rouse her. She's definitely on something. Her breathing is shallow but not thready. I took the ID from the purse next to the bed."

Shannon Gherlick. Twenty-two years old. Same blond hair. Same peek of a tattoo high on her neck in the ID's photo.

"This is his sister," Packard said. "Have EMS load her up. They can come back for Sam. It's gonna be a while before we finish documenting the scene."

He told her what he'd told Shepard about the text messages and the ringing phone in Sam's pocket. He told her more than he'd told Shepard—about calling Sam's number from Jesse's phone before he even knew Sam was involved and the one-sided conversation they'd had. Thielen stared at the ground, nodding. She had short blond hair that she could rake into place with her fingers. No makeup. Dressed business casual with a sheriff's department windbreaker. She had a husband almost twenty years her senior. No kids. She was a great cop who was always on the lookout for people who wanted to use her gender or her size to take her down on the job. She put up with no bullshit.

"I feel like I was minutes too late this morning. I might have passed whoever did this on the way out here."

He looked at the ambulance guys dressed in black and white who were standing next to their rig waiting for someone to tell them what to do. Shepard was checking the batteries in the digital camera and scratching at a stain near the crotch of his pants.

"You're in charge," Packard said to Thielen. "Keep an eye on Shepard and make sure he doesn't make a mess of things. Get in touch if you find anything interesting." He nodded in the direction of the body under the car. "I have to go tell his folks."

CHAPTER FOURTEEN

EMMETT WAS WEARING A brown pair of pants with a broken zipper and a belt that helped keep them up. On top he wore a yellowed tank that exposed his hairy arms and shoulders. He shook out a whole pill from the bottle by the kitchen sink, swallowed it, then put another pill and a half in his pocket.

The girl's lunch, a fried chicken TV dinner, was cooling on the counter. She'd told him that morning she couldn't keep eating breakfast sandwiches.

"I need more protein, more fiber," she said. "My body needs less insulin when I eat real food."

"Like what?"

"Whole meats, oatmeal, carrots and broccoli, sweet potatoes, Greek yogurt."

He had none of those things. Everything he ate came in a box or a can. He had to think of what even came close. "There's a fried chicken TV dinner."

"What else is with it?"

"Mashed potatoes, peas and carrots, apple pie."

"I could eat the chicken and the vegetables," she said.

Emmett put the chicken on a plate, used his finger to scrape out some of the peas and carrots, and went down the basement stairs.

The girl looked and smelled better since her shower the day before. She'd said her pain was still a six or a seven when he'd asked that morning. He'd given her another half pill of oxycodone and some ibuprofen with her breakfast, and left her with the lamp and a stack of *Penthouses*. It was the only reading material he had in the basement.

She set aside the magazine in her lap and took the food from him. She was still shackled to the wall, able to sit up and stand but unable to move more than a foot or so from the bed. The lamp in the corner was on a timer now—on from eight in the morning until nine at night—and far enough away that she couldn't reach it if she tried.

"What are you reading?" he asked.

"I'm mostly just turning pages," she said, picking up peas and bits of carrot one at a time and putting them in her mouth. "I'm having a hard time…tracking what I'm reading. My vision is blurry. I don't know if it's the pills or my blood sugar."

"The pills will fog your head for sure." The best part of giving her pills for her pain was an end to all the moaning and sobbing. That alone made it easier for him to spend more time in the basement and talk to her through the open door as he did other things.

"I've been trying to read this interview with some guy named Gore Vidal."

"Who is Gore Vidal?"

She shrugged. "An author of some kind. He had a lot of opinions on politics and AIDS in"—she paused to flip back to the cover and look at the magazine's date—"in 1987," she said.

"Those magazines aren't for kids. I'll find you something else."

For a minute she was completely focused on peeling the skin off the chicken. Before she bit into the leg, he saw her spit something into her hand and place it next to her where he couldn't see it.

"What was that?"

She held up a plastic thing shaped like the roof of her mouth with a wire around the front of it. It was clear and pink and looked like something that would live in a coral reef. "It's my retainer. I usually take it out before you bring the food. The pills…I forgot."

She ate the chicken and looked like she enjoyed the change in the menu. Emmett asked her what else she liked to read. "I mostly listen to audiobooks on my phone," she said. "We're reading *David Copperfield* in my AP English class. I guess I'd like to know how that turns out."

Emmett didn't know what an audiobook was or how you listened to one on a phone. It sounded like nonsense to him. "Is *David Copperfield* in that backpack?"

She shook her head. "That's Jesse's bag. He wouldn't have a copy since the seniors aren't reading it. Maybe there's something else in there. You could probably get *David Copperfield* at the library."

Emmett left her to finish her food. The blue backpack was sitting on the workbench where Carl had set it the first day after bringing it in from the car. Emmett unzipped it and saw a textbook and a spiral notebook inside. The pocket in front was so full it was hard to pull back the zipper. He took everything out: pens, gum, a pack of cigarettes with a lighter tucked inside, a small wad of bills held together with a binder clip. A metal can of breath mints had tiny plastic bags inside with individual pills in each bag.

Emmett lit one of the boy's cigarettes, a better brand than he smoked. He recognized some of the pills in the tiny bags as ones he took. Others were a mystery without any marks or a label to identify them. Did they really sell a pill at a time? For how much? Seemed like a lot of trouble to individually wrap them.

He took the textbook and the notebook out of the bag and saw something glowing in the very bottom. He reached in again and pulled out a black cell phone.

"Sonofabitch," he said.

He set the backpack on the bed next to her. "Open it up," he said.

He watched her set aside the plate and make space on the blanket between her legs. She pulled the zipper around the U-shaped top, then grabbed the backpack by the bottom and dumped it toward her. He walked out of the room before everything slid out. When he came back after making a loop of the basement, she had the textbook in her lap. It said CHEMISTRY in huge letters over a picture of a test tube with red liquid inside being heated over a blue flame. She put her hand on the cover and stared at it like she was seeing something other than what it was.

"Is that what you wanted?"

She shrugged.

"Looks less interesting than Gore Vidal," he said.

She blinked a couple of times and set the book aside. "Jesse and I met in chemistry class. He failed it last year and had to take it again. The teacher assigned us as lab partners."

Emmett grunted. "You two should have done more studying and less robbing."

"We never robbed anyone before. I tried to talk him out of coming here. I told him there's other ways of earning money, but he said it wasn't about money."

"It was about stealing my pills."

"It was about protecting his sister. Sam threatened that something would happen to Jesse's sister if he didn't get your pills. Jesse was willing to do anything to pay Sam the money he owed, but Sam wanted the pills. Jesse had never done anything like this before. I swear. He was scared to go up those stairs."

Emmett grunted. "You were only thinking about yourselves. Not one thought about me or what I would do without my pills," he said as he carried out the toilet bucket.

Back in the room, he smoked and watched the girl finish her food. She put the peas and carrots in her mouth one at a time. It reminded him of watching a squirrel eat.

"Were you ever married?" she asked after a minute.

"I was. She left a long time ago."

"Did you have kids?"

"No."

"Did you want to?"

"Wasn't a matter of wanting or not wanting," Emmett said.

"What's that mean?"

Emmett stared at the end of his cigarette. "It means you don't always get to decide. It's not up to you."

"Like me being your prisoner."

Emmett shook his head. "I don't know about that. It's one hundred percent your fault you're here."

"It's one hundred percent my fault you caught me in your basement, but it's one hundred percent your decision to keep me here. You could let me go and this would be over."

"Can't do that."

"Why not? I've never seen you in town before. I have no idea where I am. Jesse drove and drove and drove the other night. I kept falling asleep because it was so late."

"You know enough," he said. "Were you born around here?"

"I was born in Minneapolis. We moved here when I was five and my parents opened their restaurant."

"What restaurant?"

"The Sweet Pea."

Emmett knew the place but had never been inside. The girl was too young to remember the fear that had gripped the locals when Wanda and the jogger both disappeared within a couple of years of each other. Cops moved like a cloud of black flies from one long-shot suspect or theory to another. Boats spent weeks dragging the lakes for bodies. Local women were constantly warned not to go out alone at night, to be extra cautious around strangers. The girl's parents might remember those days, but she wouldn't have any idea.

"You finished with that?"

The girl picked at the last of her chicken, then handed Emmett the plate. He gave her a half pill from his pocket and watched her swallow it with the last of her water. She found her pump under the blanket and started pushing its buttons.

Emmett held out his hand. "Give me that," he said.

She looked at him, confused. "My pump?"

"Give it to me," he said. "Take it off like you did when you went to the shower."

She reached under her shirt with her good hand and unhooked the pump from her port. "I need that," she said as she watched him wrap the tube around the device. "I have to have insulin now. I just ate."

"I've been taking care of you for three days. Food, shower, carrying your shit out in a bucket. What do I get in return?"

"Maybe you should have built this room around the toilet so there'd be no bucket."

Emmett stepped forward and smashed her in the mouth with the back of his hand. "Don't get smart," he said.

She touched her mouth with the tips of her fingers, checked to see if she was bleeding. She had furious tears in her eyes.

"What do you want from me?"

"I want your pump," he said.

"You can't," she said. "I'll get so sick if I don't get insulin."

Emmett stared at the pump in his hand like he was evaluating its worth. "Then trade me something for it."

"What? The chemistry book?"

Emmett shook his head.

The girl looked at him like he was asking for the impossible. "What? My retainer? I don't have anything else."

"Never mind then. I have what I want."

They stared at each other like a pair of battling mind readers. The sounds of the evening frogs and cicadas suddenly seemed very loud.

The girl folded back the blanket, grabbed the phone, and held it out. "Here."

Emmett took the phone, gave her the pump in exchange.

The tears she was trying to hold back rolled down when she blinked. She shook her head like she was trying to deny them. "You knew it was in the bag. You knew I had it this whole time."

Emmett opened the phone and bent it backward until it snapped in half. The tiny screen went dark. "Nothing is going to come in or out of this room that I don't know about. Everything that does come in is going to have a price. I wanted to know what you valued more, the pump or the phone."

"Some choice," she said as she reconnected the pump to her port. "My life or my freedom. One's useless without the other, you know." The device made three loud beeps as she pushed its buttons. Her face screwed up like she was about to cry again. "That's the low-supply alarm. I'll be out of insulin tomorrow. I have enough to bolus this meal and maybe get through the day tomorrow. That's it."

Emmett smoked his cigarette and regarded the pieces of phone in his hand. "I don't know what to do about that."

"I can tell you what to do. It's not complicated."

"Everything about this situation is complicated."

She opened and closed her mouth, trying to figure out how to respond. After a deep, hitching breath, she said, "Jesse should have had money in this backpack. Enough I would think for what I need right away. More than enough."

"It's not just about the money."

"You can buy insulin over the counter. There's a kind that's not expensive. I'll need needles. They're cheap, too. That's it. Just those two things."

Emmett took a final drag off the cigarette, dropped it, and stepped on the butt. He turned his head and blew the smoke outside the room. "Seems like a girl who needs medicine to stay alive should have thought twice about stealing someone else's."

"Oh my god! I'm sorry!" she shouted. She flinched when he suddenly looked at her. "I've never been more sorry about anything. Jesse's dead because of this stupid thing we did. I don't want to die, too. Please. Get me more insulin. If it's not about money, then tell me what's the real price."

"Some things don't have a price. Some things I have to decide whether they're worth the trouble or not," he said.

"You said everything has a price. Whether something is worth the trouble depends on what you get in return," she said. "So tell me what you want in return for bringing me insulin every single day. Am I supposed to let you fuck me? Or give you a blow job?"

Emmett made an irritated grunting sound. He dropped his head and shook it side to side. He couldn't look at her. She started clearing the things off the cot—the backpack, the chemistry book, the magazine. "Just tell me what I have to do for you to get me insulin so I can decide what I'm willing to do to save my life."

Emmett put the pieces of the ruined phone in his pocket. "What you need to realize," he said, moving toward the door, "is that you don't get to decide anything. Not one thing."

CHAPTER FIFTEEN

DAN AND PATTY GHERLICK lived in the biggest house on Lake Redwing. Approached from behind, down a long drive through a heavily wooded lot, the house looked smaller than it was. The modest back entrance and close trees hid how the house stepped back and spread its wings on either side of a towering, three-story great room that was all windows and redwood-sized logs. The lake side of the house featured a pair of gables on each wing, second-story balconies, a gently graded pebble beach, a separate boathouse, and a dock that stretched to the horizon. At night the place was lit up with more spotlights than a NASA launch pad.

Packard went up the steps, rang the bell. A five-car garage with wooden carriage doors ran perpendicular to the house. No cars parked out front. The house was enormous, but Packard had the sense that it wasn't empty. Someone was inside, making the place feel occupied. Through the textured glass window he saw a shadow pass deeper in the house, but no one came to the door. He waited a minute, then leaned on the bell. Another minute went by before Patty Gherlick finally came to the door wearing a fuzzy pink outfit that looked like something between pajamas and gym wear. At first glance he thought the loopy embroidery across the chest of the zippered hoodie spelled *Patty,* but after a second look he realized it said *Sassy.*

"Hello," Patty said. She had medium-length brown hair streaked with highlights, cut in layers around her face. She barely came up to Packard's shoulder and seemed to get lost for a second staring at his badge, as if she was trying to see her reflection in it. She ran a hand through her hair, then spun on her heel and turned away. "Welcome. Please come in. Nice to see you." Packard had the impression she was talking more to herself than to him.

Patty disappeared into the house with a slow, exaggerated walk that made her ass move. Her bare feet made sandpapery sounds on the tile floor. Packard wiped his shoes and followed her inside. They passed through a kitchen with more marble than a cemetery. A staircase on his left went up to a landing on the second floor. A three-story stone fireplace dominated the great room. He walked around the giant hearth and found a pair of camel-colored couches facing each other in front of the fireplace. A large glass coffee table separated the couches. Packard counted four other intimate seating areas arranged on top of expensive rugs in the huge room. There were lamps and potted ferns and enough throw pillows to fill a swimming pool. Doors and hallways branched off in both directions. Opposite the fireplace, tall windows framed by peeled logs looked out over the lake.

Patty had taken a seat on one of the couches and reached for a lidded thermal mug on the coffee table. Packard stood across from her. Most people got nervous when the police showed up unannounced. Patty acted like she'd opened the door to a field researcher who had come to observe her in her natural habitat. She drank from the mug in her hand and smiled at him. Her teeth were purple with wine.

"Mrs. Gherlick, is your husband home?" Packard asked.

Patty rolled her eyes and rolled her head like she was exhausted by even the mention of her husband. "He's around here somewhere. Thirteen thousand square feet of living space and twelve acres of lakeshore property, and I can still feel him. He's close. Too close." She twisted, put her arms across the back of the couch, and looked out the window behind her. "That's why I hate the weekends. He doesn't work on weekends so he's always around. I can feel him on me like a sunburn. Do you know what I mean?"

"I'm afraid I don't."

"Well, then you're lucky. That means you get to enjoy your weekends. I don't. I hate the weekends."

The fact that he was here in uniform on a Saturday didn't seem to have registered with Patty. She was rambling. Packard had the feeling she'd keep repeating the same idea endlessly if he didn't interrupt. "Mrs. Gherlick, it's important that I talk to you and your husband."

She waved her hand in the direction of the towering wall of windows behind her. "Oh, go find him. He said something this morning about…pontoon…motor…blah, blah, blah." She drank from her thermal mug again.

Packard looked around for an exit. "How do I get out of here? How do I get down to the water?"

She said, "Go down either wing and through the first door you come to." She leaped up and grabbed his wrist suddenly, trying to guide him down on the couch beside her. "No, wait—don't go," she said. He resisted and her hands slipped around his until she fell backward. "Just sit. Tell me what you want to tell my husband. I'll tell him if I think he needs to know. If not, it'll be a secret between us. Let's have a secret from my husband."

"I have a better idea. You wait here. I'll be back," Packard said.

"Whatever you say, Ossiffer," Patty said with a big purple grin. She pulled up the hood of her pink sweatshirt and pulled the strings until it closed into a tight circle around her face. Her eyes and nose and lips were scrunched into the opening. "I wouldn't want to get in trouble wiff the law." She could barely get the words out before she started laughing. Cackling. She fell sideways on the couch and buried her face in the overstuffed cushions. She laughed and rolled on her back and laughed some more. She was still howling when he headed for the exit.

———————

The Gherlicks' boathouse was painted navy blue with white trim. Inside were two slips with motorized lifts that could lift a pontoon and a speedboat out of the water. The dock looked like wood but was made from aluminum painted to look like boards.

Packard found Dan Gherlick leaning over the back of the pontoon, staring into the motor with its top housing removed. When he saw Packard in his uniform with the lake at his back, the look on Dan's face was that of a man with too many things waiting to crash down around him to know which one had just hit the floor. He looked fearful but not at all surprised. He straightened up slowly. "What happened?"

"Dan, there's been an accident."

"What happened?" Dan asked again.

"I just came from Sam's house. He was working underneath his car when it came down on top of him. He's gone, Dan. I'm sorry."

Dan Gherlick blanched. He looked like the air was being let out of him from a valve in his back. He said, "What? He what? What happened?"

"He was underneath his car when it fell off the jacks. He was pinned underneath."

Dan crumpled and went down on his elbows on the back of the pontoon. "Oh my god," he said. "My boy," he said. He moaned and made a sound like he was trying to swallow something too big to go down.

Packard waited. Below them the lake water lapped and splashed and echoed inside the boathouse. Small waves rhythmically shushed against the shoreline.

This part of the job always reminded Packard of the day a Sandy Lake sheriff's deputy in a winter coat with wool lapels had shown up at his grandparents' cabin with news about Nick. The deputy's face was long forgotten. Packard had only seen it briefly when the deputy stepped inside and stomped his boots on the rug. The adults sent the kids upstairs, then shut themselves in the family room behind sliding oak doors.

Packard, his two siblings, and Susan, their cousin, went into the second-floor bathroom and arranged themselves on the floor around the cage that covered the cold-air return. The house's ductwork funneled the voices from the family room directly to them. They heard the deputy say that they'd found

Nick's snowmobile submerged in the lake and a single glove frozen to the ice. They had divers in the water but hadn't located a body yet.

The deputy's tone was cold. He sounded as if Packard's family had this news coming, had earned it by some course of action or inaction. He wanted to know how it was possible that no one in the house had any idea where Nick was going or who he was meeting that night. There were signs warning of open water near where the snowmobile was found. Someone would have had to be high on drugs or drunk to miss them. When Packard's dad reminded the deputy it was the middle of the night and snowing when Nick left home, the deputy was silent. He closed with saying that divers would search again the next day. If they didn't find Nick then, they'd wait for warmer temperatures and decomposition to bring the body to the surface in the spring.

This was the lake where it happened. Nick could still be down there somewhere, though in later years, the lack of a body had Packard wondering if the glove and the snowmobile might have been decoys. Awful convenient, that one glove. Packard still hadn't looked at Nick's file since coming to Sandy Lake. Hadn't even mentioned his history to anyone in the department. It was another thing about himself he wanted to keep on a need-to-know basis.

After a couple of minutes, Dan Gherlick tried to straighten himself. "Take me to see Sam. I need to...to go get my boy."

"You can't see him yet, Dan. I'm sorry. Our people are processing the scene and will take Sam to Methodist when they're done. Someone will call you when you can see him. I know this is a terrible shock, Dan, but I need to ask you a few questions about Sam. I would wait but there just isn't time."

Every time Packard said Sam's name, Dan's face twitched. Something scrunched his eyes and pulled at the corner of his mouth. He slid sideways and sat across the back lounger in the pontoon. He rubbed his face. "Tell me what happened again."

Packard told him about pulling up to the house and finding Sam under the car. He told him he'd gone in the house to see who else was around and had found Shannon passed out in one of the bedrooms.

"Shannon lives here with us, but she stays at her brother's place now and then. She got a DUI last summer so she's without a license. She has to get rides from us or her friends to get anywhere. If she and Sam are being nice to each other, there's usually an ulterior motive. They're not exactly close, but they can get along."

"I'm having Shannon transported to Methodist, too. We found her incredibly sedated. Might be sleeping pills. I'm leaning more toward opioids of some kind."

Dan shook his head and stared down at his hands. "Both of my kids are recreational drug users. You don't have to be a genius to know that. They're adults now, and I have little say over how they spend their time. What was it that brought you to the house in the first place? Something to do with Shannon?"

Packard shook his head. "I went there looking for Sam. He was one of the last people in touch with Jesse Crawford before he and Jenny Wheeler disappeared."

"I saw flyers hanging in town about those two. How does Sam know them?"

"We were able to link Sam to Jesse through phone records. Sam texted Jesse about something Jesse was supposed to do the night he and Jenny disappeared. We also know Jesse was dealing drugs in the high school. I have a student who says she saw Sam and Jesse driving near a drug drop earlier this year. Any of this surprising to you?"

"Ah…hell. Should I have a lawyer or something right now?"

"I'm not asking about any of this to incriminate you. I'm not trying to pin anything on Sam either. I'm trying to find those kids. Sam was the last person in contact with them. If anyone knew where they were going, it was Sam."

"I didn't know about Sam dealing. I know he's getting money from somewhere and it's not from me. He's got a Class C driver's license, and I've been trying to get him to apprentice in a building trade but he doesn't want to work. I assumed Patty was giving him money behind my back. She can't say no to either one of those two."

"I just came through the house. Seems like Patty's flying pretty high."

Dan suddenly looked even more exhausted. Packard saw a man worn down by endlessly battling the ones who should have been on his side. Whatever came after the death of his son would be his to bear. Whether or not his family held together would depend on how much fight was left in him. He was all alone. "My wife is an alcoholic who has alienated all her friends and most of her family. Now she's bored and lonely and does whatever it takes to keep those kids on her side because they're all she's got left."

"I didn't tell her about Sam. I meant to tell both of you together but…"

Dan fought to hold back the tears and rubbed his face. "I'll take care of it."

"Who owns the blue house? Is it yours?"

"Yeah. It belonged to my folks. Sam's supposed to be paying rent but he hasn't been. There's no lease. He just lives there. The property is in my name."

"I can get a search warrant, but it would speed things up if I could get your permission to search the property. I'm sorry to show up with bad news and ask you for a favor on top of it. Like I said, I'm not looking for things to pin on Sam. I really just want to find those kids."

Dan nodded. "Yeah, go ahead. Search the house. If Sam was selling drugs, it's because it was easy money. He's always only had easy options. That's my fault and his mom's fault. I was trying to correct that, but I guess I was too late."

Packard thanked him and said he needed to get back. Dan opened the side gate and stepped off the pontoon, and they left the boat shed and walked up the dock toward the grand house spread in front of them. Packard remembered one more thing. "I saw a safe in his closet. Any clues to the combination?"

"That safe came from my office. We needed a bigger one, and Sam said he could use the old one or sell it, so I let him have it. Unless he figured out how to change the combination, it's probably the same." Dan took a bundle of small, folded pieces of paper from his shirt pocket and a pen from his pants. He scanned through the deck until he found something he could part with, thought for a minute, then wrote down four numbers. Packard asked him to write down his cell phone number while he was at it.

Packard took the piece of paper, unfolded and folded it. "I'm sorry for your loss, Dan. And I'm sorry to spring this on you and leave right away. I can send a deputy out if you need help with Patty or getting to the hospital."

"No. I'll take care of things," Dan said.

Packard left Dan Gherlick on the dock and walked up the immaculate sweep of green grass, going around the house so he wouldn't have to encounter Patty again. When he looked back, Dan had turned his back to the house and was staring at the lake, hands on his hips. His shoulders went up and down. If Patty was watching from the windows, she might have thought he was laughing. She might have wondered what was so goddamn funny.

CHAPTER SIXTEEN

PACKARD RADIOED AHEAD TO Detective Thielen with the combination to
the safe and the news that he had permission from Dan Gherlick to search the
blue house. Thielen had him wait while she tried the code. His phone vibrated
in the cup holder where he'd stashed it. Susan Wheeler wanting to know if there
was any news. There was plenty of news, Packard thought, but he wasn't sure if
it was related or if Susan should even be told. She'd have to wait.

"Combination worked," Thielen said. "It's open."

"Bag the contents and show me when I get there. I'm on my way."

The fire department crew was loading their gear when he pulled up twenty
minutes later. He stopped to talk to the shift captain, Chuck Otts, about how
they'd jacked up the car and got the body on a board so EMS could transport
it to the county hospital. EMS had taken Sam's unconscious sister separately
while waiting for the fire department to arrive and do its thing.

Thielen had dismissed Deputy Shepard after reviewing his photos on the
digital camera and supervising while he dusted for prints. The front of the red
Mustang and its door handles, Sam's iPod, and some of the tools on the workbench were all covered in black medium. Thielen had grabbed a set of prints
from the body before it left the scene.

She led Packard through the kitchen and the living room (the video game was still paused, the soldiers still unsure what to do) back to Sam's bedroom. One by one she held up the evidence bags spread out on his bed. "Five hundred fifty-seven dollars in cash. Sixty-two individual pills in small bags, sorted by kind. I don't know all the markings and colors. If we take them back to the station and show Blake, he'll know what we're looking at. A small amount of weed. There's a .22 handgun. I called in the serial number and am waiting for a call back."

She held up the last bag. "This is what's most interesting. There are five different prescription bottles all with different names on them. All dated within the last two years. No pills inside any of them. None with the last name Gherlick. No bottle with the name Shaw on it either. Four are for painkillers. One is anti-anxiety."

"So he's stealing the drugs he's selling."

"Or he's buying from kids in these families who are stealing on his behalf," Thielen suggested.

"Maybe. The more people involved in the operation, the harder it is to keep a secret. Maybe it was well known in the school that Sam was a dealer, but that's not the impression I got. It seemed like he was being more careful than that. More careful than Jesse."

Packard hunched over and looked inside the open safe. "What else is in there?"

"That thing still in there is some kind of silicone masturbation device. I made an executive decision that it didn't need to be bagged."

"Christ. Okay. Let's see what else we can find."

They spent the next hour pulling apart the bedroom. On the nightstand was an iPad with a pass code that they gave up trying to break after half a dozen tries. The closet was full of tennis shoes, jeans, sports jerseys, and hooded sweatshirts. In a dresser drawer they found four disposable cell phones with the batteries removed.

Packard gave Thielen a knowing look. "Let's bag those. We'll be able to get the numbers off them if we need to."

"Keeping old burners lying around kind of defeats the purpose of having a disposable phone. Not very smart," she said.

"Same with the prescription bottles. This is a kid who's not worried about getting caught. He thinks he's invincible because of who he is. Who his family is."

Packard brought in a step ladder from the garage and Thielen climbed up, removed one of the tiles from the dropped ceiling, and stuck her head above the suspended frame. "There's something on the tile right over the bed," she said, reaching for her flashlight. She looked again. "I can't tell which tile for sure. I think it's a gun."

Packard pushed up a couple until he found the right one. He spread apart the metal channels and lowered a tile with a gun on it down to the bed. The barrel was etched with OFFICERS' MODEL TARGET .38. A round Colt emblem was carved into its checkered walnut grips.

"A cop's gun?" Thielen asked.

"Not necessarily. Anyone can buy one of these. Looks pretty vintage. From the forties or fifties maybe." Packard rotated the ceiling tile, keeping the barrel pointed away, so they could see the gun from all angles without touching it. "It's loaded. Looks like a name scratched in the bottom of the stock."

Thielen used her flashlight to bring out the shadows. "It says D. Chambers."

"Ring any bells for you?"

Thielen shook her head. "None."

"Curious that this one is up in the ceiling while the other one was locked up," Packard said.

"It wasn't up there for easy access. Probably hiding it," Thielen said.

Packard spent the next few minutes photographing both guns and the pill bottles with his cell phone. When he was done, they went from Sam's room to the guest bedroom where he'd found Shannon Gherlick completely unconscious. There was nothing of Sam's sister's left except the smell of her in the sheets. "She had a purse, right?" Packard asked.

"She did. I put it on the gurney with her."

"Anything interesting in it?"

"I had a quick look when I took her ID out," Thielen said. "Nothing stood out. No drugs, no paraphernalia, no weapons. She had a cell phone, tampons, wallet. That's about it."

They went through boxes and closets and cabinets but turned up little else. Back in the living room, Packard found the remote for the TV and killed the power to the confused game soldiers. "I could be wrong but this feels really small time to me. We could take this house down to the studs and I bet we wouldn't find another pill. There's no big stash here. Sam Gherlick didn't even have a connect."

Thielen almost laughed. "'A connect?' I've never heard you use that term before."

"Jay Z. 'Roc Boys.'"

"I know the song. I didn't have you pegged as someone who listened to Jay Z." Thielen was shocked.

"I listen to a little of everything. My point is this is total amateur hour. Look at this place. He's living rent-free in a house his parents own, and it's still a dump. This game system is five years old. These are not the trappings of a big-time dealer. If he was pushing serious drugs, we would have had him on our radar. Sam was a lazy rich kid getting money from his mom behind his dad's back and supplementing it by selling what few drugs he could get his hands on. When he graduated he took on Jesse as some kind of partner because he still needed someone in the school. That's his only market. So what happened Tuesday night? Sam sent Jesse on an errand. Sam probably didn't know Jenny was with him. Or he didn't care. Jesse went somewhere in the middle of the night to get…what? Drugs? Was he stealing them from someone's house? Did he get caught? And if so, why didn't the homeowner call us?"

"Maybe it wasn't a homeowner with pills," Thielen said. "Maybe Sam knew of someone with a stash. Another dealer. If so, this guy couldn't very well call us and report that someone tried to steal his supply."

Packard nodded. "Has to be something like that. Someone with a reason not to get the cops involved. Sam had to stay quiet when I called him for the same reason. He knew that Jesse and Jenny were missing, and he knew where Jesse was headed that night. He might not have known what happened to them, but he knew something that he couldn't tell anyone because of the nature of what was going down."

"So...did that someone come here and kill Sam then?" Thielen asked.

Packard thought about it for a minute. "Couldn't have been the guy Sam was targeting. Why would Sam be under the car while that guy was walking around? There would have been a fight or confrontation of some kind. I guess the guy could have been lucky and just happened to pull up while Sam was working under the car, but that seems unlikely."

"Too lucky."

"Agreed. If someone killed Sam, it wasn't Jesse's target. It could have been someone associated with him that Sam didn't know."

"Still, why is he under the car while this stranger is walking around?" Thielen asked. "It doesn't jibe. It seems like if he was working on the car while someone was here it had to be some he knew, someone he was comfortable with."

"We don't know for sure that someone pushed that car on top of him, but hell—it's just too damn convenient if you ask me."

Thielen nodded. They were both quiet. Packard could tell by the look on her face that they were thinking the same uncomfortable thought. Thielen said it out loud. "If someone came here to kill Sam to keep him quiet, Jesse and Jenny could already be dead."

"That's what I'm afraid of. But we're going to keep pushing on this like they're still alive. That's what I'm going to keep assuming until we have a reason not to."

"It's been three days," Thielen said.

Packard's phone rang just then. "Only three," he said as he took a call from Kelly.

"Where are you? You called a press conference for four. It's ten after."

Packard dropped his forehead into his hand. "Shit. I forgot about the damn press conference. All right. I'm on my way. Write a statement for me to read, will ya? Just the details on Jenny and Jesse and the car. Doesn't have to be any more than that."

"It's already done."

"Thanks, Kelly."

Thielen pushed together the step ladder and leaned it against the wall. "I can finish up here."

"Thanks. Call in the gun from the ceiling and get us a list of names and addresses that go with the pill bottles. If you have time to hit any of them tonight, great. If not, we'll split them up and hit 'em tomorrow."

"I'll do what I can. Get going. You don't want to face a room full of pissy reporters who missed their deadline because you're late."

———

Ray Hanson sat in the front row at the press conference, looking smug. There were two television cameras and four other reporters besides him in the conference room at the police station. Not exactly a media event. Hanson had seen more press turn out when the new drive-through car wash in town opened. But still, everyone who was there was there because of him. Including Packard, standing in front of them behind a lectern on a table, flanked by a U.S. flag and a Minnesota state flag.

There'd have been no need for a press conference if that cocksucker had just answered his questions in the school parking lot. Since he wouldn't, Ray called his contact at the St. Cloud TV station, a reporter named Brian Davis, who initially said he wasn't interested. Ray tried to sell him on the story's more prurient angles. "The boy's mom is a known drunk; she used to appear in the police blotter in the *Gazette* damn near weekly. Works at Wellards now but back in the day, word was you could take her out behind Bob's Bar and get your dick wet for twenty bucks."

"Ferfucksake, Hanson. How the hell am I supposed to put that on TV? It's not a story for us right now."

"Don't get caught short on this one, Brian. Here's another angle—the girl's dad died six months ago. Run it from her mom's perspective—husband dies and now daughter's missing. How much more bad luck can this woman stand? I can probably get her to talk to you."

"The cops make a statement yet? They ask for the public's help?"

"Not yet."

The silence on Brian's end let Ray know he had him even before Brian agreed to have an intern call on it. Brian's wife was a reporter at the St. Cloud paper. He'd share the story with her, or at least ask her if they'd picked up any chatter on it. From there it would ripple out to other papers and stations in the region. Newsrooms leaked like old plumbing. Once word got out, they'd all want in on the story. No one wanted to get scooped.

Still, it was just a couple of missing teenagers, hence the low turnout. The pimply intern from the St. Cloud station looked like he weighed less than the TV camera on the tripod he was standing next to. The kid had to stand on his tiptoes to look through the viewfinder.

"I'm going to read a short statement," Packard said to everyone gathered. "Photos of the missing persons and a copy of the statement are available on the Sandy Lake Sheriff's Department website.

"Two juveniles from the Sandy Lake community have been missing since Wednesday, April thirtieth. Their names are Jennifer Wheeler, age sixteen, and Jesse Crawford, age seventeen. Both are students at Sandy Lake High School. They are boyfriend and girlfriend. Jennifer is a type 1 diabetic and may be seeking treatment or supplies for her diabetes. Also missing is a maroon 1996 Pontiac Grand Am, Minnesota license plates M as in Mike, D as in Delta, three eight nine. Anyone who has seen these kids or their vehicle is asked to call the Sandy Lake Sheriff's Department or their own local police. That's all the information we have to share at this time. Any questions?"

Ray raised his hand. So did the pimply kid in the back. Packard called on the kid. "Sheriff, can you—"

"Stan Shaw is the sheriff. I'm Detective Ben Packard."

"Sorry. Uh…can you tell us anything about the families involved? Any trouble or uh…tragedy they might have experienced? Uh…recently."

Packard gave the kid a look like he'd just found dog shit on the bottom of his boot. Even Ray had to shake his head at the question. Brian must have told the kid what Ray had told him about the dead husband. The kid was as subtle as a snowplow.

Packard was not amused. "The Sandy Lake Sheriff's Department and the families involved are looking for the public's help finding Jenny and Jesse," he said. "The families will be incredibly grateful for any help the public can provide."

Ray raised his hand again. Packard called on another reporter.

"Any history of violence or trouble between the boyfriend and girlfriend?"

"No. None at all. Any other questions?"

Another reporter: "I have a source at the hospital who says the sheriff's grandson was killed in an accident today. Can you tell us anything about that?"

Ray wheeled around in his seat to see who had asked the question, then turned back to Packard, shocked by the question.

"No, I cannot."

"Packard—" Ray said.

The reporter in back talked over him. "Can you confirm if the sheriff's grandson was in an accident?"

"No, I cannot."

Ray raised his hand again and said, "Does Jesse Crawford have a record? I heard he was escorted—"

Packard scooped up his papers from the lectern and said, "That's all I have. Thanks for your time."

The editors putting the video together for the six o'clock news would have to edit out the part where Ray Hanson stood up and yelled, "Goddamn it, Packard! You sonofabitch!"

CHAPTER SEVENTEEN

PACKARD WAS STUCK AT the station following the press conference. He hung around and talked to a couple of the print reporters off the record in the hall. Not Ray Hanson. Ray stomped out of there like he was looking for a house to burn down. One day Packard would push Ray too far, but until then, fuck Ray Hanson.

After saying "No comment" again and again in regards to all their questions about Sam Gherlick, he escorted everyone out through the reception area. Kelly was still at her desk.

"Thanks for coming in today."

"You owe me comp time."

"Deal. Can you do me one more favor? I need to talk to Ann Crawford. I'll take it back in my office."

He stopped in the restroom. When he came out, Kelly hollered back at him. "Ann Crawford is on line two."

In his office, he picked up the phone receiver and hit the flashing light as he went around the end of his desk and sat. "Ann, it's Ben Packard from the sheriff's department. I wanted you to know we had a news conference about Jesse and Jenny this afternoon. There should be something on the news tonight at six and in the papers tomorrow."

"What was the news? You find 'em?" Ann asked. He could hear a TV in the background and the sound of her shaking a nearly empty can, then noisily swallowing the last of its contents.

"No, we haven't found them. We would tell you before we told the press if we did."

"Just tell ME when you find my car. Tell my SON he's a shitass. Takin' my car for…gone for days."

"Whaddaya been drinking, Ann? Just beer or the hard stuff, too?"

"Whoa, who're you? The fuckin' drink police?"

"Just the regular police."

"Never mind wha' I'm drinking."

"All right. I just wanted you to know about the news conference so you wouldn't be surprised if you saw Jesse on TV."

"I ain't surprised by nothin' no more. I don't give a damn if that boy comes home or not. I jus' want my car back."

———

Packard spent another hour on emails and paperwork from the semi accident the night before. Besides the regular dispatch shift, he had a deputy set up with coffee and a phone and a laptop ready to work late and answer the tip line if any calls came in based on the news. Kelly was long gone and had locked up the administrative area. He went out the back to the sally port where he'd parked his truck.

His phone rang as he got behind the wheel. The number was local but not assigned to a contact. He answered it anyway.

"Yeah, who is this?"

"That's how you answer the phone? Not even a hello?" Gary Bushwright said.

"Gary, I'm kind of busy. If Cora's acting out again, you should—"

"Honey, I'm not calling about Cora. I'm calling about your ward you've left under my charge. I guess I'm supposed to raise him as my own. Is that the idea?"

Packard was confused. "I don't know what you're talking about, Gary."

"Let me be more clear then. I run a licensed, certified not-for-profit 501(c)(3) organization dedicated to rescuing dogs. It's called Gary's Kids. Maybe you've heard of it? You expressed an interest in taking home one of my rescues when you were here the other day. You told me to hold on to the corgi for you, and now I haven't heard from you in days."

"Ah, jeez. I'm sorry. I forgot."

"Oh, you forgot? I'm not sure I want you to have this dog if you're going to forget about him when things get busy."

"Come on, Gary. I had a dog for years. You know that. I wouldn't forget if he was mine."

"Do you know how many emails I've had about that little three-legged doll since I put his picture on my website? I'll tell you. Forty-nine. From all over the country. I sent a couple of local kids home crying yesterday because I wouldn't let them adopt the corgi. Little baby children crying the biggest tears you ever saw. You understand that?"

"I got it. I'll be in as soon—"

"No, sir. Not soon. Not when it's convenient for you. First of all, if you want me to keep this dog, Gary's Kids also provides a boarding service. It costs $25 a day. Discount rates by the week."

"Fine, I'll pay it."

"You need to come in and sign some papers if you want me to board your dog. You also need to fill out the adoption papers so you can claim him as your dog and then pay me to board him. Tonight."

"Gary, it's been the longest day."

"You heard me. Tonight. Before 10 p.m.. I turn into a pumpkin at 10. You don't come by tonight, I'm calling those little crybabies first thing tomorrow and telling them they can have the dog."

Packard sighed. He was exhausted. This was supposed to have been his day off. The job would consume his every waking minute if he let it. One more phone call, one more stop, one more question. Everything that took him away from the job of finding Jenny felt like a dereliction of duty. But he couldn't do everything. He'd put in twelve hours already. He had a deputy answering calls on the tip line. If anything credible came in, he'd notify Packard right away. That had to be enough tonight.

The idea of getting a new dog gave Packard a boost. A dog would keep him from always coming home to an empty house. A dog would give the construction zone he called a home a heartbeat. If he could find time in his schedule for a dog, then maybe he could find time for Michael, too. He wouldn't mind coming home to a dog and maybe a naked nurse once or twice.

"All right, Gary. I'm on my way."

Packard parked behind Gary's semi cab. A bare bulb burned in the porch light next to the front door. Shadows from the railing on the wheelchair ramp cast prison bars across the scrubby grass. From the rescue building came the muted, high-pitched song of barking dogs set off by the sound of his car. Packard was suddenly anxious to see his new dog.

Gary pushed open the screen door. "This way, Deputy. I got that building all closed up. After-hours business takes place in the house."

Packard zigzagged his way up the ramp. He'd never been inside Gary's house. The after-hours invitation seemed intimate and inappropriate and totally Gary. If Cora was watching, her head was probably spinning 360 degrees. She'd already made her mind up about Packard. There'd be no convincing her otherwise now.

Gary was wearing fuzzy slippers with jeans and a very old San Francisco 49ers sweatshirt tucked under his Grizzly Adams beard. "Football fan?" Packard said.

Gary looked down at his front and shook his head. "Thrift store fan," he said, letting the screen door scrunch closed.

Inside Gary's house a plug-in sandalwood air freshener and the smoke from an endless chain of cigarettes were trying to hustle the last breathable air out the door. Packard thought he felt his chest tighten when he took a breath. He cleared his throat to suppress a cough. He looked around at the dark paneled walls and the sun-faded photos hanging in frames. There was a turquoise couch and a matching armchair, both old and worn shiny, all the arms covered in antimacassars. The carpet was knotted shag nearly worn to the webbing in spots. It was as if Gary's elderly mother hadn't died, just taken off to Sarasota or Scottsdale for the winter. It looked like she was due back any minute.

"It's all Mom's stuff," Gary said, reading Packard's mind. "Just the way she left it. I can't bear to change a thing or throw any of it out."

"If you like it, then why change it?" Packard said.

"Oh, I don't like it or dislike it. Most of the time, I don't even see it," Gary said.

The only signs that Gary's house wasn't a time machine back to 1983 were the flat-screen TV set atop a credenza in the living room and a small desk pushed against a wall in the dining room with an LCD monitor on top. A computer tower hummed on the floor next to it.

"Can I get you something to drink? Scotch? Beer? Iced tea?"

"No, nothing. Thanks," Packard said. Then he took a breath and felt how dry and scratchy his throat was already from cigarette smoke. "Actually, water would be good."

Gary went to the kitchen and came back with a water glass covered in gold dots that either had belonged to his mother or came from the thrift store with the 49ers sweatshirt.

Gary picked up a half-empty Grain Belt bottle next to the computer screen and took a big drink. "Well, make yourself comfortable. I need to print out a few documents and then we can get started." He took a seat at the computer and put on a pair of plastic reading glasses on a string that split at the bridge and came back together, held by magnets.

"I saw you on the news tonight," Gary said as he pecked away at the keyboard.

"Yeah. We got a couple of missing kids we're trying to find."

"You mentioned that last time you were here. They run away?"

"That's one theory."

"They've been gone for days. I'd hate to think what the other theories might be."

Packard said nothing. He drank the tap water. His equipment belt creaked as he looked at the photos on the wall. Photos of Gary and his mother through the years, family reunions, birthday cakes, national monuments, holidays. He stopped at one framed photo of a shirtless young man in a small red swimming suit leaning over what looked like the railing of a large boat. He was smiling down at someone below holding the camera. His hair was wet and pushed back from his forehead. The photo was old and fading to greens and blues, but Packard was still able to make out the thumbprint birthmark on the man's cheek.

"Is this you in this photo?" he asked.

Gary turned in his direction and looked over the top of his readers to see what Packard was looking at. "On the boat? Honey, yes. Can you believe it?"

Packard could not.

"When was this? How old were you?"

"Twenty, twenty-one maybe. I was on the yacht of a very famous fashion designer off the coast of Majorca. A week after that photo was taken his wife rammed the boat with a skiff and tried to shoot him with a flare gun."

"Why did the wife try to shoot her husband with a flare gun?"

"I guess she saw one too many photos of us together at Studio 54 and fashion parties in the tabloids. She was humiliated. It was the late seventies, early eighties. Famous people were discreetly homosexual back then. He wasn't being discreet enough for her liking. Two deckhands subdued her and put out the fire. He gave me a thousand dollars in cash and a brick of the finest Colombian cocaine to get rid of before the *policia* showed up. That was the last time I saw him."

"Your relationship was…what?"

"It was a business relationship. He was incredibly generous in exchange for my company, if you know what I mean."

Packard drank his water, remembering what Gary had said when Packard threatened to lock him and Cora in the same cell. *She could hold my yarn while I scandalized her with stories from my wild youth when I worked in the skin trade.*

"Prostitution," Packard said. He looked at the photo again. It was Gary, no question. He noticed for the first time the bulge in the swimsuit. He felt his face turning red.

"I plead the fifth," Gary said. Then in a loud stage whisper: "But yes, prostitution."

A laser printer by Gary's feet extruded several pages. Packard took a seat at the round dining table with straight-backed vinyl chairs in a floral jungle print. Gary handed him a pen and the papers.

Packard rushed to fill everything out. His eyes burned from the cigarette smoke. He had a thousand questions he wanted to ask Gary about being a male escort in the 1970s but he bit his tongue. He'd be there all night. Then what would Cora say?

When he was done, Gary filled out some of the sections himself, then took Packard's credit card and entered it into the billing software on his computer. "How many more days till you pick up your dog?"

"Give me five more days. In five days we'll have found those kids or we'll be out of places to look."

"Five days *max*," Gary said. "That dog wants to go home with someone who will love him. Just like the rest of us."

"I understand. I'll be back."

Packard stood and headed for the door, Gary a step behind. "Some other time I want to hear the story of how you went from small-town boy to male prostitute to retired truck driver. But not tonight."

"You forgot the part where I starred in a series of all-male cinematic features of dubious artistic integrity."

It took Packard a second to figure out what Gary was talking about. He paused with his hand on the doorknob. "Porn?"

"Yes, porn, if you want to be crude about it. I was a full-on porn star, honey. Then a high-priced call girl. Then a truck driver."

"Come on, Gary."

"Johnny Hardwood. Phoenix Films. Google it. And you won't hear a word of that story until you share your own. What brought Ben Packard to Sandy Lake out of the blue?"

"That story's not nearly as interesting as yours," Packard said. He let the screen door slap behind him and started down the wheelchair ramp.

"Any connection to the Packard boy who went missing back in the '90s?"

Packard kept walking. "Another time, Gary," he said. He didn't know why Gary asking about Nick made his heart feel like it was frozen in his chest. He really did have no secrets in this town. At least not from Gary.

Gary blew smoke through the screen door and watched him walk to the truck. "Remember what I said," he called out. "We all want out of our cages. We all want to be taken home and loved. Even you, Deputy Packard."

CHAPTER EIGHTEEN

EMMETT SAT IN HIS recliner with the oxygen cannula under his nose as he watched the story about the missing teens on the nine o'clock news. The news anchor was a woman in her fifties with pale skin and a brownish gash of lipstick the same color as her hair. Side-by-side school photos of the boy and the girl showed on the screen as she read the story. Emmett got his first good look at the boy. It had been dark when he shot him in the face on the stairs.

The news anchor said, "Sandy Lake area police are asking for the public's help locating two missing teens. Jennifer Wheeler and Jesse Crawford have been missing since Wednesday. They are thought to be driving a maroon 1996 Pontiac Grand Am. Jennifer has type 1 diabetes. Anyone with information should contact the Sandy Lake Sheriff's Department."

She then went on to talk about the start of Minnesota's other season, road construction season, and a major project that was going to slow down traffic in the area for months to come.

Emmett stopped listening. He'd had a hard time breathing since arguing with the girl and climbing the stairs in the afternoon. The oxygen machine puffed cool, dry air for him to breathe but did nothing to ease the feeling that he was trying to push a weight off his chest. He closed his eyes. If he spent too much time thinking about how hard it was to breathe or tried to time his breaths with the puffs from the machine, he'd start hyperventilating.

He peeled apart the cellophane wrapper on an oatmeal cookie and ate half of it in one bite. The oxygen machine went *pff...pff...pff*.

Part of what made it hard to calm his breathing was remembering what the girl had said.

Am I supposed to let you fuck me? Or give you a blow job?

She was sixteen according to the news, but she looked like a child. Emmett knew he was a lot of things that most people despised—a pervert and a kidnapper to name only two—but he was no fucking pedophile. He didn't touch kids.

Last night he'd sat in the dark except for the blue light from the television and stared at the curling smoke from his cigarette and dredged up his old fantasies. The genie who wanted to make all his wishes come true. His harem of women who lounged on silk pillows and waited to please him. His fantasies were as worn out as his broken body. Building the pink room to live out the things he'd only dreamed about seemed like someone else's bad idea. He had no interest in the girl like that. She was no genie. No sex goddess. He needed a sex goddess now like he needed a caged elephant.

The girl was a problem and nothing but a problem. She was never going to live willingly in a cage in his basement. Never feel affection for him. Not if they lived together for a hundred years. She would run the first chance she got.

Wouldn't she?

Of course she would.

Headlights lit up the sliding door as someone came down the drive. Carl driving Frankenstein, from the sound of the exhaust.

Emmett pushed the rest of the cookie in his mouth, peeled the cannula off, and mashed the power button on the oxygen machine. Carl showing up unannounced was bad news. It meant only one thing.

He'd come for the girl.

———————

Yesterday, she had given him the name Sam Gherlick when he asked who sent her and the boy to steal his pills. The name didn't mean anything to Emmett at first. The Gherlick family owned the building and supply business. He'd had a passing acquaintance with the old man, Jack, going back decades. Jack was dead now; his kids ran the business.

So who the hell was Sam Gherlick?

Carl was at the garage when Emmett called to ask if he knew the name. When Emmett had first met Carl, his business operated in a small commercial building with a single drive-in bay not far from the detached two-car garage where Emmett was running his welding business. Now Carl's Auto & Body Repair was in a long aluminum building right off the highway. The building had four bays, a parts store, and a business office.

"Fuck yeah, I know who Sam Gherlick is. So do you. He's Danny Gherlick's boy. He's the goddamn sheriff's grandson. Drives that cherry-red '65 Mustang. He's in here all the time asking me to order him parts. Wants to get into flipping cars, building hot rods, shit like that."

The mention of the red '65 Mustang made everything fall into place for Emmett. Sam Gherlick was the kid from Meals on Wheels. A couple of years ago, during the summer months, Sam Gherlick had started bringing the pale chicken breasts and the little carton of skim milk. Drove a red Mustang and was chatty as hell. Talking about the weather or the Vikings.

The first time Sam asked if he could come in and use the bathroom, Emmett told him he could pick any tree on the property he wanted. A couple of weeks later, on a hot day, the kid asked if he could get a glass of water. Emmett relented. The house was a dump, and he knew it smelled bad from the garbage and the mold and all the other filth, but the kid didn't seem overly invested in Emmett's welfare. After that time, whenever he heard the rumble of the kid's engine as he pulled up to the house, Emmett didn't even bother to come to the door. Just told the kid to come in and set the food on the kitchen counter.

"That motherfucker was in and out of my house two, three times a week," Emmett told Carl. "The hell of the matter is that there were times back then that I thought for sure I had pills missing. This was before the goddamn break-ins. I thought I was just losing track. Cocksucker was skimming my pills the whole time."

Carl sounded grim. "Emmett, you gotta get rid of that girl. If Sam was the one who sent them to your house, then what's to stop him from telling the cops? They could show up any minute."

"What's he going to do? Tell the cops he sent them to break into my house and steal my pills? He can't do that."

"He could do it anonymously. If the cops link him to those kids somehow, they could offer him a deal."

"So then getting rid of the girl doesn't solve our problem at all, does it?" Emmett said.

"What do you mean, 'our problem'?"

"Listen to me. That room might be in my basement but we're both responsible for what's gone on in there. I grabbed those first two, but you're the one who wrecked the second one. You also brought that truck stop whore over and killed her in there."

This was almost ten years ago now. Her face was already bruised from whatever had gone on between her and Carl before he brought her to Emmett's that night and dragged her around to the back door. She was carrying her torn skirt and one of her shoes when Emmett first laid eyes on her as he came down the basement stairs. When she saw Emmett, she didn't ask for help. She asked for drugs. "He said we could score here. What do you got?"

That was when Carl punched her hard enough that she dropped to the floor. He hauled her into the pink room and Emmett went back up the stairs. When her screams got loud enough that he could hear them through the floor, he turned up the TV.

"Not to mention you came running like a goddamn slobbering dog when I called you about the girl. Sam Gherlick is *our* fucking problem. You need to do two things. One, get rid of the car and the body in my garage."

Carl laughed incredulously. "Shit. Why should I haul around a car with a body in the trunk that you killed?"

"I'm not asking you to drive the sonofabitch through town in a goddamn parade. Take it from here in the middle of the night and dump it somewhere it won't be found."

"What's the other thing?"

"Get rid of the Gherlick boy."

"No. No way. I didn't sign up for that. I might help you clean up the mess with the car and that boy you shot, but I'm not taking out the sheriff's grandson."

Emmett pushed the phone closer to his mouth, almost hard enough to mash his lips. "You don't kill that little motherfucker, you and I are going to spend the rest of our years behind bars. Is that what you want? That boy'll sink you if the cops get to him."

"He's gonna sink *you*," Carl said.

"We'll go down together," Emmett said.

———————

Emmett drank the last of his beer, then opened the sliding glass door and stepped barefoot onto the raised deck just as Carl was getting out of his truck.

"Whatchya doin' here, Carl?"

"Came to tell you I took care of our problem."

"You sure?"

"Am I sure I left the Gherlick boy crushed under a car with his feet kicking like he was dancing a jig? Yes, I'm sure."

Emmett leaned on the wobbly porch railing and hung his head. He hocked something from the back of his throat and spat away from Carl. "You did what you were supposed to. You could've called with that news."

"I want to see the girl."

Going down together was the threat it took to get Carl to do what he wanted.

The girl was the reward. Emmett had dangled her on a hook during their phone call, going so far as to tell Carl about the blue panties he'd cut off her and what he'd seen when she showered. He tried not to think about her singing or the way she'd looked like a child getting ready for bed. She was a child. Sixteen.

"It's late. I'm not letting you see her. You'll go in there like a lawn mower over a nest of baby rabbits. Won't be nothing left but blood and tatters."

Carl grinned and chuckled. "Come on now. I'll be nice. Time's a-wasting, right? Once her medicine runs out, she's a goner."

"You still got a job to do."

"What do you mean, 'still'?" Carl said. He looked both directions, then up at Emmett. "I killed that Gherlick boy for you. Did a real good job, too, so it looked like an accident. I've earned my share."

Emmett nodded in the direction of the garage behind Carl. "What about the car? That was part of the deal."

Carl shook his head, turned, and flicked his cigarette butt up the gravel driveway. "I never agreed to no deal. I took care of Gherlick to protect myself. I'm not messing with that car. It's too risky. Safer to just let it sit right where it is."

"With the body rotting in the trunk?"

"You told me to put it in the trunk."

"It couldn't stay at the bottom of my goddamn stairs."

"You drive the car somewhere and dump it. I'll meet you and pick you up. I'll do that much."

"I don't want it found. Not with the boy in the trunk. That happens and they're going to look even harder around here for the girl. Don't you get it? The car, the boy, the girl, they all have to vanish. Then no one knows where to look."

"Shit," Carl said, shaking his head. He kicked the ground and scratched the top of his head. "I might know a place. And don't ask where 'cause I'm not interested in your goddamn opinion. You come to my place and we'll come back here with the wrecker, and then you can drive your own fat ass home."

"What about your wife and daughter?"

"Don't worry about them. They both got allergies so damn bad in the spring they take Sudafed and NyQuil every night just so they can sleep."

"I don't like the chance of the two of us being seen together doing this by your family."

"Old man, you better decide what's important. I can't believe I'm letting you talk me into any of this. Everybody in five counties is looking for a maroon Grand Am."

"I had a thought about that. What if it wasn't maroon anymore when you come get it?"

"You're gonna paint it?"

Emmett shrugged. "A roller and a can of white paint ought to be enough to make it pass as something else in the middle of the night. I'll get the paint tomorrow. Paint it Monday. We'll get rid of it Monday night." Emmett pushed himself away from the railing and turned toward the sliding door. "I'm going to bed. I'll see you then," he said.

"Wait just a goddamn minute," Carl said. "I came out here to see that girl, and I'm at least getting a look at her. I'm helping you with all this bullshit, and maybe the girl isn't even alive anymore. They don't last long once you lock 'em up."

"Goddamn it, Carl. She ain't dead."

"I'm not kidding, old man. I'm putting my ass on the line for you, and I want a reminder of what I'm getting for it. I won't touch her, but I'm damn well not leaving here without having at least a look at her. You say no and you're on your own. You can take care of that car yourself."

Emmett felt his stomach clench. He pushed on either side of his enormous gut with both hands. Somewhere in there a burp or a fart sizzled on a hot stone of fear. He didn't know what was worse: letting Carl get close to the girl or losing Carl's help with the car. He thought of the boy in trunk and the smell that would come as the long, hot summer approached. There were some things he could do himself, but dealing with the car was not one of them. He needed Carl.

"Let me get my shoes," Emmett said.

Carl took off down the side of the house at the first word. In three strides he was out of sight.

"Goddamn it, Carl. Wait for me!"

Emmett took the stairs from the deck down to the ground as quickly as his rusted knees allowed. It was completely dark now. He was barefoot and the ground was cold. He couldn't see the rocks and debris he was stepping on. By the time he rounded the front corner of the house, Carl was still out of sight. Emmett went down the stone steps dug into the sloped grade beside the foundation. The pavers were pitched and cracked after years of freezing and thawing. "Carl! You sonofabitch! Wait for me."

He was only halfway down the steps when he heard the girl scream. He couldn't go any faster if he wanted to. A fall and a broken leg meant he'd have to be shot like a horse. He couldn't have an ambulance out here or spend weeks recovering in the hospital with a girl locked in his basement.

The girl screamed, "No!" just as he made it to the basement door. The door to the pink room was wide open. Light from the lamp made the interior look like flesh lit by fire. He still couldn't see Carl. Emmett had a vision of him hunched over the cot with the girl's throat in his jaws, shaking her like he was trying to break her neck.

What he found was the girl standing on the cot, backed into the corner, her head and shoulders rolled forward against the low ceiling. She was still wearing the manacles and the big yellow T-shirt with the Ferris wheel and *Sandy Lake Labor Day Festival 1986* on the front. Her insulin pump dangled by its tube from beneath the hem of her shirt. She had her bandaged hand braced against the ceiling. In the other was a twelve-inch length of the slack boat chain doubled up and hanging down like a club. The blanket had been yanked to the floor. Carl was on his ass, back against the wall opposite the cot. His cheek was already swelling where she'd bashed him with the swinging chain.

Emmett looked at Carl and looked at the girl. His breath came in ragged, wheezing gasps. The girl had a wild, dazed look in her eyes. She fell to her knees on the cot. The old springs went *ehhh-ehhh, ehhh-ehhh.*

"You should've waited for me," Emmett said. He had a laugh inside him he knew needed to stay there. Humiliating Carl would mean the end of the girl, right here, right now. There'd be nothing Emmett could do to stop him.

"I think she broke my fucking cheekbone, Emmett."

"What was she supposed to do? You attacked her. You wanted to see her and you saw her. Now get up and get out."

Carl pushed himself up and half turned in Emmett's direction. Just as quickly, he turned again and lunged for the girl. He got her throat in one hand and her bandaged hand in his other. He was close enough that long strands of his hair fell over his eyes and brushed against her face. "You and me are gonna have a good time together," he hissed at her.

Carl rapped the girl's bandaged hand hard against the wall, then let her go. She collapsed on the cot like she'd been shot dead. He and Emmett stood shoulder to shoulder in the doorway, both facing opposite directions. "I'm coming back for her, Emmett. And next time I'm going to do more than look."

A second later he had disappeared through the basement door into the night.

———

Emmett didn't have the strength to follow Carl back up the slope so he waited and watched from the corner of the house until he saw Frankenstein's headlights back up and heard its muffler recede as Carl drove away. Emmett limped to his rocker and stared out the open door at the moon rising over the mud lake while he lit a cigarette. Behind him he heard the girl vomiting in her bucket. He smoked and studied the dirt caked to his feet from walking outside. The bare skin on his shoulders and arms was damp against the chair's leather back. He worked his hand beneath his undershirt and scratched in places where his fat overlapped.

Carl had a lesson coming to him. You didn't treat another man's property like that. It reminded Emmett of when Carl was just starting his shop and couldn't afford the equipment he needed for certain jobs. Emmett loaned him tools a few times but stopped in short order because Carl never brought things back. Or if he did, something was wrong with them. No apology. No respect. No sense of obligation. If that sonofabitch thought he was going to ruin this girl, he'd better think again.

Emmett stabbed out the cigarette, heaved himself up from the rocker, and opened the door to the room. The timer on the lamp had clicked it off. In what little light got by him from the basement, he saw the girl on her side, head hanging over the bucket. He saw her convulse in pain and retch again. She had nothing left in her to come up.

"How bad are you hurt?"

She didn't respond.

"How's your hand?"

She twisted her red face in his direction. "It's fucking killing me!" she yelled. "What do you think? He smashed it."

Emmett flinched as she retched again. He tried to think of something to say to her—about Carl, about keeping him away from her, about anything—but couldn't find the words. He had a whole pill he'd meant for himself in his pocket. He went into the room and pushed the pill into her good hand until her fist closed around it. "Take it when you're done throwing up. I'll check on you in the morning."

As he locked her in, he knew he wasn't going to let her die by running out of insulin. For selfish reasons, he needed her alive and well enough for Carl to think he had something waiting for him once the car was gone. If Carl insisted on looking in on her again before loading up the Grand Am, the whole deal would be off if she was dead or dying. And yes, maybe he was growing attached to her. She was a lot of work. She was also someone to talk to. It had been an eternity since he'd had anything close to that.

"I'll get your insulin tomorrow," he said through the door. He waited for a response.

Nothing.

"And I'll look for *David Copperhead* at the library," he added.

As he went up the basement stairs, the pain in his back knifed him with each step. He had to stop halfway and catch his breath while he held the rail. In the kitchen, he took two pills and rinsed them down with a glug of beer. He belched and looked out the kitchen window at the moon and its reflection on the still lake. He thought about everything he needed to get the girl tomorrow. Insulin and better food to eat. That didn't bother him. If there were two places in town Emmett knew front to back, they were the grocery store and the pharmacy.

The library, though.

What the hell do I know about getting a book at the library?

CHAPTER NINETEEN

SUNDAY MORNING

PACKARD CALLED THE STATION to find out about the calls that had come in after the first news reports went out. They were pretty much exactly what he expected. People who saw a maroon Grand Am or what they thought was a Grand Am. *Might have been a Taurus now that I think about it. Didn't see a license plate. Didn't see who was driving. I have a neighbor who has a red Grand Am and I don't trust the guy. You should check him out.*

Nothing concrete. No positive ID or even a pretty good ID of the two kids. He assigned a deputy to make follow-up calls but he didn't expect anything to come of it.

He found the piece of paper from yesterday with Dan Gherlick's phone number on it and called.

Dan was at the hospital. "My daughter is in a room on the third floor. My wife's in a separate room on the second."

"What happened to Patty?"

"She went into a frenzy when I told her about Sam's accident. She was drunk, of course. I tried to get her to sit on the couch with me, but she ran around like she was trying to chase a bat out of the room. She twisted her ankle and banged her head on a table. I had an ambulance come out and pick her up. She's got five stitches in her forehead. I asked them to keep her overnight so she could sleep it off. My sister-in-law is coming by to pick her up and take her home this morning."

"How's your daughter?"

"Shannon is sedated. They put her on a ventilator to protect her airway from aspiration. The doctors said it was good you found her when you did. They think she was hypoxic for some time. She had pinpoint pupils and blue lips by the time they got her to the hospital. She's on an IV for fluids."

"I really need to get in there and talk to her about her brother."

"She doesn't know about Sam yet. She's barely been awake since I've been here. Her doctor said they'll take out the breathing tube later today."

Packard knew he should sympathize with Shannon's addiction issues and the loss of her brother, but all he could think was that she was impeding his investigation. He needed to know what she knew about her brother's drug business. Everything else was secondary.

"Thanks for the update, Dan. I'll call you again later today to see how she's doing."

Packard went down to the lake in his wet suit and swam. The weight of the case felt like a drag on him in the water. He tried to put it out of his mind while he rewarmed his cold bones in the sauna. At the bottom of the narrow window in the sauna door, Packard could still see the smears from where Jarrett used to rub his nose while Packard was steaming inside. In the end, he'd had Jarrett, Marcus's dog, longer than he'd known Marcus.

When he looked back on it, Packard knew fleeing from Minneapolis to Sandy Lake had been what they call in recovery circles a geographical cure. He thought his problems were with the city and the job and the rumors about him and Marcus. He'd expected to leave his troubles behind, but two years on he still hadn't resolved his feelings about Marcus. In death, Marcus had become perfect. Untouchable. Packard was the asshole who kept him at arm's length during their year together, wary of what his life would be like coupled with another man.

One of things he missed most about Marcus was hearing him sing in the bathroom as he got ready to go somewhere. Marcus liked looking good and smelling good, and took his time doing it. He could spend an hour in the bathroom wearing nothing but a white towel, his black skin glistening with steam from the hot shower he'd continue to let run while he went through his ablutions. Nobody would have guessed that the rough, tough cop had more moisturizers and colognes than Macy's.

Packard thought he'd built this bathroom as a retreat for himself, but now, looking through the narrow window in the sauna door at how he'd spent almost $20,000, he saw it for what it was—a shrine to Marcus. A gift for someone who was never coming around to receive it.

———————

The lead investigator from the Minnesota Bureau of Criminal Apprehension had called a meeting for 10:00 a.m. to share the findings so far on the drug runners killed by the overturned semi. No one had called Kelly, so an inordinate amount of time was spent finding the keys to the conference room, figuring out how to turn up the heat on a Sunday and make enough coffee for the half-dozen people assembled for the meeting. Packard had to laugh at how some of the best investigators around could be so confounded by a commercial-grade coffee machine with only two buttons.

Once everyone was seated, the BCA agent in charge, a guy with the last name of Parks, went around the table and gave each person a stapled brief. Parks was tall and bald, dressed in a white shirt and khaki cargo pants. Age had hollowed out his face and slackened his neck. He smelled like cigarettes as he passed behind Packard.

"The driver's identity has been established and confirmed with authorities in Fargo." The packet had a photocopy of a North Dakota driver's license belonging to a white male with short, wet-looking hair cut across his forehead in a severe line. "His address is a trailer on a lot owned by an oil-drilling operation. We've got local eyes on it in case anyone shows up looking for our victim or his cargo, but so far it's been quiet. We still don't know the identity of the female. The body was too damaged to get a good photo for identification purposes."

Packard flipped through the pages, only half-interested in the presentation. The conference was a courtesy more than anything. By the end of the day, everyone who wasn't local would be gone, the investigation split to focus on Fargo and Duluth. The destroyed car and the weed in the trunk would be gone, too. Packard was happy to let it all go. The victims weren't locals. If they'd made it five more miles down the road, they'd have been in another county and this would have been another sheriff's problem.

Thielen peeked through the window in the door while the meeting was in session, and he gave her a nod so she'd know he'd seen her. The meeting lasted an hour while they went around the table and every other agent reported on their part of the investigation. It took another hour of conference calls back to Minneapolis headquarters, side conversations, and general bullshitting about the weather and the bass-fishing season before Packard could disengage.

He found Thielen typing at a computer in the squad room. Mac Davis was standing behind her, holding a Diet Coke and wearing his dispatch headset.

"What have you got?"

Thielen got up and went to the printer and came back with two pages and handed one to Packard. "As best as I can research for now, these are the names and addresses from the five pill bottles we found yesterday."

Mac noisily sipped his soda and looked at Packard's copy of the list with him. "I can tell you right now that Eunice Amberson died in January. She went to my church. You could talk to her family but you won't get much out of her."

Packard reached over and plucked a pen from behind Mac's ear and scratched out Eunice's name. "Two of these addresses are farther out. Two are at Graveside Manor."

Graveside Manor was the nickname for an apartment building in town by the lake that had been remodeled and rebranded as assisted living residences for independent seniors. The actual name of the place was Lakeside Manor.

"Did you pull any info on the guns?"

"The .22 is registered to Dan Gherlick," Thielen said. "Nothing came up for the .38 we took out of the ceiling. Mac offered to keep researching online for a D. Chambers in the area."

Mac said, "Tomorrow we can get into any city records not online. I know the gals over there."

"I'd rather have it today."

"You'd rather have it yesterday but it's Sunday. Normal people have the day off."

The pills felt more important than the gun at the moment. Packard made a mental note to ask Dan about it when he called him later. It might be another family gun that hadn't been registered. "We may find out talking to these four that the gun came from one of their houses." To Thielen: "Let's split these up. You want the two at Graveside or the others?"

"I'll take the other two. I know Martin Hughes. I'll visit him and Emmett Burr."

"Call me when you're done. Sooner if you turn up anything interesting."

The day was passing quickly. Too quickly. Packard got pulled back into the overturned semi business again before he could get out of the station. The marijuana found in the car had been stored in the narcotic evidence locker. Now it needed to be bagged in serialized evidence bags, meticulously weighed and logged in DEA ledgers, then signed off by Packard and another witness to create a chain of custody record.

He stopped for a late lunch at the Spot Café and sat at the horseshoe counter.

While waiting for his burger, he got a text message from Susan offering dinner at the restaurant if he wanted to stop in and give her the latest. Packard put the phone away, thinking that Susan wasn't prepared for the latest. Susan was better left in the dark. The idea that someone might have killed Sam Gherlick to cut the connection between him and wherever Jesse and Jenny had gone that night was not going to reassure his cousin about her daughter's situation.

A pair of old guys whose names Packard couldn't remember started talking his ear off about the bad traffic and how it wasn't even full-on summer yet and how many drunks they saw on the roads at all hours. Elaine Wilson moved around the inside of the horseshoe, a barge of a woman in a white apron. Her hair was shorter and oranger than usual. She winked at Packard, glad the old farts were hassling him instead of her for once. Packard noticed she'd traded her typical Vikings sweatshirt for a long-sleeved Twins jersey.

"How are they looking this year?" he asked, nodding at her shirt.

"Terrible, as usual. My daughter and I are going down next weekend for three against Seattle."

"Professional sports is nothing but overpaid drug addicts and wife-beaters," one of the old-timers said.

"Oh, here we go," Elaine said.

"And here I go," Packard said, sliding his credit card across the counter. "I'll take the check."

It was late afternoon when he pulled up in front of Graveside Manor. Figuring out how and where Sam got his drugs might have looked like it was taking him away from finding Jesse and Jenny, but Packard didn't think so. Drugs were the through line connecting everyone involved in this case. Sam knew where Jenny and Jesse were going that night, and now Sam was dead. Interviewing old ladies about their missing pills might not lead him directly to the target, but it was a step in the right direction. Packard was sure of it.

Manor was a generous description for the simple two-story building with a central lobby and wings to either side. An outer door led to a secured foyer. He saw a reception desk inside with a dark computer screen and no one sitting at it. Packard picked up a handset and dialed the security code for Apartment 105 where Olivia McDonald lived. He waited a full minute before a thin, trebly voice said, "Hello?"

"Ms. McDonald. I'm Deputy Packard from the sheriff's department. I'm calling from the lobby. I was wondering if I could come in and ask you a few questions?"

"Is this for fundraising for the police department? I'm on a fixed income."

"No, ma'am. I want to ask you some questions related to a case I'm working on. Won't take long."

"But I can't see you. How do I know you're a real deputy and not an ax murderer?"

"I can show you my badge if you let me in."

"But by then it'll be too late for old Mrs. McDonald. Hacked to bits, they'll say."

She seemed to be having fun with him. He said, "If you look out your window, you'll see my vehicle parked in the lot. It says Sheriff on it."

There was scuffing and clattering at the other end of the phone, then silence, then more scuffing and then the security door buzzed and he was inside. A sign pointed him to the right for apartments 100–105. He was halfway down a carpeted hallway that smelled like dusty potpourri when he saw a white head poke out from the door at the end. He called out, "Hello, Mrs. McDonald."

She was a tiny thing with hiked shoulders, a thick waist, and a rounded neck that made him think it had been years since she'd been able to look up and see the sky. She wore a pink turtleneck, green pants, and house slippers. She looked up as far as she could to take in as much of him as her neck would allow. "Well, aren't you handsome," she said.

Packard gave her his best smile. "Thank you for agreeing to meet me."

"If I'd known what a looker you were, I would have suggested you take me for a ride in your police car."

She stepped back and he followed her inside her apartment. There was a tiny galley kitchen and a small dining table just inside the door. Beyond that was the living room with a newer green couch and a padded rocking chair arranged across from a sliding patio door. She had framed needlepoints and a simple wooden cross on the walls and an older television. The apartment reminded him of a college dorm room the way a few meaningful things from home did nothing to make it feel any less temporary.

They sat down at the dining table where Olivia had the frame of a 500-piece puzzle nearly complete. The top of the box showed snowy owls in a winter tree. At the other open seat was a half-eaten meal in a cardboard tray and a small carton of skim milk.

"I'm sorry for interrupting your lunch," Packard said.

"It's nothing. I usually heat it up and pick at it. Hot or cold doesn't seem to make much difference to the taste. God forbid you give old folks salt in their food. They might run naked into the street like crazy people."

Packard took out his phone and pulled up the picture of the pill bottles then slid it across the table. "This is what I wanted to ask you about. Do you recognize this bottle?"

She picked up the phone and stared at it for a minute through the bottom of her glasses. "Well, that's my name for sure. I don't take any prescriptions for anything. I'm as solid as a rock. Those pills are from two years ago when I broke my foot. Why do you have a picture of my pills?"

Packard ignored her question. "Do you know the name Sam Gherlick?" he asked.

Mrs. McDonald thought for a minute. "I know the name Gherlick. I've known a few Sams in my day. I'm trying to put the two together."

Packard gave her a short physical description. "Teenager. About six feet. Blond hair. Muscled. He's Dan Gherlick's son. Sheriff Shaw's grandson."

"I remember him now," she said. She pointed at the half-eaten meal at the other end of the table. "He brought Meals on Wheels for a while last summer. I remember the first time I saw him that he looked familiar. I used to teach in the middle school, and I had his dad and his uncle in my class. The first time I saw him I said, 'Now, whose boy are you? I know that face.'"

"Did you get to know him at all?"

She shrugged. "Not exactly. He was kind of...nosy, I thought. I'm sure they train them to be personable and to check up on us crazy old folks to make sure we're not living in our own filth or petting a dead cat. He always wanted something. A glass of water or to use the bathroom. I thought it was a little bit intrusive. I wrote it off as a generational thing. Are you saying he stole my pills?"

"Unless you gave them to him."

"I did no such thing. To be honest I never noticed they were missing. I took a couple of them and didn't like how dizzy and sleepy they made me and got by with ibuprofen after that."

"When's the last time you saw Sam?"

"A year ago? Maybe longer. You learn not to get too attached to the people who deliver the food. They rotate routes or get busy and quit volunteering. They probably try not to get attached to us either. One day we're answering the door and the next..." She rolled her eyes back and stuck out her tongue, then gave him a big smile.

"What happens if they bring the food and you're not here?"

"We're supposed to put a cooler outside the door for them to leave the food in if we know we're not going to be home."

"Do you leave your door unlocked when you're not here?"

Mrs. McDonald nodded, looking slightly embarrassed. "There's probably a key to the front door down in the depths of my handbag, but I wouldn't want to swear on it. I have nothing worth stealing."

"You don't own a gun, do you?"

"A gun? Heavens no. All my husband's guns went to the kids after he passed."

"Do you know anyone with the last name Chambers? First initial is D?"

She thought for a minute and shook her head. "Doesn't ring a bell."

Packard said, "There's a bottle with Elizabeth Marsh's name on it. She lives here at Lakeside Manor, too. Do you know her?"

"Used to live here," Mrs. McDonald corrected. "They moved her to memory care about three months ago. She was in our bridge club, but I'd say she doesn't know trump from Go Fish at this point. We were partners a lot. She started bidding nonsense about a year ago. That's when we knew she was declining."

"Did she get Meals on Wheels?"

"She did."

"Would she have let Sam into her apartment?"

"Elizabeth would have let the devil himself inside if he asked nicely. The woman didn't know the word no. Forty years of marriage to a sonofabitch makes you agreeable to just about anything, pardon my language."

Packard picked up his phone and stood up. "Mrs. McDonald, I think I have the information I need. Thank you for meeting with me."

She followed him to the door. "Now don't forget you promised me a ride in your police car."

"Did I?"

"If you didn't, you meant to. And I accept. Just don't keep me waiting too long."

Packard had to laugh at how easily he was being manipulated by this little old lady. She could talk him out of his wallet and car keys if she had a mind to. "It's a date. We'll do it in the next couple of weeks."

Mrs. McDonald touched her cheek. "Really? Well, I better get a hair appointment, a new frock—"

"I wouldn't go to all that trouble."

"Now hush. Don't tell a woman that making herself look nice is trouble. Come by and see me again soon. I'll be here."

He called Thielen from the Lakeside Manor parking lot. "I'm done here. Sam used to volunteer for Meals on Wheels. That's how he had access to these people's homes."

"I found out the same thing. I'm just leaving Martin Hughes's house on my way to Emmett Burr's. I ate two doughnuts and drank more coffee than is sensible this late in the day. Martin tried to get me to stay for dinner. He remembers Sam all right. Said he called the Meals on Wheels program and complained about the kid being too pushy. Always wanting to come in for one reason or another."

"Mrs. McDonald said the exact same thing."

"Martin said he thought there were times when his pills were going faster than he thought they should have and was pretty sure someone was going in his home when he wasn't there. He hadn't put that together with Sam but he said it made perfect sense. He doesn't get meals anymore. He quit when he got a new lady friend who cooks for both of them most days."

"What do you know about the program?"

"My husband volunteers with them. They do the cooking out of the kitchen at the senior center. The funding and volunteers are arranged by Lutheran Social Services. The director's name is Kate Freeman."

"We should talk to her. Sounds like Sam quit volunteering with them a while ago, but I still want to know what other houses he used to visit. How many were there? He couldn't keep hitting the same handful of seniors again and again. They'd notice. He had to have another source for the pills he was selling."

"I can get Kate's number."

"Call her. Find out the soonest she can meet us. By the way, Susan Wheeler offered to pay for dinner if we stopped by the restaurant tonight."

"She offered to pay for both of us?"

"Well, no, but I'm not going to let her buy us dinner regardless."

"That place is kind of pricey."

"I'll pay. Are you in?"

"Sure. I'll get Kate's number from my husband and let him know he's on his own for dinner. Meet you there."

CHAPTER TWENTY

EMMETT GAVE THE GARAGE a nervous glance as he gunned his Cadillac across the yard. It wouldn't have surprised him a bit to see the dead boy's pale face staring out from the broken window. Telling Carl he was going to repaint the car before they hauled it to the quarry had been a lie. He wasn't going in that garage for the same reason he never followed the trail through the trees and down to the water where they'd buried the women.

Ghosts.

Some nights, paralyzed by pills, he'd hear them down in the basement—a woman crying, or a heavy chain sliding through a metal ring. In bed, he'd lie frozen with terror at the sound of dripping water and the thump of bloated footsteps coming up the stairs, and he'd wait for Wanda or the jogger to come through the door, glowing like old lanterns and smelling of the swamp. He couldn't move, couldn't make a sound. He had a scream stuck in his throat like a fist.

In town he stopped at Alco and got a motorized cart from where they were charging near the front. He pushed up both of the arms, arranged himself in the seat, and thumbed the button that made it go. He bought frozen meals and packaged cookies and potato chips and a case of beer. It took him forever to find the girl's food. The prices were shocking. Six dollars for Greek yogurt. Eight dollars for frozen blueberries. Raw sweet potatoes were a dollar sixty-nine a pound. At least the oatmeal was cheap, and a pound of carrots was only ninety-nine cents.

He rolled slowly past the section of women's clothing. A tall woman in cutoff shorts that showed the backs of her veiny legs was looking at flannel shirts on the clearance rack. Emmett wondered if buying the girl new clothes was a step too far. The thought of trying to decide what she might like out of all the T-shirts and pink shorts made him thumb the button and keep scooting.

The Alco had one shelf of books and no *David Copperhead*. Sonsofbitches had everything from tubs of cheese puffs to salt licks for cattle, but they didn't have the one goddamn book in the world he needed. As he rolled toward the pharmacy, he realized he should have gone to the library first, before he had a trunk full of frozen food.

At the back of the store, he picked up a new toothbrush and some shampoo that looked like it was for ladies and smelled like coconut and lime when he flipped up the top and sniffed. He bought more hydrogen peroxide and bandages and the biggest tube of antibiotic ointment they had.

He rolled the motorized cart up to the pharmacy window. A tall, skinny man with gray hair parted on one side asked if he could help him.

"I wanna buy insulin. The cheap kind."

The pharmacist looked at Emmett over the top of his glasses. Emmett saw him scan the contents of his shopping basket. Emmett looked, too. It was a Jekyll and Hyde mix of the absolute best and absolute worst foods for a diabetic.

"Did your doctor call in the prescription?"

"Not the prescription insulin. The other."

"I have that if that's what you want. Are you out of your regular? If insurance is an issue, I can try to get you cleared for more of your regular brand."

Emmett's heart was racing. This wasn't his normal pharmacy. He usually went to the drugstore in town where all he had to do was give them his name and make his copay. No chitchat.

"I don't... I just want what I asked for."

The pharmacist nodded. "Did you want the N, the R, or the seventy-thirty mix?"

This the girl had prepared him for. She'd told him what to get. "The last one. Seventy thirty."

"How many vials?"

"How much are they?"

"Twenty-nine dollars each."

"One. And a box of syringes."

The pharmacist disappeared behind his shelves and came back a minute later with two boxes. He jabbed a finger at the monitor in front of him and then scanned the bar codes on the insulin and the syringes.

"These qualify as covered items for payment with funds from an HSA or an FSA if you have a card."

Emmett didn't know what the hell half of those words meant. "Just credit card," he said.

"Are you a member of our rewards club? Over-the-counter drugs count toward your points."

For fucksake. Emmett sighed and leaned sideways in his cart, grimacing as he lifted his hip and reached for his wallet. "Yes, I'm in the goddamn club."

———————

He left the motorized cart in the store and limped his groceries to his car and put them in the back seat. Sitting behind the wheel, he pawed his shirt pocket for cigarettes and watched as the owner of the silver hatchback parked directly in front of him approached her car. It was the tall woman in cutoff shorts with veiny legs. She had short gray hair that matched her T-shirt. On one arm he saw brightly colored flowers tattooed on her old flesh.

He recognized her just as she got behind the wheel of her car and saw him staring from inside his. The mutual recognition felt like a shock wave that would have knocked them both down had they been standing.

It was Myra.

Emmett froze, trying to comprehend all the ways the woman across from him looked different but was definitely still his ex-wife.

Myra acted like she couldn't get away fast enough. He watched her fumble for the seat belt, then let it go, never taking her eyes off of him, as she backed up and drove away.

———————

It was four thirty when Emmett parked next to the handicap spot in front of the library. He'd lived his whole adult life in Sandy Lake and never once had he been inside the library. Not the old one in the two-story brick building paid for by Andrew Carnegie, and not when it was spread out through several classrooms in the decommissioned elementary school, and not this new glass and steel version that looked like cells in a honeycomb.

His back and leg were killing him as he stepped into the air-conditioned building and approached the three-sided central desk. A woman hiding behind a computer screen showed her face. It was his neighbor, Ruth.

He almost walked out right then. First Myra, now Ruth. Talk about ghosts from his past.

"My word. Emmett, what are you doing here? Can I help you find something?"

He wanted to say no and keep walking like he knew exactly where he was going. The pain in his left butt cheek was like something sharp had pierced him to the bone.

"I'm looking for *David Copperhead*," he said.

Ruth cocked her head like she hadn't heard him right.

"What?" he said. "That's the name of a book, right?"

Ruth clasped her hands and smiled. "I think you mean *David Copperfield*. Such a great book. You really can't do much better than Dickens. He's a master storyteller."

He followed her to another part of the library, down a narrow aisle between shelves of books. She knew where she was going based on how quickly she went right to the shelf with the Dickens books. "I'm afraid there's just one problem," she said as she ran a finger across several of the spines. "Unfortunately, all our copies are out. The AP English class at the high school is reading *David Copperfield* right now. They've got all our copies tied up." She looked at him through thick glasses with an expression he couldn't decipher because he was frozen in place.

Emmett moved his mouth but no sound came out. He forgot about his pain. Forgot about his dislike for Ruth. He felt like he'd all but confessed to having a high school girl locked in his basement.

Ruth walked away, saying something about another option, and he followed nervously. They went back to the main desk and she told him to wait there and then disappeared through a door. She was gone for several minutes. He got more nervous when he saw a stack of yellow flyers beside Ruth's computer with pictures of the boy and the girl on them and the word MISSING.

He'd walked into a trap. The girl had tricked him by making him come to the library and request the book. Ruth was probably calling the police right now. They'd probably warned Ruth to be on the lookout for suspicious characters with a sudden interest in Dickson or Dickerson or whatever his name was.

He was about to flee when Ruth finally came back with a paperback in her hand that she slid across the counter to him. It said DAVID COPPERFIELD on the cover over a painting of a timid-looking boy sitting in a large chair with his hands folded.

"I remembered seeing this come in the donation bin for next month's book sale. Usually we charge fifty cents for a paperback but since the sale isn't on, you can have it. Just come back and tell me what you thought. If you like it, I'll recommend something else for you." She took one of the yellow flyers, folded it in half, and stuck it in the book. She smiled at him without a hint of suspicion in her expression.

Emmett was still unnerved, almost delirious with the feeling of exposure.

He'd seen Myra for the first time in almost twenty years. She was old and sagging, her hair buzzed to nothing. And tattoos? Now Ruth, who had been good friends with Myra before she left him, was giving him the book the girl had requested with her photo on the missing person's flyer tucked inside. He didn't know whether to back away slowly or shit in his hat. The only word he could get out was *Myra*.

Ruth said, "Pardon me?"

He said it again. "Myra. I saw her. Have you seen her?"

Ruth pulled back slightly. She scratched her scalp and licked the back of her teeth. She said, "She's...well. Yes, I talked to her a couple of days ago."

"Where?"

"She came by the house. We had a nice visit."

Emmett saw black flashing lights at the edges of his vision. The idea of Myra being so close to the house made him dizzy. He thought she hadn't been back to Sandy Lake since the day the moving truck drove away with all her things inside. Why now?

"Why is she here? What does she want?"

"She doesn't want anything, Emmett. She comes back every couple of years. Haven't you seen or heard before now?"

"No, I never."

"She comes with her lady friend, Connie. They stay at a cabin on another lake. I wouldn't be surprised if you didn't recognize her. She—"

"You tell her to keep away from my house," Emmett said through a jaw clenched tight.

"Now, Emmett, she's not—"

"Tell her to stay away. There's nothing of hers left there. I burned it all. I signed those papers she sent so she's got no right. If I even see her looking over from your place—"

"Emmett! That's enough. You're talking nonsense. She hasn't even once so much as asked about you, and that's the truth. Now take the book before I change my mind."

He palmed the paperback and headed for the door. Every step hurt. He was aware of all four hundred of his pounds and the effort it took to move them.

He pushed through both sets of doors into the late afternoon sunlight. He couldn't get home fast enough. So many things could go wrong. Things he hadn't even considered until now. Myra showing up. Carl coming back while he was out of the house. Ruth calling the police because of his sudden interest in *David Copperfield*.

He opened the car door and tossed in the book and backed ass-first into the front seat, half in, half out of the car, while he lit a cigarette and tried to take a deep breath. He needed a minute. Just a minute and then he'd go home and check on the girl. In just a minute.

———————

Just when he thought things couldn't get any worse, Emmett came up behind a black Dodge Charger a couple of miles from home. It wasn't marked but he could see the emergency lights in the back window. Some kind of law enforcement for sure. It made all the same turns he planned to make. The chance of it going anywhere but his house decreased with each one.

He followed the black car on the gravel road that went by Ruth's house and then his. At the end of the two ruts of his driveway, the car pulled ahead and let him turn first, then backed up and followed. It stayed far enough back that he couldn't make out who was driving. Just a pair of mirrored shades that reflected the pattern of light and leaves from the windshield.

He felt strangely relaxed. Now that the worse thing he could have imagined was happening, he felt more clear about what had to be done. The first thing was to stay calm.

Emmett pulled past the garage, closer to the house but not too close. He turned off the engine and felt in his pockets. He had his knife. The cop would have a gun. He looked at the painted portrait of the child in the oversized chair on the cover of *David Copperfield* and wondered again if the girl had tricked him. The folder flyer with the word MISSING just visible felt like a confession. It was Ruth. She called the police before or after he left. Why else would they show up just now?

In the rearview mirror he saw the cop get out of the car. It was a woman. She wasn't wearing a uniform. Short and stocky. She walked with her arms out like a bodybuilder. He pushed open his car door, turned in the seat. The pain in his lower back made his left buttock feel like a glowing jack-o'-lantern full of fire and bent nails. He stood up slowly and closed the door, noticing the cop had left her car idling.

"Help you with something?"

"Are you Emmett Burr?"

"I am. Who wants to know?"

"I'm Detective Thielen with the Sandy Lake Sheriff's Department." She was dressed in gray pants and a white, long-sleeved top. She had a badge on her belt, a gun and a radio, too.

"If Ruth called you because I blew up at her at the library—"

The detective looked confused. "I'm not here because of a call from Ruth. I have some questions I want to ask you."

It was no relief to find out Ruth had nothing to do with this. If not Ruth, then who?

"Do it quick. I've got frozen food I need to get inside."

"Let me help you carry things in."

Emmett sagged against the car and dropped his head. He worried that the girl might hear their voices and start making noise of her own. He turned away from the house and lowered his voice. "No, I can't let you in. The house is not... It's not suitable for visitors."

Detective Thielen took off her sunglasses, like she needed to see him in the light. The sound of her car changed as she crossed in front of it and went halfway down the passenger side of his. He saw her look through his car windows. He pulled his ears back, straining to hear any sound coming from the basement at all.

"You sure? I can at least carry things up to the landing."

"No. I don't want any help. What's this about?"

The detective looped around the front of his car and came up to him holding a cell phone. She showed him a picture of a prescription bottle with his name on it.

"Recognize this?"

"I recognize my name."

"We found this bottle at Sam Gherlick's house. You know him?"

"I know who he is. Used to deliver my Meals on Wheels."

The detective nodded. "You ever let Sam in your house?" The way she asked made it sound like she was accusing him of something. Of letting Sam in but not her.

Emmett pushed the pain away and tried to focus on his words. Was she trying to trick him with the question? He licked his lips and tried to take a deep breath. He wanted a cigarette but was reluctant to light up in front of this lady cop who looked like she wrestled bears for the circus. "He helped me move some stuff around in the basement and in the garage a couple of times. I think that's it."

"Would he have had access to your pills any of those times? Did you notice them missing after any of his visits?"

"I don't remember. It was a while back."

"You don't notice when pills you need for pain go missing?"

"I take pills for every goddamn thing you can imagine. There's too many to keep track of."

Detective Thielen stared hard at him while he talked. She didn't blink. He felt like he was being scanned by a medical machine. She put her phone away and adjusted her belt. The radio at her side was turned down so that he could hear voices but not make out what they were saying. She looked back at his house and at something over his shoulder.

"You had any problems with break-ins out here?"

He felt like there was no right answer to her questions, no way to soften the hard glare she kept giving him. His hand went to the knife in his pocket. Could he take her down if he had to? Get the knife out, get the blade open? No. Besides, she looked like she could take a knife to the back and keep charging.

"No. No break-ins."

"You got a boarded-up window on the side of your house. The side door on the garage looks like it won't stay shut because of the splintered frame. That's why I ask."

"I broke the window when I fell against it standing on the bed trying to hang up a curtain I pulled down. Was cheaper to put a board over it than get a new window."

Detective Thielen nodded. "And the garage door?"

"That damn door's been like that forever. I don't remember what the hell happened. Look around. There ain't nothing out here to steal. I live on a union pension and social security. Anybody wants any of this shit, they can have it."

"Mr. Burr, you take narcotics for pain. That makes you a target for addicts and anyone else looking for easy access to prescription drugs."

"If Sam Gherlick took those pills from me, then I didn't know it. If you caught him with my pills, you have my permission to arrest him. Is that what you want?"

The detective shook her head. "I'm not looking for your permission for anything. Just wanted to know how a prescription in your name ended up in Sam Gherlick's house."

"Did you ask him?"

"Sam Gherlick is dead."

Emmett turned away and looked longingly at his house. He rubbed his thumb along the smooth side of the knife in his pocket. "I'm hurting right now, Detective, and could use one of those pills you keep asking me about. It's too bad about the boy. Like I said, I haven't seen him in a long time. Barely knew him."

"I understand. Just one more question. Are you married, Mr. Burr?"

"No," he spat out.

"Any children? Family nearby?"

"No."

"I'm concerned about your pain and your mobility. You should have someone come by once in a while to check on you. Does Meals on Wheels still come?"

"No. I've been getting by on my own for a long time. I can manage."

"All it takes is one fall."

"I don't need a babysitter, Detective. If we're done I'm going inside."

"What about your groceries?"

Emmett started walking toward his house. "Fuck 'em," he growled, waving a hand behind him as he shuffled closer to the stairs up to the house. "I'll get 'em later. Just go away."

He didn't look back as he slowly climbed the steps. He pushed the sliding door open and slammed it behind him, yanking the curtains across it, almost frantic as he limped to the fridge for a beer, to the kitchen sink for his pills, then back to the recliner.

His hands shook as he tried to light a cigarette. Killing the Gherlick boy was supposed to have cut the connection between him and the kids. Instead it brought a sheriff's detective right to his door. What kind of fucking shitfor-brains steals people's prescription drugs, then keeps the labeled bottles?

He heard footsteps coming up the stairs outside. He jammed the cigarette in his mouth and scrambled for the shotgun beside his chair and laid it across his thigh with the stock jammed into the cushion behind him.

How much could the girl hear from inside the cage? Two sets of footsteps up the stairs? Voices inside and outside the house? Any sound from her and he'd blast the cop right through the sliding glass door. Three women had already disappeared out here. No reason to believe he couldn't make it four.

He heard the thunk of cans and the rustle of paper bags being set down. His finger hovered over the trigger.

"I'm leaving your groceries right here, Mr. Burr. Get 'em when you're ready. Please take care of yourself."

The cop's steps retreated down the stairs. Emmett waited with the gun in his lap until he heard her drive away.

She hadn't said anything about coming back, but he didn't believe for a minute that she wouldn't. The whole plan needed to move up.

The car and the body inside had to go tonight.

CHAPTER TWENTY-ONE

TWO GATSBY-GREEN LIGHT BULBS in copper shades hung on either side of the sign over the Sweet Pea's door. Packard stood just out of view of the two front windows, watching as Thielen approached from where she'd parked on the street, wearing a zippered blue Under Armor hoodie with neon highlights and tennis shoes. Her hair was still damp from the shower.

"You had time for a workout?" he asked.

"Yeah. Ran a 5K and did legs. I'm starving."

"Try not to eat the glassware while we wait for the food to come."

"I'll do my best."

At the door he stopped and said, "I'm not sure yet what to do with the news about Sam Gherlick."

"Susan might have already heard about Sam," Thielen said. "Word's out. Peggy Simpson was walking on the treadmill next to mine. She asked me if it was true what she heard about the sheriff's grandson. I said nothing, of course."

"Even if Susan has heard, she doesn't know the connection to Jenny and Jesse."

"True," Thielen said. "Let's play it out. We'll see how it goes."

They went in together, stood awkwardly by the PLEASE WAIT TO BE SEATED sign. Packard wondered if it looked like the two of them were on a date. He was wearing jeans and a short-sleeved polo shirt and a black jacket. Anyone who knew them knew Thielen was married. He didn't know why he felt so awkward all of a sudden, like everyone was looking at them.

Susan pushed through a swinging door from the kitchen carrying two large white plates. She looked like a scarecrow made from old clothes and a wooden cross. She did a double take when she saw Packard, and for one second it felt like the restaurant went dead silent. That's why everyone was staring at them, Packard realized. They knew about Susan's daughter, and here were two detectives to see her. He should have thought of this before. Everyone in the place was going to leave with neck strain from pretending to not be trying to overhear their conversation.

"You're here," Susan said as she approached. "I'm down a server so it's hectic right now. Have a seat at the bar and we'll talk when I have time. Angie will take care of you."

The restaurant was about three-quarters full, but the long bar was open except for a couple at the end closer to the kitchen, and Ruth Adams, the librarian, around the corner at the other end drinking something brown and reading from a pile of printed pages in front of her. They took seats near Ruth, who smiled and said, "Evening," then returned to her pages.

They ordered beers and then food. The lack of privacy kept them from talking about work or anything to do with the case. They talked about Thielen's training for an Ironman triathlon she had coming up in July in Canada. She'd been bullying Packard for a year to train for an Ironman, too, but he wouldn't take the bait. He knew his limitations. The swim and the bike ride wouldn't be a problem. He knew he didn't have a marathon in him.

"I'm getting a dog again," he said just after Angie set down his roast beef with pureed potatoes and parsnips and grilled asparagus.

Thielen bent over and inhaled the scent from her gnocchi with orange and cauliflower. "You're kidding," she said. "Another golden?"

"Nope. It's a corgi. Only has three paws."

"Interesting. Puppy or full grown?"

"Still a puppy for the most part. I'm getting him from Gary's shelter. I was out there on a four one seven the other day—"

"Four one seven?" Thielen asked. She knew four one seven was code for someone with a weapon. She wanted to know who had a weapon at Gary's.

"Yeah, him and Cora at it again. Anyway, I made the mistake of letting him walk me through the kennel. He got me."

"Good for you. I think you'll be happier with a dog."

Packard ate his food, wondering why Thielen thought he was unhappy or less happy than he could be. She told him about her husband's new job as an online psychologist. His previous job was as a caseworker for the county, but he had taken early retirement and was now making three times the salary. Good for him, bad for the county, which now had one fewer person on the payroll who gave a shit.

Susan went in and out of the kitchen door but didn't stop by. People came in and people left. Ruth had flipped over the last of her pages and was making notes on the back. "Ruth, any good book recommendations for me?" Thielen asked.

"What do you like to read?"

"Jane Austen and crime novels set outside the U.S."

"Have you read Jo Nesbø?"

"No, who's that?"

"Norwegian writer. If you can get past the fact that his detective's name is Harry Hole, you'll probably enjoy his books. Well written and some exotic locales."

Packard said, "Harry Hole? Really?"

Ruth said, "It's a Norwegian name. Spelled like a man's name Harry and 'hole' like 'hole in the ground.' It's supposed to be pronounced HOO-LEH, but all you say in your mind while reading it is Harry Hole."

Thielen had taken out her phone and was typing Joe Nesbow into it. "I'll check him out," she said. "What are you working on there?" She nodded at the pages in front of Ruth.

"I'm writing a book," Ruth said. "I come in once a week and have a drink and review what I've written. Gets me out of the house."

"What kind of book is it?"

"A memoir. My true confession."

"What do you have to confess?" Packard asked.

Ruth was a second too slow putting on a smile to cover the dead-serious expression the question elicited. "Terrible things," she said with a laugh.

Packard realized he wasn't in a laughing mood. He dug into his pot roast and watched Ruth finish the last of her drink. You didn't have to be a cop and witness people on their worst behavior day after day to realize that pretty much everyone was capable of terrible things. Even the librarian.

Ruth paid her bill and scooped up her papers and wished the two of them a good night. Pretty soon it was just Packard and Thielen at the bar and two booths with couples lingering over dessert and coffee. Susan came from the kitchen, wiping her hands on a towel. She set up two small glasses and poured from a bottle of Laphroig 18. Packard thought they were for one of the booths until she used a metal scoop to drop a single cube in each glass and then pushed them in front of him and Thielen.

She hadn't made eye contact or asked if they were Scotch drinkers. Maybe she thought she had. Maybe she didn't care. She looked like she hadn't eaten or slept for days. This was how a rationalist like Susan went off the rails, Packard thought. Not with wild emotions and erratic outbursts but by the neglect of self through the mindlessness of work. The comfort of logic and reasoning she was used to was gone. There was no making sense of Jenny's disappearance.

"Tell me the latest," she said finally.

Packard told her about the news conference and the unhelpful calls that had come in overnight and the deputy he had following up on anything that sounded promising.

Susan poured herself a glass of water from the gun and took a long drink. "Where could they be?"

"I don't know," Packard confessed. "What we've been looking into lately is the identity of Jesse's recent contacts. We put together a list based on the phone records and the interviews I did at the school after I saw you at Subway. We've been able to determine that the last person in touch with Jesse before he and Jenny disappeared was Sam Gherlick."

Packard paused to let Susan put together what he'd left unsaid. The look on her face said she knew the name and what had happened. "Sam Gherlick died yesterday."

Packard nodded. "He was working on his car and it fell on him. I'm the one who found him. I went there to talk to him about where Jesse was going that night. Sam might have known."

Susan reached up and pinched the spot between her neck and shoulder. "The one person who could have helped us is dead now? Is that a coincidence?"

Packard didn't want to answer that question. He felt Thielen holding her breath, waiting to see how he would respond. "We're actively investigating what happened to Sam," he said.

"Does 'actively investigating' mean you don't think it was an accident?"

"We're keeping our minds open to all possibilities," Packard said. "I'm not a big believer in coincidence when it comes to investigations. I believe in cause and effect. Things don't just happen independently in parallel."

Susan's gaze was fixated on her empty water glass. "Someone might have killed Sam to keep him from telling what he knew?"

Packard nodded. He didn't want the Scotch anymore. It felt wrong to be drinking Susan's booze while indicating her daughter's situation might be more dire than anyone wanted to admit.

"Could Jesse have killed him?" Susan asked.

"It's possible. Is Jesse a killer? Does he have a reason for killing Sam? We don't know that yet."

Susan looked at Packard and Thielen, back and forth, like she couldn't tell who she wanted to talk to or what she wanted to say. "So now what?" she asked.

Packard said, "We have to accept that something could have happened to Jesse and Jenny. There's no pretending that's not a possibility. They could also be hiding. They could want to call home but can't for some reason. We don't know. But we're not out of options. Sam's sister was at the house yesterday when I found him. She nearly overdosed on drugs. I still haven't had a chance to talk to her."

Susan made a face. "She has the neck tattoo, right?"

Packard nodded. "How do you know her?"

"She works at Hanson's."

Thielen sat up straight suddenly. Packard didn't know why.

"Hanson's Drug?" Thielen confirmed.

"Yes," said Susan.

"How do you know that?" Thielen asked.

"You make a lot of trips to the pharmacy when your daughter is type 1 and your husband is dying of a brain tumor. I asked her about the bandage on her neck that never went away, and she told me they made her cover her tattoo while she was at work. I asked her what made her think it was a good idea to get a tattoo that high up her neck. She didn't like that."

Packard asked, "You're saying she works in the pharmacy?"

"I've seen her all around the store. Stocking shelves and cashiering up front. I only ever talked to her at the pharmacy desk. She'd hand over the bag and ask if you had any questions for the pharmacist. Probably not a great place for a girl with a drug problem to be working."

"Not at all," Packard said. He took out his phone and sent a text message to Dan Gherlick, then gave Thielen a look that said it was time to go.

Packard left his Scotch unfinished, thinking about what he still wanted to do that night. "Susan, the sister working at Hanson's is new info that we didn't have before. We need to go so I can look into that. What do I owe you for dinner?"

"There's no bill," she said, moving their dirty glasses beneath the bar.

"We didn't come here to get a free meal. Let me pay."

"It's not me. I planned to comp you but someone else paid."

"Who?"

Susan pointed to the empty seat where the librarian had been sitting. "Ruth. She slipped Angie a note and asked for your bill. She paid it with hers."

Thielen asked Susan to thank Ruth for them next time she came in. Packard left two twenties on the bar for Angie or the Scotch or whatever Susan decided to do with them. Outside, he and Thielen zipped up their jackets and stopped to figure out their next move.

"How the hell did we not know Sam's sister worked at the pharmacy?"

"I've lived here ten years and I didn't know," Thielen said.

"The sheriff mentioned the other day that she was a cashier. It didn't even occur to me to ask where." His phone buzzed with a text message.

Thielen said, "It would have come out eventually. It's barely been twenty-four hours since you found her and her brother. Neither one has been in any condition to talk to us."

She was right but it didn't make him feel any better. "Dan just texted me. He's still at the hospital with Shannon. Tell me quick about the last guy you went to see today. Anything new from talking to him?"

"Emmett Burr? No, not really. He's like the others. Elderly. Lives alone. He's morbidly obese and in terrible physical condition. He remembers Sam and said he didn't care for him much. Said he didn't realize his pills had been stolen."

"What about Kate Freeman at Lutheran Social Services? Did you get hold of her?"

"I did. I caught her waiting to board a flight at O'Hare. She's on her way home from a conference. Won't be back until really late tonight. She told me they had gently suggested Sam find another volunteer opportunity after his second summer with them. They'd had complaints about him but nothing specific about stealing drugs or anything like that. Kate said she'd meet us at the office tomorrow morning if you want to look at the addresses that Sam used to deliver to. She still has that information in their files."

"That one's yours. I'm going to the hospital to talk to Shannon Gherlick."

"Right now?"

Packard nodded. "We're already a day late on this information. Dan said she's awake and knows about her brother. I want to catch her before she's had too long to think about things. It's gotta be tonight."

"I can come with you."

"No, go home. I'll text you if I get anything meaningful from her. We'll touch base in the morning."

"I hope she doesn't clam up."

"She won't. She's gonna talk. I'll make sure of it."

CHAPTER TWENTY-TWO

JENNY WAS SITTING UP in the bed and wouldn't look at Emmett when he came in with her dinner: a baked sweet potato with a glob of plain yogurt and an oxycodone pill on the side. It had been the same when he'd come down earlier with the insulin and a new syringe. She was angry about being kept prisoner in this room, about Carl smashing her hand, but she hadn't been able to hide her relief at the sight of what he was carrying. Didn't mean she had to talk to him, and she didn't. Not even a thank-you. He'd smoked in the doorway and watched as she read the tiny print instructions that came in the white box. After a few minutes her only words were to ask him for a pencil so she could do the math to figure out the right dosage. He found a flat carpenter's pencil in a drawer under the workbench and used his knife to expose the graphite.

She looked almost as relieved by the sight of real food as she had at the box of insulin. She swallowed the pill with some water, then picked at the still-hot potato with her good hand while he slowly unpacked a grocery bag filled with the other things he'd brought down for her: a cleanish towel, a new toothbrush, the girly shampoo. He saved the book for last. He'd taken the MISSING flyer out and thrown it away. She wouldn't reach for the book when he held it out to her.

"You don't want it now?"

She kept staring at her food.

"I'll take it back," he said.

"Don't," she said.

"I went to a lot of trouble to get this stuff. The insulin, too. You could at least say thank you."

She refused.

Emmett dropped the book. He didn't know if he should stay or go. He picked up the shampoo bottle and smelled it. "Do you want to eat first or shower?" he asked.

She gave him a look like she was trying to figure out whether this was a trick or not. "Shower," she said.

He put the leg restraints on her, then undid the manacles that kept her chained to the ring in the wall. She took off the Sandy Lake Labor Day T-shirt and he put the regular handcuffs on her. She was naked and he couldn't help but look again as she walked stiff-legged to the shower. She carried the new shampoo in her good hand, and the thin towel over her shoulder. She had a dark mole on her right hip and a birthmark on her back the color of an old tan.

He watched her clutch the shampoo bottle under one arm and pop open the top with her good hand. She tried to keep her back to him but there was no missing her small, pointed breasts and the fawn-colored hair between her legs. The girl squeezed a blob of shampoo on top of her head, then set the bottle on the floor and scrubbed her hair with her good hand. The basement filled with the smell of the tropics.

He let her take as long as she wanted under the warm water. The wounds on her hip were still bruised and red, but she seemed to flinch less from the water this time. She spit her retainer onto the back of her bandaged hand and balanced it there while she brushed her teeth and spit on the floor. He went back for her bucket and dumped it in the toilet. Something electric passed through him as she stepped aside so he could rinse the bucket under the shower hose. It used to be a fantasy of his to stand close to a naked woman wet from the shower. Not while holding a stinking toilet bucket and her with a foamy toothbrush sticking out of her mouth, but close. He stared at her, waiting for the feeling to come back until she turned away from him and hunched her shoulders, protectively.

When she was clean, they went back to the room and he undid one side of the handcuffs so she could put on a different T-shirt, red and full of little holes, probably from welding sparks. She still wasn't speaking to him. He dragged the rocker into the room and sat across from her and unwrapped the soggy bandages on her hand. The sight was still gruesome. Red and tattered flesh. Her wrists were raw and abraded from long hours in the heavy manacles he kept on her. He prodded gently with his stiff fingers for any bits of shot that might have worked their way to the surface. He found one on the back of her hand that popped out with just the slightest bit of pressure, followed by a slurry of pink pus. The girl's face was damp with sweat.

"Can you move it?" he asked.

She could make somewhat of a grip with her thumb and first two fingers. The ring and pinkie wouldn't move at all.

"Needs more peroxide," he said.

She nodded and braced herself for the pain as he poured right from the bottle over the back of her hand and on to the floor. "Show me the palm. We need to hit it all."

Again with the peroxide. Tears ran down her cheeks but she kept from crying out. He held the clean bandage in place and helped her wrap the new tape. Next to hers, his thick fingers, stained with tobacco and knobbed with arthritis, looked like those of a rock creature. Between the two of them they had about one and a half good hands.

When her hand was rewrapped he sat back and smoked a cigarette and watched as she ate. She had the blanket pulled up over her legs with the sweet potato in her lap.

He didn't appreciate the silent treatment. The least she could do after he got her everything she asked for was talk to him. "Let me ask you something," he said. "How come you don't ever ask about the boy?"

She flinched like she'd been hit by something wet. She kept eating. "What would I ask? I saw what you did to him."

"You don't want to know about the body?"

She looked like she was thinking. "What did you do with it?"

"Put it in the trunk of the car you all came in."

"Where's the car?"

"In my garage."

"What are you going to do with the car?"

"Carl has a tow truck. He's going to haul it away and get rid of it."

She picked up a piece of the potato skin and used her teeth to peel away the orange flesh stuck to it. "Why does Carl help you? What does he get?" She looked at him sideways while she waited for the answer he didn't want to admit. He ignored her question and studied the end of his cigarette instead.

"It's me, isn't it? He said he was coming back for me when he smashed my hand against the wall. He expects you to let him have me for helping you."

"That's what he expects."

"Are you going to let him do whatever he wants? Rape me? Kill me?"

"I'm not keeping you locked in here for Carl's benefit," Emmett said.

"Then why are you?"

"Maybe I'm going to rape you. Maybe I'm going to kill you."

She gave him a flat, cold stare that seemed like a dare. "What are you waiting for?"

Emmett leaned forward in his chair. "You don't want to challenge me. What do you think happened here before? Why do you think I built this room?"

Her boldness wilted. She turned back to her food. "Carl said you killed three women and buried them in the woods."

"That's not true. There are three women buried in the woods. Carl killed one of them. One of them killed herself."

Wanda, the girl from the gas station. Three months after he grabbed her. He thought time would make her grow to like him, but all it did was make her realize he wasn't going to let her go. The end of the chain that went through the ring on the wall was padlocked around the handle of a one-hundred-pound dumbbell underneath the cot. Emmett could barely move it so he had assumed it would be too heavy for a woman. He hadn't counted on a woman who used to stack plywood for eight hours a day before getting a job at a gas station.

Wanda got the weight up on the cot, wrapped the slack chain around her neck, then rolled the weight over the edge. He found her on her back, head hanging off the side of the bed. Her face was dark blue. Her tongue stuck straight out of her mouth like a stamen.

"Carl said you shot one."

"I put that one out of her misery. The news said she had quit taking her schizo pills after her husband left her. She thought she could control her craziness with exercise and jogging. Between that and the things Carl did to her, she went nuts. She clawed the walls until her fingers bled. She smeared shit all over everything, including herself."

They both looked around the pink room with the low ceiling. The girl looked like she was trying to imagine what had happened. Emmett didn't have to.

The girl said, "I don't understand. You keep women locked in this room and then Carl does what he wants to them?"

That's how things had more or less turned out with the pink room. The space he'd built for himself and Wanda had become Carl's playground. After Wanda, the whole terrible history of it belonged to him. Now history was about to repeat itself. Carl was practically pacing outside, waiting to pounce.

"Don't worry about Carl."

"How can I not? Can you explain it to me? I don't want to die in here, and that means you have to bring me insulin, and now I realize it also means you have to protect me from Carl. If he killed those other women, he'll kill me. Why bring me insulin if Carl can just do what he wants?"

Emmett didn't say anything. He stared at his enormous belly and watched it go up and down with his breath.

"Are you going to protect me?" she asked. "I need your help, Emmett. You have to have a plan to stop him."

The sound of his name coming from her mouth made the hair on his arms stand up. Had she said it before now? He didn't think so.

Emmett grunted. "I'll bring your medicine and protect you from Carl, but there's going to come a day when I want something in return."

"Like what?" she said.

"I'm still deciding. Might be what a man usually wants from a woman, might be something else. When I decide, I don't expect a fight. You'll owe me. The price for fighting me is the light goes out, I lock the door, and I don't come back."

The girl's face was a mask. "I understand," she said. Silence filled the room like so much cigarette smoke. Emmett scratched the back of his neck and looked out the door like something out there had caught his attention. Neither one of them knew what to say next.

The girl set her plate aside and reached for the book. "Do you want me to read to you? I can start at the beginning if you want."

"Do what you like."

She laid the book in her lap and used her good hand to get it open and turned to the first page. She read aloud, her voice growing more sure with every sentence:

Whether I shall turn out to be the hero of my own life, or whether that station will be held by anybody else, these pages must show. To begin my life with the beginning of my life, I record that I was born (as I have been informed and believe) on a Friday, at twelve o'clock at night. It was remarked that the clock began to strike, and I began to cry, simultaneously.

He let her read to him for half an hour. She was more animated than he'd seen her the entire time. She moved her bandaged hand in the air while she read. Occasionally, she looked at him over the top of the book. After a while, he was lulled by the sound of her voice and the pictures it made in his head. The saddle of fat around his neck bulged between his chin and his chest as his head dropped.

"Emmett, are you tired? Do you want me to stop?"

"No, keep going."

He sat up, smoked one more cigarette to wake himself up, and then told her it was time for bed. He got her more water to drink and dragged his chair out of the room.

"Can I keep these handcuffs on instead of the others?" she asked as he got ready to chain her to the wall again. She showed him her red, abraded wrists where the manacles had rubbed her skin raw.

"Yeah, okay," he said. He unhooked the manacles from the wall chain and looped the end of the chain around the connector between the handcuffs she was wearing. He secured the chain with a padlock through two of its links.

"I feel like we made a deal earlier about the insulin and about Carl," she said. "Do you want to shake on it?" She stuck out her good hand. Emmett grunted in agreement. Her small, soft hand curled around his rocky mitt. "Thank you for the insulin, Emmett. And the food and the book," she said.

"All right then. Maybe you can read me more tomorrow."

He locked the door to the pink room. It was dark out. Bugs attracted by the lights flew through the broken window in the basement door as he picked up the phone extension and called Carl.

"We gotta move the car tonight. I'll be at your place just after midnight."

"You said tomorrow night."

"That was before a lady cop showed up here asking about the Gherlick boy."

"The hell you say. How'd that happen?"

"He had a pill bottle with my name on it in his house. Cop came out here to ask me about it. That car's gotta go now in case they decide they got more questions they wanna ask."

Carl didn't say anything for almost a minute. Emmett imagined his deep-sunk eyes flashing in the blue light of the television, his wife moving around the kitchen with a dishrag or sitting nearby with a basket of laundry. If she was anything like Myra, she had no idea the thoughts that went through her husband's mind. She didn't know the man sitting next to her at all.

"I'm coming over tonight," Emmett said. "Midnight."

He hung up before Carl could argue.

CHAPTER TWENTY-THREE

PACKARD TEXTED DAN GHERLICK again before he pulled out of the Sweet Pea parking lot. Asked him to meet him in the hospital lobby in ten minutes.

He parked in a spot for emergency vehicles and found Dan inside the double automatic doors holding two paper coffee cups in front of the canteen that was just closing for the night. A heavy-set girl with a red ponytail and a blue visor was turning a key that lowered the security gate over the shop's entrance.

"Free coffee," Dan said, extending one of the cups to him. "She said she was going to dump it out."

Packard took a sip and tried not to flinch. The coffee was five degrees warmer than body temperature and had simmered into a sauce.

"How's Patty?"

"She went home this morning. My sister-in-law is staying with her. I found a rehab center just north of the Cities for Shannon. They're sending a van to pick her up first thing tomorrow morning."

"She agreed to go?"

"She did. They took out her breathing tube and cut back on the medication earlier today. I told her about Sam when she woke up. She's heartbroken and mad at herself for being out of it while he was trapped under the car. She thinks if she was awake she would have heard him calling."

"You know as well as I do that if that car slipped off the jacks, he wouldn't have had time to yell."

"I told her. I tried to get her to talk to me about her drug use and what's been going on in her life, but she doesn't want to talk about it."

They headed for the elevators. Further down the hall, a short old woman and her same-sized husband stood in front of the hospital's pharmacy window. Packard pushed the button for the elevator.

He told Dan about the pills and the prescription bottles they found at Sam's house, about connecting Sam to those people through Meals on Wheels. Dan stood frozen. Packard said, "I just found out tonight that Shannon works at the drugstore. There's no way she's not involved somehow. Being a dealer in pre-scription drugs and having a sister who works in a drugstore would be a missed opportunity. The fact that she's a user is leverage he has over her. She has to help him if she wants him to help her."

Dan ran a hand through his hair and held the back of his head. "These are my kids that I raised from babies. This is who they grew up to be?" he asked in disbelief. He sighed and shook his head. "So what did they do? How did it work?"

"That's what I'm here to find out."

The elevator came and they rode up. Packard saw himself drink his coffee in the blurry reflection from the steel door in front of him. "Damn, Dan. This coffee is terrible."

"I know. Want me to find a microwave and reheat it?"

"God, no. What I want you to do is run interference for me with the nurses if necessary. I'm sure visiting hours are long over but I need to talk to Shannon tonight, especially if the plan is to ship her out to rehab tomorrow. I also need you to stay out of the room so I can talk to her alone. Can you do that?"

"If that's what you want. You're not going to arrest her, are you? Has she done anything that she can get arrested for?"

The doors opened. Packard exited without answering.

———————

Shannon's room was three doors down from the nurses' station. Dan pointed to the door and then went down to the desk to ask about the plan for discharging his daughter. No one noticed Packard or saw him go into her room.

It was dark inside. The room's single window was black except for the hole punched in the night sky by the waning moon. Ambient lights behind the bed gave off a sleepy yellow glow. A TV mounted near the ceiling was on with the volume low. The air was sharp with cleaning products and sweat from the woman cranked up in the bed.

At the sight of him, Shannon's expression collapsed like a hand was crumpling her features from inside her skull. She knew who he was, even out of uniform. She turned away and cried soundlessly. Packard pulled a chair close to her bed and sat down without a word. He brought the coffee cup to his lips, remembered what it was, put it back down. He watched the television while the girl with the neck tattoo and the unwashed face and the IV in her arm cried and gasped.

When she finally got herself under control and turned her face toward him, she opened her mouth to say something but he held up his hand.

"Listen to me. You think you know why I'm here, but you don't know the half of it," he said. She tried to say something but he stopped her again. "I'm going to start by telling you everything I know. Don't bother trying to tell me that I'm wrong or that any of it isn't true. I know better. When I'm done with that, I'm going to ask you some questions and you're going to tell me everything you know. No lying. No withholding. Understood?"

"Where's my dad?"

"It's not time for your questions yet. That comes later."

"I want my dad."

Packard shook his head. Shannon reached blindly over her head, looking for the call button clipped on the corner of her elevated mattress.

"Shannon, if you push that button I'm going to arrest you. I'll leave if the nurses come in here and tell me to, but I'll find a deputy to sit outside your room, and as soon as you're discharged, he'll take you straight from here to the jail. You'll detox in a jail cell instead of a treatment facility."

Her hand froze where it was, then dropped back to her lap.

Packard laid out everything. Jenny and Jesse's disappearance late Tuesday night/early Wednesday morning. The text from Sam to Jesse. The eyewitness who saw Sam and Jesse together in Sam's car. Sam's Meals on Wheels history. The drugs and the prescription bottles they found at the house.

"You're involved in this through your job at the drugstore. I know you cover the prescription counter sometimes. Tell me how it works."

"I'm not involved. You're making assumptions."

"Bullshit. Let me give you one more reason to tell me the truth. There's a chance what happened to your brother wasn't an accident. I think there's actually a very good chance someone else figured out the connection between Sam and Jesse and got to your brother before I did. If he also knows your involvement in all this, then he could come looking for you next."

Shannon fought to keep from crying again. Packard stared at her without sympathy.

"Tell me how it worked between you and your brother."

"If I tell you, I'll lose my job."

Packard shook his head. "Shannon, you lost that job the minute we found you OD'd in bed. You're never going to work there again. Now, for the last time, how'd it work between the two of you?"

Shannon hung her head and scratched the tattoo on her neck. She snuffled snot and wiped her forearm under her nose and rubbed her wet eyes with the back of her hand.

"It was Sam's idea for me to get a job there. A lot of what he sold was stuff he bought from other kids who were selling their own prescriptions. ADHD drugs, things like that. Sometimes it was pain pills from someone else in the house, old meds they found in a medicine cabinet or a hall closet. Sometimes they skimmed pills from Grandma and Grandpa or a friend's house. After he graduated, Sam couldn't keep those connections up and Jesse wasn't as good at making the deals."

"Sam set Jesse up in the school to take over for him."

"Yeah, I guess."

"Did you see them together a lot?"

Shannon shrugged. "I'd see Jesse at the house now and then. They played video games together. Got high. You know."

"What else?"

"You already know about the Meals on Wheels, how they kept moving him around because people didn't like him. That's exactly what he wanted. It gave him more places to skim. Eventually they asked him not to come back, so that dried up. I was using him to score by then. He said if I wanted to keep getting high, I needed to help with the supply. He said if I got a job at the drugstore and could tell him what he wanted to know, then he would owe me."

"What did you do?"

"I got the job at the drugstore. After a few months they let me start covering the register in the pharmacy. It was my job to show people the instruction sheet that comes with their pills and ask them if they had any questions for the pharmacist. I was the last quality check to make sure what was in the computer matched what was in the bag. Sam gave me a list of drugs he was interested in. I memorized the list and watched for who was getting the good stuff. And then I told him."

"How long was this going on?"

"I've been working at the drugstore for a year. Only at the pharmacy counter for maybe the last six months or so."

"How often did you give him a name?"

"Rarely. We'd get caught if everyone who came into the pharmacy for the good shit got ripped off right away."

"Did you text him the names?"

She gave him a look. "No records. Nothing in writing."

"Did you tell him about somebody right before Jenny and Jesse disappeared?"

"I don't remember. Maybe."

"Who?"

"I don't remember."

"Male or female? Young or old."

"Everyone who gets prescriptions filled is old," she declared. "This whole fucking town is full of old people, taking pills and waiting to die."

"Is that what you were doing the night before we found you? Taking pills? Waiting to die?"

"Yeah. Welcome to fucking Sandy Lake."

Packard sipped his cold coffee. The burned flavor was more prominent now that there was no heat to hide behind. "It's not this town that's the problem. You've been raised to always get everything you want, no effort on your part, no consequences. You recoil at the word no. On the rare occasions you don't get what you want, you make your world smaller so you don't have to deal with that person or that situation again. Your options get more and more limited. Every day becomes the same as the one before it."

Shannon picked at the tape holding her IV in. "Are you a cop or a shrink?"

"I just say what I see. Who did you tell Sam about last week?"

"I told you I don't remember. I didn't even see who came to pick them up. I saw the prescription bagged with a name on it in the cage where we keep the opiates for pickup. I called Sam and told him the name. I don't know if I was even working when they went out the door."

"What was the name?"

She sighed, rolled her eyes. For a second her face went blank as she time-traveled back to that day. "I don't remember the name. I can't even say if it was a man or a woman. That's the truth."

"What was the prescription for?"

She stopped to think again. Packard knew his chances of getting a court order forcing the pharmacy to show him a list of everyone who picked up a prescription for narcotics in the last ten days was almost zero. Even if he could get a judge to sign off on something like that, the pharmacist would have to get signed permission from everyone on the list before releasing it to comply with patient privacy regulations. That could take days, if not weeks, and be incomplete if people refused to cooperate.

"I think they were for eighty-milligram oxys. Sam always wanted to know about those."

"How did Sam react when you gave him the name?"

"I don't think he did. When I called him about this stuff, it was with a name and what they were getting. He'd usually hang up on me without even responding."

Packard took out his phone and pulled up the list of names they had from the prescription bottles they'd found in the safe in Sam's bedroom. "Tell me if any of these names ring a bell. Eunice Amberson? Martin Hughes? Emmett Burr? Olivia McDonald? Elizabeth Marsh?"

Shannon stared at him blankly. None of the names caused even a twitch in her expression. "I don't know who any of those people are. I mean, you know some of those last names from living in this town forever, but I couldn't put a face with any of them."

"Could one of these names be the name you gave Sam?"

"Maybe. I don't remember."

Packard felt his frustration rising. *I don't remember. I don't know. Maybe.* He had a feeling if he asked her questions about the idiots on the television up in the corner, she'd be able to catalog Kardashian minutia in excruciating detail.

"Am I going to be charged for any of this?"

"That's not my decision. It'll be up to the DA once everything comes to light. It won't hurt to have me on your side."

"How do I do that?"

"Make better decisions than the ones you've made so far."

"I'm not holding out on you."

"I'm talking about the drug overdose and the neck tattoo."

She tilted her head and raised her shoulder to hide the tattoo, sighed. "An ex gave me this tattoo a couple of years ago when we were super fucked up. He wanted everyone to know I was his princess. He marked me and I was too wrecked to stop him. I'm waiting for the lasers to get better so I don't have a princess-shaped scar on my neck instead of a princess tattoo."

"Did you press charges?"

"He wasn't worth the trouble. Pressing charges wouldn't undo what he did to me."

"What are you going to do after rehab?"

"Stay in the Cities maybe. I need to get the hell out of this town."

"What's stopped you? Can't be money. Your folks could bankroll anything you wanted to do."

"I don't know where to go. I don't have any skills. I didn't even graduate high school. My mom wanted us to hang out and party. She would say, 'Books are for losers. You don't need a diploma—we're already rich.'"

Packard's opinion of her was changing. He came in loaded for a spoiled rich girl who'd never given a thought to anyone other than herself. She wasn't so much selfish as she was vulnerable. No one to look out for her and unable to look out for herself. Every relationship she'd had—with her mother, her brother, the ex—was at her expense.

Shannon stared at her hands in her lap. "And I don't want to leave my mom. She'd be miserable without both of us."

"You can't let your mom hold you back. She's got her own substance-abuse issues. You have to break the cycle. Keep going down this road and the next thing you know you'll be pregnant and there'll be a third generation in your family struggling with the same thing."

The look that came over her just then, the same time he noticed her clenching her fists, made him think she was about to take a swing at him. "Who the hell are you to sit there and judge us? Tell me how to fix my life? Like you're some kind of model of having your shit together."

"This has nothing to do with me."

"You know what people say about you, right?"

Packard braced himself. No one wants to hear what others say about them when they're not around. Her tone made it clear this wasn't going to be a list of his best traits.

"It's important you try to remember—"

"You're the hot gay cop who lives alone and goes for an ice-cold swim in the lake every day because he's got no one to get him off." She made a crude gesture with a nearly closed fist. "Everyone knows you were a cop in Minneapolis—you can google that much—but no one knows what brought you here. People figure it must have been something big for you to hide out on that lake and live like you're the last of your species. No mate. No prospects. Maybe Gary Bushwright. People think maybe one day you two will hook up."

Packard laughed in spite of himself. "Jesus," he said. He looked around the hospital room and at the dark night outside. *Him and Gary?* He thought about Cora accusing him of being the same as Gary, and about Gary's casual chatter about bathhouses and gay porn, like these were things they had in common. Packard had assumed the liberties they took were based on a false sense of familiarity. He was out there mediating things between them every other goddamn day. But it wasn't just Cora and Gary. The realization made him feel exposed. He turned his phone over and over in his hand nervously. He felt like someone had been looking through his windows and seen him in his most private moments. Not someone. The whole town.

Shannon wasn't done. "When you first got here, half the single women in this town, and some of the married ones, too, would have pulled their knees up to their ears with just a look from you. Once Karen's story got around, that pretty much stopped. Anyone who hasn't figured you out quickly gets brought up to speed by everybody else in the room. *Don't waste your time. He doesn't look it but he's...*" She flopped a limp wrist in his direction.

It took Packard a second to remember who Karen was and what her story might be. Karen Roth. Before she finished her nursing degree, she was another EMT, like Sean White Cloud, he would run into responding to calls. Last fall, at the Sandy Lake Labor Day carnival, she had come up to him, put her hands on his waist, and said, "Ben Packard, I would like to go out on a date with you. Would you please ask me out?"

He'd been strolling Main Street with Thielen and her husband. The two of them were riding the Ferris wheel and he was watching by himself. He was off duty, dressed in jeans and V-neck sweater, but suddenly he felt like he'd just been shot at. He wanted to duck behind something and pull his weapon. He looked over Karen's head at the Ferris wheel slowly spinning cars full of couples and kids.

"Why don't you let me buy you a beer?"

She'd looked at him sideways. "Instead of a date or in addition to a date?"

"Let's start with the beer, see what happens."

They'd had a beer, walked up and down the length of the tiny street carnival a couple of times, then he told her he had to find Thielen and her husband again since they'd all come together. She gave him her number and told him to call. He never did.

Shannon said, "So why don't you tell me how it goes when you just move somewhere and figure it out when you get there? You have a job, obviously. You pretty much have Grandpa's job as sheriff without the hassle of an election. And you have a whole town of people who gossip about you behind your back. But what else you got? Anything? Anyone?"

Packard stood and dropped his coffee cup in the garbage can by her bed. "You just made my point for me. I did the same thing I'm advising you to do. I didn't say it was going to be easy. You have to decide what's important and then do the work to make a life for yourself. I can live with gossip. I've got no secrets, just untold stories."

He took out his wallet and give her a card with his numbers on it. "I've also got two kids I'm trying to find. If you remember a name or anything else, call me. Anything at all."

Shannon stared at him with a nervous triumph in her eyes that collapsed in the next second. Attacking him had done nothing to change her current circumstances. It might have cost her an important ally.

Packard checked the time on his phone. It was almost 11:00 p.m.

"I'm sorry," she said. "People don't—"

"Shannon, enough. Don't be sorry," he said.

———————————

Dan Gherlick was standing outside the room, leaning against the wall and scrolling through his phone with one hand. Somehow he looked like he had aged since Packard had gone in. "What do you know now?" Dan asked.

"More than I knew before, but not what I was hoping for."

He quickly gave Dan a summary of Shannon's confession. "She gave Sam the names of the people who came in to get prescriptions for pain pills. He or Jesse would break into their house to steal it. She gave him someone's name a week ago right before those kids disappeared but she can't remember who."

Dan looked like more weight had been added to the yoke around his neck. "I hate that drugs and alcohol and thievery are all you know of our family," he said. "I'll do what I can with Shannon in the time remaining. The van comes to pick her up first thing tomorrow. The program is sixty days. No contact with the outside for the first thirty."

"You'd be smart to keep her and Patty separated, especially if Patty resists getting help."

Dan nodded knowingly. "I appreciate the advice. It's a lot to manage on top of having to plan my son's funeral—"

His voice cracked and he looked away for a moment. It struck Packard how tears could suddenly make a man look like a boy again.

Dan said, "I have to plan my son's funeral and then I'm going to see about getting Patty into treatment. If there's anything I can do to help find those kids, let me know."

Packard put his hand out and they shook. "Push Shannon to try to remember the name she gave Sam. That'll be the biggest help."

CHAPTER TWENTY-FOUR

IT WAS CLOSE TO midnight as Emmett raced his white Cadillac down the empty roads leading to Carl's house. The big moon was plastered to the cracked windshield like a sales flyer. On the radio a man talked in a hushed tone as if he were broadcasting from a hiding spot and trying not to be overheard. *We know for a fact that the government and the extraterrestrials are using secret tunnels to go between an underground military base and the inter-dimensional portal near Sedona. Hikers have reported being threatened by soldiers with M-16s patrolling the perimeter. How much more of this are we going to allow before we rise up and demand answers from our elected officials?*

The Cadillac was the first thing Emmett bought for himself after Myra left. The previous owner had put it in the ditch and bent the frame. Carl bought it from the insurance company for scrap, then had his guys straighten the frame well enough to drive and put a new radiator in it. He sold it to Emmett without a title for slightly more than he had in it.

At first, Emmett saw the Cadillac as a symbol of his freedom and his new life. Over time it became one more thing that he didn't take care of. It had rusty rocker panels and missing chrome trim. Someone stole the hood ornament. The hinge that kept the driver's side of the bench seat upright broke after a few years of Emmett's punishing weight. Now it stayed propped up thanks to a pipe-and-steel-plate brace he'd welded together to fit in the foot well behind him.

Emmett killed his headlights as he approached Carl's property. The land, more than twenty acres, had been cleared of trees years ago and was nearly naked all the way to the property line. The house was a rambler with a shaded front porch and three garage stalls.

Emmett crossed the gravel driveway that bridged the ditch and pulled up in front of the third garage door. A red Ford F-450 with a Dynamic towing hoist was parked in front of the garage stall closest to the front door. Already Carl was fucking things up. The stupid sonofabitch had a flatbed tow truck at his shop. Why not bring that one so they could throw a tarp over the car?

Emmett got out and felt the bite from the night air. He'd left the house in a mishmash of clothes put together for comfort and warmth: a stocking cap in yellow wool that looked like a bottle nipple, a red-and-black flannel coat that was too small to close around the middle of him, sweats with the elastic around the ankles cut off, and his smashed-flat house shoes.

Almost immediately Carl came out of the front door with a cigarette in his mouth, dressed in a Carhartt jacket, dirty jeans, and steel-toe boots. He was carrying gloves and keys and a bottle of Coke. His cheek was swollen where the girl had hit him with the chain.

They didn't bother with hellos. Carl got behind the wheel of the wrecker and watched as Emmett tried to haul himself up into the cab. It took him three tries.

Carl just shook his head. "Let's get this fucking over with," he said.

———————

The moon was at Emmett's back now as he smoked and watched the front end of the wrecker swallow the yellow lines in the road. He'd made a silent checklist of the night's activities in his head so he could cross things off as they were done.

Drive to Carl's. Drive back home. Load the car. Dump the car. Drive home. Only one down and it was almost 1:00 a.m. They had a long night ahead of them.

"How come you didn't get the flatbed?" he asked when he couldn't keep quiet any longer.

Carl looked at him as if he'd heard the part Emmett had left unsaid. *How come you didn't get the flatbed, you dumbfuck?*

"Flatbed went on a call today and still has two cars loaded on it. Not enough notice to get it unloaded for tonight. I had to have one of the guys from the shop drive this out to my place and drive Frankenstein home to save us a trip going into town."

Carl cracked his window and pushed his cigarette butt out with his thumb. "You were gonna paint the car but I'm guessing you didn't do your part either."

"Nope. We were supposed to do this tomorrow night. No time to paint the car."

"That's fucking great."

"Don't worry about it. It's Sunday night. I didn't see a single car on the way to your place. We still haven't seen one."

Carl drank from the Coke bottle between his legs and got another cigarette burning. "I almost bailed on this whole fucking shit show, sitting around, waiting for midnight to come. I'm getting pulled too deep into your bullshit. Blackmailing me to take out the Gherlick kid was pretty low," he said.

Emmett said nothing. They'd known each other too long to be surprised at anything the other did. There was no loyalty between them. Every interaction they'd ever engaged in was a matter of carefully weighing the outcome and trying to break even or be the one who came out slightly on top.

"But then I changed my mind," Carl said. "You know why?"

Silence from Emmett.

"Because after tonight that girl belongs to me. We're gonna ditch her boyfriend's car, I'm gonna get a good night's sleep, and then tomorrow I'm coming back to your house to get what's mine. She and I are gonna have so much fun together."

Emmett forced himself not to look at Carl or say anything in response. He heard Carl chuckling to himself.

"So much fun," Carl said into the bottle and took a drink and laughed some more.

———————

Back at Emmett's, Carl backed the wrecker up to the garage door and killed all the lights except for the running lights.

"You need me to get out?" Emmett asked.

"Keep your fat ass where it is," Carl said, putting on his gloves. "It'll take you longer to get back in the cab than it will for me to hook up the goddamn car."

Emmett stayed in his seat and smoked his cigarette. He took off the yellow hat and let the top of his sweaty head breathe. There were no lights on at Ruth's. He realized too late that moving the car in the middle of the night was more suspicious than doing it in broad daylight. If Ruth woke up and looked outside, she'd have a dozen questions. In the driver's side mirror Emmett saw Carl lit by the red taillights as he lifted the garage door and used the levers at the back of the truck to lower the wheel lift and extend the wrecker boom.

Turning his head the other way, Emmett looked at his house and thought of the girl asleep inside, like an egg in a nest. He remembered the smell of her island shampoo and imagined the library book open like a tent where she'd put it down before nodding off. He was getting more concerned about her wounds. The lead bird shot needed to come out of her. He remembered going to the hospital years ago after a grinding wheel had flung a metal splinter deep into his leg. The doctor had given him a shot to numb the area, opened the wound with a scalpel, then pulled the sliver out using a pair of forceps with a long slender tip. Maybe he could get a pair of those at the drugstore to extract the lead in the girl's hand and leg.

Tomorrow he'd put a padlock on the cage door to keep Carl out if he had to.

Her current wounds would be the least of her troubles if he couldn't keep Carl away from her.

The girl's voice was loud and clear in his head.

You have to have a plan to stop him, Emmett.

Carl got in the truck, backed up a couple of feet, got out again. Emmett heard the rattle of chains as the tow sling was hooked under the back end of the boy's car. Still no lights at Ruth's. A minute later the hydraulics whined as Carl used the levers to lift the car's front wheels off the ground. Emmett imagined the boy's body rolling inside the car's trunk.

Emmett rolled down his window and dropped his cigarette butt. Carl got back in, put the truck into gear. "You better hope we don't pass anyone between here and my place or we're both fucked."

"Just drive this sonofabitch," Emmett said.

In his head, he checked another box on his list.

Load the car.

———

Five miles into the fifteen-mile trip back, Carl spotted headlights in the rear-view mirror. "Motherfucker," he said.

Emmett turned as best he could to look out the back window but said nothing.

The wrecker's engine revved louder as Carl stepped on the gas and pushed it up to sixty-five. Ahead of them was nothing but empty road. No lights anywhere. Just scrub trees and every once in a while the flash of a white NO TRESPASSING sign or blue driveway reflectors.

Behind them the car was getting closer.

"This guy is gonna run right up on our ass and see a maroon Grand Am hitched to us."

"Then drive faster or turn off the sonofabitching road."

"There ain't nowhere to turn that gets us to where we're going without adding another ten miles to our trip."

They were going seventy miles an hour, seventy-five on a two-lane black-top road. Towing the car was nothing for the F-450 but everything was less stable the faster they went. Eighty. The boy's car was a shimmying rudder that wanted to steer the truck. The road curved and the headlights behind them disappeared for almost ten seconds but came back and seemed even closer now. Someone in as big a hurry to get where they were going as he and Carl, but in a fast car and not towing anything.

Carl pushed the wrecker faster. They passed an intersection and kept going, both of them watching to see if the other car might slow and turn. It didn't.

"Next intersection has a stop sign," Carl said.

"Don't stop," Emmett said. He held his breath as they got closer to the inter-section. He looked out his window watching for headlights approaching the four-way stop. "Clear this way," he said.

The wrecker was going ninety as it raced through the intersection. They hit a dip on the other side. Emmett felt his stomach fall away and rise up again. The boy's car banged behind them like it had been dropped.

Carl didn't slow down. They both watched the headlights get smaller and smaller as the distance between them and the other car increased. The last they saw of the car was its turn signal coming on and the sweep of its headlights in another direction.

Neither one of them said anything. Carl backed off the speed and lit a ciga-rette. "I've been thinking about what I'm going to do to that girl tomorrow," he said.

He meant later today but Emmett didn't correct him.

"I like how you have her in those manacles chained to the wall. I'm going to get her on her knees and shorten the chain so she can only hold herself up by her elbows on the mattress, and I'm gonna loop it around her neck so she can't back up from the wall without choking herself. Can you picture what I'm saying?"

Emmett stared out his window. "She's not gonna be much fun if you choke her to death."

"I ain't gonna choke her to death, but she's gonna have a mighty hard time breathing during some of it."

You have to have a plan to stop him, Emmett.

He tried to change the subject. "Where are we taking the car? Not back to the junkyard at your place."

Carl ignored him. "I like that she's a fighter, but she's gonna pay for hitting me with that chain. I'm going to take my time with her."

"You'll ruin that girl like you did the last one."

"That's what she's there for, Emmett! Goddamn. Are you fucking simple? You don't put a woman in a cage and wait for her to learn to like it. Do you still not know that yet?"

He did know that. He knew it after Wanda killed herself. He had grabbed the jogger anyway, thinking she would be different somehow. She never had a chance, thanks to Carl. Emmett knew he couldn't keep the girl around forever. That didn't mean he wanted to see her broken down like a deer carcass.

"I'm gonna do you a favor and show you just how to take care of that girl. I'll come back the next day and do it again. And again the next day. When I'm not there, you can try to do like me or the two of you can have a tea party or whatever the fuck it is you have in mind for her."

A padlock on the door wasn't going to be enough to stop Carl, Emmett realized. He could weld the door shut with the girl inside, and Carl would bull-doze his way through the block wall to get to her. She was his now. Emmett stared at the cigarette in his hand and tried not to think about it.

They were almost back to Carl's when he suddenly realized Carl's plan for the car. "We're going to the quarries," Emmett said.

"Bingo, genius."

When they made the turn onto Carl's driveway, Carl veered to the right of the garage and picked up a dirt trail that followed a post-and-wire fence near the

property line. After the small backyard lawn and a garden with an eight-foot
deer fence around it, the land turned to wild prairie, still brown and beaten
down from winter. Carl drove slowly. The wrecker bounced against the uneven
terrain, and the chains holding the car sang like wind chimes. The trail went
straight back for two hundred yards to a shelter belt of arborvitae trees hiding
an unpermitted junkyard of wrecked cars lined up door to door and stacked on
top of each other two high. There were giant racks built from timbers stocked
with more car bodies and long, rusting parts.

They turned left, behind the vehicle graveyard. In the headlights Emmett
saw skeletal chassis and old engines laid open like dissected hearts, their valve
covers and pistons missing. Thick trees bordered their right where the clearing
of the land had stopped. They drove another tenth of a mile and turned right.
Now they were in a wide clearing, ugly as a scar on the landscape, planted with
scaffold utility towers. Three electrical transmission lines hoisted high overhead hummed with the menace of a wasp nest.

The land was once owned by the Great Northern Mining Company starting
in the late 1800s. Quarrying ended in the 1950s. When the pumping stopped,
the two dozen granite quarries filled with groundwater. At one point, the fed-
eral government had wanted to use the site to bury radioactive waste. Now
the land was owned by the state and largely neglected. In the summer, people
ignored the NO TRESPASSING signs and sunned themselves on large slabs of granite and swam in the quarries' coffee-colored water.

Carl slowed down and edged the truck through a narrow gap in the trees.
Just a few yards later, a high wall of stacked spoil blocks on the far side of the
quarry came into sight. Behind it, a towering pile of grout rock rose taller than
the surrounding trees.

Their side of the quarry was an exposed outcrop, faceted and fractured by
a fault where red and gray granite came together. There was just enough room
around the edge for Carl to maneuver the wrecker around and back the boy's
car up to the rim of the gaping hole. He put the truck in park and got out without a word.

Emmett's back hurt from the rough ride and from sitting too long in the same position. He shifted in his seat, staring at the gap in the trees they'd come through. This pit didn't get much use because the high sides all around made it too hard to get in and out of the water. It was the ideal place to dump something you didn't want found.

The hydraulic arm buzzed as Carl lowered the front end of the boy's car to the ground. He came back and opened the driver's door. "You got your knife on you?"

"I do."

"Come out here and cut the tires," Carl said.

Emmett put on his hat and eased himself to the ground. It was cold enough that he could see his breath. He got a cracked thumbnail under the knife's spine and pulled out the blade until it clicked. He stabbed the sidewall of the front tire, yanking the handle back and forth to widen the gash as he pulled out the knife. Same to the back tire. The water in the quarry smelled like iron and wet vegetation.

He walked between the trunk and the edge of the pit. Carl was waiting for him on the other side of the car.

He had a gun in his hand.

"I had some other thoughts today about our situation," Carl said. "I'm not sure it's in my best interest to let you keep calling the shots."

"You dirty cocksucker. Put that gun away," Emmett said. His sudden anger kept him from being as afraid as he should have been.

"I'm serious, Emmett. The cops are too fucking close. They were at your goddamn house today. They're gonna get you for the girl in the basement, and when they see what you have built down there it won't take long for them to find the bodies by the lake. The first chance you get to make a deal, you'll turn on me for killing the Gherlick boy and the whore. If I kill you now, there's no connection between us. No deal to be made."

"You stupid sonofabitch. There's a million connections between us. Your employees have seen us together. Your family has seen us together. The girl has seen you."

"I'll take care of her, too."

Emmett bent over and stabbed the rear tire of the boy's car like the gun pointed at him was meaningless in the face of the work still to be done. From the trunk came a whiff of rot. He stood upright, knife in hand like a weapon. "You better think some more. If I go missing right after the Gherlick kid is killed, it's going to be too many fucking coincidences. They'll start looking for my known associates. They'll be at your door first."

"They won't find anything. I'll play dumb."

"You are dumb. There's no playing about it. You think you can lie to the cops over and over? Your story will change before you finish telling it the first time."

The gun in Carl's hand started to drop as Emmett's indifference to it ate away at his resolve. "Of the two of us, I'm the only one smart enough to keep the cops off our backs. They look at me and see an old man with chronic pain who lives in a shithole on the ass end of a mud lake. I'm a victim of that Gherlick boy. *You poor old man. Living with all that pain and having your medication stolen.* That lady cop carried my groceries to the front door and all but rubbed my goddamn feet she felt so sorry for me. If I go missing, then I stop being a victim of that Gherlick boy and become a victim of someone else. Someone connected to me who's connected to the Gherlick boy who they've probably already connected to those kids. They'll come for you, Carl. I'm the only one standing between you and that happening."

Carl lowered the gun to his side. "You fat fuck. I don't know if I should believe you and kill you anyway, or if I should let you live on the chance that what you say is true."

"I can protect both of us but only if I'm alive to do so."

"You won't protect us," Carl said. "You'll protect yourself. I'm only safe as long as you are."

Emmett didn't bother denying it.

Carl put the gun in his coat pocket and looked lost now that his plan had changed. Emmett handed him the knife. "You get that last tire. I can't bend over again. My fucking back." He went around the front of the truck and got back in, stepping on a hunk of rock just high enough to give him the leverage he needed to make it the first time. Carl got in on his side, handed Emmett his knife, and lit a cigarette.

"How deep is this quarry?" Emmett asked.

"Probably about forty feet right below this wall."

Emmett held the knife and wiped the blade on his pants. A thin twist of tire rubber was wrapped around the flipper. Carl put the wrecker in reverse and eased off the brake. He turned away from Emmett to look in his side mirror and check his alignment. Emmett saw the long line of Carl's throat, the hair from his beard that covered his neck like vegetation, the cigarette pinched between his big lips.

Emmett twisted in his seat like he was trying to look out the back window, then leaned across the space between them and buried the knife in Carl's neck to the bolster. It dragged against something that felt like cartilage on the way out, followed by a gush of blood that leaped at Emmett like a snake.

Carl stomped the brake and reached for his neck with both hands. The amount of blood running down his neck and into his shirt was shocking. It pulsed between his fingers with the force of his pumping heart. He made a wet sound in his throat like he was trying to gargle.

Emmett saw him reach for the gun in his coat pocket. "No, Carl. Leave it." He slashed the back of Carl's bloody hand with the knife. "It's too late for that. You were right. We're not in this together. It's every man for himself."

The inside of the cab was steamy with the mineral heat of Carl's spilled blood. He let go of the hole in his neck and made a bloody print on the driver's side window as he fumbled for the door latch. Blood dribbled from between his lips and sprayed the dashboard when he let out a wet cough. He turned toward Emmett and gave him one last look that flashed a thousand emotions—regret, confusion, fear. He reached for the front of Emmett's shirt before collapsing in his lap.

The wrecker was still inching backward. Emmett felt it collide with the

Grand Am behind them, then stop. He looked down at the back of Carl's head and saw maybe the only thing in the truck not covered in blood. He got his hands under Carl's shoulders and pushed him off of his lap. Emmett could feel Carl's blood soaking through his clothes and getting next to his skin.

Emmett threw the knife to the floorboard and pushed the wrecker's shifter back into park. He opened his door and rolled out like wet laundry from a basket. He wiped his hands on his shirt and adjusted his yellow stocking cap as he walked back to see how close the car was to the edge. Maybe five feet but there was a slight incline. Too much work to try to put his back into it and push the car himself.

He went around again to Carl's side and opened the door. Carl's bloody handprint on the window was already darkening and drying. Emmett reached across the body, looking for the gun in Carl's pocket, found it, and put it in his own. He reached between Carl's lap and the steering column for the shifter lever and pulled it down into reverse. The truck lightly backed into the front of the Grand Am again and then stopped.

Emmett stopped for a minute to catch his breath. With the dome light on, the inside of the truck looked like a slaughterhouse. Carl's eyes were open. His face was a blood mask with a beard.

The truck needed a little gas if it was going to push the car hard enough to overcome the slight incline at the quarry's edge. Bending so he could get his head under the steering wheel, Emmett found the cuff of Carl's right pant leg and lifted his size fourteen boot to place it on the accelerator. Immediately the engine revved and the truck started to move back. The driver's side door pushed against Emmett and knocked him to his knees. The bottom of the door hit him in the ass and scraped up his back, pushing his shirt up around his shoulders before he finally flattened himself and let it pass over him. Another inch and the front tire would have gone over his left hand.

Emmett lifted his head just in time to see the boy's car curve to the left instead of going straight back. It went over the quarry's edge sideways and looked like it was going to land on its roof. A few seconds later the wrecker followed it. The front end pitched straight up and the headlights swept toward the sky. There was a crash and a splash. Emmett got to his feet and went to the ledge. Water frothed and moved in overlapping waves. The boy's car was upside down, the weight of its engine compartment pulling it toward the bottom. Carl's wrecker was going straight down, ass end first. The air rushed from the cab in a hiss of bubbles and the headlights went under the surface, two owl eyes staring back at him as it sank deeper into the churning, cola-colored water. One light went out and then the other, and then there was just the sound of the agitated water and his own heavy breathing.

Emmett looked around this place where he suddenly found himself all alone. Light from the moon made the trees cast shadows in the dark. He could feel Carl's blood drying and tightening against his skin.

He took out his cigarettes, relieved to see they had stayed dry. At least the sonofabitch had the decency not to bleed all over his smokes. He had three left.

After a minute he headed for the gap in the trees, back the way they had come in the truck. The realization that he'd just taken care of all his troubles buoyed him. The boy, the car, Carl—all gone. The girl was going to be fine. He'd take care of her wounds and bring her the insulin she needed. He didn't think about how far he had to walk or how cold he was. He didn't think about how much he hurt or was going to hurt by the time he got home.

Emmett lit a cigarette and kept walking.

CHAPTER TWENTY-FIVE

PACKARD COULDN'T SLEEP. EVERY time he got close to letting go of his racing thoughts, the dip in consciousness would goose him awake again and start the loop playing from the beginning.

They'd almost closed the gap between what Sam knew and where Jesse went with Jenny five nights ago. Shannon had given Sam the name of someone picking up a prescription for eighty-milligram oxys, Sam's pill of choice. Sam sent Jesse to steal them. It was the only solution that made sense.

Packard sat up and reached for his phone. He pulled up the photo of the prescription bottles they'd found in the safe at Sam's house. Two were for Percocets. One was for thirty milligram Roxicodone. One for ten milligram generic Valium. No eighty-mil oxys.

They were so close. Packard felt like a racing wolf straining for those last few inches that would finally give him the mouthful of hide that would take this beast down. He put the phone down and stared at the ceiling.

He was still awake at 2:00 a.m. when he got a call from Sean White Cloud.

"I thought you might want to know we just brought Susan to the hospital in the ambulance. She's been in an accident."

———————

Susan had a private room on the hospital's second floor. Packard wondered if it was the one Patty Gherlick had been discharged from earlier in the day. One floor up, Shannon Gherlick was sleeping or nervously waiting for the rehab van that would take her away in just a few hours.

The doctors had given Susan something to help her sleep. Packard sat in the chair beside her bed in the dark room and didn't wake her. From what he'd gathered, Susan had fallen asleep behind the wheel and driven her car into a ditch. She had a broken nose from the airbag. Her eyes were already turning black.

He finally nodded off and was awakened when someone tapped him on the shoulder. Karen Roth—the woman who had asked him on a date at the carnival—was standing in front of him in navy-blue nurse's scrubs.

"What are you doing here?" she whispered. She looked put out by the sight of him. Their encounters on the job were awkward after he never her called for that date. They'd hardly crossed paths since she'd quit her EMT job and moved to nursing.

Packard looked out the window and wiped his face. "Waiting for her to wake up. What time is it?"

"It's seven thirty. Shift change. I'm coming on. Is she your… Are you guys dating?"

Packard shook his head. "She's my cousin."

Karen said, "I was gonna say…"

"You were gonna say what?" Packard asked. "That you thought I was gay?"

"Well, aren't you?"

Packard shrugged. "Under the right circumstances, I guess."

Karen rolled her eyes and wrote her name as the nurse on duty on the whiteboard across from Susan's bed. "You guess. Under the right circumstances— Gwyneth Paltrow and two bottles of chardonnay—I might step a foot over the line, but I'm not gay. No guessing about it."

"All right, yes, I am," Packard said. "I should have told you. I was trying to keep it on a need-to-know basis. When I first moved here, I didn't think anyone needed to know."

"I've got news for you. It's a small town. Everybody knows," she said.

"It's not news. I've heard."

Karen woke Susan so she could take her blood pressure and give her a pill. On her way out, she slugged Packard in the arm. "You 'guess,'" she repeated, shaking her head. She was smiling.

Susan hadn't said anything. She blinked slowly, and for a second Packard thought she was asleep again.

"Sean called you," she said as she struggled to keep her eyes open.

"He did. Tell me what happened."

"I was out looking for Jenny and Jesse. I've been going out every night after the restaurant closes. I fell asleep at the wheel."

"Susan, you don't need to do that. You need to take care of yourself and get some rest. I'm going to find Jenny."

He had no right promising such a thing, no matter how confident he was in his abilities or what leads remained to be followed. They both knew people went missing and stayed missing.

Susan turned her head and looked out the window. "Something bigger is going to come along and you'll have to move on. You're not the Wheeler family's personal deputy."

Packard scooted the chair closer and reached for her hand. "Hey, look at me. This isn't going to be like it was with Nick. Those guys didn't care. We were out-of-towners back then, and Nick was just another case to them. That's not going to happen with Jenny. I won't let it. We still have leads to follow. I'm still looking."

Susan studied his face. "What was the worst part of Nick's disappearance for you?" she asked.

Packard didn't have to think. "It was that we'd spent our last moments together fighting. We fought all the time. I was still a kid and he was practically an adult. I always wanted to hang out with him and he didn't want me around. I acted like a total shit that night. We fought, he took off…and I never saw my brother again."

"I would have thought it was the not knowing. All these years with no answers."

"Mom says he's alive until it's proven he's not. I wish I had the same faith."

Susan closed her eyes. "Faith doesn't produce results. Actions are what will find my daughter. I went to you for help; I'm hanging flyers and looking for her myself. If we don't find her soon, I'll think of something else. I'm not going to sit around and rely on hope."

"I'm not asking you to have faith in me, Susan. I'm asking you to believe me when I say that I'm not going to quit looking."

Susan didn't say anything. She pulled her hand away from his and turned her head. In a minute she was asleep.

Packard left the hospital, driving home into the sunrise, hoping a swim would keep him going after being up most of the night.

The water was still bracingly cold. Shannon Gherlick's words came back to him as he did his laps.

You go for an ice-cold swim in the lake every day because you've got no one to get you off.

He'd never thought of his morning swim as a cold shower before. Maybe she was right.

Sitting in the sauna, he realized he had no plan for the day. Thielen was going to meet the woman from Lutheran Social Services in charge of Meals on Wheels. They could pull a list of all the people Sam ever visited. They might find the eighty-milligram oxy user that way, but their user might also have never been registered for Meals on Wheels.

Mac, the dispatcher, called while Packard was waiting for the water in the shower to get hot. "I came in early to work on that name etched on the stock of the .38. Carol in the Recorder's office looked it up in her files. I think we have a good idea where Sam got the gun."

"Tell me."

"The stock was carved with D. Chambers. We found a marriage license for a Donald Chambers of Irving and Gertrude Nelson also of Irving. Married in 1949. They had one daughter that we found a birth certificate for named Myra Chambers."

None of the names so far meant anything to Packard. Irving was a tiny town in Sandy Lake County about twenty miles north. It was little more than a post office, a flag pole, and a bar across the street.

"Myra Chambers of Irving married Emmett Burr of Sandy Lake in 1978. Emmett Burr was one of the names on the prescription bottles."

"Thielen went out and talked to him yesterday. Who is he?"

"Emmett used to own the welding shop in town. It's that old building with the red peeling paint that looks like the roof is about to fall in over on Elm. Sign out front says Burr Welding."

"I know that place."

"He closed up shop maybe ten, twelve years ago. I think he had a lot of physical problems that made it so he couldn't do the work anymore."

The bathroom was filling with steam. Packard wiped his hand across the mirror and stared at the circles under his eyes. "So my next question is—"

"Whether or not he reported the gun stolen. Or reported anything stolen."

"Exactly," Packard said.

"He hasn't. No record of any calls out to his place, either from him or from anyone else."

"Do you think that's odd?"

"Kind of," Mac said. "Unless he didn't realize the gun was gone."

"And his pills, don't forget. His pain medication and a handgun go missing and he doesn't notice either?"

"Maybe he'd quit taking the pills. Maybe the gun was tucked away somewhere and he doesn't realize it's not there anymore."

"But not somewhere so hidden that a teenager breaking in can't find it," Packard said.

"Right."

"All right. It's curious. Thielen mentioned he lived alone yesterday. Is Myra not still in the picture? Dead? Divorced?"

"I don't know," Mac said. "I'll have to go back to Carol and ask her to look. We stopped when we hit on Emmett's name."

"Thielen didn't know about the gun yesterday. I think it's worth another visit to ask him about. I'll get hold of her. One of us will go visit him again today."

———————

Packard showered. Ate hard-boiled eggs and a bowl of cereal for breakfast. Put on his uniform. He felt the idea of something starting to coalesce in his mind, just over his right eye. They had pills and a gun that had come from Emmett Burr's house. It didn't make him any more involved than the other three whose names had shown up on the prescription pill bottles in Sam's house, but it still made him stand out. Packard wished he'd been the one to interview Burr yesterday. Thielen had described him as elderly and in terrible physical condition. Mac said he was in bad shape years ago and had to quit working. Bad enough to need eighty-milligram pain pills? The prescription bottle at Sam's with Emmett's name on it was for something else. That didn't mean there weren't others.

Packard also knew Emmett's address was north of town, which was the direction the kids had gone according to the location of the cell tower Jesse's burner phone had pinged. So was Martin Hughes's place, the other guy Thielen had visited yesterday. Seventy percent of the population outside of the town of Sandy Lake lived north. It wasn't much to go on.

He was zipping his vest over his uniform shirt when Michael, the nurse from Minneapolis—the nurse he did want a date with—called.

"You didn't tell me you were a cop."

Packard closed his eyes and dropped his head. In Sandy Lake, he wanted to be known as only a cop. Away from work, his job was the last thing he wanted to talk about with strangers. "I didn't tell you I wasn't a cop, did I?"

"No, but… I saw you on the news this morning. Detective Ben Packard, it said on the screen. You were talking about a couple of missing teenagers."

Packard wiped a hand across his face. "Yeah, that was me."

"Why didn't you tell me?"

"Wait a minute. Today's Monday. That press conference was Saturday. It's news in the Cities two days later?"

"I saw it near midnight last night on the suburban station that mostly shows infomercials and syndicated reruns. I didn't have time to call until just now. It might have been a rerun of the Saturday news considering the channel it was on."

Packard was conflicted about whether he should be happy the story was running in the Cities or pissed that it was little more than filler on a low-rent station almost no one watched.

"Why didn't you tell me you were a cop?"

Packard pinched the phone between his shoulder and his ear as he strapped on his equipment belt. "We didn't spend a lot of time talking about our careers when I was down there."

"You said something like you worked for the county."

"That's a true statement. Sheriff's deputy is a county job."

"I thought you worked at a desk and dealt with potholes and road salt."

"Yeah, well…it's more than that."

"No kidding. Any chance of seeing you again soon?" Michael asked.

"Yes. Couple of weeks maybe?"

"Cool. And hey, I'm not mad, just so you know. I'm just shocked that I had sex with a cop. I've always wanted to do that."

Packard's other phone was ringing now. Mac calling back.

"Well…okay. I'm glad you're not mad. I gotta take this other call."

"One last thing."

"What's that?"

"Bring the uniform when you come next time. You looked hot as hell all geared up like that on TV. Damn."

"Deal."

He hung up on Michael and answered Mac's call. "Did you find out what happened to Emmett's wife?"

"No, something else has come up."

"Now what?"

"Cora Shaker keeps calling for you. She wants you to get out there immediately."

"No. Tell her I don't have time for her and Gary's nonsense right now. Not today."

"This isn't about Gary. She said her husband's missing and there's blood all over her front door."

"How long's he been missing?" Packard asked.

"She said he was home last night when she went to bed."

Packard turned off the coffeepot and the kitchen lights. "Come on, Mac. There's a difference between him being missing and her just not knowing where he is."

"I know. But what about the blood?"

"How much blood? Is she sure it's blood?"

"She said it's all over the front door, like someone covered in blood was trying to push their way in," Mac said.

"So send someone to talk to her and check it out. I'm pretty sure I'm not the only one on duty today."

"I did. I sent Shepard. She keeps calling back and insisting on you." Mac dropped his voice. "She keeps saying, 'I don't want the stupid one. Send Packard.'"

"Typical. Last time I was out there she threatened me with the Lord's vengeance."

"Are you going? Can I tell her you're on your way? She keeps calling every two minutes."

"Yeah, goddamn. I'll go. It's gonna take me half an hour to get there."

The sun was up, drawing out green things hidden below the soil. The endless brown and white monotony of winter was over. Packard was getting too familiar with the roads and the turns out this way. He'd read somewhere that five percent of people cause fifty percent of health-care expenses. Cora and Gary were the law-enforcement equivalent of that.

He got his phone out and called Thielen's number. When she answered, he could tell she was driving, too. "Where are you?" he asked.

"On my way to see Kate at Lutheran Social Services. What did you get from Sam's sister last night?"

"Not much." He told her about Shannon's role in her brother's drug operation and about the prescription for eighty-milligram oxys waiting to be picked up right before Jenny and Jesse disappeared. "She also said everyone in town thinks I'm a sad homo and that I've blown my chance to nail all the single ladies, and one day I'll probably marry Gary Bushwright."

Thielen made a sound like she was choking on something. "Jesus, Packard. You almost made me drive in the ditch. Why are you... What did you say to that?"

"What do you think I said? I said Gary Bushwright is not my type."

"So...is this your big coming-out?" Thielen asked.

Packard adjusted the visor to get the sun out of his eyes. He'd never imagined a scenario where he was out at work because he never imagined himself taking the initiative to be so. If Shannon and Karen were telling the truth, the hard part had been done for him. All he had to do was confirm or deny. It was definitely easier to finally admit these things to Thielen than it was to keep dancing around them like they'd done for the last year and a half. He also knew he would conveniently forget this truth as soon as it became uncomfortable to put it into practice again. "I don't know if I was ever in if the whole town knows. I just wanted privacy."

"That was your first mistake," Thielen said. "Moving to a small town and expecting privacy. I, for one, don't think you're sad."

"You said the other night I should get a dog and be happier."

"I didn't mean because you're sad. I meant you could be happier. We can all be happier."

Packard came to a stop sign, looked left, turned right. "I get it. I've been unhappy for a while. I just haven't figured out what to do about it."

"Want to know what I think?"

"Sure."

"No one is happy not being themselves. If you can quit worrying about what other people think and live your life, the rest will work itself out."

He remembered Shannon asking him if he was a cop or a shrink and how he'd told her exactly what he thought she needed to do to fix her life. It was easy pointing out the error of other people's ways. Harder to see your own. "You're right. There's a whole history of things you don't know about, but we'll talk about it over beers some time. Back to the matter at hand. I feel like we're closing in on something. At that same time, it could all blow apart in the wind. It's vague. We need something more."

"I'll get the complete list of Sam's Meals on Wheels customers," Thielen said. "We'll interview every single one of them if we have to."

"We might. Did you get Mac's message about the gun from Emmett Burr's house?"

"Yeah. It's weird that he didn't report it missing. On the other hand, I carried his groceries from his car to the front door of his house yesterday. He wouldn't let me in. If the inside of his house is anything like the inside of his car, it's probably just this side of a dump. The whole place looks like it's one wet spring away from sinking into the ground."

"Can you drop in on him again today?" Packard asked. "Tell him we found his gun and let him know how he can get it back. I'd go but I'm on my way out to Cora Shaker's place."

"She and Gary at it again?"

"Not this time. She says her husband's missing. Says there's blood all over the front door."

"Blood?"

"Blood," Packard repeated.

"Damn. Call me when you know more."

"I will."

CHAPTER TWENTY-SIX

EMMETT'S BELIEF THAT THE worst was behind him lasted as long as it took him to walk a hundred yards. He shuffled away from the quarry, arms swaying as he propelled himself forward one step at a time on knees that barely bent. He'd dressed with the idea of staying warm while riding in a vehicle, not warm enough to walk a mile and a half at night covered in blood through damp grass.

He'd had the foresight to bring two Vicodins in his pocket. The pills came out stuck together and felt fuzzy to the touch. He worked up a mouth of spit and then swallowed the pills without confirming whether it was Carl's blood that had made them sticky or the damp night air. Better not to know.

He walked beneath the transmission towers clutching their thick cables on each side like giants marching toward the horizon. It took him more than an hour to reach the wrecked cars Carl had stacked in his junkyard. Feeling like he couldn't take another step, Emmett sat down in the front seat of a Chevy Blazer with no doors and no wheels. The shattered windshield had a forehead-shaped dent in it that pressed out from the inside.

He took off his yellow hat and set it on the seat beside him. How could he be sweaty and freezing at the same time? He pulled up the legs of his sweatpants and saw how full of fluid his feet and calves were. Cracks and sores in the tight, red skin radiated heat. His left foot was numb except for the tingling in his toes.

He lit a cigarette and stared over the trees at the top of Carl's house up the hill, dark save for a single bulb beside the back door. The cold weight of Carl's gun in his pocket made Emmett think it might be a good idea to kill Carl's family once he got up to the house. If Carl had told them anything about his plans for the night, mentioned Emmett's name at all, the cops would be right back at his place once Carl was reported missing.

Emmett sat for as long as he dared. He listened to frogs and things moving in the tall grass. The sun was far from coming up but he could tell the darkest part of the night was over. The bloodstains on the front of his clothes looked darker and were still wet from the moisture in the air. He rubbed his hand on his front and it came back red and damp. He wiped it on the side of the seat and rubbed his tired eyes, knowing he was getting blood all over his face but unable to do anything about it.

He still had a long walk ahead of him, all of it uphill.

He started walking again, keeping his eyes to the ground so he wouldn't have to see how much farther he had to go, or how the ground rose up the closer it got to Carl's. The Vicodins did nothing for the pain he felt. The insides of his thighs were chafed raw. His hurt was so intense he felt like he was glowing in the dark from the heat of it.

Finally, he reached a point where he could see his white Cadillac, and the distance remaining felt conquerable. He looked behind him and saw the low land filled with fog. He was going to make it. He heard dogs barking in the building behind Carl's neighbor's house. Did they smell him? The blood on him?

At the house, it took everything he had to walk by his car and go for the front door, gun in hand. His shoes were soaking wet, his feet ice cold and completely numb. Every breath was a gasp.

He grabbed the door handle and pushed. Locked. He leaned all his weight on the door but it didn't budge. Shoot the door? Shoot the lock? He'd lose the element of surprise and end up chasing two women around the house, trying to shoot them like pigs in a pen. He looked at the wide smear of blood he'd left on the front door where he'd leaned against it. The sound of the dogs barking seemed to get louder. This whole night was two minutes from going tits up. If he didn't get out now, everything he'd accomplished since leaving home would be for nothing.

He wiped the door handle with his sleeve and got in his car. He started the engine, backed away from Carl's house, and pointed the Cadillac in the direction of the slowly brightening horizon.

It was full-on dawn by the time Emmett eased past his garage—wide open and free of dead bodies—and stopped in front of his house. Relief overcame him almost to the point of tears. He was home. It was over. Check the last box on the list. *Drive home.*

His knees screamed as he climbed the front stairs to the deck. Inside, he bumped the thermostat up, stepped out of his wet shoes on the way to the fridge to get a beer and his pills by the kitchen sink. He took an eighty-milligram OxyContin and washed it down with half a beer that burned his parched throat like battery acid. He let the bubbles fizz out, finished the beer in two more gulps, and opened a new one. To the bedroom, whimpering with every step. *Oh, Jesus Christ. Goddamn.* He dragged the blanket off his bed back to the recliner and pulled it over himself. He drank the second beer and lit a cigarette. He smelled sweat and blood and the stink of his body raised by the heat of his efforts. He belched and smelled beer.

He smoked the cigarette halfway down and lost consciousness with it pinched between his fingers. His neuropathy was so bad, his fingers so gnarled and callused that he didn't flinch when it burned down to the filter and seared his skin before going out.

———

It was 10:00 a.m. when he snorted himself awake. The cold cigarette filter dropped from between his fingers and left a streak of ashes on the blanket on its way to the floor. Emmett rubbed at the dried blood on the back of his hands and watched it come off like dead skin.

The rawness between his thighs, his swollen legs, and his aching feet were on fire. He wanted to grab every spot that hurt, squeeze it, fan it.

He smoked a cigarette and finished the warm beer beside him, then heated up two breakfast sandwiches in the microwave. He took a pill and put four more in his pocket so he could keep taking them at regular intervals. The microwave buzzed and counted down the seconds while he absently rubbed his burned fingers.

Going down the basement stairs with the sandwiches on a plate, he felt like he was seeing things with new eyes. It had been less than a week since he'd thrown open the door and blasted the boy standing where he was now with the shotgun. The wall at the bottom was cratered from the second blast. There was still plaster dust and smears of blood and rolling bits of lead shot at the bottom of the stairs.

He caught of glimpse of himself in the mirror by the sink and realized too late that he was still in his clothes from last night and that he had Carl's blood all over him, even on his face. He looked at what he was carrying and saw too that he'd made the girl the old food, not anything that he'd bought yesterday. If she didn't want a sandwich, maybe she could read him more of that book while he ate. He'd bring her oatmeal or whatever she wanted later.

He pulled the bolt back and opened the door. It took him a second to figure out what was wrong. It was the darkness. The timer for the lamp was set so the light would be on by now. He opened the door wider until he could see the empty bed where the girl was supposed to be.

"Where are y—"

Something wet splashed him in the face. He dropped the plate. The girl slipped between him and the doorframe just as he realized he'd been hit with the contents of the toilet bucket.

He was a second too late reaching for her. She was unsteady on her feet as she tried to get her bearings. She wobbled and leaned against the side of the cage, long red T-shirt, bare legs, a newborn foal trying to stand and walk for the first time. The rocker he'd pulled inside while she read to him last night blocked the shortest path to the back door. She stopped, pivoted, her foot slipping on the wet floor, then stumbled toward the long way around, grabbing for anything she could reach for balance, pinballing in one direction then another. She made it to the toilet and the sink, around the shelving unit, heading toward the light from outside coming through the basement door.

He was after her now. When she stopped to paw the door handle with her good hand, Emmett shoved the towering stack of shelves between them in her direction. Cement blocks and sagging planks and everything stacked on them—tools and magazines and cardboard boxes and paint cans—smashed to the floor. The higher shelves came down closest to the girl. Cement blocks skidded in front of the door. She crouched with her hands over her head, then reached again for the door handle. Even if she could have unlocked the door, there was too much blocking it, and she only had one hand to move it.

When she turned in Emmett's direction, he had Carl's gun pointed at her. He saw her glance toward the basement stairs—the direction she should have gone instead of toward the promise of the outside light.

"You ain't fast enough, girl," he said.

She started wailing, knowing she had failed. She sank to the floor in her red Coke T-shirt, holding on to the door handle like there was still hope.

Emmett smelled the piss and shit on him. He smelled Carl's blood and those goddamned microwaved breakfast sandwiches. He stared at the girl down the length of the trembling barrel.

You knew it was always going to come to this, old man.

He closed his eyes and pulled the trigger.

CHAPTER TWENTY-SEVEN

PACKARD PARKED JUST BEYOND Cora's driveway. Shepard had pulled his car practically to the front door, doing a nice job of obscuring any tire tracks that might have told them if someone had come and gone during the night. That fool would drive over a dead body if it meant fewer steps to the crime scene.

Packard got out just as Shepard came through the door with Cora and Greta right behind him. Cora looked like a gray-haired mouse between them, wearing a plain, green house dress with large front pockets that looked like she'd made it herself. Greta was as big as a door with greasy hair pulled back in a braid, wearing camouflage pants and a gray hooded sweatshirt with a Green Bay Packers jersey over it. Her unibrow was so pronounced it seemed confrontational. It dared you not to stare at it.

"It sure took you long enough," Cora said. She was holding a television remote in one hand that she jabbed in Shepard's direction. "This one ain't done nothing but walk around the yard and scratch his ass since he got here. You pay this guy a salary? For what, I'd like to know."

Packard often asked himself the same question, but he wasn't about to take Cora's side against one of his deputies. "What do you know so far?" he asked Shepard.

"Cora says her old man was home when she went to bed last night. Earlier in the evening, one of the guys from the garage dropped off the wrecker and drove home in Carl's truck. This morning Carl and the wrecker are gone. They've been calling his cell phone and the truck's radio because they had tows scheduled and there's no response. No sign of Carl at either scheduled pickup."

"What did Carl need the wrecker for last night?" Packard asked.

"How should I know?" Cora said. She tucked the remote into one of the huge pockets on her dress. Out of the other one she pulled a tangled tissue and wiped her nose.

"So he didn't come to bed last night?"

"No."

"Did he spend the night in front of the TV?"

"When he falls asleep in his chair, he's usually still there when I get up at six thirty. He wasn't in his chair and the TV was off when I got up. And the truck was gone."

"Greta, did you see or hear anything last night?"

"Uh-uh. I took some Sudafed and NyQuil like every night so I could sleep." She had a deep voice, adenoidal, like she never wasn't suffering from allergies or struggling to breathe.

Packard was studying the wide concrete pad in front of the three garage doors. "You usually park in front of this far door?" he asked.

"No, me and Greta park in the first two stalls. Carl parks outside. The boat's in that third one."

"Was the wrecker parked here last night?"

"No, it was kittywampus across the other two."

"Someone parked here recently," Packard said, squatting down on his haunches and rubbing his finger through a dime-sized drop of engine oil.

"If they did, I didn't see or hear 'em," Cora said.

He walked to the edge of the driveway and wiped his oily finger in the grass, looking at the dirt tracks by the side of the house.

"Cora, what's back there? What's behind those trees?"

"It's storage. He's got car bodies and parts he's saving."

"Would he take the wrecker down there?"

"He would if he was towing a junker."

"Get in the car, Shepard," Packard said. "Let's drive down and have a look."

He let Shepard drive. The idea of sitting in the same seat Shepard filled with his farts all day made Packard shudder.

"It smells like cigarettes in here," he said.

"I haven't been smoking in my patrol car," Shepard huffed. He reached between them and yanked down the immaculate ashtray.

"I don't care how clean the ashtray is. It stinks in here."

"It must come off of me after I been smoking outside."

"That's a pleasant thought."

The trail through the grass was rougher than busted cobblestone. Shepard drove too fast. Packard held on to the handle over the door and rolled with the rocking car.

At the bottom of the hill they both got out. Packard made a mental note to look up whether you needed a permit of some kind to have this many junked cars and rusted car parts stored on a residential property. He noticed the new green grass coming up through the dead stuff from last year. Broken straw clearly showed footsteps to and from a navy-blue Blazer sitting on cement blocks to keep its chassis off the ground. No door, no wheels. Busted windshield.

Packard stuck his head inside the cab. In the seat was a yellow stocking cap with what looked like blood on it. The black streaks where a cigarette had been rubbed out against the dashboard smelled even stronger than the cigarette odor in Shepard's car. Getting down on his haunches, Packard spotted the butt in the grass and a swipe of something reddish brown on the side of the Blazer's seat. More blood.

"There's a hat in here with blood on it. Blood on this seat, too," he told Shepard.

"Yeah? New blood? Or from when it was wrecked?"

"Don't know for sure but I'm guessing new. Not sure how long a bloody hat would sit in an open vehicle like this out here in the wild. The cigarette smell is fresh. I think someone sat here last night and smoked a cigarette. Someone with bloody hands."

"Carl smokes."

Packard walked past the rows of stacked cars. Where the dirt tracks gave way to tall grass he stopped. "Someone drove through here recently. You can still see the tire tracks. They went that way. All the grass is laid down in that direction."

They got back in the car, Shepard driving again, and followed the trail, made a right turn into an electrical tower clearing, kept going until they saw the tracks make their way into the trees. "We're by those quarries, aren't we?" Packard said.

"Yup."

Packard told him to stop. They got out and covered the rest on foot, walking through the trees that surrounded the pit. Packard studied the tire tracks in the dirt around the rim. "There's two different tracks, but you can see where they came in, did a turn here, then backed up to the edge." He squatted again where there were the most footprints, where people got in and out of the vehicle. He saw several spots that were darker than the rest of the dirt. He cut through where he imagined the invisible vehicle had been parked and saw more spots where the driver's door would have been on the other side.

"Hey, Chief. You should see this."

Packard walked to the lip of the quarry where Shepard was staring down at inky-black water that started about twelve feet below them. The surface shimmered with oil and gas rainbows.

"That doesn't look right," Packard said.

"Sure doesn't."

Packard got on the radio and requested a member of the dive team to Cora's address. "Whoever can get here the quickest. Tell him it's a quarry dive and to bring a good light."

He had no choice but to overcome his resistance to driving Shepard's car so he could get back to the house. "I need to talk to Cora. Stay here and wait for the diver," he told Shepard.

Shepard looked like he was being abandoned on the side of the road miles from anywhere. "How am I supposed to get back?"

"You can ride back with the diver or walk."

"What am I supposed to do until then?"

Packard popped the trunk and took out the camera and the evidence collection kit. "Document everything. Everything you've seen and heard from the minute you got to Cora's. Try not to walk over the tire tracks or the blood."

"There's blood?"

"There's blood. Find it and photograph it."

Packard drove with the windows down. Past the junkyard he spotted the back of Gary Bushwright's house and the cab of his semi parked beside it. T-shirts and several pairs of overalls hung motionless from a clothesline in the backyard.

He had a bad feeling about what was hiding in the black water back at the quarry. Cora's husband could have taken the wrecker anywhere between the time she went to bed and now. He could have been out of cell phone range all morning, and that's why no one could reach him. It wasn't hard to do up here. He might also have been deliberately not responding. Packard would have held fast to either of those options if he hadn't noticed on the way to the quarry that the bent grass was all lying in one direction.

Based on the tracks, two cars went down there. Neither one came back.

Back at the house, Packard had a seat at the kitchen table. He asked Cora and Greta to tell him everything about the night before. He made notes in tiny script in his notebook. After twenty minutes he had a few more names, times, and details but no new information. When they were done, he asked Cora to try to call Carl's cell phone again from their home phone. After four rings Carl's voice told her to leave a message. She called down to the garage, too. Still no word from Carl there either.

Dave McCarthy, a local diver in his early fifties with a tumbleweed of thinning hair, showed up in a battered white pickup with oxygen tanks riding in a custom wooden rack behind the cab. Packard met him on the driveway and gave him directions back to the quarry. He told him about the gas and oil on the surface of the water. "I think there's one or more vehicles down there."

"Bodies?" Dave asked.

"I sure as hell hope not," Packard said.

Back in the house, he and Cora and Greta stood on a small square of linoleum looking at the smear of blood on the front door. It was a steel door painted gray with a peephole drilled through it. In part of the blood, near level with the doorknob, he could see the weave of the fabric of whatever had pressed against the door. Higher up was a swipe where it looked like someone had leaned a shoulder against the door, then turned away.

"How tall is your husband?"

"He's big. Six four," Cora said.

"Same as me," Packard said. He looked at Greta, who was maybe an inch shorter than her dad. For some reason he had a sudden vision of her in a singlet, climbing the turnbuckle in a wrestling ring and coming down on top of her opponent like a landslide.

"Whoever rubbed up against this door was a lot shorter. If this swipe here is near his shoulder height, then I'm guessing this person was five eight. Maybe less. Either one of you touch this outer doorknob?"

They both shook their heads, but he could tell neither one was sure she was telling the truth.

"Keep it that way."

Cora found the tissue in her pocket again and wiped her nose. The three of them stared at the shape on the door like they might recognize who left it if they squinted long enough. Packard debated whether to share what was coming together in his mind. Not yet, he decided.

Motion outside caught his eye right then. The sound of barking dogs got noticeably louder as Gary came out of the kennel's steel building pulling a wire basket on wheels.

"Cora, put your shoes on and come with me," Packard said.

"Why? Am I arrested?"

"No, you aren't arrested. Why would you think I'm arresting you?"

Cora threw her hands up. "You're always threatening to arrest me."

"Yeah, well, whose fault is that?"

"The sodomite's."

"The last time I was here was because you shot the sodomite's house with a crossbow."

"On accident," Cora insisted.

"I don't care. You're not arrested, but you're not going to like where we're going."

"Where are we going?"

"Next door to Gomorrah."

———————

They caught up to Gary in his backyard by the clothesline. Cora was wearing rubber rain boots and an orange quilted vest over her green house dress. She walked five steps behind Packard to make her reluctance known to Jesus and anyone else watching. In her arms she had a black bound book with the words HOLY BIBLE facing out like a talisman. Packard was surprised she'd left her crucifix and wooden stake back at the house.

Gary kept one eye on them while he pinned up the laundry. His wheeled wire basket was full of wet blankets.

"I see the two of you coming, and I don't know if I should bar the door or put out tea."

"Gary, I need a favor. When I was here after the incident with the crossbow—"

"Accident with the crossbow!" Cora blurted out.

"You said you had a security system watching your property."

Gary had wooden clothespins in his mouth. He took one out and pinned the corner of a blanket, shook out the rest of it, and pinned the other corner. He was wearing Carhartts and a flannel shirt over a black T-shirt that said Eagle on the front. "I do. I can see all back here, my rig, and across the way to Cora's. I got cameras on the kennel, the dog run, and the front of my house. Full coverage, as they used to say when I was in the movie biz." He gave Packard a knowing wink. Cora was looking away at the cameras mounted under the soffits of Gary's house and missed it.

"Is it always on? Does it record?"

"It does. Got a big old hard drive that takes two weeks to overwrite itself. Why do you ask?"

"I want to look at the video from last night. Something strange might have happened next door. I want to know if your cameras caught any of it."

"Something strange? Like what?"

"Can we just see the video?"

Gary hung up the last blanket and pulled the wire basket behind him. Packard followed. Cora stood her ground, looking up like she was seeing blue sky for the first time.

"Come on, Cora."

"I'm not going in that house."

"Yes, you are. I want us both to see whatever Gary's got on camera. I'm not running back and forth to describe it for you."

Gary waved her over. "Come on, Cora. It's not like you've never been inside. You used to visit with Mom all the time."

"That was before."

"Honey, it ain't changed one bit. I got all the same doilies on the furniture, the same dusty bowls of potpourri. Still smells like cigarettes and Mom's hair spray. It's in the walls."

Cora looked seriously conflicted. She held the Bible up with both hands, leaned her forehead against it, and mumbled something to herself. Packard caught Gary rolling his eyes. "Not a word," he warned.

"Honey—"

"Shut it."

Cora came along and they followed Gary and his rolling basket up the ramp. Packard held the door for Cora, who looked like she was being prodded into an animal's lair. Her shoulders were up to her ears. She looked to her left and to her right, Bible clutched to her chest. When she saw everything as Gary had described, maybe as she remembered it, her shoulders dropped. Half an inch.

Gary took a seat at his computer, pecked at the keyboard. Cora said, "Your mother didn't have a computer there. That was her sewing table." She said it like she'd caught him in a lie.

Gary turned in his chair toward Cora. "That's true. Mom's grasp of technology pretty much ended with her 1970s Singer sewing machine. She wouldn't even touch a TV remote. She left the TV on twenty-four hours a day. Said all those buttons scared her to death."

Cora pulled out the remote she was still carrying in the front pocket of her house dress. "It's not that hard. You really only use two or three buttons most of the time. The rest are just for looks, if you ask me."

"Can we just look at the video from last night?" Packard prodded.

Gary double-clicked and double-clicked. He brought up video from the camera that captured where his semi cab was parked on the side of the house and also almost all of Cora's front yard. "What time do you want to start?"

"What time did you go to bed?" Packard asked Cora.

"Ten o'clock. Carl was still home and the wrecker was in the driveway then," she said.

Gary moved the slider until the clock showed just after ten the night before.

The footage was in black and white. "This is the night vision. It's color during the day and much higher resolution." Gary clicked until the video started playing at four times the speed. White streaks flew across the screen every once in a while. "Bugs," Gary said.

It was almost 1:00 a.m. when a white car eased in front of the third garage door. Packard made a mental note of the fact that the car's headlights were off when it turned into the driveway. Like it didn't want to be seen.

A fat man in a stocking cap got out of the car. Carl came out of the house at the same time, and they stood in front of the wrecker almost out of sight of the camera. After a minute they got in the truck and it backed up the driveway away from the house.

"Who was that?" Packard asked.

"Emmett Burr," Cora said.

Packard felt every hair on his body stand on end. "How do Carl and Emmett Burr know each other?"

"Emmett had a welding business in town. He used to do work for Carl in the early days of the garage."

"They're friends?"

"Carl doesn't have friends," Cora said. "He knows people and people know him."

Packard told Gary to keep the video moving. An hour later, bright-white light entered from the side of the screen and the wrecker came into frame towing a car behind it. "Pause it right there," Packard said. He already knew the answer to his next question before he asked it. "What kind of car is that?"

Cora had relaxed a bit. She had her Bible by her hip and was leaning over Gary's left shoulder to get a closer look at the screen. "That's a mid-nineties Pontiac Grand Am."

Both Gary and Packard looked at her, surprised.

"What? I worked the front desk at the garage for years. I know cars, thank you very much. That's a mid-nineties Pontiac Grand Am. You can tell by the fluted panel on the side."

"Jesse Crawford was driving a mid-nineties Pontiac Grand Am the night he and Jenny Wheeler disappeared," Packard said.

"Those local kids that have been missing? Is that who you're talking about?" Cora asked.

Packard nodded. The three of them stared at the car frozen on the screen. Cora was tense again. She grabbed the zipper on her vest and pulled it higher. "Could be another Grand Am," she suggested.

"Start the video again," Packard told Gary. After a second the wrecker drove off the side of the screen and was gone. "What about the camera in the back? Let's look at the view from that."

Gary clicked and brought up another window with the video that showed the view from the backyard camera. He moved the slider until the time lined up with the time from the other video, and they watched the wrecker's headlights move down the property line. The junkyard was well out of the range of the camera and its night vision. All it could pick up was lights against a dark background. They could make out the headlights when the wrecker made a left, kept going well past the junkyard, then turned right and disappeared. "Where were they going? We don't have nothing back there," Cora said.

Packard kept what he knew to himself.

They went back to the other view, four times the speed, saw nothing happen for hours, and then suddenly Emmett Burr limped past the three garage doors, looking like he was fighting a current. He was lost in the dark under the porch overhang for a minute; then they saw him go back to his car and drive away. Gary let the video run for another couple of hours until the sun came up and the footage changed to color. Near the end, Cora came out the front door with a coffee cup in one hand, looking like she was checking if anyone was parked in the driveway. Gary stopped the video.

Cora was confused. "Where'd they go? Where's Carl and the truck?"

Packard took his phone out and called Shepard. "Is McCarthy in the water yet?"

"Yeah, he's been down ten minutes or so."

"Stay on the line. I have a feeling he won't be down long."

Gary was saying, "Lots of people park on the road out here and cut through my property to hike down to those quarries in the summer."

Packard left the two of them and stepped outside.

"Anything yet?" he asked Shepard.

"I can see his light now. He's heading up."

Packard listened as Shepard asked McCarthy what he found. He could hear the sound of McCarthy's response but not what he said.

"Jesus Christ," Shepard said.

"What is it?"

"He says there's two bodies."

Packard's blood turned to ice. Jesse and Jenny. He'd promised Susan he'd find her daughter. Not like this. "Is it the boy and the girl?"

"Hang on a second," Shepard said. Packard waited an eternity for Shepard to ask the question, then repeat back what he'd been told. "There's no girl. He says there's two vehicles in there. A maroon car lying on its side at the bottom. The trunk is partially open like it might have popped when it hit the water. He said there's a male in the trunk who looks like he's been dead a while. The second vehicle is a tow truck from Carl's Auto. It's almost on top of the car, ass end down. Carl is in the cab up against the windshield. Dave says he's got what looks like a stab wound in his neck."

Packard was too cautious to be relieved that there was no sign of Jenny. If Jesse was in the trunk of his car, where did that leave her? Just because she wasn't in the pit didn't mean she was alive. "No sign of the girl? Could she have been in the trunk and fallen out?"

He waited again while Shepard asked. "He doesn't think so. The trunk is only a little ways open and the body is fully inside. He can go down for a second look if you want him to."

"Tell him yes. Call and request fire, EMS, and crime scene. Make sure everyone knows where you are so they know what equipment to bring. Not a word about who's down there over the radio. Understand me?"

"Got it."

———————

Carl Shaker had helped Emmett Burr hide a car that every cop in five states was looking for. So why was Carl dead? Something had gone sour between him and Emmett. That was the problem with trust among criminals. The quality of their character was incompatible with the integrity necessary not to murder each other.

So where was Jenny? Was she alive? Was she what had come between Emmett Burr and the one person he could trust to help him dump Jesse's body?

Emmett had killed Jesse and Carl. Jenny had to be at Emmett's. And right now Thielen was on her way there alone, knowing none of this.

Packard tried her phone and got no answer. He didn't have the number of the lady from Lutheran Social Services to find out if Thielen was still there or had come and gone already.

He called dispatch and got Mac. "I need another deputy out here at the Shaker place. What's Thielen's status? Where is she?"

"She was ten twenty-three maybe fifteen minutes ago."

"Where?"

"Emmett Burr's residence. Didn't you send her out there to talk to him about the gun?"

"Goddamn it." Packard felt like he was being drawn and quartered. He needed to be in four different places at that exact moment. "Cancel the deputy for out here and route everyone to Emmett Burr's address. He should be considered armed and dangerous. Send EMS, too. Keep trying to get hold of Thielen. I'm on my way."

Back inside, Gary had a photo album open over the top of his keyboard, pointing at old photographs held in place behind yellowing plastic. "Here's one of you and Mom drinking Tab at the picnic table that used to be out back. What year is this?"

"Probably late seventies," Cora said. "Way before Greta was born. I'm holding a cigarette like a hussy. I quit when the Lord blessed us with her."

Packard hated to break up this moment, but there was no time. "Cora, I need you to come with me. We have to hurry."

Cora snapped to like she'd been under some kind of spell. "What is it?"

He held the front door open. "Let's go. Gary, thanks for your help."

"Honey, it was nothing. Bye, Cora. It was nice visiting with you."

Packard hurried her down the ramp. He waited until they were back in her yard, then grabbed her arm. "Listen, Cora. Something happened last night between Emmett and Carl. Carl's been killed."

He waited but Cora said nothing. The sun was in her eyes. She squinted and dropped her head.

"I have a diver in the quarry back there. He said the tow truck is at the bottom. Carl's inside."

"What about the Grand Am?"

"It's at the bottom of the quarry, too. There's a body in the trunk I'm guessing is Jesse Crawford."

Cora started walking again. "My husband did not walk with the Lord. He had wicked urges. He thought he kept them hidden from me but he wasn't as smart as he thought. I've prayed and prayed for him. But I didn't know about those kids. I'll swear on a stack of Bibles," she said.

Packard found empathy for Cora he hadn't felt before. His primary concern was still Thielen. "I believe you, Cora. I don't know what Carl's involvement was in all this, but I need to get to Emmett's right now and find out. I'm sorry to leave you with news like this—"

"Go. I have Greta and we have the Lord. Isaiah 41:10 says 'Do not fear, for I am with you; do not be dismayed, for I am your God.'"

"All right then. I had Shepard request an ambulance and more investigators from the sheriff's department. They'll be here soon."

Cora put her hand on him. "God bless you," she said.

Packard nodded and ran for the truck.

CHAPTER TWENTY-EIGHT

EMMETT KILLED THE SKID loader's engine, lit a cigarette, and stared into the hole he'd spent the last hour making in the reddish-black soil. Groundwater was leaching in from the bottom. It'd be a foot deep by the time he came back with the girl's body in the bucket and tipped her in.

While digging, he'd added up the number of deaths he was responsible for. Wanda. The jogger. The girl's boyfriend. The Gherlick kid. Carl. Hell, even the whore from the truck stop. He'd always blamed that one on Carl, but he certainly hadn't done anything to help her. That made six. The girl would be seven.

He'd missed when he fired the gun at her. He knew better than to pull the trigger without aiming, but she'd dumped the goddamn toilet bucket over his head! He had piss in his eyes. A second shot was a bad idea considering he could see fishing boats on the water from where he stood.

It only took the threat of the gun to get her to walk back to the cage. She'd gotten loose by taking the wire from the thing in her mouth and using it to release the handcuff's ratchet. He put her back in the manacles, and stuck his finger through a hole in her red T-shirt and ripped it wide open to the collar. She looked sick and broken to him now. Bruised and covered in sores and bleeding through the bandage on her hand. He clawed at the things she had taped to her abdomen until the adhesive lifted away like scabs. He looked around for her pump, found it under the cot, and smashed it. Everything was for nothing. All the time he spent taking care of her, all the things he'd bought for her. He'd killed Carl for no reason. He should have let him have her.

She twisted and fought him as he hooked a finger in her mouth, pulled it open, and fed her the pills in his pocket like he was putting quarters into a slot. Her can of water was half-full. He emptied it into her mouth and pushed her chin up with the heel of his hand.

He saw in her eyes she knew what he was doing.

"Swallow," he said.

She sputtered, sprayed him, puffing out her cheeks, trying to hold everything back. He pinched her nose shut until her face turned red, then suddenly let go of her chin. She sucked air like a drain cleared of a clog. That many pills at once was probably enough to kill her. Definitely enough to put her in a state where she wouldn't fight him when he came back to load her in the Bobcat. If she was still alive when he put her in the hole, she wouldn't be by the time he finished filling it.

The sun came down in rays through the trees and lit the green undergrowth surrounding him. Emmett felt strangely calm, like things were on their way back to normal. He looked at the cigarette he was smoking, checked the pack in his pocket, and realized it was the brand from the boy's backpack. He inhaled deeply, really tasting the gritty warmth that inflated his chest. A good cigarette was one of life's true pleasures.

He thought he heard a woman call his name just as he started the engine again. Wanda and the jogger were buried directly beneath where he was sitting in the Bobcat. He thought of the coming night and hearing them call his name in the dark, the sound of their footsteps on the basement steps. Would Carl be there with a hole in his throat that whistled as he breathed in and out? How long before the girl joined the parade?

Some things would never go back to normal, he realized. Some things would stay with him the rest of his days.

He followed his tracks back to the garage, steering the 'cat through the gap in the bushes, and stopped short at the sight of the black Dodge Charger that had followed him home yesterday parked behind his Cadillac.

One look at the open door at the top of the stairs, and he knew nothing would ever go back to normal.

CHAPTER TWENTY-NINE

THE FIRST CHANGE THIELEN noticed at Emmett's place was that the garage was open. She spotted sheets of bowed plywood leaning against one wall, heavy chain hanging in a loop, and cement blocks sitting on top of a crushed pallet.

She parked behind Emmett's Cadillac and radioed in her location. Getting out, she noticed a gap in the bushes behind the garage that looked like the start of a trail where matted leaves and a fallen tree gave it its shape. The rapid-fire staccato of a woodpecker sounded nearby. It took her only a second to locate the bright-red head against a white paper birch. She heard a cardinal chirp and saw a pair of black-capped chickadees swoop over the top of Emmett's house.

Her attention came back to the white car and a partial palm print on the doorframe. She'd seen enough dried blood in her life to know it when she saw it. At the top of the door, where someone might have held on while trying to lift his considerable bulk out of the seat, were bloody fingerprints. Thielen peered through the driver's side window. Yesterday, when she grabbed the book from the front seat, she'd noticed the ring of gray grime on the car's white leather interior that outlined where Emmett sat. Now she saw smeared blood on the seat back, on the steering wheel, and against the interior door panel.

She unsnapped the retaining strap on her holster. The feeling of familiarity from her trip yesterday was gone. Her antenna was fully up, heartbeat steadily rising. She had a hand on her firearm, now aware of every sound, every movement.

She drew her weapon as she approached the house, went up the warped stairs to the landing, and knocked on the glass sliding door. She called Emmett's name. Standing off to one side with her back against the wall, she slid the door open by pushing it away from herself. "Emmett? It's Detective Thielen. We met yesterday. Are you okay?" She waited. Nothing.

She entered the house.

The smell made her gag. She brought her arm in front of her nose to block the smell and keep herself from sneezing. Mold, mildew, garbage, cigarettes. She saw a shotgun on the floor next to a battered, brown recliner that looked like it had been dropped from up high into its current location. There was a console TV like she hadn't seen since she was a kid, a VCR and a stack of video cassettes on top, mostly pornography. A couch with a sagging middle sat against the wall. Dust was thick on every flat surface. The windows were hazy from cigarette smoke, the carpet streaked with stains and dropped ashes.

On an end table next to the recliner, among empty beer cans and an overflowing ashtray, was a prescription bottle for 80-milligram oxycodone. The date on the label was only a week old. It matched what Packard had learned from Sam's sister about someone picking up a prescription for these exact pills last week.

She swept the upstairs rooms quickly, looking for anyone. A bathroom covered in black mold. A bedroom with plywood screwed over the window and clear plastic taped over that, the bed covered in clothes and linens with just enough space for someone to sleep on the side closest to the door. Emmett didn't really live in this house, she realized. He moved from spot to spot, huddling out of the elements. It was a lair. A burrow.

Back to the kitchen. She opened a green door with a porcelain handle. The light bulb at the top of the stairs was on. The handrail was splintered. At the bottom of the stairs she saw swipes of old blood that looked like someone had tried to clean up with a dry rag.

She started down the stairs. "Emmett, it's Detective Thielen. Are you down here?" The steps flexed and creaked beneath her. On the fifth stair she was low enough to squat down and survey the basement over the top of the handrail. She saw toppled cement blocks and long boards and deduced the stacked shelving that had once segmented the room. Looking from up high, she spotted a rocking chair, a cascade of dirty magazines, the cluttered workbench. In the nearest corner she saw a wet floor near a toilet and a sink with a green hose running from the faucet. At the other end of the room, in the far back corner, was a steel door to a cement-block room.

She went down the rest of the stairs. It smelled worse in the basement, if that was possible. Like damp rot and an unflushed toilet and more cigarettes. Also faintly like shampoo. Like coconut shampoo.

Thielen moved past the exposed bathroom toward the room in the back corner. The toppled shelves had to be a recent occurrence. She saw beer cans sitting in puddles of spilled liquid. The back door was ajar and had what was clearly a bullet hole through it two feet up from the ground.

The toilet smell was worse by the steel door. She looked down and saw smeared feces and what she had to assume was spilled urine. She pulled the sliding bolt on the door, bracing herself for the worst but still not prepared for what she saw.

A tall lamp with no shade threw harsh light on horrifically pink walls streaked with stains and moisture-blistered paint. It looked like a jail cell for a mad dwarf or a little girl's bedroom in hell.

Jenny Wheeler was on a thin cot with her arms stretched overhead, chained to the wall. One hand was wrapped in bloody bandages. She had tape over her mouth. An oversized red T-shirt was ripped up the middle and only held together at the collar. She thrashed at the sight of Thielen, tears running from her eyes.

Thielen holstered her gun and pulled the tape off the girl's mouth. "Jenny, I'm Detective Thielen. You're going to be okay. I'm going to get you out of here," she said.

Jenny pushed the wad of what looked like part of her red T-shirt out of her mouth. "He forced me to swallow...pills so I overdose. I already feel..." She couldn't finish the sentence.

"How long ago?"

"I don't know. I can't..."

The manacles were heavy, crude things closed with padlocks that would need a key or bolt cutters to remove. Thielen pulled a blanket from the floor to cover the girl's nakedness. She spotted the copy of *David Copperfield* she'd brought up from Emmett's car yesterday.

"Where'd Emmett go?"

"I don't know. I tried to escape but he caught me," she said, sobbing harder at the memory.

"You did great, Jenny. You're alive. You survived. I need to call for backup—"

"Don't leave." Her eyes were getting heavier, her words slower.

"Jenny, stay with me. Don't go to sleep. I'm just going far enough to get on the radio. You'll hear my voice."

"He's got...gun," Jenny warned.

"I know. I'll be right back. Keep listening to my voice."

Her radio was in the car and her cell phone had no bars in Emmett's basement. She stepped outside to see if the reception was any better. It wasn't. On the opposite side of the house she heard the growl of a small engine and knew right away what it was. Yesterday there'd been a Bobcat skid loader by the garage. It wasn't there when she pulled up.

Thielen drew her weapon. She heard a crash just as she peeked around the corner of the house. Emmett was inside the Bobcat's cage maneuvering the teeth of the bucket under the side of her vehicle. The car went up on two wheels as he raised the bucket and pushed in closer with the skid loader. Black smoke poured out of its exhaust.

Thielen scurried up the hill beside the house, keeping low. Emmett saw her coming, raised the gun in his lap, and fired it. Neither one of them had a good line on the other as the black car went higher between them, then rolled on its side with the sound of crunching aluminum.

Thielen retreated to the basement, kicking herself for not calling for backup sooner. The blood in Emmett's car had made her assume he was the one who was hurt. Jenny needed Narcan if she was overdosing on opioids. Thielen carried it in her car but there was no getting it now.

She looked around Emmett's basement for a solution. Her eyes went by the wall phone beside the door several times before she realized what she was looking at. She lifted the receiver in disbelief.

Dial tone.

CHAPTER THIRTY

PACKARD WAS DRIVING NINETY with lights and sirens while Mac in dispatch described for him the layout of the property based on what he could see on Google Maps. "It's the last lot on the southwest side of the bay. The road goes another hundred yards but nothing else is developed. Probably too swampy. There's a garage near the road, and the house is set back beyond that, closer to the lake."

On the long straightaway behind him, Packard saw lights and emergency vehicles forming a line half a mile back. Despite having requested backup before leaving Gary's, Packard had beaten them all because Emmett's house was closer to Carl's than it was to Sandy Lake.

His phone rang with a number he didn't recognize so he ignored it. He slowed as he made the left turn onto the gravel, then accelerated again, the sound of the tires different on the dirt. The truck bounced over the uneven surface.

Mac said Emmett's was the fourth turn on his left.

Packard turned onto the property, looking everywhere for Thielen. He recognized Emmett's Cadillac from the video at Gary's. No sign of him. No obvious explanation for why Thielen's car was on its side, spilling gas and other fluids onto the ground.

He pulled far enough away from Thielen's car that they wouldn't lose both if hers caught fire for any reason. Packard scanned the upper deck of Emmett's dilapidated house and the trees surrounding the property. He felt exposed sitting in his vehicle.

On the radio, Mac said, "I've got Thielen on the phone. She calling from a landline inside Emmett's."

"Thielen, what the hell is going on?"

"I'm in Emmett's basement with Jenny. I need the Narcan from your vehicle right away." She told him about Emmett flipping her vehicle with the Bobcat and that he'd fired a handgun at her.

"I don't see him out here anywhere," said Packard. "There's no Bobcat."

Deputy Wilson pulled on to the property. Packard motioned him to go on the other side of the cars. Wilson put the nose of his car into a slight clearing just past the garage.

"I'll be coming around the east side of the house," Packard said to Thielen. The land was thick with brush in that direction, but he had a clear line of sight to the house next door. There was nowhere on that side for Emmett to be hiding.

Packard pocketed the naloxone spray from the center console and got out of the truck, taking care to keep it between him and Emmett's house while he called out to Wilson. "Do you see a Bobcat?" he asked.

"I hear it," Wilson said. "Sounds like it's down closer to the lake."

Packard warned him about the gun, then ran across the open yard and alongside the house. He squatted low and peeked around the corner, saw the lower-level doorframe but not Thielen.

"Thielen, can you hear me?"

"Yes. I'm here."

He tossed the box of naloxone at the woodpile beside the door. "Grab the spray if you're clear," he said. "Wilson is in position back by the garage."

Thielen peeked out, gave him a nod, and snatched the box.

To Wilson, via the radio. "Can you see Emmett?"

"He's driven off the path and deeper into the brush. I can still hear the engine. I'm seeing clouds of smoke move through the sunlight. I don't know if it's a cigarette or exhaust."

Packard took a long look. He saw something white with straight lines through the brush, but it was too dense to make anything out for sure. He yelled, "EMMETT, COME OUT OF THERE WITH YOUR HANDS UP!"

No movement in the brush. Later in the summer the mosquitoes would have chased Emmett out of there in less than a minute. Now they might have to wait as long as it took for Emmett to smoke all his cigarettes. They knew he had a gun but not what kind or how many rounds. He was a slow, overweight old man from what Packard had seen on the video back at Gary's. Still, you didn't reach blindly into a snake hole, no matter how old the snake.

Wilson on the radio: "Something's happening. I hear him revving up. He's moving."

Before Packard could ask a question, he saw a belch of black smoke rise up through the brush. The tops of the smallest trees and saplings shuddered. A second later, a green wall fell in a shower of leaves as the scoop laid everything flat and the Bobcat leaped forward. Emmett started raising the arms and tipping the scoop down as soon as he was clear of the brush, angling himself toward the basement door, where Packard could see Thielen squatting with her firearm drawn.

Emmett was focused on covering himself from Thielen and Wilson the way he kept edging the Bobcat back toward the lake while swinging the front end in a narrow arc between the two. Packard realized Emmett hadn't spotted him on the other side of the house. The Bobcat arms were raised all the way up, the scoop pointed straight down so that it blocked most of the cage where Emmett was sitting. Packard could see him struggle to see around it.

Packard stepped forward with his gun drawn. As soon as Emmett saw him, he backed up farther and swiveled the front end in Packard's direction while he reached for something between his legs.

Packard heard Thielen and Wilson both shout "Gun!" at the same time.

Emmett got off one shot, not even bothering to aim.

He knew he was seeing his house for the last time. Myra was the one who had wanted to live on a lake. He told her if she could find a house in their price range, then all right.

You could do a lot worse than Myra, Emmie. She'll keep you a good home. You two could be happy together.

His mother's voice.

He'd done everything she told him to do. Married Myra. Settled. A boy like him could only expect so much. The pink room, Wanda, the jogger were all attempts at grabbing more than he deserved. He'd forgotten himself.

The ringing in his ears from firing the gun muffled the return fire that immediately followed. He felt a bullet rip through his thigh and another punch his gut. He dropped Carl's gun. He was hit a third time. He reflexively pulled back on the Bobcat's levers, trying to retreat.

The Bobcat lurched backward and the rear wheels dropped off the edge of the eroded shoreline. The heavy bucket raised above the center of gravity pulled the skid loader over backward. Emmett saw his sad brown house and the bright-blue sky rush by him, and then he was suddenly underwater. He felt all his weight press the safety bar across his lap; then he was slammed against the side of the cab. Something heavy fell across his back. He strained his neck in every direction looking for the surface. He gasped and sucked muddy water into his lungs and stomach. His arms flailed. He tried to sit up but all the weight in the world was on top of him.

Myra, he thought.

This was all your fault.

I would never...

Packard's last glimpse of Emmett before he went upside down and disappeared underwater was of his hands flying off the controls, his arms spread wide like wings.

Packard approached the water cautiously, watching for Emmett and his gun. Standing on the dock was as close as he could get to the Bobcat. Exhaust belched out from under the surface of the churning lake as the overturned Bobcat's engine died. The cab was completely submerged, the weight above it pushing it deeper into the soft mud.

There was no point getting into the water. He'd sink to his waist in muck two steps from the shore. Packard squatted to steady himself on the shaky dock, ready to reach for Emmett if there was any sign of him. The Bobcat's upside-down tires were motionless. After a minute, Packard stood up, looked at Thielen, and shook his head. He radioed the all clear and requested the ambulance be sent in.

"I'm sure I hit him at least twice," Packard said, coming off the dock. "I don't know if there's anything we could have done to save him," he said.

Thielen stared at the water like she dared Emmett to come out. "You haven't been inside yet and seen what I've seen. The sonofabitch responsible for that"—she hiked a thumb over her shoulder—"gets to save himself."

Packard went inside Emmett's house and sat with Jenny in a pink room that smelled like cigarettes and urine while they waited for the firemen with the bolt cutters. She was barely conscious. He stepped out when the EMTs arrived, but watched as one of them checked her blood and shook his head at the numbers.

They rolled Jenny on a gurney out the back door. Packard called Susan from Emmett's landline and stretched the cord outside so he could watch them push Jenny up the hill to the ambulance.

Susan was still at the hospital waiting for the doctor to discharge her.

"Stay there," Packard said. "We found Jenny. They're bringing her in now."

CHAPTER THIRTY-ONE

PACKARD WASN'T ABLE TO leave the scene at Emmett's until well after dark. It was late evening by the time he made it to the hospital.

The door to Jenny's room was open, the lights dimmed. Jenny was asleep with Susan in the chair by her bed, reading a book. Susan had two black eyes and a splint over her nose from the car accident. "How's she doing?" he whispered.

"Okay, all things considered. They gave her something to help her sleep. She's getting lots of fluids to get her blood sugar back in line. And antibiotics for the infection in her hand. She's going to need surgery on it when she's stronger."

Packard had a lump in his throat, looking at Jenny asleep in the bed, knowing how close they'd come to a different outcome. Another hour would have changed everything.

Susan was reading his mind. "You said you'd find her. You did."

Packard shook his head. He didn't know what to say so he told her some of the details from earlier in the day. About finding Jesse and Carl in the quarry, and Carl's connection to Emmett.

"When she was coherent, she talked about Carl and that there are bodies buried at Emmett's."

"We figured as much when we saw his basement. We've got people searching the property." He didn't tell her about the pink room or the hole Emmett had dug for Jenny or that the cadaver dogs had already picked up the scent of two, maybe three sites. She would know it all eventually, then wish she didn't.

"You might still be questioning your decision to move to Sandy Lake, but I'm glad you did," Susan said. It clearly embarrassed her to say so. It was probably the closest he'd get to a thank-you. He was fine with that.

"I'm here to stay. There's work to be done. And you have to let me help with whatever the two of you need. I don't want this to be like it was after Tom died. I call. You don't call me back. We shouldn't live in the same town and only see each other at the family reunion."

"We don't have family reunions."

"Exactly."

"I'll do better," Susan promised.

There was no other place to sit, and Packard was dead on his feet so he said good night. He was almost out the door when he turned around.

"I almost forgot. I stopped at the station and got her phone from the techs. I'm sure she'll be wanting it."

Susan closed her book and took the phone he'd had in his pocket. "Thank you," she said.

CHAPTER THIRTY-TWO

A WEEK LATER, PACKARD had a date.

He knocked and stared at his shoes while he waited. After a minute the door opened, and Olivia McDonald stood there in purple pants and a short-sleeved yellow blouse. She had a white sweater over her shoulders and a beaded clutch in her hand.

"Mrs. McDonald, you're as pretty as a spring flower."

"*Pishh*," she said. "I'm older than oil, but thank you for the compliment. My granddaughter helped me pick the outfit."

"It's very nice. Shall we go?"

She let the door close behind her. He stuck out his elbow and she put her hand through it. "Still not locking your door, I see," he chided.

"Still got nothing worth stealing," she said.

They walked slowly down the hallway. The attendant at the reception desk was waiting for them with the front door held open. "Have a nice time, Mrs. McDonald. Please have her home before dark, Deputy."

"No promises."

It was the perfect summer day. Low eighties and sunshine. Standing next to the department vehicle, he put her clutch on the dash, then held her hand

and her elbow while she got both feet on the step up, then eased herself into the passenger seat. He helped her with her seat belt, then closed the door and went around the front and got behind the wheel. Mrs. McDonald took a pair of oversized sunglasses out of her purse.

"My granddaughter said I had to wear the sunglasses to complete the outfit. She said all the celebrities nowadays wear sunglasses this big."

"You look very sophisticated."

Mrs. McDonald lowered the visor on her side and looked at herself in the mirror. "I look like Jackie Onassis, the nursing home years," she joked.

He drove them through town, around the Sandy Lake shoreline, then headed north. Mrs. McDonald told him about teaching math to sixth graders for forty years and about her husband who was a farmer for all that time and how he died of a brain aneurysm a decade ago while milking one of their cows. When he didn't come in for his breakfast, she went to the barn and found him sitting on the ground, leaning against a heifer like he was listening to its heartbeat.

"How's the Wheeler girl?" Mrs. McDonald asked.

"She's home now. Her hand is going to require multiple surgeries to try to undo some of the nerve damage, but she should be fine physically. Mentally—we'll have to wait and see, I guess."

Jesse Crawford had been cremated. His mother held off on the funeral until Jenny was able to leave the hospital and attend. Jenny and Susan sat next to her and Alissa in the front. Most of the other people there were high school kids, friends of Jenny or Jesse or his sister. Packard saw Virginia Stevens there, the straight-A student with the tiny gold cross who'd bought Adderall from Jesse. The scrawny, unshaven man in the gray T-shirt and dirty jeans crying in the back was probably Jesse's dad.

Jenny still hadn't sat for an interview with anyone from the sheriff's department or the district attorney's office. With Emmett and Carl both dead there was no rush.

"That poor girl," Olivia McDonald said. "I never knew Emmett Burr. My husband did. He came out and did some welding for us in the barn. Feed troughs and pen doors, things like that. I never would have imagined such a monster could live among us."

Emmett had died from his gunshot wounds. There was some water in his lungs but not much, according to the coroner, meaning he was damn near dead by the time the Bobcat tipped over and sank into the mud. It had taken more than an hour for a truck with a winch to arrive, and another two hours before they were able to pull the Bobcat out of the lake. Emmett sat slumped inside the cab, covered in swamp mud and lake weeds, like a movie monster. It took six men to get him out and load him into the coroner's van.

"How long before they identify the other women?" Olivia asked.

Packard made a noncommittal noise. A search of the area where Emmett was digging the hole for Jenny had turned up three bodies. Two of them were all but identified based on local missing persons cases and an initial examination of the remains. Dental records would take a bit longer. "A few days, I guess. You'll hear about it on the news once they know for sure."

Olivia pulled her sweater together in the front, suddenly chilled. "Listen to us talk about such horrible things as casually as the weather. And on such a beautiful day. You have a difficult job, Ben. I don't envy you."

"It's usually not this bad, but you're right. We should find more pleasant things to talk about."

"How about this? You still haven't told me where we're going."

"I have an errand I've been putting off that I thought you might enjoy."

"Does it have anything to do with the dog cage in the back?"

"It does indeed."

Gary Bushwright was in his front yard walking a three-legged corgi on a retractable leash and smoking a cigarette when Packard pulled in behind his rig. The dog stopped sniffing the ground long enough to watch the SUV pull up, then bounded straight up in the air when a white moth suddenly flushed in front of it. Packard smiled in what felt like the first time in weeks. He was about to be a dog owner again. It was time.

Gary thought so, too. "Honey, it's about time. I mean—It's. About. Time," he said as Packard climbed out of the truck.

"Give me a break, Gary. You know I've been busy."

"We're all busy. Busy living, busy dreaming, busy dying. Who's this you brought with you?"

"This is Mrs. Olivia McDonald."

"Oh Lord. Olivia, I didn't recognize you behind those giant sunglasses. I thought you were a movie star. Olivia and my mother worked on the church fundraising committee together," he said to Packard. "Olivia, I still bolt up in bed some nights and call out for your chocolate cake with cream cheese frosting. You still make that?"

"I don't but I've taught my grandkids how to make it. You can ask them. They volunteer at the church."

"I'll be at the next bake sale with bells on," Gary promised.

Packard took a seat on the front steps and held his hand out for the leash. It was harder to look Gary in the eye since he'd googled Johnny Hardwood—the name Gary used for his adult film work. Packard would have never known it was Gary if he hadn't seen pictures of him as a young man in his house. Turned out Johnny Hardwood was somewhat of a gay porn legend in the late seventies and early eighties. The photos and movie clips Packard had seen made it clear why.

"Got everything you need at home?" Gary asked.

"I got your email and bought everything on the list that I didn't already have." Packard pulled a twisted plastic bag with dog treats from his pocket and fed one to the corgi. The dog gobbled it down, then sat and looked at him expectantly. "Dog food has gotten more expensive."

"The good stuff costs money. You can feed him what you want. I only make suggestions."

The three of them and the corgi took a stroll through the kennel, mainly so Olivia could see the other dogs under Gary's care. He let some of the dogs out one at a time for Olivia to pet and feed treats. *Oh for heaven's sake*, she said. *Well, aren't you the cutest thing*, she said.

"I imagine you always had a dog or two at the farm," Packard said.

"Oh yes. My husband loved dogs. We always had a good herding dog and then another one, usually a mutt of some kind, to keep that one company. Corgis are good herders, I've heard," she said and laughed at her own wordplay.

Back outside, Gary helped Olivia into her seat while Packard opened the rear door to the SUV and put the corgi in the dog kennel with a treat and a toy to distract it. He glanced over at Cora's house as he closed the door. All the blinds were drawn. No vehicles out front. "You seen or talked to her lately?"

Gary shut Olivia's door and shook his head. "Not a word. She and Greta are around. I heard they opted not to have a public funeral."

Packard nodded. He wondered how long it had been since Sandy Lake had so many dead to bury at once. Jesse. Sam. Carl. Emmett. Plus the bodies from Emmett's property that would need to be reburied.

"Seemed like you two might have had a thawing of the ice when we were looking at the security footage," Packard said.

Gary shrugged, shook out a cigarette from the pack in his pants pocket. "We'll see. I'm not going to hold my breath, or hold it against her if she's crazier than before. She's been through a lot."

"That's big of you. I'd appreciate not having to come out here and use the hose on you two."

"Honey, come by any time. Bring your hose, bring your fur friend. I always like to see how my former charges are doing."

"All right then. We'll be back."

"Listen to you," Gary said as he lit his cigarette. "Already a 'we.' That's what I like to hear."

Already a "we."

Gary's words stuck with Packard over the next couple of days at home alone with his new dog. He still hadn't come up with a name. He didn't want anything obvious, like Tripod or Tilt. It would take some time together to decide on the right one. There was no hurry.

He brought the dog down to the lake when he went swimming. It was full-on summer now. The trees around the lake had exploded with leaves, and the water was warm enough that he didn't need the wet suit. The great gray owl still watched over him and her nest from her spot high in the trees. He hadn't seen any of the fledglings take flight yet, but he often saw their heads above the swirl of the nest when the smaller male swooped in at feeding time.

In the evenings, he took the dog for a walk and thought about Marcus and the years that had passed since he was killed. Packard had spent them like a monk lighting candles at an altar to a forgotten saint. It was time to let his regrets go, stop cataloging the whys and the what-ifs. That's not what Marcus had asked of him.

The remorse he felt about moving to Sandy Lake was rooted in the realization that there was no outrunning his past or his problems. It was also hard to imagine making a life here if he couldn't be himself. Knowing his big secret was out made it easier. His skin was thick enough to take the name-calling that was sure to come. If anyone wanted to take a swing at the faggot cop, they'd find out in short order that he was ready for them.

He'd come to Sandy Lake for a reason, he decided. His family had known good times here once. They might again if he could find out what happened to Nick. The women they'd found on Emmett's property were proof that secrets don't stay buried forever. Their families had gone without answers for almost as long as his family had. It took two teenagers breaking into the wrong man's house to set in motion the events that uncovered the truth. The same could happen with his brother.

Packard didn't have to wait for chance. Cold-case files were stored in a locked room in the lower level of the city building. Kelly had the only key. She also maintained the log of people who requested files, when she pulled them, and when they came back.

"There's no file with that number," she told him after he requested it.

"What do you mean? It's in the system."

"I know. I see a space for it on the shelf but it's not there. I make the work-study kids do an audit every year comparing the system to the inventory. According to the audit, the file was there in February. There's no record of it going out in my book since then. What's the case?"

He thought back to the night when Gary asked him if he was related to the Packard boy who went missing. If Gary had made the connection, it stood to reason others had, too. Nick's disappearance hadn't come up in any of Packard's interviews for the job. It hadn't been mentioned by anyone in the department in the last eighteen months. Who else was suddenly interested in his brother's case? Why pull the file without leaving a record? And why now?

"Never mind," Packard said.

They were questions for another time. He was just coming off a case involving his family, and there was still a lot of work to do before Emmett's file and the related cold cases could be closed. Packard needed a break before he took on something that intense again.

He called Michael, the nurse in Minneapolis, on his way home from running errands in town. "I have some time off but here's the deal. I have a new dog and I can't leave him behind to run to the Cities. What do you think about coming up here?"

"I could do that. When are you thinking?"

They compared schedules and made a plan for a three-day weekend. Michael asked if he would get to see him in uniform while they were together.

"I'll see what I can do," Packard promised.

Back at home, with a drowsy dog pressed against his leg, he sat on the couch and stared at his unfinished living room and the makeshift kitchen that looked like something out of a deer camp, and thought about how it would look to Michael when he showed up. There wasn't time to do much about it between now and then. He needed a better plan, some way to prioritize all the construction that remained and a logical order for getting it done.

The dog, sensing Packard was about to stand up, raised its head, but Packard forced himself to stay sitting. These were the quiet moments he needed to learn to enjoy. The idea was to relax, not replace one kind of work with another.

He worked his fingers through the dog's scruff. "You need a name," he said.

His unfinished house had him thinking of all the work his grandfather had done to build the two-story family cabin they used to spend summers at just miles from here. Grandpa Frank had been a man of infinite patience, who never seemed happier than he was while spending time with his grandkids. He'd been the one who taught Packard how to fish and ride a bike. He'd taught him to be a listener rather than a talker. Grandpa's favorite solution for settling disputes between grandkids was with a toss of a Kennedy half-dollar he always carried in his pocket. Once Grandpa flipped the coin and you called it, there was no more arguing.

"I'm going to name you Franklin 'Frank' Packard, after Grandpa," he said to the dog, putting his face close enough to be licked. "You're now heir to the Packard estate and all the untaped drywall and exposed wiring you see before you. What do you think?"

The corgi rolled over and showed its belly.

Packard gave him a rub and stood up. "All right then. Let's go for a walk, Frank."

READING GROUP GUIDE

1. Despite a family connection to Sandy Lake, Packard wonders whether the decision to move there was the right one. Why is he conflicted? How does his reasoning about his motivation evolve over the course of the book?

2. Characterize the feud between Gary and Cora. How do they each feel about the other at the beginning of the book? Has anything changed by the end of it?

3. Though they were together for over a year, Packard and Marcus never openly discussed their relationship. Why do you think that is? After Marcus dies, how does Packard feel about the relationship?

4. Why did Emmett kidnap Wanda and the jogger? What did he want from them? Do you think he's being honest about his intentions or his recall of what happened?

5. Describe Packard's relationship with the locals (Gary, Cora, the sheriff, Susan). Do any of them really know him?

6. Emmett is a morally complex character: he somehow manages to play both the role of perpetrator and victim. Did you ever feel sympathy for him? Why or why not?

7. While he's not ashamed of his identity, Packard assumes that his sexuality could complicate his job. How does Shannon's revelation that the whole town already knows he's gay confirm or contradict those assumptions?

8. Emmett and Carl have been begrudging allies for years. Outline their similarities and differences.

9. The bond that Emmett starts to feel for Jenny is a strange one. Describe his feelings. How does his opinion of her change, and why?

10. What do you think happened to Packard's brother?

A CONVERSATION WITH
THE AUTHOR

Ben Packard was a long time in the making. When did you first develop him as a character, and why did you decide to give him his own series?

I wrote a novel before *And There He Kept Her* with the same setting of Sandy Lake. Packard was an insignificant character in that book—a deputy another character describes in crude terms as being gay. Why I made the deputy gay when he only appeared on two pages and was in no way central to the plot is still a mystery. That book was good enough to get several agents to read the whole thing, but they all had issues with the plot. I was so tired of the story that I couldn't find a solution to the book's structural problems. I set it aside, but Ben Packard stuck with me. I wanted to know how he ended up in Sandy Lake and what it was like to be a gay man in a small town and in a position of authority. I wrote *And There He Kept Her* to find out.

Turning the victim of a robbery into a retired serial killer flips the script on readers' expectations of victimhood. What made you think of a twist like that?

I started with the idea of a man being victimized in his own home and the reasons why he might have to fend for himself. What secrets did he have that he couldn't call the police for help? I started thinking about a killer who had never been caught, who was old and weak and vulnerable to being preyed upon, just like the women he used to target. There had to be evidence of his past crimes and that's when I imagined the room in the basement, the chains on the wall, and the door with no handle on the inside.

The landscape of Minnesota and the culture of the small town play a huge role in this story. As a Minnesotan yourself, it seems natural you'd be drawn to the setting. But were there any other reasons you chose Sandy Lake as a backdrop?

I was an Army brat as a kid. My mom was in the military, and we moved every three or four years with no permanent place that felt like home. My dad, on the other hand, has spent most of his life in the same small South Dakota town (population 1,300) where he grew up. We spent summers there as kids.

I've always been fascinated by life in small towns—the options for creating community, finding love and meaningful work, the reasons why people stay or come back to small towns, and how the things that we need to consider a place *home* change over time.

Some authors need a regimented writing schedule, while others work best in marathon writing sessions. Can you talk a little bit about your process?

This is the third novel I've written. There were times when I'd put away the book I was working on and not write for months. Eventually I realized if I ever had hopes of publication I needed to be more diligent. I have a day job, so most of my writing is done in the evenings and on weekends. I'm a slow and steady grinder from the first word to the last, and then a heavy reviser. This book took many, many revisions because I had no plan, no outline, and often couldn't see more than a chapter or two ahead. I don't recommend it.

Strangely, the reader finds themselves rooting for Emmett when Carl enters the scene. Did you expect this reaction? What were you thinking when you came up with their dynamic?

The same things that made Emmett vulnerable to being preyed upon by

Jesse and Jenny also weakened him as a villain. At some point, I realized the story needed an even bigger threat than Emmett. Once I introduced Carl, I wanted there to be a dynamic between him and Emmett where the one with the power over the other kept shifting. Adding Carl also changed the dynamic between Emmett and Jenny. At different points in the story, Emmett is a kidnapper, a murderer, an elderly victim, and a protector all in one. I didn't assume readers would feel sympathy for Emmett (he's still a horrible person), but I wanted to challenge their perception of him as the story evolved.

Sometimes authors must put themselves in the headspace of their characters when they write. Did it feel different writing Packard's perspective versus Emmett's? Did you find one to be more difficult?

Emmett's headspace sounds like a radio tuned to static. He has very base instincts—eat, drink, smoke—that drive him. In the background is the constant hum of his pain. I needed his actions and the basic need for self-preservation to propel his chapters rather than rely on a lot of internal thoughts to justify his motivations. It was definitely more fun getting to know Packard. He's got a backstory and unresolved issues that will carry into the next book. He's pretty uptight, but I'm hoping he learns how to relax and live a little more as his adventures continue.

What books are on your bedside table right now?

I've followed Hanif Abdurraqib on Instagram for a while, read a book of his poems, and just started reading *A Little Devil in America*. My friend Lisa said reading George Saunders's *A Swim in a Pond in the Rain* was life-changing, so that's also on deck. She gave me a copy of Haruki Murakami's new collection of short stories, *First Person Singular*, that I will get to sooner than later.

In thinking about a character like Jesse or Sam, who steals medication from the elderly, or a character like Emmett, who kidnaps women but wants to

protect Jenny, it seems like most of these characters aren't *entirely* bad. Can you talk a little bit about the moral ambiguity that comes up in this story?

All-good or all-bad characters aren't interesting. They can't surprise us when they have only one way of reacting. It helped me as the author to instill them with moral ambiguity by seeing them beyond their primary function in the story. Emmett is a kidnapper, but he was also someone's son, someone's husband. Sam is a small-time drug dealer, but he's also from a wealthy family and the sheriff's grandson. Giving them a backstory and knowing something about the other forces in their lives helped create that push-pull that I hoped would make them multi-dimensional characters.

Do you have any advice for aspiring authors?

I'm going to be older than the average debut novelist by the time this book comes out. So what? It takes as long as it takes. After a lot of years working as a project manager, I realized I could manage my writing goals like a project by defining what success looked like, identifying the deliverables I needed to create, and devising a schedule for completing them. I know how contrived that sounds, but it worked for me. When life threw me curves, I adjusted the plan. The important thing was having a strategy for completing what I wanted to do, which was publish a novel.

Even more important than the plan was finding a writing community. The feedback I got from other writers helped keep me motivated and ultimately made this book what it is. Thinking and talking about other people's work helped me see my own writing in a new light. Find a thoughtful reader or another writer whose opinion you respect, and trust them when they tell you what is and isn't working. Keep writing. Keep dreaming. Follow the plan.

ACKNOWLEDGMENTS

When I was a kid I thought books came from libraries. I thought the librarians went in the back room, put on hairnets, and manufactured the books, just like grocery stores made all the food on the shelves and hospitals made babies. It took longer than it probably should have for me to grasp the idea that books were written by writers. (Still not really clear on all the baby business.)

I was ten or eleven years old when I got tired of the kids' section at the library and started wandering the adult stacks. A book with a weird title on the spine—*Cujo*—and a snarling dog face on the cover kept catching my attention. Stephen King was only eight books into his career then and was probably the first person I recognized as a writer. He was the first writer whose books I sought out because of the name on the cover. I distinctly remember thinking that if writing about a dog that wants to eat people was a real job for a grown-ass man, then I wanted to do that, too.

A lot of years passed between then and now. Life moves to its own rhythm. I majored in English at the University of South Dakota. I moved to Minnesota. I started to get an MFA in creating writing, then dropped out. I started to get a master's in rhetoric, then dropped out. At the Loft (loft.org) in Minneapolis, I met author Mary Gardner, who taught a novel-writing class that I took several times. Mary became a friend and a mentor for many years. She told me I could write when I needed to hear it the most. The world lost a generous writer and teacher when Mary died of COVID-19 on Christmas Eve 2020.

I met my friends Lynn Filipas and Barbann Hanson in one of Mary's classes. They read the two books I wrote before this one and encouraged me to keep going. Gretchen Anthony and Laska Nygaard read this book a chapter at a time, then draft after draft. There'd be no book without their friendship and support.

My undying gratitude to my agent, Barbara Poelle, for making my writerly dreams come true, and to my editors, Anna Michels and Jenna Jankowski, for connecting with the story I was telling. Thanks to everyone at Sourcebooks who turned the voices in my head into the book in your hands.

Thank you to the Scott County Sheriff's Office for allowing me to attend their virtual community academy. I learned a lot about the work of a sheriff's deputy and how a department is run. The rest I googled or made up to suit the needs of the story.

My mom and dad kept books in my hungry, hungry hands and gave me the love and guidance I needed to keep pursuing this dream for as long as it took.

This book is for Chris. I've spent my whole life imagining the lives of others, but I never dared dream a story like ours. I love you.

ABOUT THE AUTHOR

Joshua Moehling works in the medical device industry by day and writes at night. *And There He Kept Her* is his first novel. He lives in the Twin Cities.